CRACKER

MEN SHOULD WEEP

D0499343

CRACKER

MEN SHOULD WEEP

Jim Mortimore

First published in Great Britain in 1995 by
Virgin Publishing Ltd
332 Ladbroke Grove
London W10 5AH

Cracker © Granada Television and Jimmy McGovern

Text copyright © Jim Mortimore 1995
from a screenplay by Jimmy McGovern

Cover photographs © Granada Television

ISBN 0 86369 916 2

Typeset by Galleon Typesetting, Ipswich
Printed and bound in Great Britain by
Cox & Wyman Ltd, Reading, Berks

For Mum and Dad
For instilling a sense of values . . .

'To suggest there is anything racial in a primary school pupil refusing to hold hands with another primary school pupil is ridiculous.'

(Conservative Councillor Mike Summerby,
13 March 1987)

BIG BROTHER AND TINY TOTS
[This] gallumping project . . . sounds about as sensible as unleashing a bloodhound in a dolls' house.

(*Daily Mail* headline and editorial in response to the publication of Hertfordshire County Council's 1988 initiative to tackle racism in all its educational institutions. Headline and editorial appeared 11 October 1988)

The typical image of a rapist, derived primarily from crime statistics, is that of a young, black, urban male, often of lower class status. However, other information suggests this image is incorrect. Several investigators have found no significant differences in the incidence or prevalence of sexual assault as a function of race, social class, or place of residence.

(Ageton, 1983)

Acceptance of beliefs that foster rape has been demonstrated among a variety of groups including typical citizens, police officers and judges.

(Feild, 1978)

The Myths

'No really means yes.'
'Women love to be swept off their feet.'
'Women love to be taken by force.'
'Nice girls don't get raped.'
'It is impossible to rape an unwilling woman.'
'You cannot thread a moving needle.'
'She deserved it.'
'She dressed like that kind of woman.'
'Rapists are mentally deranged strangers.'
'You cannot be raped by someone you know.'

PART ONE

Anticipation

ONE

11.30a.m.–1.30p.m.

It was the year they privatised the benefit system.

Not content with Railtrack, the water, electricity and British Gas, not content with taking away what should by rights have belonged to the people and then cynically selling it back to them at crippling prices, they started in on the social. Take away people's homes. Take away their ability to earn a living, to keep a roof over their head. Take it all away and *throw* it all away, knowing *them*.

It wasn't just that, though. It was the pious hypocritical attitude of it all. That was what made him mad. The way they looked at you and smiled their thin smiles that never touched their eyes and told you they knew what was best for you without ever knowing you. Told you they knew what was best and then told you they were investigating you or suspending you, withholding your benefit, taking away your freedom, your individuality, any choice you might have had about the way you lead your life.

And the questions. Always the questions. Have you worked? Have your circumstances changed? Do you have any dependants? Is there anything else we should know? Have you read the back of your UB40? Do you understand the statement that you are signing? Do you understand that to lie is an offence?

Understand? Oh yes. He understood all right. Understood that to keep your head above water nowadays was like walking through a minefield on crutches. So yes, he lied. He lied and he was proud of it. Proud to be able to play the system at its own game, to survive by understanding the

3

rules, obeying them when necessary, circumventing them whenever he could. He took joy in it. He was good at it. He knew all the forms by now. Oh, the numbers changed, whenever *they* had enough money to waste redesigning and reprinting the forms; the numbers changed but the information remained essentially the same. What hours are you available for full- or part-time employment? Do you live alone? Do you or your partner have any savings? Do you or your partner have any other income? Any children? Any outstanding loans? What is your rent or mortgage? What are your monthly outgoings? Ticks in boxes. That was what Floyd Malcolm was. That was what anyone was to these shop-dummy clerks with their condescending attitudes and their fake sympathy and their forms and their questions.

And somewhere deep down in his heart, right down inside him, where the bitterness sat uneasily on a cheap and unnourishing breakfast, he knew it was never going to change. Not in his lifetime. It was never going to change, nor would it improve. He was in this system for life, such as it was. In it, smothered in it, suffocated by it.

A life sentence.

Floyd stared at the clerk in front of him. A neat man of middle height and middle weight with a neat haircut and a neat expression. A box-ticker if ever there was one. He was perfectly in place in this neat room in this neat, privately run building. In a moment of craziness (which actually wasn't so very crazy when you got right down to it) Floyd thought the only things out of place here were the people the place was supposed to support. Support? That was a joke. The staff here didn't have the zap between them to support a bloody football club.

Floyd stared at the clerk and the clerk looked right back at him. His eyes blinked once, neatly, not seeming to see him, Floyd, at all. Something in that neat expression told Floyd the clerk didn't see him as a person at all, not even as a punter. Just another coon. Another golly.

A threat to his white, middle-class life.

The clerk arranged a pen and notepad on the desk

4

between them, making a neat rectangle beside the stack of forms. Forms in which he would soon be busily ticking boxes, no doubt.

'Mister Malcolm? Mister Floyd Malcolm?'

Somehow the neat voice, the open mouth and the neat rows of white teeth in that white face made Floyd want to laugh.

'I see my fame goes before me.'

The clerk nodded. A small, dapper movement. His lips curved in a polite smile which, as expected, came nowhere near his eyes. 'My name is Andrew Wiley. I'm a benefit adviser.'

Floyd studied the clerk. 'I don't need to see a benefit adviser. I just come here to sign on.'

'I understand.' The clerk selected the top form from the stack and laid it out on the desk in front of them. He picked up his pen. 'Now then, Mister Malcolm, if you could just fill in this form.' He slid the form across the desk towards Floyd.

'What's it for? I brought me UB40. I know you have to do that now, or you can't sign on.' Floyd produced the small booklet and dumped it on the desk, on top of the form the clerk offered him.

The clerk looked at the booklet. Floyd thought he saw a glimmer in his eyes. Something beyond the neat expression of professional concern. Something animal. He'd seen that look often. A reaction to his colour, his voice. Particularly his voice. 'Mister Malcolm, you missed your last signing date. There was no communication from you to us. Under the circumstances the rules are very clear –'

Floyd frowned. 'I didn't miss it. I was ill.'

'You should have notified us.'

'How could I? Was ill, wasn't I?'

'Don't you have a phone?'

'Me can't afford a phone on what you pay.'

'You should at least have produced a doctor's certificate.'

'I got one. I gave it to me mate to bring in. Wilson. He's me mate. He brought it in, you ask them,' and Floyd jerked a

5

thumb over towards the signing desk, the two clerks busy there.

'I'll have to check.' The clerk stood, scooped up Floyd's UB40 and vanished behind a partition screen into the rear part of the office.

Five minutes went past.

Floyd sighed. He tapped his feet. He tapped his fingers on the desk. He looked at the clock. 11.30. Practically the whole morning wasted. Could have been forty or fifty quid in his pocket by now. Well. Maybe thirty quid. Fifteen after the cab controller took his cut. Then again, fifteen quid was fifteen quid. It would buy food for the table. Maybe a little something to share with Trish later. A little smokeable something.

The clerk came back. He sat, placed Floyd's UB40 back on the desk.

'You had flu?'

'Yeah, man. Summer flu, you know the babe. She hug you round the lungs and don't let go.'

The clerk nodded, closed the form he'd got out earlier, placed it back on the little stack. Selected another, laid it out in front of Floyd.

'Have your circumstances changed since your last interview, Mister Malcolm?'

I told you, I was ill. The shakes. Puking my guts up from both ends for two days.

'My bowels have improved.'

The clerk did not smile. He drew the form towards him and placed a precise tick in a box on page three. He looked up. 'Have you done any work over the last four weeks, Mister Malcolm?'

Cleaned the toilet once or twice.

'Yeah, man. Understudy to Arnold Schwarzenegger.' Floyd flexed one whipcord thin arm. The clerk didn't respond. 'Next week I'm the Milky Bar Kid.' That got a response. The age-old look of fear and hatred, a spark buried deep in those mundane clerk's eyes, a spark waiting to be fanned alight.

Floyd held the clerk's gaze. After a moment the spark died. No. Not dead. Just held in check. Controlled.

Then the clerk put aside the form, placed his pen on the desk. 'Where were you born, Mister Malcolm?'

Floyd blinked. He should have expected it. Should have bloody well expected it. 'Manchester.'

'You speak with a Jamaican accent.' The clerk's voice was carefully modulated, no hint of emotion. Just observing the rules here. Just ticking the appropriate boxes.

Floyd grinned. 'Man, it feel good to speak with a Jamaican accent. My old dad, he was Jamaican. Me, I'm British. Mancunian. Scary thought is it not?'

The clerk thought for a moment. 'I'm afraid we'll need to see your passport, Mister Malcolm.'

Floyd felt the old heat well up inside, the anger an old and comfortable friend, with him since childhood. Best buddies. To do or die for. 'I'm British. I haven't got a passport.'

The clerk sighed. 'In that case I'm going to have to suspend your claim until you can produce –'

'I told you. I ain't got no passport. I'm bloody English, man, like you, I was born here. I got a birth certificate –'

'– either a passport or a birth certificate. Until then I'm going to have to terminate this interview. I won't suspend the claim, but we'll have to start again when you have the relevant documentation.'

'– and me need my money. How can you expect me to live with no money? How can you expect me to eat with no money?'

The clerk simply folded his arms. 'Mister Malcolm, the benefit system is designed to help those who need it.'

I need it, you bloody ignorant white fool, I need help.

'If you want to claim benefit, you have to ask us in the right way.'

Floyd's mouth twisted bitterly. 'The only help I'd get from you would be a leg up onto a burning cross.'

'Would you like to see a supervisor, Mister Malcolm?'

But Floyd was away, flinging aside his chair and barging through the queue of people waiting to sign on, ignoring the angry words and stares, past the neat modern display racks less than half full of job cards, through the doors and onto the street.

Once out of the building he turned left and charged along the high street, heading round the corner to Percy Street where he'd parked the wheels. The street, man, that was his home. His beat. With his wheels he could go anywhere. But even the job bled him white. Now there was an irony. Bloody Tom Trantor's taxi cabs? Bloody vampires, more like. Fifteen per cent of his fares to take home plus tips. Plus bloody tips. That was a laugh. Tip a cabbie? A black cabbie? I should cocoa. Bloody white liberal bleeding heart hypocrite vampires. Tip a black cabbie. Ho ho ho.

He walked down the street, feet thumping, head down, shutting the world out. Imagine how he must have looked to the shoppers, the women with pushchairs, the OAPs getting on the bus to town, the kids scabbing around town in the lunch break. Tall. Young. Moody. Whipcord thin.

And black.

Black.

Frightening? Did they find him frightening? No-one would meet his gaze. No-one would look at him. Oh some kid in a pram waved a sherbet lolly at him and gurgled happily but his mother or sister, or whoever she was, just spun the pram around and headed back into Valubuys, face breaking into that 'Oh, I've left my purse at the checkout' expression.

Oh I've left my purse at the checkout so I'll just nip back in and get it and then I won't have to look at that tall, young, moody black man thumping along the pavement towards me. I won't have to worry about what he might be thinking, won't have to think about what he might do.

There was more good news waiting for him when he logged back on in the cab.

'What do you mean, no work,' he snarled at the handset as he slammed it back onto the cradle. 'You guys running a cab company or a bloody mortuary?'

The handset didn't reply. Floyd sat there in his wheels in

the car park of Valubuys, hands locked around the wheel, mind locked onto a single thought.

Black he was black he was moody he was dangerous he was black black and dangerous –

Bollocks.

It was like Wilson said: Why couldn't people celebrate the differences? Why the oppression, the political necessity to jam people into the same mould of equality? Wilson was right. People weren't equal. They weren't. They were different. People should be proud of the differences. Proud of them. Not frightened.

It was one spark of common sense in a world that, to Floyd, seemed to rage ever more out of control by the day, the hour. The great machine of society grinding down upon him, on Wilson, on all of the brothers and sisters, gears locked, flywheel spinning, all control gone.

Floyd put his face in his hands and struggled to get himself under control. *Shape up. Someone sees you here they'll probably think you're some kind of weirdo. A child molester or something. Some kind of pervert.*

They do that. Wilson had once told him of how he'd been accused of loitering outside a school. Waiting to pick up his kid, that was all. But he'd been in the cab. And it had been a new school. Someone had seen the cab parked outside the school fence and had phoned the bill. Two police cars. Four coppers. Fifteen minutes radio time in which he'd been taken from the car and searched, in which his car had been searched, right there, outside the school, and when he'd finally been checked out clean there had been one half-hearted apology smeared across an expression that said, 'We'll get you next time', and he'd turned to see eight-year-old Roselyn standing at the kerb staring at him with frightened eyes in a crowd of friends, and of them all she was the only one who wasn't laughing.

Floyd dug his fingers into his scalp. Some days it got you bad. You felt your head was exploding with the noise, the insane pressure of it all.

But you had to cope. Had to deal with it. So dig in those

fingers, my old sport, and *calm right on down there*. That's better. Chill factor five. Easy. Easy.

Floyd felt the muscles of his arms relax, not for the first time felt the pain of cramp there. Pain that seemed to spread through his mind, come out of his head, fill his muscles, his arms and legs and stomach with a bilious tension.

And then a thought. Did they really do this to him? Or did he do it to himself?

'Oy, mate, you can't hang around there, you know.'

What?

Floyd looked up. A middle-aged man dressed in the uniform of a Valubuys car park attendant was peering in through his windscreen.

'I'm waiting.' The words squeezed out thin, sounded muddy to his unfocused mind.

'I've been watching you, mind. You haven't been in the supermarket. You went out onto the street. This parking facility is for Valubuys customers only.'

'Fine.' Floyd jammed his key into the ignition. 'I'm leaving.'

'You'll have to pay if you haven't got a receipt.'

'Fuck you, asshole.'

Floyd slammed the wheels into gear and roared away, the rage hot within him once more.

Then he grinned. Fuck you, asshole? Maybe he could understudy Arnie at that. He stared at the car park attendant in the rear-view mirror and mentally flipped him the bird.

Fuck you, asshole. I'll be back.

For you and everyone like you.

Real soon.

2.00p.m.–7.30p.m.

Floyd's life was full of things he couldn't change. Staring at himself in the mirror before the evening meal he was more aware of that than ever.

The rest of the day had been about what you'd expect. For want of anything better to do he'd gone round to Wilson's to shoot the breeze a little, maybe shoot a little extra something too. Helene had been there though, so that had put paid to that. What Wilson was doing married to a woman like Helene he couldn't even begin to imagine. She was black and beautiful. That was good. She was smart too, university degree. That was also good. The problem was she was a bit too sensible for Floyd. And far too sensible for Wilson. To be honest, he'd never understood quite what the attraction between them was. But then they'd been married for nearly seven years now. Seven years. That they worked together was obvious, their daughter Roselyn the proof of their compatibility, if any were needed. But man. Wilson did dig a little toke now and then. Well, rather more now than then, if you could understand that. And Helene, well, she may have smoked the odd joint or whatever, but frankly, that was all well and truly in her past. And she didn't hesitate to let you know it.

Nice as Helene was, sometimes Floyd thought Wilson was on a short leash. What she didn't understand was that there were times when he and Wilson needed to chill.

Today of all days he'd really needed to chill.

The problem was Helene had been spending the day at home with Roselyn so that had been a washout. Wilson had been apologetic, but adamant. Family was everything. Floyd had left Wilson to his family and driven to Fallowfields. He'd spent a couple of hours in a local pub, taken some grief from the barkeeper, then headed back to Salford in time to catch the rush hour.

Halfway home it had begun to rain. Half a mile from the house he'd got a puncture.

By the time he arrived home he was soaked to the skin. His mum had insisted on a change of clothes and a bath before dinner, after which he was due for a couple of hours' work. At some point during the evening he would scab off and meet Trish, then back to work for the late travellers. The businessmen from London, the party-goers out for a kicking Friday at the Boom Box or some other rave club.

Floyd gazed at his reflection in his mum's bathroom

mirror. He had no time for the rave scene. The techno parties. There was no discipline there. No control. He believed in control. Totally. The odd little something, sure, just to loosen up, but on the whole, control was the thing. He half turned, looking over his shoulder to examine his legs. They hadn't changed. Not since the age of twelve.

Floyd forced himself to stare at his thighs and buttocks. The skin there. The scars.

Some people wore their hearts on their sleeves. He wore his ideology on his arse.

Control.

That was the ticket.

And one day . . . well, one day the Movement would have the power it deserved and the cause of those scars would be sorted right out.

I'll be back.

With friends.

There came a banging on the door then, impatient. A voice called, 'Yo Floyd, man, you starting a new career in there or what?'

Floyd shook his head at his own reflection. The voice belonged to his brother. At eighteen Marv was three years younger than Floyd, the baby of the family, a bit idealistic. He tended to view Floyd and his friends with suspicion and no small amount of sarcasm. Floyd was unconcerned. Marv'd grow up soon enough. His first serious run-in with the bill would sort him right out, show him where they all stood in relation to the power structure of this country. Just let him spend too long outside a school, let him smoke a little weed, hang with the wrong crowd. He'd see. No qualifications, no accent, no classy job, no good intentions could overcome the prejudice engendered in those in authority by the colour of his face.

He grunted a reply to Marv, slung a towel around his waist and opened the bathroom door. Marv held his hand out for a high five, then when Floyd went for it ducked to whip the towel away from his waist. Marv was grinning from ear to ear.

Floyd sighed. 'Don't you be doing that to me now, brother,' he said warningly.

Marv's grin widened. 'Well don' you be speakin' in dat cod accent to me den, mon,' he drawled. 'Anyway,' he added in more normal tones, 'it's good to see you, even if you are an idealistic bastard.'

Floyd snatched the towel back without replying, turned to walk along the upstairs landing to his room.

Marv followed him.

Floyd paused at the door to his room. 'I thought you wanted the bathroom.'

'That was then, this is now.'

Floyd's lips narrowed to a thin line at his brother's deliberate misuse of the catchphrase of the Movement. He didn't reply. He didn't move either though.

'How is the dear old Movement these days, anyway?' Marv pressed the point.

Floyd licked his lips. Marv liked to play word games. But somewhere during the last few minutes it had got beyond a game. It was out of control. Floyd couldn't countenance that.

'Out there are people who want to burn our homes, to destroy our lives. They distribute their literature in primary schools to indoctrinate the kids. *How to recognise a red teacher. How to deal with a red teacher.* They hate us. They must be stopped.'

Marv shrugged. 'Oh, that's easy enough. Shove them all into Salford and nuke the ruddy lot.'

'It's easy for you to mock, isn't it? You've never been arrested for waiting to pick up your own kid from school.'

Marv laughed out loud. 'Neither have you! You haven't got any kids. If the amount of times you've brought Trish home is any indication you probably never will!'

Floyd fumed, fist wrapped around his door handle, body soaked and cold, but hot inside, raging inside. Oh dear Lord allow me one shot. Just one shot to make him understand. That's all I ask.

Something in his expression, in the set of his body must

13

have filtered through to Marv. 'You've been listening to that bloody Wilson again, haven't you?' He didn't wait for an answer. 'Things must be pretty bad for you to think about belting your own brother.'

He turned, headed for the stairs at the end of the landing. 'See you at dinner, man. In the meantime, chill out. You don't endear yourself to Mum, Bev or me like this.'

Floyd opened the door to his room without replying, went inside, into the dark, shut the door firmly behind him.

Control.

By the time Floyd got his head together enough to show his face at the dining table Bev had stuck the radio on. Some chat show. Not even music. Mum had let her get away with it. Bev was Mum's golden girl. She could do no wrong in her eyes. She was seated at the table with Marv as Floyd entered the dining room. Dining room. There was another joke. As if his mother's house was big enough to boast a separate dining room and lounge. There was an extra bedroom upstairs now that Dad had gone, but downstairs . . .

Bev looked at him as he came in. 'Something funny baby bro'?' she asked, a hint of a smile curling the edges of her mouth.

Floyd frowned. Was it his imagination or was the whole world leaning on him today? He shook his head. 'Just looking forward to grub.'

'I should think so too.' His mum came into the room carrying a plastic jug of gravy which she set down beside the roast.

Marv smacked his lips appreciatively. 'This looks cool, Mum. What's the special occasion?'

Floyd watched his mother arrange the table and then sit. 'Just having you lot back together again for a few hours.' She grinned, handed a carving knife to Floyd. 'Going to be dad?'

Floyd looked at the knife. Slowly took it. Began to carve the roast. Mum was in a slushy mood. This was going to be bad.

He wasn't wrong.

The next hour passed in a daze of smalltalk and gossip, backed by the annoying blather from the radio. The chat show just seemed to go on interminably. Every so often they played a bit of music, some crap sixties thing, nothing with any groove to it. Nothing you could move to. Floyd smiled inwardly as he shovelled down a last forkful of Yorkshire pudding. He imagined some senile old DJ playing hide and seek with the beat in some middle-of-the-road radio shack somewhere in the middle of town. Last year he and Wilson had watched a video called *Talk Radio* by Oliver Stone. It was about some late-night phone-in DJ who wound up his audience until one of them broke into the station and tried to kill him.

This was hardly in the same league, of course. Some pot-bellied, armchair-hugging psychologist winding up a bunch of OAPs about their day-to-day lives. There was one on there now, claiming to have shoplifted from Valubuys. Floyd grinned. Take the whole damn store, dear, he thought to himself. On the radio the disembodied voice blathered on and on, 'The goods are laid out like that to tempt you. Don't feel guilty about it. How old are you? God, it's not you, Mum? Sorry. My little joke. Are there any shoplifters listening? Here's a seventy-eight-year-old woman driven to attempt suicide by Valubuys Supermarket . . .'

Despite himself Floyd began to giggle.

Bev looked at him. 'You on something or what?'

And the voice on the radio said, 'All shoplifters. Calling all shoplifters. Report to Valubuys and clean them out. If you're not a shoplifter, please consider becoming one for the day. You are the voice of the people. Obey your social conscience . . .'

Floyd exploded into laughter. 'Jesus. This guy. Who is he? He should have his own show.'

'He's just some idiot taking the piss, Floyd. Taking the piss out of people like that poor old lady who can't answer back.'

Bev's voice was loaded with disapproval, but Floyd was too far gone to notice. 'Driven to suicide,' he gasped through a mouthful of brussels sprouts. 'By Valubuys . . .'

Floyd's laughter stopped when his mother switched off the radio.

'That's better. I can hear myself think now.'

Floyd nodded. He lifted another slice of roast onto his plate and filled in the gaps with some vegetables.

Bev grinned. 'You'll explode.'

Marv took up the call. 'Growing lad, our Floyd. Gotta keep his strength up. You know. For those clandestine midnight meetings.' Here he winked broadly at Floyd.

Floyd put down his fork, his lips thinning. He was on the point of snapping out a comeback when his mother spoke instead.

'Did you go and see the benefit people today, Floyd?'

Great, mum. Hit the only other sore point in my life, why don't you.

'Yes.'

'Did they sort your claim out?'

'No. But what do you expect from a bunch of bleeding-heart white liberals?'

Bev groaned.

Marv whispered, 'Jesus, Floyd.'

His mother didn't move a muscle. This was an old story in her house. 'What happened then?'

Floyd put on his fake Jamaican accent and said, 'Wanted to see I passport, didn't they?'

His mother sighed.

'Doesn't matter, anyway,' Floyd continued in more normal tones. 'I've got some work.'

'Cabbing?'

'Yeah.'

'You'll get caught.'

'Yeah right. Sure. They're too busy trying to get me deported to worry about whether I'm doing a bit of moonlighting on the wheels.'

'Someone'll tell on you.'

If only you knew how right you were.

'Why?'

16

'Because that's the way people are.'

'It's just a few hours on the wheels. It's that or starve.'

Marv frowned. 'Go without *that* more like,' he trapped an imaginary cigarette between two fingers and took a drag, blew non-existent smoke across the table.

Floyd stood, anger etching his face. 'What are you saying, man? I don't have to take that from my own brother, man, not in this house!'

Marv didn't rise to the bait. He stared calmly at Floyd until he sat down again.

'You can't work and claim social security,' said his mother.

Floyd turned on her. 'So I stop signing on, right? Is that what you're saying?'

'Yes.'

Now Bev joined in. 'Mum, don't be ridiculous. Floyd can't live on what the cab company pays him.'

'It's nothing to do with you.'

'Right. Floyd's just my brother and you're just my mother and right now it looks like you're both going to rip each other's teeth out. Of course it's got nothing to do with me.'

Marv shrugged. 'Let 'em go to it, Bev, if that's what they want. Floyd's on one, and you know what he's like when he's on one.'

'I'm not on one, all right? I'm not bloody on one!'

Bev shot her brother a nasty look. 'If he doesn't claim the social what happens to it?'

'Listen to her, man,' Floyd rounded on Marv. 'She's nailed it.'

Bev went on, 'It stays in London, that's what happens to it.'

'It's stealing.'

'Mum, it's not stealing.'

'Oh for God's sake, there's loads doing it!'

And Bev was right there with him. 'It's a few quid spent here rather than in London, that's all. We should all be doing it.'

'He'll get caught.'

'Why?'

'You know why, Floyd, now don't answer me back. I'm your mother!'

'Why should I get caught when there's millions doing it?'

'*Because you're not white.*'

There was a long silence.

Floyd looked at his mother. She seemed to crumple slightly. 'There. You went and did it, didn't you? You made me say it. You know how I hate to keep saying it.'

Floyd was on his feet again, that old heat surging inside him again. 'I've told you before,' his voice was tight with anger. 'I'm not "not white".'

But his mother was gone too, off into some interior landscape of memories. 'White people watch you. They watch you because you're not one of them. One of these days one of them will pick up the phone.'

'Mum,' that was Bev, mediating as per normal.

'Pick up the phone and –'

'Mum, that's enough.'

'– and . . .' Mrs Malcolm ran her hands through her hair. 'I only wanted a few hours. Just a few hours with you all together. One meal. One evening a week. It's not too much to ask is it?'

Floyd pushed aside his chair and headed for the door. 'Mum, you're just like all the bloody rest.'

He didn't need to say any more, it was all there in his expression, hatred, bitterness, he could see it reflected from his mother's face, it splashed out into the room, fizzed out like electricity from a sparking wire.

You're just like all the rest. Condescending. Paranoid. Scared.

But he said it anyway. 'You're white inside as well as out.'

8.00p.m.–8.30p.m.

Trantor's Cab Company was located in Fern Street close to Manchester Victoria station. It consisted of one tiny waiting room and an even tinier office into which were usually

18

squashed Tom and Nellie Trantor, the owners and controllers, and any number of cab drivers sneaking a gossip or cuppa between fares.

By the time Floyd joined the queue of wheels parked outside, his temper was flaring intermittently. This was a good sign. Another half an hour and his anger would probably have abated altogether. Balancing the anger he felt at his mother with calming thoughts of Trish, whom he hoped to see later on in the evening, Floyd got out of his wheels. He locked the doors. That wasn't normally the practice, considering the cars were always within plain sight of at least two or three drivers on station outside the office, but Floyd had had car trouble here in the past. Oh nothing the police would consider serious. Just little items of theft. His tapes, mainly. Floyd took pride in his collection of tapes. Everything from banging hardcore to ragga, even a smattering of the more intense garage underground.

The only other thing in the car worth nicking was the CB and that belonged to the cab company. If it wasn't for the fact that everything in the car had to be covered by his own insurance policy he would have left all the doors and the windows wide open.

As it was he made sure they were locked.

He walked heavily along the pavement to the office, past the Chinese chippy, the local community housing action shop and a pub with its main window boarded up. The window was boarded up because of a fight that took place there just last week between some pissed punters and a couple of drivers. Dee Edwards and John Carter had sorted that out. Or rather – according to rumour control – Eddie had had to sort it out because Carter had started it. Floyd found that easy to believe. Carter was a white bastard with a quick line in abuse, while Eddie was also white but not such a bastard; he only laughed at the jokes, he didn't tell them. Eddie had stitches from that encounter. Just three but they were going to leave a scar along Eddie's jaw. Floyd shook his head. There were no medals in this job for heroes. And no sick pay either.

John Carter was with a couple of other drivers, all white boys together, lounging outside the office, cigarettes in hands and smiles on their lips. Great. Carter was telling the joke again.

As Floyd approached he could hear Carter's voice rise a little. Into the joke then. The old joke. Must be a rookie started on the wheels tonight. The old joke came out every time a rookie started. It had come out for Floyd and it had come out for every new driver since. Sometimes, if Carter had been drinking it came out at other times as well. Floyd tried not to listen, tried to think of Trish instead, her calming influence, but the voice with its irritating masculinity and intermittent sniff hammered away at his mind until he had to let it in.

'So I drop the golly in the front off. That leaves three in the back, one of them pissed as a rat, unconscious. I go another mile, drop another one off . . .' Carter saw Floyd then, stopped speaking, took a drag on the cigarette instead. He blew smoke, grinned at the rookie. The rookie looked from Carter to Floyd and back to Carter, unsure how to respond.

Floyd closed his eyes for a moment. *Let it go.* 'All right?'

'All right, Floyd?' Carter's voice was friendly enough.

Floyd howled inside. They were the worst sort. The friendly ones. The ones that pretended.

With an effort he controlled his temper. 'Not much doing?'

Carter shook his head. 'Nah. Not much on at all mate.'

There was another moment of silence, then Floyd began to move past Carter, heading for the office.

Carter turned back to the two drivers he was with, continued, 'I go another mile, drop another one off. He tells me where to take the last golly. The one who's pissed. He's gonna pay me.'

Floyd had paused with his hand on the office door. He was motionless, listening, thinking it over. The heat inside billowing up again, despite all attempts at control.

He turned. 'What were you talking about?'

Carter turned, affecting surprise at being interrupted. 'Do what?'

'I came up, you stopped talking. Why?'

Carter shrugged. 'No reason in particular.'

Floyd took a pace back towards Carter. Inside his head something was hammering away, something was being forged in the heat, another link in the chain, another link of hatred, of persecution.

One of the other drivers, obviously the rookie, was beginning to look a little nervous.

Floyd grinned inwardly, accepted the heat, let it burn him from the inside. The heat was the truth, pure and simple. It wanted out. Soon.

The new driver began to shuffle from foot to foot. He looked from Floyd to Carter. The driver was quiet, staring at Floyd, meeting his gaze with an irritating calm. A calm that only fuelled the fire inside.

This isn't the way. This isn't the place or the time.

Abruptly Floyd turned away.

Carter sniffed. Floyd heard the sound of a shoe grinding against the pavement as Carter stubbed out his cigarette. Almost before he'd taken a pace, Floyd heard the voice again, the irritating masculinity, the presumptuous superiority.

'So anyway, I get there, right, ask the last golly in the car for the fare. Twelve pounds fifty on the clock, but the wog doesn't answer, right? So I gets out to take a look, thinking he might've puked up in the back or something, and fuck me it's not a wog at all –'

And despite his intentions, despite any control, Floyd lost it. He turned, fuming inside, the heat gushing out in a flood that made the rookie take a step backwards, to slip on the kerb before flailing his arms wildly to regain his balance.

'– *it's a tailor's dummy.*' Floyd spat the words into Carter's face, nailed the man with his eyes.

For a moment Carter didn't move, didn't react at all. Then he looked away, groping in his pocket for another high tar.

Floyd turned to stare at the rookie. 'That's right. I know

21

the punch line.' Every word came out pinched, dripping anger. 'Heard it before like.'

Without waiting for a response from either driver, Floyd turned on his heel and went into the cab office.

The satisfaction he felt was a tiny spark next to the flame that still burned inside. The anger. He was a big charge on a short fuse tonight; God help the next person who got in his way.

11.15p.m.–Midnight

Under the circumstances it was tantamount to social suicide to see Trish; he did it anyway. If there was one person guaranteed to calm him down it was Trish. She had that way. That inner something.

How was he to know that tonight it wasn't going to be enough?

The heat was rising; the nightmare was coming back.

Trish worked the late shift at the Boom Box, one of three behind the bar. The club occupied a basement beneath a middle-class Italian restaurant not far from the centre of town. Floyd's usual thing was to catch Trish on a break around ten thirty, eleven, before pub chucking-out time. Chill out for a bit, maybe grab a quick drink, if Trish could blag one on the house. Tonight when he entered the club at about eleven fifteen, Trish was waiting for him on his side of the bar.

She stood as he approached, medium height, medium build, with a cute bob and an impish grin. Floyd felt the old heat evaporate as he saw her. Evaporate, and be replaced by a new heat.

Trish offered her lips for a kiss. Good start.

'What's the special occasion?' he asked, nodding towards the bar.

She grinned, a little shyly, he thought. 'Us,' she said.

'Oh yeah?'

'Yeah.'

Somebody cranked up the sound system. More people

were coming in off the street now; it was ten minutes after usual chucking-out time. The press of bodies was thick around the bar.

Floyd took Trish's hand and drew her away, found a space by one of the support pillars. When he spoke he had to shout above the music. Jungle tonight. Appropriate. 'What's the plan then; bop or blow?'

Trish grabbed him around the waist. 'I want to dance,' she squeezed. 'But not here.'

Floyd licked his lips. Inside heat fought heat, confusion, conflict. Peer pressure was telling him this should be easy, the most natural thing in the world. Somehow the facts never fit the rule book. 'That's a bit sudden isn't it?'

Trish looked up at him. 'Floyd. We've known each other for three months now.'

Floyd drew back a little. She felt his body tense; responded by clinging a little tighter. 'Yeah.'

'So.'

'So what?' The tension between them was crackling now, fizzing in time with the beat, garage jungle, bordering on hardcore, thrash rhythms slashing along his nervous system and into his brain. His feet were tapping. All around him the crowd surged, calls for drinks, laughter, chat, beery catcalls, all merging together into a chaos of white noise.

Trish rolled her eyes. 'So do you want me to draw you a picture?' She grabbed a handful of arse. Floyd jumped, every muscle tense.

Naked, she wants me naked, together, in bed, she wants –

'Nervous, huh?' Trish grinned, renewed her grip on his buttocks. 'Dominant women scare you do they?' Abruptly she fished in her purse, frowned when she came up with a crumpled pack of Silk Cut. She shook the box; empty. 'Come prepared did you?'

Floyd blinked.

– wants me naked, in bed, wants me –

'What?'

'Got a smoke, have you?' She sighed, grinned. 'We're in dreamland tonight aren't we?'

23

Floyd groped for an answer and Trish cast a look around the club. Trish shook her head. 'Let's go back to mine,' she said with a direct look.

'Oh right. You took the evening off then?'

'Of course. If I stay here now not only will I lose any peer respect I may have, but I'll probably be collared to get back behind the bar as well.' Here she nodded to the woman working behind the bar. The girl tossed her a quick grin and winked at Floyd.

'Yeah. You know. I could do with a drink. We're all right here for a bit?'

Trish's lips firmed. 'We are not. Now do you want to take me home or not?'

Floyd hesitated. 'Yeah. It's just that work –'

'Screw work.' Trish's look shook him to his feet. She leaned closer and he caught a hint of her perfume. 'Then screw me.'

Trish rented the ground floor of a Victorian mid-terrace a mile from the town centre. The house was on the main drag and the rumble of traffic was a soothing backdrop to their conversation, such as it was. Floyd left the wheels parked directly outside – the other occupants of the house were a couple who Trish told him were so ecologically sound they should paint their arses green. She didn't seem to notice when Floyd didn't join in her laughter at the absurd state-ment. She took him downstairs to the stone-walled kitchen, and made him a cup of tea. The kitchen was sunk beneath the level of the garden, so that cool moonlight glimmered through the overgrown lawn and cast monochrome shadows across the old-fashioned gas stove and kitchen units. The sink had a permanently drippy tap, and the sound, together with the soft rustle of weeds against the kitchen window, and the muted rumble of traffic from the front of the house worked a kind of soothing magic on Floyd – for a while.

Only for a while. Drinking the tea was fine, but he knew sooner or later Trish was going to make a move. True to form it was sooner rather than later. 'You've nursed that tea like it had cancer,' she said after ten minutes passed in silence. 'I'm beginning to think you don't want to be here.'

Floyd shook his head, an automatic reaction.

Trish smiled. 'Good. Look. Why don't you take a shower. Unwind, yeah?'

Floyd nodded mutely. Eyed the half-empty mug of tea as if it was the last straw thrown to a drowning man.

'It's through there,' Trish pointed to an alcove at the far end of the kitchen.

She got up, took Floyd's hand, guided him towards the alcove. As she walked him through the kitchen she began to unbutton his shirt.

He took her hand in his, stopped the movement. 'I can manage.' He contrived a half-hearted grin to defuse the tension. 'I'm a big boy now.'

Her smile widened. 'That's what I'm hoping.'

In the shower he finished removing his shirt, folded it neatly, hung it over the towel rail. He started the water running. Steam filled the glass cubicle. He took his shoes off. His socks.

As he bent he caught sight of his reflection in Trish's full-length mirror. Good skin. Firm expression. Good teeth and eyes. Neat hair. A good body.

From the waist up.

His fingers moved to his belt. Hesitated. Fumbled with the catch. Hesitated again.

The door to the kitchen opened and Trish came in wearing a huge fluffy bath towel.

'Thought you'd be nice and wet by now.' She moved closer, ran her hands across his back. Then she lowered her head against his shoulder and put her arms around his waist. 'You want to get wet?' Her fingers moved across his groin. He tensed against her.

She wants me she wants me naked she wants me –

Her fingers moved upwards, to his belt. Found the buckle. Undid it.

– in bed wants me naked wants me in bed naked –

25

And he was moving, out of her arms, out of the bathroom, out of control.

She followed, hurt, not understanding. She didn't say anything, just stood on the cold flagstones of the kitchen as he put his shirt on and did the buttons up, grabbed his jacket, headed for the door, the stairs, the street.

Then, as he was on the stairs, the old-fashioned wooden risers, she spoke. 'Is it something I did? You're shy right? I know that, it's obvious. But why —?'

'You wouldn't understand.' The words came out pinched and bitter.

'At least come and have a cup of tea. We can talk it through.'

Floyd turned then and the heat was back inside, boiling up, molten emotion, unstoppable. And he didn't want to stop it, welcomed the heat, drew strength from it, let it fizz out into the house, a spray of words.

'We're friends, Trish. Yeah. Good friends. I like you. I fancy you. But tonight. Ah, man, tonight. You want me in bed. Naked. You want me naked in bed.'

'Fuck yes, I want you naked, I want you in bed, in the hall, on the staircase, on the fucking ironing board, wherever you like. I love you.'

'You want sex. I don't. There's a word for that.'

She blinked, uncomprehending for a second, then fury blasted across her face. 'You selfish wanker!' She gasped for a moment, fish out of water, his words bringing a boiling heat to her face. 'You selfish . . . *wanker*.' She struggled for control, found it eventually. 'How would you know? You've got no idea what you're talking about! How *dare* you accuse me of —'

But Floyd was already moving, up the stairs, out, away. Her self-righteous fury washed over him, a cool, soothing trickle compared to the heat inside.

'There's a word for that,' he said again, over his shoulder.

'Oh yeah? Well how the fuck would you know?' she screeched after him.

But he was gone, leaving Trish to collapse on the staircase, alone with her shame and confusion, alone to look into herself, to look for the truth while he stormed away. Both of them alone. One with the truth, the other with his anger.

His anger and the night.

How would you know?

TWO

Doctor Edward Fitzgerald stared at the woman sitting across the desk from him.

A middle-height, middle-aged woman who might once have been pretty. Who would still be pretty if she could get past the present. Then again, that was what she was here for, wasn't it? To regain her self-confidence. To overcome her guilt, her fear, her humiliation.

Except that, judging by her level of agitation, she wasn't going to be here long enough to discuss five across in *The Times* crossword, let alone the fact that she'd been assaulted and raped.

Fitz leaned a little closer across the desk. Grey daylight filtering in through the blinds across the office window cast horizontal bars across his face. He gave a jowly squint, realised what he must look like. Cute.

'Mrs Holmes. Gaby. I know what you're thinking. You're thinking it might have been a mistake to come here. To see me. That I won't understand because I'm a man. Because my wife's left me. Because I have no experience of being raped.' He felt the woman's eyes on him, imagined himself as she saw him: six foot two, twenty-one stone, mid-forties, short-cropped jet black hair. Aggressive body language. A pile of neuroses wrapped up in a crumpled suit. He lit up a high tar and sucked deeply. He reckoned she probably thought he looked more like a very seriously gone-to-seed private detective than a leading psychologist. There were days when she'd be right, too.

He pressed on, pushing ever so slightly. 'But you need to

talk to someone. Your husband definitely doesn't understand. Your girlfriends won't talk about it. They're embarrassed. You hate them for that. And your family. Of all the
people who could help, it should be them. Should be them.
But they refuse to visit any more, get uncomfortable on the
phone, won't talk to you any more. But you need to talk
about it, Gaby. That need is fundamental to the human
psyche. No man is an island. No woman either. You need to
talk about it. You'll go mad if you don't, but no-one is
prepared to listen. It's called secondary victimisation. It
makes your husband, family, society, even me, as guilty of
aggression towards you as the man who raped you.' He
sucked once more on the high tar, blew smoke at the
window. 'Did he smoke?'

She nodded, captured, a moth to his flame. He had her and
he knew it. He stubbed the high tar out, three-quarters
unsmoked, left it in the ashtray on the desk, one among
many unemptied throughout the cluttered office.

All right. She'd bitten. It was time to reel her in. The first
step in the healing process, Fitz-style. 'You need to talk.
That's understandable. You don't have to feel guilty about it.
Society wants you to, but you mustn't. Talking about it will
help. It's the first stage of recovery. You need to talk. You
need to talk; I'm here to listen.'

She seemed to crumple in the chair. Just for a moment he
thought he'd lost her. Then she straightened, and he saw that
look in her eye. That look that told him he'd played the
winning hand again.

She began to speak. Her voice was quiet, a whisper in the
grainy silence of the office. 'I remember feeling stupid. I
remember that and I remember thinking

how stupid
   How stupid to be scared.
   This man would never do *that* to me.
   His voice is warm. It's a nice voice. He's a nice man. It's
stupid to be scared. He wouldn't do that to me. Not to
me. Not here. He wouldn't. He wouldn't touch me like

29

that wouldn't touch

*my mouth his hand is over my mouth and his skin is warm
and his face is so close and his breath is Colgate sweet that
ring of confidence sweet and oh God he's a nice man he
won't do this won't do this to me if I stay still if I stay*

calm.

Must stay calm.

Don't provoke him and he won't do that to me.

Stay rational and he won't do that to me.

He'll see I don't want him to and he won't do that to me
not that not to me no he can't if I stay calm he won't he
mustn't he mustn't do that to me no oh no oh I can't I
can't

*see there's something covering my face something cover-
ing me he put it there put it on me he put it on me put it on
me oh oh I can't see him but I can feel him feel the muscles
moving against me I can smell him I can*

talk.

Perhaps if I talk to him reason with him he won't do that
to me stay calm and talk to him and reason with him and he
won't he won't do that to me to me he won't do that to me
he's a nice man he won't

put a hood on me and gag me and

wouldn't do that to me not to me he wouldn't he wouldn't
he wouldn't he wouldn't do that he wouldn't do that to me
he wouldn't touch me like that he wouldn't

rape

he wouldn't

rape me

he wouldn't

rape me oh God he's going to rape me he's going to

please

rape me's going to

please God

going to

please God please God please please please no please God
no please no please don't take not my skirt oh not my skirt
no don't take it off don't do that don't

kill me he's going to
do that to me don't
  *kill me he's going to rape me and kill me murder me
drown me right here in the canal in the water right here
where the children play oh God the children the children
there'll be blood in the water in the water with the children
blood in the water and I'll be in the water in the canal
floating*

INSIDE ME HE'S INSIDE ME OH GOD OH JESUS
HE'S

inside me he's
  *dead in the canal dead in the water floating dead because
it hurts oh God it hurts it hurts make it stop hurting stop
hurting please make him stop hurting me stop*
  pushing pushing pushing inside me
raping me he's
pushing me he's
raping me he's
pushing inside me he's
raping me
pushing
raping
pushing
raping
  pushing me into the water we're in the water I'm in the
water in the canal and the taste of it is washing away the
sweat and the Colgate smell of him but the pain the pain
won't wash away the pain of him won't wash away it's
inside me even though he's not any more inside me and I
want to open my mouth and let the water in let it in to wash
him out from inside me wash the pain of him out from inside
me I want to open my mouth but I can't because of the hood
the gag I want to open my mouth and let the water in I want
to
  drown
  I want to

die
I want to wash him out of me I want to
die
I want to

run, to hide, to get away where no-one can see me, where none of my friends can see me, Christ I can't stand it any more, the pain, the humiliation, the fear, the looking over my shoulder, I want them all to go away, just go away, I want to die, God help me, I want to die!'

Fitz reached for a high tar. The packet was empty.

As usual he'd got the prize.

But as her words trailed away into tears, he began to wonder, not for the first time, exactly what he'd won, and what this first step on the road to recovery would ultimately cost Gaby Holmes.

2.00p.m.–7.00p.m.

The day had begun badly for Fitz. Ho hum. A late morning, blue fuzzy stuff on the bread, half-dead can of beans in the fridge. So much for the self-catering holiday. Perhaps he should have stayed at home. Then his nineteen-year-old son Mark came in trailing the smell of alcohol and self-abuse from the night before and reminded Fitz he was still at home. At home minus half the family. His wife gone, his daughter. Judith. Katie. He had replacements though. Things to stop him getting lonely. He had his son. Boom-boom. He had the dust, the dirty laundry, the faulty plumbing in the upstairs loo. Oh yes. Katie's fish tank and paraphernalia. Mustn't forget those. What else? Ah, he had himself, as was abundantly obvious from that glorious another-night-spent-on-the-sitting-room-couch odour.

And that was just the start.

Following the session with Gaby Holmes Fitz cancelled all non-emergency appointments for a few days while he concentrated on the case Charlie Wise, the new DCI at Anson Road, had bunged his way. Sitting back in his comfortably upholstered chair, Fitz thought that cancellation was probably just as well – for his clients. Professional respect for a psychologist who was in worse shape than his patients was pretty thin on the ground these days.

A virulent disease this non-respect thing.

He spent a lazy half-hour wondering if there was a cure and, if there was, whether it was available in litre bottles from the drinks counter at Valubuys.

Well. It seemed like a logical theory. He called in to Valubuys on the way home, spent the rest of the afternoon testing it; the old suck-it-and-see approach.

Mark banged in around three, took one look at his father's empirical reasoning and empty bottle, and promptly went out again, the banging door an angry counterpart to the disgust on his face.

At three thirty the phone rang.

He stared at the phone, allowing the ringing tone to get into his head. There was a wealth of hope tied up in the shrill electronic bleep. Anything could be waiting for him on the other end, anyone. Judith. Katie. He stared at the phone. It might even be Officer Panhandle, calling to say why she hadn't spoken to him for a month. Oh, he thought. Life is exciting. He reached for the phone.

Tripped over the cable.

The phone went dead.

It took him five minutes to put the plug back in the wall. The phone remained stubbornly silent. He watched it for a while. Nothing. He thought about ringing the BT Lastcall service, then didn't. If whoever it was wanted him that badly they'd call back. He'd bet on it. Well; he would if he'd had any money. He picked up the bottle of Bell's and shook it. Three fingers of whisky left in the bottom. Nice, satisfying gurgle.

Tell you what, he said to himself, *I bet you these three fingers of Bell's whoever it was phones back.*

Oh yeah, he replied. *What'll you do if they don't? Drown your sorrows?*

Don't you cliché me, you middle-aged, self-loathing old bastard, you.

Then promise me no promises, you middle-aged alcoholic old bastard, you.

Fitz's argument with himself was about to get violent when the phone rang again. It was the local radio station. They wanted to put Fitz on the air. Better still, though no less absurd, they wanted to pay for the privilege.

So he spent the remainder of the afternoon with a producer and a DJ, neither of whose names he remembered after being paid. Oh yeah, and a dozen disturbed callers, among them an old lady driven to attempted suicide by Valubuys supermarket.

Sometimes life was strange.

He got home around six thirty, fist full of tenners, head full of commercial breaks and microphone technique, to find the phone ringing again. Fitz had grabbed the phone quickly, half hoping it would be Penhaligon, but it was Judith's estate agent. Would seven thirty be OK to show a prospective buyer around the house?

Fitz yelled. Actually screamed would be a better word. 'Seven thirty would not be convenient. This century would not be convenient. A man's home is his castle, you know. Come near it and you'll get an arrow up your arse.'

He slammed the phone down. Had a drink. Had another. Lit up a high tar. Had another drink. Sucked on the high tar. Looked at the phone. Balanced the smoking high tar on the packet, on the sofa beside him. Picked up the phone. Dialled her number.

'Hello?' Her voice was light, smoother even than the whisky. As smooth as her skin had been to the touch. So long ago.

'Panhandle? It's Fitz.'

Long silence. Then her voice again. 'Fitz? I haven't hung up.' *Not like Judith does when you try to talk to her.* 'You could try speaking to me if you like.'

Panhandle. Jane. I think I love you. That's bad because I love my wife, I love Judith, and my kids, but I love you too. I'm really confused. Can we talk? Please? Just a few minutes would do. Maybe an hour. Over a meal, perhaps? A drink. Or two.

'I suppose a quick one's out of the question?'

A sigh from the phone. 'Fitz.' His name like a breath of wind. A zephyr. 'Fitz, why are you doing this to us? I thought we were on stable ground. You're pulling the rug out from under again.'

I'm pulling the rug? Who is it that hasn't called who around here? Come round, just for a bit. Let's get it sorted. Please.

'That's Fitz-speak, Panhandle. You're so besotted with me you even talk like me.'

'Oh yeah? Well get this, Fitz: I'm going out tonight. The Blue Mountain. And I'm not going with you. That's Jane-speak. Plain enough for you? Goodbye Fitz.'

Fitz stared at the phone as the front door banged open and Mark barged in. Fitz put the handset back on the cradle. 'I could sue British Telecom. Accessory to murder.'

Mark sniffed, looked around, pointed to the cushion where Fitz had balanced his high tar on the packet. The cigarette was no longer there, but a curl of smoke was seeping from between the cushions beside Fitz's leg.

'You've set light to the couch.'

'Shit!'

Fitz reacted without thinking. He picked up the fish tank and emptied it over the couch.

The water ran through the cushions and drenched the floor. Fitz glanced at Mark and grinned smugly. 'It's out.'

Mark pointed to the couch. 'So are Katie's fish.'

'Oh Christ!' Fitz made a hopeless grab for the flopping and jerking fish. 'I thought she'd taken them with her!'

Mark shook his head and left the room.

'Where are you going?'

'To call the fire brigade. Get them to check out the couch.'

Fitz chased Mark into the hall, both hands full of fish. 'It's out.'

Mark picked up the phone. 'You get fumes. It can light up again. I'm calling.'

'You're over-reacting –' Fitz reached for the phone,

remembered the fish he was holding, made a dash for the downstairs loo.

He heard Mark talking on the phone as he ran water into the sink, dumped the fish into the cold water.

Then he walked back into the hall, placed a dripping finger on the cradle, cutting off Mark as he was about to give their address.

Fitz glared at Mark. 'The fish are all right.'

'They're tropical.' Mark fielded the glare and shot it right back. 'They're gonna die anyway.'

The inevitable argument followed about whether he should have phoned the fire brigade or not. Then Mark stomped out again, banged out into the evening with a scowl that was becoming depressingly familiar, and Fitz was left with the lingering smell of burnt cloth and a head full of guilt.

Eventually the smoke went away; the guilt remained in his head, persistent, a nagging reminder of his own inadequacy. He finished the Bell's, hunted through the drinks cabinet, found it bare of everything except glasses, sat down in a depressed daze, only to find he was sitting on the dripping couch.

Then he remembered the money in his wallet. The money from the radio show. He grinned. Suddenly the evening had potential.

11.15p.m.–Midnight

The potential evaporated twenty-eight quid and ten shorts later at the Blue Mountain Club, right about the time that Detective Sergeant Jane Penhaligon walked in with a man on her arm who would have made the Chippendales crawl *en masse* to a plastic surgeon and beg for priority placement.

Fitz watched them for an hour. Why did he do it? Masochism? Voyeurism? He was not prepared to admit he couldn't see a reason, so he blamed the alcohol. Losing control made him more depressed than ever. Finally, with just a tenner left in his wallet, he got up, threaded a less than steady path through the crowd to where Penhaligon and her partner were dancing.

He watched her for a moment before she noticed him, watched the way her skin glowed in the lights, thought she seemed to pulse in time with the music, pulse with life and vitality. He thought of that skin and hair spread out across his pillow. He turned to leave.

That was when she saw him.

Time seemed to unravel. She'd brought him the news of Joanne Barnes's murder, dead in Manchester Central, pumped full of alcohol and antidepressants, a lethal mixture, her body covered with magic marker symbols, techno graffiti for the age of Chaos, a seventeen-year-old schoolgirl seduced and screwed, knocked up and finally murdered by the priest of a local church, his brother and both their wives.

Jealousy. Penhaligon herself had looked no older than seventeen herself then; for some reason Joanne's death had hit her hard. Perhaps she felt some connection. That attraction for an older man. Tragic. Except that he had been the older man.

And sex had been just too good.

Now she looked at him, her red hair and lips accentuated by the lighting, looked straight through him.

The club seemed to fall silent around him. Fitz fell into the gravity well of his own memories, banked around the event horizon, felt himself whipped in a vicious orbit back to a present dominated by the thought of her, the memory of her, dammit even the smell of her.

I think I love you. He'd thought that afterwards, not just before. *Jane Penhaligon, I think I love you.*

'Why, Panhandle. What a surprise. Are you going to introduce me to this god of male sexuality?'

Penhaligon bit her lip. Her companion looked steadily at Fitz, his expression carefully neutral.

Fitz spared him a casual glance. 'It's OK, the old bugger's twenty-one stone and pissed as a fart, he's no threat.'

37

'Fitz!' Penhaligon pushed her fingers through her hair. Fitz thought he detected no small amount of despair in her voice. He imagined those fingers running through his own hair. Imagined kissing them. Tasting the creamy skin. Had it really been as good for her as he'd thought?

'You must be Peter.'

He looked at the man. The perfect skin, the cobalt eyes and square jaw. Dear God, the man was a walking cliché. Then Fitz grinned. The orbit was complete, the event horizon of his memories slung him back out again, fizzing, pinwheeling through a starfield of his own emotions, free at last.

'I bet you can't do this,' he said.

And waggled his ears.

And he was away, shuffling backwards through the crowd, a fat drunk doing the Michelin Man Moonwalk away from her, away from the picture they made together.

Midnight–1.30a.m.

As he stepped out of the cab, thirty minutes later, Fitz read the name off the ID card in the window. 'Floyd?'

'Nah, man. Wilson. Shared cab.'

Fitz nodded. 'Sure, man. Tell me, Wilson, how old would you say I am?'

Wilson shrugged. 'Late forties.'

Fitz sighed. 'Bang goes your tip.'

He grabbed his change, counted it, stuffed it into his pocket, grappled with the front-door lock – almost an intelligence test, these Yale double locks, but he'd crack it – stumbled into the hallway.

Mark was on the phone as he slammed the front door. 'Say hi to the brigade for me,' mumbled Fitz.

Mark looked up. 'Surprise me, Dad. See if you can get as far as your bedroom before you crash out.'

It was as much of a surprise to Fitz as Mark when he actually managed it.

An hour later Fitz tossed and turned on his bed. Alone on

his bed. Got up. Pulled open the curtains. Stared out at the moon, the light drifts of silver clouds coasting silently over Manchester.

The truth was that sex was too good. Too good to miss at all, let alone like this. Because of fear.

Not his fear. Hers.

That must be the reason: she liked sex. She liked sex with him. It was frighteningly good. The look on her face had told him that much. That was why she practically hadn't spoken to him since. The fear. But it was so long ago. Now the look was fading; his memory of it gradually overlaid with more recent events. It should remain etched in his mind. Etched in stone. No. That was a cliché. The truth was different. Always different from what you'd expect. The fact of the matter was that the truth was a stranger these days, hadn't dropped in for some time, in fact. And it was getting lonely here, inside, especially now that the memory of her expression was fading. Worse still – and he had to admit it, had to be *truthful* about it – now that the memory of sex with her was fading.

Oh. God. Fucking. Dammit.

It was all bollocks anyway.

Judith. Jane. Sex. The whole kit and kaboodle.

All of it.

Fitz reached for the bottle on the dresser, reached unconsciously, without looking, knew exactly where it was, to a gulp how much was left in it. Bell's. Seventeen pounds and ninety-nine pence worth. He tilted the bottle up, stared at the moon through the sloshing fluid as it ate into his throat. Stared at the moon and felt like howling at it. Felt like an animal.

He drank like an animal too, guzzled the liquid fire, breathed in the fumes, splash of gold, rippling craters, Tycho there, and the Sea of Rains, wobbling crazily as the whisky sloshed, nine point eight on the Richter scale, and did the earth move for you, too, darling? Oh yes, like a JCB on heat.

And then the gold was inside him, molten, the heat an old

friend, comfortable, familiar, and the moon wasn't the moon any more it was her face, and then her face turned gold, gold and weightless and gravity tricked him, tripped him up and claimed him for its own.

3.30a.m.–4.00a.m.

When Mark shook him awake Fitz became aware that he was asleep on the bedroom floor, his head cradled on his own shoes. He blinked, grumbled awake, stared up at his son. 'What's for breakfast?'

Mark's lip curled in disgust. 'It's three thirty in the morning.'

'It may come as a surprise to you, my eldest and dearest, but I am currently wallowing in the throes of a bleak depression. So I'd be terribly grateful if you'd sod off, OK?'

Mark gritted his teeth, somehow managed not to give vent to his anger. 'The doorbell was ringing for ten minutes.'

Fitz jerked upright. 'Judith?'

Mark sighed. 'Your bit on the side. The copper.' He stood up, turned, left the bedroom. Fitz heard him speak from the other side of the room.

'He's in there. Rat-arsed.'

The sound of Mark thumping back along the landing, disapproval evident in the slam of his bedroom door. Shutting him out. Shutting them out.

And then she was there. In the room. Her face. Those eyes.

Fitz rubbed his face, felt ridges in his cheek where the laces of his shoes had indented the skin.

'It's all right, Panhandle. I understand. You're racked with guilt. You couldn't stand to be away from my body for another night.'

Penhaligon's lips narrowed to a thin line.

'It's all right, Panhandle. I forgive you. I do.'

And then her voice, dry, brittle with tension. 'There's been another rape. Wise wants both of us at the scene . . .'

40

Fitz sat down again, missed the end of the bed, landed arse first on his shoes. *Matching cheek patterns. Chic.* 'Coffee. I need coffee.'

Penhaligon stared at him without an ounce of sympathy. 'You've got time to wash and get dressed.' She tossed him a packet of Trebor Extra Strong Mints. 'You don't want to be smelling of whisky.'

Fitz licked his lips, scowled at the taste. 'Thanks.'

She nodded. 'And when I get the chance, I'd like to explain.'

Sure. I'm old, fat, a wreck. You fancied a fling, maybe for the novelty of it. Perhaps you were attracted to my intellect, an older man, a different viewpoint on life, God knows, it's all I've got going for me these days. I understand.

'There's nothing to explain.'

Then again maybe you just fancied being out of control.

He almost made it to the bathroom before throwing up.

4.00a.m.–4.30a.m.

The case had been in progress now for nearly fourteen weeks. It had begun two days after he and Penhaligon had slept together with the rape of Helen Robins, a thirty-two-year-old pharmaceutical assistant who had been walking through Centenary Park on her way home from work.

A month later Gaby Holmes had been assaulted on her way home from work.

Two weeks after that Danielle Sumner.

Three weeks after that Joanne Harris.

The attacks had taken place less than five miles apart, in the same section of central Manchester. According to Wise, the police were treating the cases as connected. The start of a promising career for a serial rapist. There were other similarities too: all the victims were white. They were all within the same five-year age bracket.

And the *modus operandi* of the rapist had been the same in each case. The victims had been made to wear a hood. The victims had been comforted afterwards by the rapist. He had talked to them. And other things. He combed their pubic hair. The rapes had taken place near running water. A lake in Centenary Park in the case of Helen Robins, a canal in the case of Gaby Holmes. Both women had been immersed in the water by the rapist after intercourse had taken place. The other victims had been thoroughly washed.

The profile was building slowly. Fitz knew the danger of making snap judgements in cases such as these. In the past, he had himself collaborated on a textbook dealing with the psychological traumas associated with rape, during the course of which more than a few rape myths had been exploded. As a consequence he was fully aware of the possible processes involved, both of the victim and the rapist. He had interviewed both Helen and Gaby – the only women who would consent to speak with him – on different occasions; he'd been careful to explain the process of secondary victimisation associated with the recovery process. Had emphasised the fact that neither Helen nor Gaby had been responsible *in any way* for their attacker's behaviour, no matter what the press or society as a whole had to say about the matter. He had counselled Gaby Holmes when she was diagnosed as having contracted Hepatitis B from being thrown in the canal after her ordeal. Apart from that both victims had been clean as a whistle. No signs of gonorrhoea, AIDs or any other sexually transmitted diseases. The rapist had been almost professional in his approach. He knew the ropes. And he knew police methods, too. So far the only evidence he'd left behind had been a queue of badly traumatised early middle-aged women.

Fitz felt almost physically sick when he thought about the case. He felt a rage in him, the heat of shared guilt. He was a man. The rapist was a man. It had to stop. And he knew that his feelings were nothing at all compared to the physical pain, misplaced guilt, and absolute terror the women concerned had felt, not only during their ordeals and in the immediate aftermath, but were likely to continue feeling, possibly for years to come.

Fitz's thoughts were still rattling loose in his head when Penhaligon steered her Volvo into Arnos Leisure Complex car park and braked to a halt.

The car park was almost full. A couple of unmarked police cars. The forensics van. A couple of striped Rovers, all with lights on to combat the night. More lights bobbed like will-o'-the-wisps across the building as uniformed officers examined the exterior and grounds, checking doors and windows for any signs of forced entry. Another van had been set up as a control centre. Crackly radio voices carried distantly on the wind.

'All we need is a hotdog stall,' Fitz muttered as he clambered stiffly out of the Volvo. He glanced at Penhaligon to check her response. A grin would be good news. Even a hint of a smile would do.

Nothing. She led the way up the concrete steps and through the wide glass double doors, flashed her ID at a uniform on duty there, introduced Fitz.

Fitz looked around. He smelled chlorine and changing rooms. There was a pool here. It was starting to add up.

He also smelled smoke. Only one copper he knew who would smoke at the scene of the crime.

Jimmy Beck was waiting with Harriman beyond the uniformed constable, lounging against a wall full of posters advertising everything from the forthcoming swimming gala to aerobics for beginners to advanced Tai Chi.

Beck and Harriman had their differences. Beck was a Detective Sergeant, old school, a hard man, balding, moustached, rollup tucked into a perpetual scowl. Harriman was newly promoted. Still on the green side. A bit under-ripe, some would say. A bit gullible. Both men wore plain suits, Beck's grey, to match his complexion, Harriman's a neat brown. There were other similarities too. Harriman tended to look to Beck for guidance.

Both of them now looked towards Fitz and Penhaligon. But not for guidance. For a bit of a laugh. The fact that Penhaligon and Fitz were a – sometime – item was a source of boundless mirth to her workmates.

43

Beck took his rollup out and straightened as Penhaligon led Fitz towards him.

'Earth move did it?' That was Harriman, chipping in with the comment that should by rights have been Beck's. The older man, sensibly, said nothing, allowed Harriman to fend off the weight of Penhaligon's irritable stare alone.

Fitz grinned at Harriman as Penhaligon swept past. 'Eight point nine on the Richter scale; and these Krauts are accurate . . .'

That earned him a foul glance back over the shoulder from Penhaligon.

Shit.

Beck and Harriman led them through the main foyer, past the ticket office, following signs to the changing rooms. They passed more uniformed officers. A whole gaggle, thought Fitz. A gaggle of uniforms, clustered around the swing doors to the main pool. Fingerprint dust. Little brushes. Santa's little helpers.

Beck opened the door to the changing rooms. He ushered Penhaligon and Fitz through the doors. Fitz caught the glance he gave Penhaligon, then found himself on the receiving end of a knowing grin. Beck closed the door between them before Fitz could respond.

In contrast to the bustle outside the changing rooms, particularly around the pool area by which they had passed, inside was almost cathedral calm. Fitz could hear the sound of Penhaligon breathing. His own breath chuffed in his throat. And there were other sounds. Dim, distant, a word, muted, the sound of sobbing, choked back, the scuff of a shoe, all rippling gently through the warm air from behind a wall of lockers.

Behind the lockers was a row of wide plastic benches. Seated on them were two women. One a uniformed PC, the other a slight woman wrapped up in a huge bath towel. Her feet and face stuck out from the towel. Her hands clutched the material to her chest. She was shivering. Her hair was ash blonde, streaked, darkened with water. She was staring at the plastic-tiled floor.

Another figure stood some yards away, a bear of a man, beard, piercing eyes behind glasses above a serge suit. DCI Wise. The new boss at Anson Road.

The WPC glanced up. Wise beckoned to Penhaligon with his eyes. They walked over to him, allowed themselves to be drawn off to one side.

'Her name's Catherine Carter,' Wise said, his voice a soft purr, at odds with his bear-like appearance. 'She's the manager here.'

Penhaligon asked, 'Is it the same man?'

Wise nodded. 'Superficial evidence bears that out. I'm hoping you can corroborate the supposition, Fitz.'

Fitz chewed his lower lip thoughtfully. 'I should do this at Fallowfields.'

Fallowfields Family and Child Protection Unit, one of many set up around Manchester, was a twenty-minute drive away. Procedure was very clear now. If Catherine agreed she should be taken to the unit, given a medical examination and then interviewed. The key word here was: if she agreed.

Wise frowned. 'We're not really getting much from her. I don't want to get her there and find the evidence is worthless because she won't follow through. See what you can do, eh?'

Fitz weighed up the odds. Doing anything here at the site was a risk. A risk for the police, but more importantly a risk for Catherine. He considered. It was long odds on anything panning out. What did they have to lose?

He gave a little half nod, groped in his top pocket for his bifocals, rested them lightly on his nose. 'Thunderbirds to the rescue then,' he said in a voice so quiet it hardly registered.

He caught the WPC's eye and moved towards the two women, settled himself on the bench a casual distance from the betowelled woman.

She looked up straight away. Fitz expected fear. There was none.

I'm not a threat to her. Not a man to her. Not that kind of man.

'Catherine?'

She nodded, pushed back a limp strand of hair that fell across one eye.

'Would you rather speak to DS Penhaligon?' Fitz nodded towards Penhaligon standing quietly with Wise some yards away.

Catherine shook her head. 'No. Thanks for asking. You're the psychologist.'

Fitz nodded. Waited. Waited for that look from Catherine that said she was ready to go on. Got it after ten minutes or so. 'Can you tell me what happened?'

'I . . .' she sniffed. Wiped the back of one hand across her face. Her eyes seemed hooded, deeply shadowed. Fitz stared deeply into the darkness there, found something that gave him a little hope. A certain strength. A certain resilience. 'I . . .' Again she tailed off. It was just too soon. From the corner of his eye Fitz caught sight of Wise. The DCI folded his arms, somewhat impatiently, Fitz thought. Well tough. You'll have to wait, mate.

'I understand, Catherine. It's hard to talk about. You don't want to talk about it. You don't want to think about it.'

'No. I don't.'

'He hurt you. Violated you.'

'He . . . talked to me. Afterwards. Said my name. My name. He said my name. Afterwards. Before. All the time. All the time.'

Again Fitz nodded. 'And that makes you cringe. You associate your own name with this awful thing that's been done to you and you can't bear to hear the name, think of yourself as separate from the event.'

Catherine shivered, suddenly, clutched the towel more tightly around her. A single drop of water flung from her hair struck Fitz's bifocals dead centre on the left lens.

He took off the glasses and cleaned them on a handkerchief.

'Sorry.'

'It's OK.'

'I know what it's like. Get water on your glasses, they're a devil to clean.'

46

'Do you wear glasses?'

'Contacts. Used to though.'

'I'm a minus three on the left eye. Not so bad.'

'You can have that corrected with laser surgery these days.'

Fitz nodded. 'I know. I've been thinking about it. Do you mind if I use your name?'

A pause.

'No.'

Fitz smiled. 'I have to ask you these questions, Catherine. I hope you understand.'

'Yes.'

'If you'd rather DS Penhaligon asked them . . . ?'

'No. You ask them.'

Fitz nodded. *Bingo.* 'All right then.' A breath. 'First of all I'd like you to describe what happened to you. One sentence will do. Take it slowly. You can take as much time as you need.' A glance at Wise. Practically tapping his foot with impatience. Insensitive bastard.

'Uh . . . I . . . um. I was swimming. Working out. I'm the manager here. I sometimes use the pool after we're closed to the public. I shouldn't really, it's against the rules, but . . . well, there's no harm in it, is there?' Catherine paused. Fitz waited patiently until she continued. 'I'd finished swimming. I was walking to the changing rooms. Um . . . he . . . he was . . . he was waiting in the corridor. He was . . . wearing a hood. A black hood. He made me put one on as well. He . . . he . . . oh God . . . he . . . um . . . pushed me up against the wall. Roughly. Had to show me who was in charge I suppose. Then he . . . um . . .' Catherine bit her lip. She turned to the WPC. 'Could I have a towel please? For my hair?'

The WPC smiled, nodded, handed Catherine a towel from a nearby rail. A moment passed while Catherine wrapped her hair in it. Turbanned, she stared at Fitz and continued. 'When I was against the wall he spoke to me. Told me he wouldn't hurt me. Not if I didn't struggle. So I didn't. I couldn't believe it was happening. I kept thinking it would

47

stop, but it didn't. It didn't stop and then he told me to lie down so I did as he said I lay down on the tiles just beside the door to the pool I lay down and that's where he . . . that's where he did . . . did . . . that's where he did it to me. That's where he assaulted me.'

Fitz remained quite still, taking in the woman, the set of her body, the withdrawn expression, saw how hard it was for her to say the words, knew how hard it was for her to say them because to say them made it happen again for her.

And now she was looking at him. Straight at him, some kind of light in her eyes, maybe just a reflection from the neons, but oh God it looked like the hot light of hell in there. 'I have to say the word? It has to come from my lips?'

Fitz didn't prompt her.

'I lay down on the tiles, by the door, and that's where he raped me.'

Catherine shook suddenly, so badly that the WPC was forced to catch her around the shoulders, to hold her as she dealt with it, dealt with the memories. Another five minutes passed, each tick of the clock bomb loud and far apart. Eventually she looked up again. Fitz hadn't moved.

'There's more? You want more from me?'

Fitz nodded slowly. Chewed his lip again. 'There's a possibility this man has raped before.'

'Oh God.'

'You've said he wore a hood and that he put a hood over you. Did he do anything else?'

Catherine opened her mouth, shut it, shivered slightly.

'Things happen in a rape, Catherine.' There, say her name. Restate it. Bolster her identity before she loses herself in those memories. 'Things that are difficult to talk about. I know that. Did anything like that happen to you?'

Catherine nodded dumbly, looked at the WPC, at Penhaligon, finally back to Fitz, hands shaking where they gripped the towel around her.

'He combed my hair.'

Another silence.

'Not this.' Catherine put one hand to the towel wrapped

around her hair. 'After he finished, he combed my hair.'

Fitz glanced at Penhaligon, beyond her to the look of satisfaction on Wise's face. He looked back to Catherine, to see she had clocked the glance.

'He's done that before?'

'Yes.'

Wise and Penhaligon had been talking quietly together. Now Penhaligon nodded. She came forward. 'We'd like you to take some tests. Is that OK?'

Catherine snapped her head around and Fitz could see why. Penhaligon's voice was soft but her words, oh, her words were hard.

The single word that came from Catherine crashed into the silence, a brittle thing, volatile. 'AIDs?'

Penhaligon spoke quickly, but calmly. 'It's just a precaution. There's no evidence he's got it.'

'The other women were clear?'

'Yes.'

Catherine nodded. Looked back at Fitz. He met her gaze. She was emoting on all wavelengths; a white noise of hurt and pain and guilt and more pain.

Penhaligon continued, 'Are you married?'

A nod.

'Would you like to phone your husband?'

A shake of the head.

'Would you like to tell him in person?'

The laugh that exploded out of Catherine was more like a bark – a sudden release of tension, an expression of fear, pain, anger. Her simple 'No,' was utterly redundant; it threw Penhaligon for a moment. Then she recovered enough to continue.

'Would you like me to phone him?'

A release of tension. Catherine nodded, looked gratefully up at Penhaligon. 'He'll be at work. Trantor's minicabs. The number's in my purse.'

Ten minutes later Penhaligon and the WPC helped Catherine to stand, took her out to the line of waiting cars. Fitz shuddered as he imagined Catherine walking the

49

gauntlet of uniformed faces, bland, sympathetic, none of them with the slightest idea between them what was going on inside her head.

He didn't have to imagine very hard either; the line began directly outside the changing room doors, began with Beck and Harriman. Beck, lounging, sucking on his rollup, Harriman upright, his eyes flickering attentively between Beck's expression and Catherine's receding form.

Beck's expression said it all, but as usual, he left Harriman to make the comment.

'Well. We're looking for someone with *taste*.'

Fitz shuddered.

4.30a.m.–5.30a.m.

For Catherine Carter the journey to Fallowfields was as much of a nightmare as the rape itself had been. All these people. These strangers. They knew. They knew all about it. Knew what had happened. What he'd done to her. They knew her as intimately as he had.

The police car glided around a corner and she stared out into the night, the rain pebbling the glass, felt almost as if the rain were calling her, summoning her from her body and propelling her back to relive the terror all over again. The last walk around, securing the premises, waving hello to the late-shift cleaner, taking one last look around the pool, walls and ceiling glimmering in dim light reflected from the chlorinated water, and all the time he was waiting, there and waiting, following her from foyer to changing rooms, to pool, to office and back to pool, stalking her, hunting her, and then the attack, the hissing breath, the punches, the stabbing pain of penetration, the terror, the humiliation.

And afterwards she opened her eyes inside the leather hood to the sound of his voice, and the realisation that he was

talking. He's talking to me. Why? Why is he doing that? He's been inside me once, now his words are inside me again.

50

Inside me and oh God I want to be sick I want to throw up I want him out of me out of me I want him out of me out out—

'It's good to get the sex out of the way, isn't it?'

What? What? Jesus Christ you're insane. You're talking to me. You're talking to me and you've just done that to me just raped me just been inside me and come inside me and now you're —

'Sorry. Didn't catch that.'

Bastard pervert rapist, inside me, rapist, inside me, I'll kill you I'll fucking do that to you oh God it hurts I'll do that back to you you bastard fucking pervert rapist I'll get you and I'll —

'Yes.'

'You know it's got to happen. The relationship's not gonna progress until it does.'

Progress? You were inside me. I didn't want you but you were —

'So do it, get it over with, that's what I say. Do you smoke?'

Smoke. Oh God. He wants to know if I smoke. Smoke. Do I smoke? Do I smoke? Dear Lord I can't remember.

'Pardon, love? What was that you said?'

'No! No. I don't smoke.'

'What about John? Does he smoke?'

Oh God, it's one of John's friends. One of his friends has done this to me.

'Do you know him?'

'What does he do?'

Drives a cab. He drives a cab and you'd know that if you knew him, you'd know that so you don't know him, can't possibly —

'Drives a cab does he?'

Did I say that? Must have. Thoughts and words all the same now. All the same. Can't tell them apart. Can't tell what's really happening. Is it in my head? Is this a friend of John's? Wish I could get this hood off. Maybe it's better if I keep it on, do what he says. Is this a friend of John's?

'Is he the jealous type?'

51

'I want to take the hood off.'

'Is he the jealous type?'

'Please. I want to –'

'Is he the –'

Sometimes. Yes. What do you want me to say? Sometimes he's the jealous type. Yes! Sometimes he is, all right? Why are you doing this to me? Why are you raping me again? Raping me with your words? Penetrating me with your words?

'If I was married to you, Catherine, I wouldn't let you out of my sight.'

Oh.

'Was it too fast for you Catherine?'

Oh dear God.

'Over too soon?'

Does he want to do it again? Is he going to do it again?

'Is it Catherine or Cathy?'

Please.

'Is it –'

Not again. Please.

'Catherine! It's Catherine.'

'When we lived in caves, Catherine, we were vulnerable during sex. Take too long and there was a tiger at your throat. Do it fast and you'd live to do it again. Have you ever thought of it like that?'

Thought. Of it. Like –

'Do you want to live, Catherine? I said do you want to –

'– get onto the examination table please? That's fine. Thank you.'

Catherine blinked rapidly as she looked up from the hospital bed, realising, as she looked straight into the eyes of the nurse, that the balance of the journey to the recovery suite had passed already. And the trip through the lounge, the removal of the towels she wore, the bagging of her swimsuit, all these had passed her by as if she'd been unconscious.

The police surgeon – an older woman – kept her expression

carefully neutral; no condemnation, no support. Just functional efficiency. A robot. Catherine herself felt like a robot. Like something with no feelings. Just a robot going through the motions. Going through the

motion. There's someone behind me! Oh. It's just the doctor. With a tray, medical instruments. What's she going to –

'Penetration took place?'

on the tray what's on the

'Yes.'

'Vaginal?'

are those things on the

'Yes.'

'Rectal?'

she going to do with

'No.'

'Oral?'

comb it's just a comb just a little silver comb like the school nurse used to have and

'No.'

'Did he use a condom?'

little balls of cotton wool and

'What?'

'Some do.'

touch me there not even gently don't you put that

'He didn't.'

'Did he ejaculate?'

inside me hot inside me hot and wet inside me

'Yes.'

'Thank you.' A moment. 'It's so much easier when the victim's educated.'

Educated? Educated! What's that supposed to mean?

The doctor winked. *Nothing to worry about. Just our little joke eh?* Catherine suddenly realised she didn't even know the woman's name.

A flash of silver. The clink of metal on metal. The slosh of metal in a glass of antiseptic fluid.

Catherine couldn't look at the older woman. She fixated

on the tray instead, the little silver tray, the tray with all the

was that? who's that behind me? Oh. It's just the redhead. The policewoman. I wonder if she's called John yet. Oh God. John. What am I going to tell him? What will he think? Will he hate me? Support me? Will he care? Will he understand? Oh God it hurts. It hurts inside. It hurts it

Something else swam into Catherine's vision. Glass. Tubular. A hypodermic.

A nearby WPC tapped the glass, pressed the plunger so that a little fluid was

inside me he's inside me he's coming inside me

ejected to patter onto the floor. The WPC offered the hypo to the doctor, who took it and approached Catherine.

'This is just a precaution against venereal disease.'

Catherine began to shake. Another penetration. A stinging sensation. Fluid

inside me hot and wet and coming

inside her and the needle was withdrawn, the hypo placed in a glinting dish, and that too, seemed to drift out of her line of sight under its own power. Out of sight along with the rest of the pieces of her they'd taken. The hair, the blood, the endless swabs, the scrapings from beneath her nails, her clothes. Was there anything of her left? Anything of herself left to call her own any more? Just her name and even that had been taken from her. Taken from her and used by . . . by *that man*. Used as Catherine herself had been used. Used and discarded.

What could I have done to change it, to prevent it?

Then more movement. A shadow beneath the bright lights. A shadow with red hair. Red hair and a carefully neutral voice. Another doctor?

No. The policewoman. Penhaligon. That was her name. Penhaligon. Jane.

'You owe it to yourself to catch this man, Catherine. Otherwise he'll always be out there.'

You think I don't know that? I'll carry the memory with me to my grave. I'll

'Yes.'

be sick with the memory of him inside me. Sick to my grave.

'Yes. I know.'

From somewhere nearby came the sound of a pen scratching on paper. That would be the WPC labelling the

pieces of her

swabs, the cuttings, the hairs.

And Penhaligon again, her voice rattling gently in Catherine's ear, textbook calm, soft, gentle, persuasive. 'I know this is horrible, Catherine, but it will help women everywhere because that man's a threat, Catherine, a threat to us all –'

Catherine finally found the will to focus on something. She sat up, despite a warning look from the doctor, sat up, pulled her gaze back from the edge, back from the void of memory, focused it and thrust her attention at the redhead. At Penhaligon. 'Jane.'

The redhead nodded. 'Yes.'

'You know it all by heart don't you?'

Catherine watched the other woman recoil from the accusation in her voice, the *truth* in her voice. She took a step backwards, her eyes widening in realisation; a sudden understanding of how she must have appeared to Catherine.

'I do. Yes. I'm . . . I'm sorry.'

Catherine nodded. Pulled the medical robe more tightly around her and swung her legs over the side of the examination table, tried to ignore the burning sensation between her legs. 'Where's Fitz?' She ached as if she'd just run a marathon.

'He's outside. He's waiting for your husband.'

John. Oh God. What will he think? What will he do?

'I want to see Fitz.'

He was outside, a wall of a man, perfectly still, dwarfing one of the little plastic chairs which stood in a neat row along one wall of the rape suite corridor. Catherine stepped from the examination room and he looked towards her. It was odd really, just his eyes moved, the set of his head on his neck didn't alter, his body didn't move. And the way his arse was hanging over the edge of the chair made her want to giggle, despite everything. There was something about him both absurd and magnificent. With the redhead trailing behind her, Catherine started down the corridor towards him.

Seeing her Fitz rose.

That was when John entered the corridor through a door at the far end, face a thundercloud, eyes questing towards her, carrying her small holiday suitcase, the one with the broken handle, under his arm.

Fitz moved easily aside as they embraced. Or rather, as she embraced John. And she knew. She knew in that moment when his muscles tensed, tensed as she touched him, she knew that it wasn't over yet. Not by a long way.

When she stepped away from John, he still hadn't moved, a bulldog of a man, tall but thick with muscle. The holiday case was still clamped under his arm, the other hung stiffly at his side. There was no reaching out from him. Not with his arms, or his eyes. No comfort. No sympathy.

Fitz stepped forward. 'Mister Carter?'

John looked at him, eyes flashing. Was that anger there? Rage? Was he angry because the woman he loved had been hurt, or because his property had been violated? Angry because Fitz was a man? Because she wanted him here in this moment of intimacy?

'Edward Fitzgerald. Psychologist attached to the police.' Fitz studied John minutely, eyes scanning him from head to foot. Catherine was suddenly sure that although they'd only just met Fitz understood John at least as well as she did herself. 'Let them take your case.'

'I can manage.' The words snapped out, his anger a beacon.

Fitz nodded. 'Of course you can.' Catherine watched him look back towards her, no, past her to where

behind me who's that behind me

Penhaligon waited. The policewoman came past Catherine, opened the door to another room. Through it Catherine caught sight of a small room, its pastel walls a stark contrast to the antiseptic glare of the examination room. The room was furnished with a comfortable three-piece suite, a dining-room table and chairs. The lighting was concealed. There was a Turner seascape on the wall, a row of absurdly fluffy teddy bears on the windowsill. The room looked very soft, warm and safe. It looked like a nice room.

With a look towards John she followed Penhaligon into the room. Fitz brought up the rear. Penhaligon gestured to a seat. Catherine lowered herself gingerly into it. John looked at her as she moved, painfully slowly. His face creased. What was he thinking? Was he thinking anything? Or was he in shock? She supposed she was in shock, or everything wouldn't have that dreamlike quality she associated only with the bad horror flicks he loved so much, the ones he liked her to watch with him, on occasion, even though he knew she hated them.

When he saw John wasn't going to sit, Fitz shot him a sidelong glance and lowered himself into a chair on the other side of the table. After a few moments John put down the suitcase. The WPC came in then and asked if anyone wanted tea. She was looking right at Catherine when she said it.

Catherine shook her head. 'I couldn't.' Her guts churned at the thought.

The WPC nodded. 'I'll just be down the corridor if you need anything.' She closed the door quietly behind her.

As if the sound of the door closing had broken a spell, John sat. He moved suddenly. No indication. He was like that. Like a spider. You never knew which way he would jump. He sat opposite her. Stared at her. Said nothing.

Catherine looked at him for a moment. Felt Penhaligon's gaze on her. Felt Fitz's too. A gentler look. No judgement there. No accusation. Just support. His gaze buoyed her up. Kept her afloat. John looked like he wouldn't have been too unhappy had she sunk without a trace. Fitz knew that too, he looked at John, then at her and somehow Catherine knew that he knew.

And then he spoke. That soft voice, a hint of far north in

57

it, shaping the words, giving them a rhythm all their own.

'Why me? Was it my fault? What did I do to provoke him? What could I have done to prevent it?'

Catherine felt tears well up, splash out. She wiped them away with the back of one hand. He knew. Oh God he knew. She nodded, mute; the tears would be answer enough for Fitz.

John looked from her to Fitz, anger blooming on his face. He didn't understand.

'It's all right, John.'

'Christ.' He subsided into the chair. 'You've some definition of all right.'

'Overcoming misplaced guilt is a major step to recovery.' Fitz was looking at her but his words seemed to be aimed equally at her husband. Did John realise that?

'He combed your hair to remove strands of his own. He pulled you into the pool to destroy traces of his semen. He knows police procedure inside out. That means he's done it before. He's been caught, learned the hard way to destroy as much evidence as possible.'

And John was turning in his seat, arrowing in on Fitz's words, the anger blooming again on his face. 'He's done it before?'

Penhaligon said, 'A number of times that we know of.'

'Then what are you playing at, for God's sake?' John's anger was a palpable thing, it splashed out into the room, went through Catherine as it had so often in the past. She felt it fizzing in her blood like the bends. 'He's raped before, he's got a bloody record and you –'

Oh God, John, not now, not here. Not in front of these people. Not in front of Fitz. He wants to help. Let him help, please let him

'– still can't catch him.' He turned to Fitz. 'If it was your wife, you'd catch him, I'm bloody sure of that –'

'John.' God was that her voice? It was so tired. The voice of an old woman. Her mother's voice. 'Please.'

And Fitz was speaking again. 'He knew your name. You said he knew your name.'

58

'Yes.' Somehow Catherine found the strength inside to keep the memories at bay. 'He knew my name. And he used it. All the time. Catherine this. Catherine that. All the time. He asked me about John –'

Fitz threw a quick glance at John but didn't interrupt.

'He said he was good, that if I didn't
move didn't fight him just let him do that to me and not struggle, I'd enjoy it . . .'

'We could leave it there.' That was Penhaligon. Concern lining her voice. Catherine wondered how much of it was for John.

'I want to carry on.'

John stood suddenly, the movement spastic, almost uncontrolled. He went to the door. He looked back, the door half open. 'I want a cup of tea.' He blinked. 'All right? I want a cup of tea.'

Catherine was beyond John now, her memories coming back, flooding back like the water in her mouth, the chlorinated water, and the taste rose in her throat, threatening to make her sick. 'He tried to be nice. Talked to me for ages. It was as if he hadn't raped me.' And then she put it all together. As Fitz watched her with gentle, understanding eyes, she finally put it all together. The truth. The truth was –

'In his mind it wasn't rape.'

5.30a.m.–7.00a.m.

Penhaligon watched as Catherine left the recovery unit with her husband, got into a red Austin Allegro and drove away. Wise had already headed back to the station, along with Beck and Harriman. That left her to liaise with the medical staff. Doctor Jordan was co-operative. She promised to rush through the results of all the tests; Penhaligon arranged to have them picked up early the following afternoon. Doctor Jordan returned to her shift, leaving Penhaligon to go to the car park alone. No. Not alone. There was still Fitz.

He was waiting by the Volvo, a great hulking shadow in

the headlights of the remaining vehicles, looming at the passenger door.

'I suppose you want a lift.'

She watched him make that little movement of his head, that quirky sideways glance. Then he nodded.

'Get in.'

The presence of Fitz next to her in the car made her edgy; the temptation was to shove her foot to the floor, get it all out of her system with a little speed, a little recklessness. She resisted temptation. It would be all he needed to have yet another dig. Another little poke at her psyche. Even as her foot eased off the accelerator he was looking at her, a frank expression, *I know you Panhandle. I know what you want. Would you take it if I offered?*

'You go left here.'

She scowled. Jesus. Was she that easy to read? Did he enjoy doing it to her? Showing her how transparent she was? Come to that, did she enjoy having him do it to her?

'I know Fitz.'

'Just thought I'd . . . you know.'

'That's unusually self-effacing for you, isn't it?'

Fitz snorted. 'You really are beginning to sound like me.'

'It's nothing I couldn't get from the back of a Weetabix packet.'

Fitz glanced at her and grinned. She took her eyes off the road for a moment, stared him down.

'Panhandle. The road . . .'

'Far as I know it's still where I left it. Under the wheels.'

'Yes and that's where we'll be, under the wheels of some bloody lorry if you don't –'

She tapped the brakes, slid the car to a halt outside Fitz's drive. He was out of the car almost before it had stopped moving. It never ceased to amuse her how fast he could move when the fancy took him.

He peered in through the window as he shut the door. 'Thank Christ you're a copper and not a bus driver.' He came round to her side, opened the door. 'Think of the generation of psychologically traumatised kids we'd have on the roads. It'd be just like Paris.'

Penhaligon smiled. Her scary smile. 'Why are you holding my door open, Fitz?'

'I'm inviting you in, Panhandle.'

'Why?'

'Because you need to explain why you haven't spoken to me in a month. You need to tell me all about Fidel –'

'Peter.'

'You fancy me Panhandle, you fancy me like mad. Sex was great and I understand that can be scary. He was a sex god. What if he doesn't want to see me again? What if I can't handle that? You have to absolve yourself of the guilt you feel at enjoying my body. I feel it's only my duty as a responsible citizen to allow you the privilege.'

Penhaligon shook her head. Fitz's words left her dazed. The arrogance of the man. Christ. What had she ever seen in him? What had his wife ever seen in him? What did his kids see in him? What did anyone see in him, ever?

She shook her head again. Got out of the car.

'I'm going to put my shrink on overtime.'

Fitz mugged, a superb Cagney. 'Honey, I *am* your shrink.'

Inside Fitz shovelled a little coal on the fire, grovelled around on his hands and knees for a while until it was lit.

'Doesn't get any smaller does it?'

Fitz looked around. 'My sex appeal, you mean?'

'No Fitz, your arse.'

Penhaligon nodded towards the open drinks cabinet.

Fitz followed her gaze as he rose to his feet, drew himself up to his full six feet two. His expression turned serious, then. It was almost as if the game he played called life stopped there, right there at the drinks cabinet, at the Bell's. The half-full glass, the almost empty bottle. He chewed introspectively on his lower lip as flames began to crackle in the hearth. 'The voice of my conscience.'

'Try the voice of your liver.' Penhaligon felt what little humour there had been in the moment evaporate, to be replaced by a liberal dose of tension. Tension and no small amount of concern.

Fitz met her glance, looked right through her. He picked up the half-empty glass. He swirled the liquid inside around, golden shards of light flashed across his face, reflections from the fire. 'A pessimist would say the glass was half empty.' Fitz lifted the glass to his lips. 'No, no, not the whisky, please, not the whisky,' he cried in a falsetto squeal. He downed the liquid in one gulp, continued in that high tone, 'No, no. Don't swallow. Please don't swallow.' Grab the bottle. Tip, another gulp. 'Oohhh. Don't metabolise. Don't metabolise.' He stared at Penhaligon, his gaze as hot as the fire. 'The voice of my liver.'

'Fitz.' She looked away, unable to bear the self-pity in his voice, the set of his body. No. Not the self-pity. The self-understanding. 'I don't want to have an affair with an alcoholic hell-bent on self-destruction.'

Fitz chewed his lower lip again. 'The suicidal psychologist,' he quipped. 'Ought to have my own show. People could ring in. I could counsel them on how to mend their marriages, cure their addictions. How to deal with their lives, and their livers, how to keep their families together.'

Why did he do this? Did he do it to everyone? Or only to her? Why did it affect her so much? Why did she let it affect her so much? Christ!

Penhaligon tapped her fingernail against her front teeth. It was a stupid habit, one she'd been trying to kick since first year secondary.

'I thought you were good. With Catherine, tonight. I thought you were excellent.'

'My ego thanks you from the bottom of its furry little cerebellum.'

Was he ever going to stop?

'Fitz. Listen. Judith's gone. Katie's gone.' She gave an odd little tension laugh. 'The whisky's almost gone.'

'What about you, Panhandle? Are you gone?'

'I'm here aren't I?'

Though Christ alone knows why.

'Yeah. You're here.' Abruptly Fitz sat down. He sat on the sofa, kicked his shoes off, began to massage his feet. 'It's obviously a guilt thing, right?'

And she snapped. Right there, with the heat from the fire lapping at her feet and the heat from Fitz scalding her head. Snapped down the middle, no greenstick fracture this, a clean break.

'Bollocks to you, Fitz. If you don't want me to explain, why did you invite me in?'

He didn't have an answer for that one, of course. She let out a breath. That at least was a start. She turned away from him, looked into the fire. 'I need a drink.'

Fitz stirred on the couch.

'Don't panic. I'll get it.'

The whisky burned its way down.

'Jesus, I hate this stuff.'

Fitz laughed. A lost child's laugh when he realises the magic path home has vanished and the mall looms over him like a gothic palace, filled with wonder and loneliness.

'First couple of litres always get you like that.'

And she set down the glass on the mantelpiece, turned to find herself sandwiched between Fitz and the fire. 'I've known Peter four years, Fitz. What do you want me to say to him? "I've met a middle-aged married man, slept with him once while his wife was away so, I'm sorry, Peter, four years of friendship's down the Swanee?" '

Fitz took another slug of whisky, straight from the bottle this time, let the glass slip from his fingers to the carpet. That's another thing Judith would've quietly berated him for. 'Did you sleep with him?' The change of expression from accusation to contrition was almost comical. 'Ignore that. It came from somewhere down here.' He tapped his chest somewhere close to his heart. Unfortunately he tapped it with the hand holding the bottle of Bell's. He stared at the wet patch on his jacket and shook his head. 'Engage the brain. It's your body Panhandle, do with it as you wish. Who am I to ask a question like that? What happens when Judith comes back? Won't I do exactly the same as I did before? Won't I leave you at the airport again, bags in one hand guilt in the other?' And he was working himself up again, the

63

way he always did, hyping himself up with the words, she could see it in the set of his shoulders, the ruddy glow in his cheeks. 'No good, Panhandle, because this,' and here he slopped more whisky over his chest by way of indicating his heart, 'the great green emotion monster's growling at me, sod the bloody brain, *did she sleep with him?*'

And Penhaligon looked away. On any day of any week she could walk into the home of a total stranger and tell them, as part of her job, that their loved one had been raped or murdered, violated, but she could not stand here, in front of this great, fat, alcoholic self-loathing lump of lard and tell him the truth.

Except she had to. Had to tell him and watch it eat away at him. So, 'Yes.' A breath. A slug of whisky. 'I'm sorry you found out, Fitz. I'm sorry I hurt you. But that's all I am sorry about.'

She watched the words burrow into him, her apology, saw how little comfort he drew from it.

'Did it have to be somebody so bloody perfect? Couldn't there have been the slightest hint of a pot belly? He spoke to me. Fidel. He didn't utter one intelligible word but he spoke to me. He said, "You're just a dirty old man, Fitz, the grave beckoning, desperate to get your hands, one last time, on a bit of young, firm flesh." '

Penhaligon blinked. It was too hot in here. She felt sweat start out on her neck, her forehead and cheeks. A complex flush composed of equal measures of guilt, anger, sympathy. How could he affect her like this? What was it about him? For crying out loud, what the fuck was it about him that had her on this bloody emotional hook?

'Fitz,' she began.

But he was gone, off in his own little world, his words more of a cry for help than a suggestion worth any merit.

'Let's have sex.'

'Christ almighty, Fitz!' She rubbed the back of her hand across her face. It came away wet. Tears? Or just sweat from the fire?

Of all the things you could have said, of all the bloody

64

things. I was going to stay, I really was. I wanted to stay. I really did.

'How can you say that to me, Fitz? After tonight. Catherine. How can you say that to me like that?'

She was sure he was building up to an answer, but she didn't wait to find out.

THREE

5.00a.m.–5.30a.m.

If he'd ever considered it, Jimmy Beck would have had to acknowledge that as a copper he sometimes drove too close to the edge. Then again it was his job and duty. Gather the evidence. Put them away. Old school values. Something David Bilborough would have been proud of, had he still been alive.

Beck sucked hard on his rollup as he got out of bed, bench pressed a set of weights, hit the bathroom for the Three S's. Shower, shit 'n' shave. Get that right and everything else followed. Get that right and the fact that you'd only had an hour's sleep before going on shift again became irrelevant. In fact, the only thing that was relevant was the thought, no the obsession, with getting the job done. With getting the pervert whose ongoing line of rapes had continued early that same morning with the rape of Catherine Carter. Getting the bloke bang to rights, hauling him up before a jury and making him do serious time.

Hopefully with a prison full of perverts who'd take a similar interest in him to that which he'd taken in Catherine.

That thought made Jimmy Beck grin. There wasn't a lot these days capable of bringing a smile to his lips but that thought did.

Just lately he had been feeling restless and depressed, agitated, angry. He would sometimes awake with a cry of terror, night thoughts following him into the waking world. The funeral. The upcoming christening. Baby Bilborough, fatherless. Catriona. His boss's wife. His ex-boss's wife. His *friend's* wife. Husbandless. Alone in a man's world with a

66

year-old baby and a police widow's pension.

Those thoughts were bad enough but some days it was even worse. Some days Jimmy Beck would wake up with a scream at his lips, his throat hoarse with suppressed tears, his head pounding, *hammering* with guilt, with his best mate's last words ringing in his head like the interested buzzing of a coffin full of flies.

This is the last testament of a dying man . . . I know what a jury will try to do to this . . . I'm scared, I don't want to die. I'm scared but I'm thinking straight . . . get the bastard for me, Jimmy. Get the bastard . . . get the bastard . . .

And then the drive, oh God that nightmare drive, Penhaligon at the wheel, her face a mask, she couldn't have driven any faster if she'd been steering a bloody Jag instead of the Volvo, and they'd got there to find his best friend lying on his back, half in the gutter, hands clamped to his ripped-open stomach, radio through which he'd dictated his last words lying face up and bleeping gently in a pool of fast cooling blood. More blood leading in a trail back into the house. Blood smeared over the front door, the hallway, the living-room carpet. Blood everywhere. How could a human body hold so much?

According to the paramedics DCI David Bilborough had died as the cars drew up. Now he lay there. Not a man any more but a broken doll of a figure. Emptied by death of all dignity. Jack-knifed over the edge of the gutter. With the run-off. And the drains. And the dog turds. And the blood. And the greasy entrails poking clear of his jacket like two-week-old sausages. And his empty face. And eyes reflecting the raw sunshine from a cloudless sky. And

Catriona.

Waiting in the car, in Valubuys car park, with the baby, waiting for David, and

his fault it was his fault it was his fucking fault and

now somehow they all knew about it. They all knew. All of them. That would be down to her. To Penhaligon. She was the only other one who knew. She was the only other one and he had asked her, begged her, face aflame with grief and shame, not to tell anyone, begged her beside his boss's cooling body, his knees splashing in his boss's blood, begged her not to tell anyone that just four hours before he'd had the killer and didn't realise it. Had him and let him go. He'd begged her not to tell and she'd slapped him, bruised him, mashed his rollup into his jaw, damn near blacked his eye.

But she hadn't said anything. Hadn't made the promise.

Oh she knew what he was asking of her. She knew and she hadn't said anything to him.

He tried to press the point, hysterically, but then the ambulance had arrived, and Fitz; and Wise, the DCI from the swing shift at Anson Road nick, an army of cars and coppers, ringside seats the lot of them, ringside seats for the death of one of their own.

Wise, a great bear of a man who had finished the case and later been shuffled sideways by Chief Allen so that he was now Jimmy Beck's boss.

The wail of the ambulance siren became the insistent whistle of a kettle and Beck suddenly became aware that he was standing naked in his kitchen, naked and dripping from the shower, one hand clamped so hard around a packet of Shreddies that the box had burst, spilling the contents all over the floor and his feet. The other holding a cereal bowl in front of him like a weapon. A weapon or a talisman to ward off the shadows.

He blinked, put down the Shreddies and the bowl, crunched his way into the lounge, padded to the mantelpiece. On the tiled shelf was a crib board. *His* crib board; the fucking head case who had done David. Beck had lifted it just a week ago from the evidence room at Anson Road. The case was closed, no-one would miss it. The crib board had ninety-six matches set into the holes. Four of the matches had been lighted. The third stood for Bilborough, his life snuffed as easily as a match. Beck stared at the crib board. Now it was turning around, he was turning it around, the fascist ju-ju. Now the magic was working for him. One match for every guilty mother's son he put away. And when the matches were all burned why then he'd get more, another box, a whole other factory if that was what it took to fulfil David's last request.

David. Christ. Christ.

Beck rubbed both hands over his face, grabbed the skin, twisted almost hard enough to bruise, as if by pulling the flesh from his skull he would allow an egress through which the guilt could escape. Not a fucking chance, mate. That guilt was in there to stay, had come home to roost big time.

And if Beck sometimes heard David's voice, say from the bedroom, or the kitchen, or the street, or his car, and if sometimes that voice seemed edged with reproof for Jimmy's state of mind, for his actions and attitude, then he could believe that it was all his imagination. That that part of it, anyway, was down to his own guilty conscience. And that was when the voice was easy to drown out, easy to ignore in the process of living.

Something else Beck would have realised had he stopped for even one moment to think about it was that he wasn't only driving close to the edge as a copper, but also as a man. But he didn't stop to think about it. And so he couldn't see it.

Yet.

6.00a.m.–6.30a.m.

Anson Road police station was eighty-three years old; an ancient place, and dangerous, biding its time in the shadows of more modern buildings on the outskirts of central Manchester. An architectural facelift in the early seventies had left it with a strangely disjointed fascia stretched uncomfortably across an over-made-up main structure. Modular ethics were evidenced by the bolted-on look of the forensics lab and newly erected records building. The underground garage with its shuttered steel doors, and chainlink fences built over rust coloured brick around the perimeter of the building gave it the air of a thing grown old before its time. Certainly before it had outlived its usefulness to society.

Inside the fixtures and fittings were still Victorian. Heavy oak for the doors and window frames, brass for the bannisters and the stair guards. New steel doors had been fitted to the basement, sealing off the cell block and the trough, the overnight holding facility for drunks and teenage chancers. This mixture of old and new did nothing to lighten the atmosphere of the place. Still, thought Jimmy Beck as he climbed the stairs around the lift shaft to the third-floor duty room, that wasn't the object of the exercise was it? The object of the exercise was to scare the bejeezus out of anyone stupid enough to get themselves banged away by DS Jimmy Beck and his erstwhile, if somewhat soft, colleagues.

The third-floor duty room was open-plan, spacious, the windows allowing a full measure of greasy Manchester sky to peer in across the city. Beck felt the pressure of that sky on him now. Beyond the Sun Alliance building the real sun would be coming up, poking its wintry fingers across the city, having a bit of a grope around for anything interesting to shine on. Somewhere out there was a pervert, a rapist of women. A man Jimmy Beck wanted very much to fuck with. One more match on the old crib board, one in the hole for David. Soon now.

The duty room was full of people. Debbie Chandra. Mat Jennings. Geoff Renshaw. Julie Tanner. Bobby Skelton. Bobby Utrecht. The odd uniform fetching and carrying for Wise, who was standing near the blackboard beside the glass wall dividing the duty room from his office. Harriman, seated attentively on a desk, his too-earnest face gazing towards Wise as if he was a disciple and Wise the guru of police procedure. Den Jones was on the phone; he'd finally taken down Giggsy's bloody origami dinosaurs from the noticeboard. Jesus. Giggsy. There was another one for that great police roll-call in the sky. Jones's ex-partner. A year gone now, head crushed by a psychotic with a golf club. A year gone and his own legacy of a widow, a teenage son, a police pension and an origami bloody dinosaur. Oh fuck. The absurdity of it all. What was the force coming to these days? Why couldn't they just get out there and crack heads until something gave? Show them who was boss? Oh no. They wouldn't allow that. Too much common in that. He'd bottled the bastard that had done for David. Cracked a few ribs with his size elevens. The medical report had read like a shopping list for human spare parts. Four cracked ribs. Two bust. Broken nose. Fractured skull. Glass fragments in his eye from the bottle. Cheek opened to the bone by the second blow. Stitches. Concussion. Trauma.

But David was dead. Fucking *dead*, and that bastard had only got life with a recommendation for thirty. And Jimmy? What had he got? A month of fucking courses. Dealing with the public. The police and the man in the street. Techniques for apprehending suspects. Techniques for approaching suspects. How to fill in your fucking pension plan effectively.

All down to Wise.

All for doing his job.

All for putting away the fuckhead who'd done for his mate.

And even then it wasn't over. When he'd come back things had changed. The rotas had changed. He was stuck on paperwork for a fortnight. Taken off the sharp edge. 'Put all that learning to good use, eh Jimmy.' That was Wise. Smart aleck bloody gobshite. Didn't he know who did the job around here? Who got the job done. Christ. He, Beck, was a career copper. A life man. Take him off the sharp edge and he'd die faster than a begonia in a bonfire.

And then when Wise had finally had no option but to return him to the duty rota, just when he thought the worse was dead and gone, he'd been partnered with Harriman.

The thought almost made him laugh. At times he did laugh, the despairing, screechy, insane laugh of the terminal cancer victim when he realises what life has done to him. How much it has given, how much it has taken away.

Harriman was a wanker. All right he was green, but he was still a wanker. A rookie, two months out of training. His first duty shift had begun the week before David had been killed. As far as Beck was concerned the fuckhead who'd

71

got David had got the wrong bloke. If he was going to get anyone.

'Jimmy,' Wise nodded to Beck as he leaned against the stationery cupboard at the back of the room. Beck inclined his head a millimetre in response, sucked on his rollup.

Wise was in full flow.

'Have you all got a list? Bobby, will you shut it please? Have you all got a list?'

Beck watched them all nod or murmur affirmatives. He didn't need a list to know what Wise's next move would be. Get the bastards with previous. Get 'em in the cells and piss on 'em until they begged for a sponge. He felt no pride as Wise's next words confirmed his supposition; it was what he would have done. And at last the DCI seemed to be showing a bit of spine about how to do the job.

'Right. You've all got your orders. We're going in now. These are all perverts, right? Perverts with previous, right, so no one's going to complain if you lean on 'em a bit. You get me?'

And Beck felt his heart shudder as it shoved a little adrenaline around his body with the blood. Finally. Finally Wise was getting it. Thank fucking Christ.

He was smiling as he took his list from Wise, collected Harriman from his desk and hit the motor pool for a car.

7.00a.m.–7.30a.m.

Beck glanced at the jobsheet as Harriman drove the car out of the garage.

'Floyd Malcolm.'

'Where's he live?'

Beck grinned nastily. 'Would you believe with his mother?'

Howling with laughter, Harriman steered the car up onto the main drag and accelerated.

The Malcolm home was smack in the middle of the Barnfield estate in sunny downtown Salford. Harriman tapped the brakes and Beck was out of the car as it slid to a halt outside the window box of a garden.

Peripherally he was aware of curtains twitching across the street. He ignored them, banged on the door.

It was opened by a white middle-aged woman.

Beck blinked. 'Is Mrs Malcolm in?'

'I'm Sue Malcolm. Who are you?'

Beck suppressed his surprise, flashed his ID instead. 'DS Beck, Anson Road police station. This is DC Harriman. We've come for Floyd.'

Mrs Malcolm opened her mouth to reply, but Beck simply pushed past, stomped into the living room. No-one there. No-one in the kitchen either. Back door locked, key on the inside. Hm. Upstairs then. Probably still asleep. He turned, pushed past Mrs Malcolm again, ignored her indignant yells, took the stairs two at a time. On the landing he threw open the first door he came to. Bathroom. Woman in her mid-twenties. Daughter? Floyd's girlfriend? He shut the bathroom door with a grin, headed on up the landing. The third door opened onto a bedroom filled with posters and weights. Digin' at the Digin' by Praise Space Electric, Rhamoon by mammal, the rest a mixture of hardcore and garage, jungle music. Beck laughed inwardly. Jungle music for a jungle-bunny. Floyd was in bed. Beck pulled back the covers.

'Floyd Malcolm?'

'Do fucking what?'

'Nice pyjamas, Floyd.'

'Who the fuck are you?'

'Jeremy Beadle. Now get dressed.'

Beck turned at the sound of Mrs Malcolm in the bedroom doorway. 'He's done nothing. My son's done nothing. He's been home all night. What are you doing? *He's done nothing wrong!*'

Harriman appeared in the doorway behind Mrs Malcolm. Beck nodded towards the distraught woman. *Get her out of my face.*

Five minutes later Beck was manhandling Floyd into the back of the car while Harriman started the engine. Floyd banged his forehead on the roof as Beck pushed him in.

Beck grinned. 'Mind you don't bang your head, sonny,' he said.

Then he was in the passenger seat and they were away, leaving a distraught mother and daughter to console each other with a hug while across the street even more curtains twitched and eager eyes drank in the scene.

8.00a.m.–8.30a.m.

Interview room one was tiled, the lights a dazzling white. There were no windows, nothing to distract the suspect, nothing to prevent the total connection between police officer and suspect that was necessary in almost all cases to obtaining information, a confession, whatever.

Floyd sat in one of two plastic chairs set on either side of a plain wooden table on which the only object was a twin-deck tape recorder. The red RECORD light on the deck was winking on and off. Inside, gears hummed and spools of tape glided around.

Beck was standing beside the empty chair. Wise was standing beside the closed and bolted door.

Beck studied Floyd minutely. He was a cool one. Despite Beck's method of apprehension, Floyd hadn't said anything beyond his first two sentences. Until they'd got him in here. Then he'd asked for his lawyer. Beck had laughed outright. Wise had shot him a glance, but Beck had ignored that. Floyd was too cool for his own good. He was hanging loose, fast and loose, and that wasn't the manner of someone who should be surprised at being arrested in their own bedroom before they'd even eaten their Coco Pops.

That, together with his previous, gave Beck all the fuel he needed. The fire was building in him today, slowly getting out of control. But not completely, not yet.

He leaned over Floyd, sucked on his rollup, blew smoke into Floyd's face.

'What do you get out of it?'

Floyd blinked away the smoke, said nothing.

'What do you get out of it?' Beck's voice was harsher

now, grating, a machine to wear away Floyd's smooth exterior.

An answer came. 'I don't touch women.'

'That's not what the last jury thought.' Beck chewed at his rollup, blew more smoke. 'Is it?'

Floyd looked up at Beck and the edges of his mouth curled in a smile. Contempt? 'They thought that and they were wrong. The appeal court overturned the verdict. I got three months for no reason. They were wrong. Now you're wrong. You've brought me in here because you think I raped someone.'

Beck's eyes narrowed. *What was going down here?*

'You think I raped someone in 1991.'

'Didn't you?' Beck hammered out the first response that came to mind. Floyd merely shrugged.

'No. I finished with her. She screamed rape. A bunch of fascist coppers went along with it. I've never raped anybody in my life before. Can I go now please?'

Beck's voice hardened. 'No. Where were you last night?'

'Driving the cab. I went to sign on in the afternoon, had dinner at home, went to work. My mum, my brother, my sister, they'll vouch for me. The guys down at the cab firm, the Trantors, John, Eddie, they'll back me up.'

Beck blew smoke. He was starting to feel it now, a blade at the back of his throat, the smell of guns, of the night. Something was happening here. Some connection was being drawn. That was what he wanted wasn't it? What he needed in order to extract the necessary information from the suspect. A connection. A connection.

Beside him, Wise was considering everything that had been said. He was also considering the body language here. The aggression beneath the words, the subtle language the tape wouldn't pick up.

Floyd chewed on his lower lip. 'Look. I don't need to rape.'

Wise uttered a short laugh. 'The old ones are always the best, aren't they, Jimmy?'

Beck nodded, grinning. Was matey getting rattled at last?

He looked at Floyd. Said nothing. The silence stretched on.

Then, 'I drive a cab. I pick up women full of booze and I get plenty of offers. I don't need to rape.'

Inside Beck was laughing like Ed the talking horse. It was close now. Something was happening here. Something was –

'OK.'

Beck whirled, stared at Wise. What the fuck? Couldn't he see it? Was he really that soft?

'Get off home to yer mum.'

Floyd moved then, gracefully, not the movements of a hunted animal, more like a predator. Oiled. Well maintained machinery.

The door slammed behind him as a WPC ushered him from the room.

Beck turned on Wise. The DCI beat him to it. 'White women get raped by white men, Jimmy. Believe it or not the big black man in the alley's a myth.'

Wise turned to leave. Beck stopped him with a look. 'He's signing on. You heard him. He's signing on and moonlighting on the wheels. We should tell the social.'

Wise didn't say anything. He didn't need to. Beck felt his lips compress to a thin line broken only by his rollup as the door slammed behind his superior officer.

He wrenched open the door and followed Wise into the hallway.

'What d'you reckon,' he said aloud. 'With that many willing women maybe I'll take up a job on the cabs myself.'

Wise either didn't hear or didn't respond.

Either way it didn't matter; and Jimmy Beck, old school copper, life man, moved just a little closer to the edge.

8.30a.m.–9.00a.m.

When Fitz met Penhaligon in the parking space next to her flat, he was carrying a large bouquet of flowers. She was carrying a gift-wrapped bottle. He grinned, felt the grin returned.

76

Three hours wasn't exactly full recovery time for your average alcoholic but he'd made inroads. He'd ironed a new shirt. Had a bath. His head still felt like it was stuffed full of cotton wool but at least the headache had a fresh clean edge to it, a biting pain, clean and crisp and somehow *honest*, none of that muddy, all night with the windows shut and the radiators turned full on feeling.

Penhaligon saw him approaching. She'd changed her clothes too. Done something to her hair. Normally it would be tied back. Not today. Was that for him? Hm.

She waited by the Volvo for him to cruise through the car park. When he reached her neither of them said anything for a moment. Then both held out their gifts simultaneously. He the flowers and a little card. Her the bottle and a little card.

Then they laughed at the moment.

'I suspect you're more a gladioli person, Panhandle, but . . .'

She took the flowers and the card, handed over the bottle and her own card.

He looked at the card. Then looked at her.

'It says "Sorry",' she said.

'So does mine.'

Somewhere deep down inside a warm glow was spreading, not the fizzing heat of alcohol, more the gentle warmth of renewed friendship.

He became aware she was looking at him, that direct look she had. And he knew what she was thinking. Knew it even though she'd only spoken three words to him in the last three hours. Knew it as if she'd written a novel about it.

She looked at her watch. Grinned. When she spoke it was with her eyes, her body, not her voice.

Take me to bed Fitz.

He made a pretence of checking his watch. *Can I fit you in to my busy schedule?* She went along with the joke and they laughed together again. Then, linking arms they started back up the concrete steps to her first-floor flat.

The phone was ringing as they pushed in through the door.

77

Fitz glanced at Penhaligon. Smiled that quirky smile, allowed his face to fall effortlessly into that crumpled hang-dog expression.

She knew what he was thinking. 'I have to answer it.'

'No you don't.'

'I do.' A grin.

'You don't.'

But she picked up the phone anyway, cupped her hands over the mouthpiece as Fitz took the flowers from her, walked through into the kitchen to find something to put them in.

He returned to the hallway with the flowers in a disused four-pint plastic milk bottle. He held them out to her. She laughed aloud. Shook her head. 'That was Wise. We have to go check out one James Molloy. He works at the leisure centre. He's got previous.'

Fitz put the flowers, milk bottle and all, down on the kitchen table. 'When someone invents the time machine, do you know what the first thing I'll do will be? Go back in time and assassinate Alexander Graham Bell.'

Penhaligon shook her head as she led him from the flat.

As the door closed behind them, a thought occurred to Fitz. ' "We?" How did he know I was here?'

Penhaligon hit him with a smile like summer sunshine. 'Hearts and sleeves, Fitz.' She grabbed Fitz's jacket sleeve and tweaked it. 'Hearts and sleeves.'

He grinned then. The day was looking up. And not before time.

9.30a.m.–10.00a.m.

Fitz's first sight of James Molloy came in the café of the Arnos Leisure Complex. Molloy was a thin man, early forties, going bald in a big way. His demeanour was self-effacing, he walked with stoop shoulders and stared at the ground a lot. Fitz thought he was like a weed; a weed in a garden full of flowers that knew it was going to get pulled. Pulled and stuffed on the bonfire with the rest of the spring burnoff. His face was pale, freckled, his hair sandy. His voice was mild, quiet. His eyes moved around all the time. Watchful. Some might say suspicious. He was just being seated at a table when Fitz walked in with Penhaligon. A uniformed constable was beside him. Two polystyrene cups of tea rested on the table before them.

'James Molloy?'

Molloy nodded.

Fitz sat opposite him. The cafe was empty as yet. The leisure complex didn't officially open its doors for another twenty minutes. That was all to the good. Fitz had almost all the information he needed from Molloy already. All he needed was to confirm a few facts.

'It's just a few questions, James. Then you can go.'

Penhaligon glanced at him then. Fitz was pleased to see she didn't contradict him though. Maybe some of the old Fitzgerald magic was rubbing off. Some of his way of looking at the world.

Molloy looked around him, a sandy-haired squirrel of a man. He licked his lips. Looked around again.

It's all right. I'm not going to steal your nuts.

'You work the night shift here?'

'No, I work earlies. I come on at six thirty.'

'Yeah? Early start then?'

'Five thirty.'

Fitz grinned, nailed Molloy with a wink. 'Bet the missus isn't too happy about that, eh? I know what mine likes first thing in the morning.'

What she used to like, Fitz. Before she left you.

'Oh, I'm not married.'

Fitz affected surprise. 'Girlfriend?' he hesitated. 'Boyfriend?'

Molloy looked nervous.

'I . . .'

And just like that the room was full of people. Beck, with Harriman in tow like some bizarre, gangly pet. More uniformed officers. Fitz sighed. Beck. It had to be Beck. He was looking at Fitz now. And at Penhaligon. His eyes wandered between them, and a faint smile stretched across his face.

Go on, say it. Did the earth move? No, you pig-ignorant bastard, your boss put a stop to any earth moving I might have done today.

'Well, what do you know,' muttered Fitz. 'It's Dennis the Menace and Gnasher.'

'James Molloy?' Beck strode across to the table occupied by Fitz and Molloy, loomed over the man like a thundercloud.

'Yes.' Molloy was beginning to sweat.

'DS Beck. DC Harriman.' That was Penhaligon, sympathy factor five, Captain.

Beck shot her a look. Then back to Molloy. 'You're the caretaker here, Mister Molloy? Yeah?'

'A cleaner. One of the cleaners.'

'You've got four convictions for indecent assault and last night, in this building, where *you work*, Mister Molloy, a woman was raped. Now are you trying to tell me that's just a coincidence?'

'Yes.' Molloy was squirming in his seat. Fitz could see how it looked to Beck. Guilt written all over him. The guilt was there all right, but not for the reason Beck thought.

'He didn't do it.'

Beck ignored Fitz. 'Would you like to come with me down to the station, Mister Molloy?'

'I'm not going anywhere.' The panic in Molloy's voice spread out around the room. Beck heard it, closed with his prey.

'Where were you last night?'

'At home.'

'You weren't.'

How the hell could Beck know that? He was shooting in the dark.

'We knocked on your door this morning. You weren't in.'

'I was at work.'

'And last night?'

'I was in all night. Watching telly.'

80

'What did you watch?'

Fitz glared at Beck. Without looking at Molloy, he asked, 'Do you have a girlfriend, James?'

Once again Beck rode roughshod over Fitz. This time he seemed to take even greater delight in it. 'Will you answer my questions, please? What did you watch?'

'*Eastenders*.'

Beck pounced. 'Sorry. Wasn't on.'

And Fitz chipped in with, 'Have you *ever* had a girlfriend, James?'

Now Molloy looked from Fitz to Beck and back to Fitz again. The expression on his face was helpless guilt. 'No. No girlfriend. And I meant *Coronation Street*.'

'And afterwards?'

'I went out.'

That was obvious enough for even Harriman. 'You said you stayed in all night.'

'Until eight o'clock.'

'That's hardly all night.' It seemed to Fitz that Harriman had been taking lessons in interview technique from Beck. 'Where did you go?'

'The pub.'

'Which one?'

'The Admiral.'

Harriman glanced at Beck, pulled out his radio.

Fitz leapt into the gap. 'The man we're looking for forms relationships with his victims. We know that. Catherine Carter said so. Helen Robins and Gaby Holmes said so.'

Beck glared at Fitz. 'Nice one Fitz. And now he knows their names too.'

'He didn't do it.'

'Is it your local, Mister Molloy? Is the Admiral your local?'

'Yes.'

'You're well known there?'

'Yes.'

'So they'll back this up.'

Fitz glared right back at Beck, frowned, tapped a finger against his own temple. 'Anybody home?'

'Will they back this up, Mister Molloy?'

'I don't know.'

'He didn't do it.'

'Shut up, Fitz.'

'He didn't do it.'

And finally Beck did what Fitz wanted, rounded on him. 'And how do you know that, eh?'

Fitz grinned. 'It's alimentary, my dear Jimmy.'

Fitz grabbed Molloy by the shoulder, hoisted him out of his chair. Despite his bulk, Fitz could move fast when he wanted to. Now was one of those occasions. He ushered the compliant Molloy through the glass doors along a corridor and into the main pool area, talking all the while. Beck and the rest could do nothing except follow and listen.

'The man we're looking for *talks* to his victims. Talks incessantly. He forms a relationship with the victim. That means he's had relationships. Broken relationships.'

Behind him Harriman clicked off the radio. 'He lied. Nobody saw him down the pub.'

Fitz didn't break stride or flow.

'This guy's been hurt. The women he rapes are the kind of women he's used to or the kind of women he aspires to. James here – don't take this personally by the way – James here aspires to nothing, to nobody. He's a nonentity. He gets letters from *Readers' Digest* saying he *hasn't* been included in their draw. But the capper. The capper is this. Our man can swim.'

To gasps of amazement and a wail of terror from Molloy, Fitz guided the man right up to the edge of the pool, the deep end, and pushed him in.

'Twenty quid says this poor bugger drowns. Any takers?'

Beck looked like he was about to blow a gasket. 'Get a lifeguard. Get a fucking lifeguard!'

Fitz turned his back on Beck, called out to Molloy, currently going under for the third time, 'A medieval system of justice, I'll grant you. If you drown you're innocent. If you swim, you're guilty. A bit Catch Twenty-Two, really, isn't it?'

Beck was fuming, hopping from foot to foot. 'Get him out. Get him the fuck out of there. Look, you put him in there you Scottish bastard, you stupid prick, you get him out.'

Fitz just grinned. 'There's twenty quid on this, James. No-one's gonna dive in for you. So do something . . .'

Finally there was movement. Harriman turned, slipped on some water, swore, recovered his balance, limped away to find a lifeguard.

By this time Beck was doing one. 'If this man drowns it's down to you, you Scottish prick. Will you listen to me, you stupid soft sod? If he drowns it's down to you, you're carrying the can, I'm not accepting responsibility for this one . . .'

And Fitz didn't miss a beat. 'Do something, James. Don't just splash about. You're not on holiday now. Do something. Swim. Swim. Swim. Swim . . .'

But as anyone could clearly see, Molloy was not swimming. He was drowning. With that Beck took off his jacket, ripped off his shoes and dived into the pool. Fitz didn't know which he found more amusing; the ease with which he'd proved Molloy's innocence, or Beck's expression when the uniforms took him away dressed only in his jacket and shoes and a borrowed towel.

10.00a.m.–10.30a.m.

If the night had been bad the following day was worse. Catherine hadn't slept, of course. Hadn't even come to bed. She'd had a bath. That had taken an hour and a half. Then they'd talked for ages. Well. He'd talked. She had said almost nothing. When sleep finally claimed him at around six a.m. she was still hunched up on the living-room couch, dressing gown drawn tightly around shoulders raw from scrubbing in the bath, face ruddy in the light from Breakfast TV.

She hadn't moved by the time he got up a couple of hours later. She was still sitting in front of the TV, clutching the dressing gown, rocking gently back and forth as article after article of the news flashed past in silence. The light from the TV sent grainy shadows flapping across the room. The curtains were pulled tightly closed, as if to shut out the world; the last thing she had done before taking the bath hours before. He moved to open them and that was when she spoke.

'Leave them.' Her voice was hesitant, a child's voice. *Are these the right words? Am I using them the right way?*

'No love, let's open them up. Bit of sunshine'll do you the world of good.'

'Please.'

John turned to look at her. She still hadn't moved. How long could she sit like that? With her legs curled under her like that?

'Please, John. Don't open the curtains. I don't want people to see in.'

John said lightly, 'People won't look in. When have people ever looked in?' When Catherine didn't reply he continued, 'Bit of sunshine, do you good. Make you feel better.'

And God knows you deserve that, at least.

'All right?'

'No, John, I don't want them open!'

He jerked backwards with the force of her words. 'OK, all right. It was just an idea. What about the telly? You want that on or off?'

Catherine subsided back into the couch, shook her head minutely.

'Is that a yes or a no?'

Again the shake of the head. 'I don't care. I'm going to have a bath.'

Abruptly she stood. Blinked. Moved jerkily to the door.

'I'll bring you some clean towels up.'

Was that a nod?

She began to climb the stairs. He could see her ankles

beneath the bathrobe, vanish step at a time into the top of the doorway until only her feet were visible.

He followed her into the hall. 'What about a bit of breakfast? For when you come down? A nice breakfast, eh? That'll cheer you up.'

The feet stopped moving.

'Bit of breakfast, yeah. What d'you fancy? Scrambled eggs? Bit of porridge? You name it.'

'I don't want any breakfast, I just want a bath!'

The feet resumed their uneven tread. Then she was gone, leaving the sound of a closing door and running water, the sounds of normality to counter the strident pain in her voice that echoed endlessly in his head.

John had breakfast on his own. Porridge, scrambled eggs and mushrooms followed by muffins and jam, passion fruit juice, two mugs of Red Mountain.

The whole lot tasted like so much cardboard.

Upstairs, he could hear moving sounds, the occasional squeak of the bath supports, the splash of water.

And the sound of scrubbing.

All the way through breakfast, the scrubbing.

Louder than the whistling kettle, more persistent than Radio Two.

The scrubbing.

And John couldn't help but think of Domestos and Brillo Pads and Jif and Flash and Everclean and all the tiny little score marks the cleaners left on the polished surfaces in the adverts. He went back into the living room, flipped on the telly. Mr Sheen was flying his cartoon biplane around a spotless kitchen, spotless except, of course, that from a long shot you couldn't see the scratches made by the

scrubbing

cleaning agents and pads as you mashed them down on the doors and sinks, the work surfaces getting rid of every trace of

him of that bastard that raping bastard every trace of

household dirt and grime.

He turned up the sound on the telly. Now that bloke from

Neighbours and the girl from *EastEnders* were doing an ad for the Big Breakfast. Apparently Daddy G from Massive Attack was going to be On The Bed with Paula and wasn't that a scoop, kids? But John didn't care because by this time he was having a massive attack of his own. An attack of . . . he began to pace. An attack of . . . what? Guilt? Fear? Fuck that. He wasn't scared of any raping bastard. He'd prove it too, if only he could find out who the bastard was. Coming into his home like this. Messing with his wife like this. Coming into his home. His fucking *home* for Chrissakes. And what were the police doing about it? Bugger all, same as always. Bastards couldn't catch a cold standing starkers in Alaska.

In his home. In his wife. In his home.

Bastard.

John switched off the telly. The picture shrank to a dot and winked out. Like an eye winking at him. Like a man's eye winking at him.

She was good our Catherine, oh she was good. I told her she'd enjoy it. I certainly did.

In his home. His wife.

Back into the kitchen, stomach churning with the knowledge, the awful knowledge. Dishes into the sink and
scrub
rinse them clean and
scrub
wipe them dry and
scrubscrubscrubscrub
put them back into the cupboard and boil the kettle and have another brew and flap the newspaper and turnup the radio and
scrubbyscrubscrubscrubbityscrub
finally he just couldn't bear it any more.

He took the stairs two at a time, something inside him close to snapping. Outside the bathroom the sound of bristles against flesh was louder, almost obscene. He wanted to scream. Instead he knocked gently on the door. 'Catherine?'

The sound stopped. A moment passed.

'John?'

'I've brought you a cup of tea.'

'Leave it outside would you?'

'I could come in. I could
scrub
wash your back.'

'Oh. No, John. No. I . . . I don't think so.'

'I thought you liked it when I did that.'

'Yes.'

'Well then?'

'No, John.'

And then something in him bubbled up, something uncontrollable, a hot rage burst out of him and the words came despite any better judgement, any common sense; and any sensitivity he might have felt went right out the window.

'Jesus, Catherine, what's the matter with you? Can't you see I care? That I want to help? What do you want me to do, ignore you? Hang out bells? She's a leper! My wife's been raped and now she's been branded a leper! Christ, Catherine, I'm hurt too you know, don't be so bloody selfish!'

And he sagged against the wall, spent, his stomach cramped with almost sexual exertion, and the sickness spread right through him, poisoned him with self-knowledge. Worse; the moment the words were out of him he knew he'd been wrong. That he'd been the selfish one. He slid down the wall until he was in a sitting position, knees clamped against his chest, a child again seeking escape from a bullying father, an uncaring mother; the sound of crying from within the bathroom building a wall against his own tears, locking them inside him with the apology he knew she deserved, but that somehow and despite every effort to the contrary simply wouldn't . . . come . . . out.

'Catherine? Catherine?'

There was no reply.

The crying stopped and there was no sound at all.

John almost fell downstairs in his haste to get off the landing before the dreadful sound of scrubbing began again.

10.30a.m.–11.00a.m.

The sound of the front doorbell shocked him to his senses. When he opened the door Floyd Malcolm was standing there with a bouquet of flowers.

What are you doing here? What right have you got to intrude on my grief?

Then common sense socked him a good one.

He's just brought flowers. It's just flowers for Catherine, that's all.

John looked at Floyd.

Floyd looked back, the face of youth, the face of hip, the face of . . . the face of *difference*.

John struggled to find words.

In the end Floyd saw it wasn't going to happen. 'How is she?' He held the flowers out for John to take.

'So-so.'

Yeah? What else?

'Thanks for the flowers.'

'You're welcome.'

He closed the door before Floyd had even turned away. Something inside him was yelling *Abuse! He was being polite, showing he cared and you abused that!*

Then that voice of common sense rose once more. *It's the stress. Anyone would have done the same. I'll apologise to him later.*

He turned to see Catherine standing at the bottom of the stairs. She looked at the flowers.

He moved past her towards the kitchen. 'I'll put them in water.'

'Who brought them?'

He hesitated. 'Floyd.'

'Floyd Malcolm? From work?'

He nodded. 'Yeah. So?'

88

She shook her head. 'It was just nice of him that's all.' She followed John into the kitchen. 'John? It was just nice of him, that's all.'

'Yeah.' He took a glass vase from beneath the sink, rinsed it, ran some water into it, arranged the flowers, placed them on the kitchen table.

She sat at the table while he was doing this. Hands on the wooden surface, skin puffy, slightly inflamed.

Scrub.

'Bath all right?'

She nodded. 'I feel better now.'

He heard the words she didn't say, heard but didn't understand.

Now I'm clean again.

He sat, opposite her at the table, the flowers between them, a splash of colour in the grey light of early morning.

'I'm sorry. What I said. I'm sorry.'

'I know.'

'I love you.'

'I know.'

He reached across the table for her hand but before he could take it she was holding her bathrobe again, clutching it to her chest.

Jesus, what was she playing at?

'You don't want me to touch you.'

She shook her head.

'Why? Catherine, why? I'm your husband. We love each other. Why won't you let me touch you?'

She looked away, squirmed on the wooden chair. The feet squeaked on the lino, shockingly loud in the silence that stretched between them.

'Try and . . . understand.' Her voice was quiet. Her hands were shaking. 'You're my husband, yes. I love you, yes. But he did that . . . to me. He was a man and he did that to me. You're a man too. You're my husband and I love you. But you're the same as him.'

John felt the confusion inside turn to anger. 'I don't get it. Catherine, I don't get it. Are you saying I . . . are you saying that I've done . . . I've done that . . . to . . . to . . .'

Catherine ran her hands through her hair, the fingers clenching convulsively. 'No! Yes! I don't know, John. I'm confused. I know I love you. I know I hate him. Beyond that . . . I can't articulate it. It's like there's something inside. Something . . . big, something ready to blow. I'm going to blow, John, I'm going to . . . oh for Christ's sake I can't . . . I don't . . . I can't . . .'

And he was moving, circling the table, arms reaching for her, to hold her, comfort her, show her he cared; and she was up too, backing away, shoulders pressed the wall by the door, tipping the jug of fruit juice onto the floor, backing down the hallway as the thick splash of juice and the crack of breaking glass slashed the moment to ribbons, and she was half way to the stairs when the doorbell rang again.

It was DCI Wise and a WPC.

'Mister Carter.'

What is this? A three-ring circus? Rape becoming fashionable now, is it? Frightened to stay away too long in case we miss something?

'Yeah.'

'May we come in?'

Sure. I'll get Catherine. We'll jump through a hoop of fucking fire, shall we?

'My wife's not feeling up to another interview.'

'It's not exactly another interview, Mister Carter. If I could just come in for a few moments?'

Twenty minutes later he had it out of them.

James Molloy.

All four, John, Catherine, Wise, the WPC were all seated in the living room. The curtains were open (Catherine had opened them) and a generous portion of morning light filled the room, glancing from the Turner prints above the fireplace (Catherine's), the darts trophies on the television (his own), the video and satellite decoder, the hi-fi, the three-piece. Catherine had dressed (five minutes flat, a minor miracle if you asked him, obviously she was beginning to recover at

90

last), the WPC had brewed up a pot of tea, everything was cosy.

Then Wise had told them. They had a suspect. They were questioning him. They needed additional information from Catherine.

She sipped her tea now, face blotchy and wrung-out from her bath, hands still sore-looking. 'James Molloy?'

'Yeah.' That was Wise, matter of fact, keep things on the level, under control.

'The cleaner?' There was incomprehension in Catherine's voice. John was peripherally aware of it through the glare of his own steadily building anger.

'Yeah.'

He knew Molloy, had seen him around once or twice when he'd had to collect Catherine from work. The time her car had crocked on her. Well, she would buy a bloody Ford – Fix Or Replace Daily – luxury estate or no. He was about forty odd, a queer goose if ever there was one. Always looked at you. Never said anything but always looked at you. John had sometimes imagined him staring at the staff, or the punters, the schoolgirls with that vacant, no-one driving expression, and the thought had made him shiver. So it was bloody Molloy was it? Right.

'I thought it was someone younger.' That was Catherine.

'Why?' Somehow John's voice came out a little sharper than he intended.

'What?' Catherine looked at him, startled by the harshness in his voice.

'Why did you think it was someone younger?'

'John! I just did, that's all.'

'It's just you know what you're like when you get one of your ideas . . .' he turned to Wise, shrugged. 'Last autumn we had the homemade Christmas ornament fad. Six weeks and the house was full of tinsel, glitter, crap like that. The place stank of glue. Six weeks. Blue-Peter-itis I called it.' He smiled.

Wise didn't.

Neither did Catherine.

The moment stretched out.

'Yeah, well.' Wise licked his lips, obviously embarrassed.

John said, 'What led you to him?'

'He's only answering some questions.'

'Then why are you here?'

'To ask Catherine if . . . it could have been his voice you heard. James Molloy's voice.'

'I'm not sure.' Catherine's voice shook. Was it fear or uncertainty?

John blinked. 'So what did lead you to him?'

Wise sighed. 'I can't tell you that. Police procedure. You understand.'

'No. Has he done it before?'

'I can't tell you that either.'

And then the truth hit John, so powerfully and overwhelmingly that for a moment he swayed in his seat. His tea cup rattled on its saucer.

'He has hasn't he?'

Wise looked away. He didn't answer. Instead he turned to Catherine and repeated his question. 'Could it have been him?'

Catherine was biting her lip. She put her tea down on a low coffee table. Drew her knees together. Rocked a little in her chair. She licked her lips where she'd bitten them, groped for words.

'He wore a mask. He made me wear one.'

'He spoke, though. You said he spoke.'

'Yes.'

'Could it have been his voice? James Molloy's voice?'

Catherine put her arms around her shoulders, hugged herself. She blinked rapidly.

Christ. What was he doing to her? What was this bloody copper doing to his wife, making her remember like this, making her relive it like this?

'To tell you the truth . . . the way I'm feeling now . . . it could have been anyone's voice.'

Wise sighed. 'I understand that this is hard for you, Catherine. But you must –'

At that moment his bleeper went off. He let out a frustrated breath. 'May I use your telephone, please?'

John nodded towards the hall. Wise was careful to close the door behind him but still his voice carried, an indeterminate rumble rising occasionally with impatience, finally ending on a disbelieving note. Then he was back. And was it John's imagination, or was the DCI's face a shade redder? Was that embarrassment shining there?

Wise's words confirmed his guess. 'We were wrong about Molloy. I'm sorry.'

John felt overwhelmed, a mixture of amazement, disbelief, horror. 'You've let him go? He's done it before and you've let him go?'

Wise snapped, 'I didn't say he'd done it before. You assumed that. I didn't say that.'

John put down his tea and got up. 'I think you'd better leave now.'

Wise nodded, clearly embarrassed. 'I'm truly sorry to have troubled you,' he said to Catherine. She continued to hug herself, nodded slightly, but otherwise made no sign when Wise and the WPC left the room.

At the front door, Wise turned. 'You should both think about . . . you know. Seeing someone. Together.'

John gaped.

What are you saying? Are you saying, now this has happened I'm a failure as a husband? This man attacks my wife and suddenly we're the people who need help!

'People speak highly of Doctor Fitzgerald.'

You arrogant, condescending bastard, you love it don't you? You arrogant middle-class bastard, it couldn't be more fun for you if we were black.

'Yeah well. Thanks for stopping by.'

'Sure. And . . . once again . . .'

'I know.'

'Yeah.'

And Wise was gone.

James Molloy committed his first murder at the age of fifteen.

He was the second child in a family of two. The second and not exactly planned-for child. No doubt he would have been the reason cited in his parents' eventual break-up if the accident had not happened first.

His mother, Sandra Molloy, had suffered extensive damage to her womb at his birth, something the doctors claimed was as much due to conditions at home as anything else. *Conditions at home.* Well, there it was, that sentence. It could mean any number of things. For James the meaning was very clear. His parents, who loved each other very much, at least early on, wouldn't or couldn't seem to offer him that same love. Oh no doubt they had their reasons. He was an accident after all. His mother was losing the race to the change of life when she'd fallen pregnant with him. Forty-two was no time to be conceiving children, as he'd often heard his father say, but never really understood.

He was forty-two himself now, as old as his mother had been when he was born. As a child he'd seen her as the fount of all wisdom, longed for her age so that he could become privy to all the things he so desperately wanted to know. Now he'd attained that magical age and yet still life seemed to contain just as many mysteries, just as many secrets. What he'd done last night, for example. If he'd done anything at all. Had he stayed in and watched telly? Had he gone to the pub? Had he gone out but not to the pub? Had he in fact gone back to the leisure complex where he worked, there to assault and *rape* Mrs Catherine?

He *thought* he'd watched telly for a bit then gone to the pub. But could he be sure?

Parental violence had started when he was three years old. Subtle at first, often simply a tone of voice. That had gradually escalated to vague murmurings and the odd restless cry in the night, often prefixed by the phrase *that damned accident of yours.*

Accident. Blame. Even at three years old he was starting to understand all about that. Some would have said James Molloy's life never had the chance to get off right. As with most things, they'd have been both right and wrong.

James had been raised by his sister Audrey from the age of five when their mother had fallen downstairs and died of internal haemorrhaging from a compounded mixture of old wounds and new, her fall precipitating his father's own into the murky pit of self-pity and alcohol abuse.

Audrey was eighteen when James had been born, another example, if any were needed, of the unwelcome and unexpected nature of his arrival in the world. She was a secretary, one of a pool in the local foundry. At the time of their mother's death, Audrey was twenty-three and engaged to be married to a steelworker named Frank Hardacre. Frank was a huge wall of a man; even at twenty-five he had the roots of a boxer growing in him. James used to find it funny to see Frank and Audrey together. He was so big, with a heart of gold and no element of hurt in him anywhere, though he could arm wrestle two men at a time to a submission, while she was so small and fiery. After his first November bonfire party, James thought privately of Audrey as 'his sister sparkler' because that was what she did. Everywhere she went, everything she did was like a firework throwing off sparks, fizzing out into the night, the world. Where they touched things ignited, things grew. Like the love that grew between her and Frank. Between all of them, in fact, for Frank fell instantly in love with James when he met him; and the delighted grin on his face when their petition to legally adopt was granted simply knew no bounds. For one wonderful moment James, then six, thought Frank's grin was going to start by swallowing Frank's whole face and then simply gulp down the whole rest of the world.

James's father died when James was eleven, the year he started secondary school. They received notice via the police, for Thomas Kevin Molloy had vanished back to his native Ireland years before.

James's schooldays were no different than any other kid's

at that time, peopled with good days and hard lessons and bad days filled with comments about his homework by the teachers and jibes about both his inability to dress and his inability to think from the other kids. Over the next three years the number of bad days grew while that of the good days dwindled, in the same way the pond on the common got smaller in the summer. Despite this James kept a sunny disposition and took little umbrage at almost anything. I'll be nice to them, he thought. They'll be nice back. It was a simple equation, about which he could see none of the subtleties, none of the evidence to the contrary. This evidence manifested itself as digs and taunts and the occasional thump, behaviour which worsened all through his school life until finally, at the age of fifteen, it became simply overwhelming.

Nineteen sixty-five was the year his growing anger first found a voice; it was the year James stopped smiling.

Frank and Audrey had married by then, and Audrey had quit her job as soon as she'd fallen pregnant for the first time. Now Francis Hardacre junior himself was five and Audrey was expecting her second child. They'd been sensible, waited for the right time, waited for Frank to get the promotion he'd been due for nearly three years. It had come suddenly, in the wake of a miraculous and – to Frank – unexplainable boom in the steel industry. He had the chance to shoot for floor manager. He was popular, a hard worker in his own right, and no-one needed to tell him when the quality control was slipping. Men like Frank Hardacre were thin on the ground at the best of times. He had one shot at promotion; the opposition had fallen in round one.

Audrey was delighted, and immediately made plans (which James overheard one night, to his endless fascination, while midnight snacking on Rich Tea biscuits and cold milk) to have another child. The squeaking sounds from the old bedframe made James giggle with embarrassment all night long, and he went to school the next day with bags under his eyes 'like suitcases', according to a glowing-faced Audrey.

The problem was that that time, which was for Frank and Audrey probably the happiest of their lives, was also the start of the downward slide for James.

He'd been too young to understand that sometimes people change. Especially that they change in their attitude towards children who are not their own, particularly when children who are their own come along.

Certainly the change was unexpected and not only for James. Audrey too was surprised by the change in Frank towards her brother, and put it down to stress caused by the higher responsibility of his job. The thought that somewhere in Frank's mind might be a whispery voice that said *two children is enough in these times. Two's enough but now we have three, and what will you do about that Frank?*

Whatever the cause the voice went unheard until halfway through James's fifteenth year, when the frightening and hurtful alienation of him by one half of the couple he had come to think of as his parents – closer than his parents – combined with the abuse from the kids at school and the confused mass of teenage chemicals exploding in his brain, combined and grew one day into a frightful rage the way a tropical storm blows up out of a clear sky. And James was a mean old storm that summer, moody, resentful, aggressive. He stared at people when they annoyed him. He got a kind of reputation for himself which had no base in any reality other than the minds of his schoolmates but which none the less said quite clearly *Stay away. Trespassers into my head space will be severely punished.* And he got quiet. Real quiet.

His teachers thought he was internalising, but that, they said *en masse* to the police afterwards, was normal for a kid his age, wasn't it?

What wasn't normal was that, at the age of fifteen years and seven months, James Molloy murdered his best friend Eddie Pritchard in cold blood, by pushing him under a bus.

No-one but James knew the circumstances leading up to the murder. He pushed Eddie in front of a bus. That was all. And Eddie was dead. One minute he was laughing at James, the next he was an odd, blotchy shape squashed into the road, an absurd tyre mark across his burst stomach like that across Wile E. Coyote in the *Roadrunner* cartoons just after one of his crazy inventions had gone murderously wrong.

James never told anyone why he had done it, not the police, not the psychologist, not Audrey or Frank, not his adopted brothers, not Eddie's mum and dad, no-one. And if he might, one day later in life, have gone to the churchyard where his sister was then buried, and knelt beside her grave, and prayed devotedly for an hour or more and then spent five minutes whispering a reason to the cold, mossy stone, then no-one was there to hear those words except an old groundsman and the wind.

James admitted responsibility for Eddie's death. The court sentenced him to fifteen years' imprisonment and corrective psychological counselling.

When he was released from Horfield Prison at the age of twenty-five, having served ten years of his sentence, James had spent eight of those ten years in psychological counselling. As a result he was – it was generally considered – fit once more to resume a normal life.

But James had problems on the outside. His criminal record meant he found it very difficult to find work. This in turn meant his lodgings were invariably cheap, single-room bedsits in the bleakest part of town. This was bad enough. But worst of all was the knowledge that Audrey had died while he was in prison.

He'd been informed of this a year before, released for three hours to attend the funeral. It was there he found out how she'd died.

Both Audrey and her youngest son had been burned to death when a chip pan had caught fire in their home. The kitchen ceiling had been tiled with fashionable polystyrene. When the chip pan went up, the room became an inferno in seconds. Audrey herself had been overcome by smoke and fumes while wrestling with the side of the baby's cot. Her elder boy, at school by then, and Frank, now in middle management, had begun a new life together. Frank told James bitterly at the funeral that he, Frank, would have nothing to do with James upon his eventual release from jail.

Now that time had come, five years early, and James had no-one to turn to for help.

So James wandered from suburb to suburb; rejected even for dead-end jobs, signing on for months on end, no friends, no social life. And gradually whatever spark of warmth and vitality inside of him, whatever had been rescued by his sister from his wreck of a family life when he'd been so young, and which she'd carefully nurtured over the years, gradually dimmed until eventually it was extinguished altogether.

James became pale, dark rings developed around his eyes. His hair thinned and waned, his skin became mottled with middle age.

And he killed again.

Another child. A teenager. Same method. Followed him home from school, waited until there was no-one around, pushed him under a car. The car bounced over the kid, hit a lamp-post; the driver died in hospital in a coma, without regaining consciousness. The kid died instantly.

James got away with it.

The next time was four years later, and this time he tried a variation on a theme.

He raped the child before attempting to murder her.

He was caught but the girl refused to testify. Too traumatised, he supposed, with somewhat clinical detachment. He served nine months for assault and was then paroled.

He was thirty-two years old. He had no home, no job, no family.

He was a murderer and a rapist.

And, as if something had thrown a switch inside him, he stopped. Just like that, as Tommy Cooper had been wont to say. Just stopped. It really was that simple.

The first thing he did, upon wakening to find himself, filthy, derelict and sleeping in an alleyway in the streets of central Manchester, was to find a public bog and throw up.

That didn't take long, there wasn't much inside to come out.

After that he found a hospital, obtained treatment for the many superficial injuries he had sustained whilst living on the streets. He also obtained information and advice on emergency housing, social security, income support.

He was given priority placement on a private emergency housing list, and was awarded a small flat in a tower block in Salford. He got a job. Just a cleaning job, but it would do. It would do because it was honest and, though he hadn't yet really understood anything that had happened to him over the last seventeen years, he felt that he owed it to Audrey to make something positive out of whatever remained of his life.

James was now forty-two. He had spent the last decade in the same flat. He had never had a girlfriend, or indeed a close friend of any kind. He was still a cleaner, though last year he had been lucky enough to land a job at the local leisure centre. To do that he had to admit he had a criminal record; the manager there, Catherine Carter, had thought for several weeks about this record, and eventually decided to employ James under the equal opportunities directive then in progress.

James was overwhelmed. His life, for so long an empty shell, at last begun to take on some meaning. He was determined to do well. He became, in fact – and he knew this because he looked the phrase up – a *walking cliché*.

And now this.

Mrs Catherine, assaulted, raped. Right where he worked.

And he'd been accused of it.

He wondered if he had done it. If in some fit of madness and forgetfulness he had let the past overwhelm him again. If he had stayed behind last night and attacked her and done *that* to her, had raped her.

He knew he was capable of it. That and much worse.

He knew he didn't really think like other people.

He walked through the sculpted green surrounding the flats where he lived, these thoughts and others churning slowly through his head. He'd come home from work this morning after the psychologist had pushed him into the pool – the police had given him a lift and hadn't that amused the neighbours? – changed his clothes and taken the wet ones down to the launderette. On the way home he had noticed a silver-plated Thomas the Tank Engine piggy bank in the window of the local toyshop. He had stared entranced at Thomas's glittering smile for a good long while, then had gone in and asked the price. He had no children, and knew none, but he liked to buy this kind of trinket. He liked to play with them a while and then take them to his sister's grave. He had always felt sure she would prefer these gifts to flowers, which got old and died. She had always told him it was the thought that counts. Well, he was thinking, wasn't he? Thinking of her.

As he entered the lobby of the flats, the stink of urine and fresh sprayed-on graffiti and the odd burned newspaper assaulted his nostrils. He smiled anyway. He hadn't done anything to Mrs Catherine. He would have remembered if he had.

He was still smiling, and thinking about placing the silver-plated Thomas on Audrey's grave, when the fist looped out of the shadowy stairwell by the lift and broke his nose.

He sat down, surprise flickering across his face. Then the pain started and he cried out. The cry was stopped even before it had started by another blow, this one to his mouth.

He felt teeth break.

The pain from this new blow didn't hang around. It dug in, there for the duration.

He choked on blood.

Once more a gloved fist looped towards him. He held up his hands to protect himself. The hands with the brown paper bag containing the boxed Thomas.

Someone wrenched both bag and box from his fingers.

He heard breathing, soft laughter. 'Thomas the Tank Engine? Thomas the fucking Tank Engine!'

James felt himself move. He realised a second later it was

101

because he'd been kicked in the ribs. He fell over, wailing, banged his head on the urine-soaked ground. The world exploded in his head. Something cut loose in there, some last bit of sense.

He began to crawl.

He crawled right into a wall, sending a scalding pain through the crown of his head.

The second kick caught him in the ribs. The third turned him over, the fourth caught him across the right cheek.

He was crying now, blood and tears mixing on his face, running freely onto the ground. He tried to rise. Collapsed instead. Felt hands grabbing him by the feet, grabbing him and pulling him. He heard the sound of a button, the metallic chime of the lift arriving. Then the scrape as the doors opened. He felt a rough metal texture against his face.

He was in the lift.

The door began to close.

And then a thought filtered into his screaming brain: *if the lift door closes I'm dead.*

He reached out for the door; it closed on his arm, bounced open, crunched shut again.

He tried to call out but his voice was dead in his throat.

And then his attacker laughed again, a short bark without humour.

James heard the sound of cardboard and paper tearing. Something cold and heavy crashed into his back, his neck and head. His face smashed against the metal floor. He felt himself turned over, saw something flash towards him in the dim yellow elevator light.

Thomas the Tank Engine.

He was smiling.

There was blood on his silver lips.

FOUR

1.00p.m.–1.30p.m.

Pub lunches were hardly the norm among the staff at Anson
Road. Though anyone who saw them at it now, thought Fitz
ruefully, was going to be apt to think otherwise.

An hour earlier, after Beck and Molloy had been taken
home from the leisure complex in separate cars, Molloy to
take the rest of the shift off, Beck simply to change and
report back for duty, Penhaligon had driven him back to the
police station. Wise wanted a summary of his thoughts on
Molloy before the official report was typed. Fitz gave him
that summary in thirty seconds. Molloy may have committed crimes in the past, but Fitz was betting those crimes
were connected with his inability to form relationships;
a fact which absolved him of all blame in the case of
Catherine Carter's rape. The fact that he couldn't swim also
weighed in his favour. Marginally.

'He could've been faking,' Wise mused thoughtfully.

Fitz cocked his head on one side, a favourite angle from
which to launch a verbal attack. 'If James Molloy raped
Catherine Carter, I'll never bet again.'

Wise held his hand out. 'Is that a bet, Fitz?'

Fitz looked Wise straight in the eye. 'I'm right. I'm right
and you know it.'

Wise sighed, removed his glasses and rubbed the bridge
of his nose. 'Yeah,' he acknowledged the fact begrudgingly.
'Yeah, I suppose so. What are you going to do now?'

'Well,' Fitz glanced thoughtfully at his watch. 'I thought I
might go for a bit of a drink before lasties. What d'y'reckon?'

Wise looked around the duty room. 'Bit of morale-boosting might be in order.' He beckoned to Penhaligon. 'The reconstruction with Helen Robins. It's scheduled for four thirty, right?'

Penhaligon nodded.

'Well then, my lads and ladies,' Wise turned to the duty room as a whole. 'I suggest anyone that wants to can piss off down the pub for an hour.'

Jones looked up from a stack of files. 'Eh up, guv, Christmas come early has it?'

That got smiles.

Wise nodded towards Fitz. 'First round's on Santa here.'

Fitz grinned at Wise. *I haven't stung you for the sub yet, matey.*

At that moment Beck walked into the duty room.

Fitz's grin widened into a delightful beam. 'Nah. I know. I reckon the first round ought to go to the cleanest person in the room.'

That got a result. Everyone including Wise and Penhaligon turned to look at Jimmy Beck.

The door swung closed behind him. He fetched up against the wall of stares. 'What are you lot looking at?'

Fitz licked his lips. 'The cleanest copper in Christendom,' he quipped.

More laughter. Skelton whipped his sleeve around in a scrubbing motion over Beck's receding hairline, making squeaking noises as he did so. 'Mister Sheen shines every-thing cleaner,' he quipped.

'Removes follicles other cleaners leave behind,' giggled Chandra.

Beck jammed a rollup in his mouth and lit up. 'Oh piss off,' he muttered to the room at large.

'Said the master of witty repartee,' Jones retorted with a grin.

'Whose idea is this then?' Beck asked over the laughter.

Fitz modestly raised his hand. 'Please, sir, it was mine,' he said in a trembling schoolboy voice.

'Might have bloody guessed. We've got work to do, in

case you haven't noticed. There's a pervert running around out there, you know.' The look Beck directed at Fitz said even more. *Thanks to you, Fitz.*

Wise clocked the look, said, 'I'm authorising a bit of R and R, Jimmy, OK?'

Beck returned Wise's glare with no hint of a smile. 'New broom sweeps cleaner, eh guv?' There was a moment's silence as the import of his words sank in. *Bilborough would've kept us all on the case until the case was closed.* No-one in the duty room, even Harriman, who'd known Bilborough the shortest time, was immune to the moment.

Fitz shot a sideways glance at Wise. If the new DCI noticed the real motivation behind Beck's quip, he chose not to respond to it. Not directly anyway. 'There's no escaping it, Jimmy. The first round's on you.' Wise chose his next words carefully. 'You can show us your swimming medal, eh?'

And the moment broke, laughter spilling out once again as Beck scowled, sucked on the rollup, turned and walked out of the duty room without another word.

Wise leaned closer to Fitz, rubbed two fingers together in the age-old symbol for financial gain. 'And a lucky escape for you, eh Fitz?'

Fitz looked back with a level expression, 'Can I have a sub, guv?'

'No, you bloody can't.' Wise turned to follow the general exodus through the door. 'And I'm not your bloody guv. All right?'

Fitz grinned. Some days the game was simply a joy to play.

1.30p.m.–2.30p.m.

The Robin Hood was situated less than a hundred yards from the car park exit to Anson Road station. It was a small pub, cosy; this time of year there was generally a fire roaring in the grate. The fixtures and fittings were even older than those in the police station, mostly made of heavy oak.

There was an incredible variety of brass pots, pans, plates, kettles, bedwarmers and other paraphernalia hanging from the beams.

Sitting around a table right at the back of the saloon bar were Wise, Penhaligon, Skelton, Jones, Chandra and Harriman. The jukebox was bleating out *When You're in Love with a Beautiful Woman*. Fitz sat at the back of the table facing the saloon; he hated having his back to open spaces. Also it was a good position from which to observe the interplay between the police officers. And a great place to watch Penhaligon. She was sitting side-on to him. Her profile did crazy things to the inside of his head.

The conversation bubbled merrily around him, flitting from topic to topic with as much sense as you'd expect from any team of good mates who worked hard and as a consequence had to play hard.

Chandra was muttering about her husband to Jones, something about divorce, an affair. Fitz wondered if Jones would pick up on that. His mate Giggs had been killed during a one-night stand; Jones had had to pick up the pieces afterwards. And God knew, there was mess enough in the average separation without bringing murder into it.

Shifting his gaze slightly Fitz saw Harriman was listening intently to Chandra's conversation, wearing the same eager, slightly ingenuous expression he always wore. Fitz worried sometimes about what might be going on inside Harriman's head. He'd once seen Penhaligon catch Harriman staring at her legs. She'd pulled her skirt up, a typical Penhaligon response. Aggression. At least Harriman had had the grace to blush.

Skelton was having a dig at the system, mumbling on about overtime and how there wasn't any. He was aiming his comments at Penhaligon. She was soaking them up, a sponge to water, but Fitz could see she wasn't really listening. Fitz studied them hard, fascinated by the moment. They were perfect opposites: he black, she white, he a man, she a woman, he expressive, she . . . well. That politically correct part of him was loathe to use a word such as attentive. And he knew she wasn't passive, from personal experience. Fitz grinned, suddenly realising just how well he really knew Penhaligon. Beyond the bluster, beyond the professional bullshit there was something there, something tender. Was it just friendship? Could it be love? If it was, what should he do about it? Christ, if the genie popped out of one of the many brass kettles hanging from the oak beam above his head now he'd only have one wish. Shaking his head slightly, Fitz returned his attention to Penhaligon. It was obvious from the set of her shoulders that her attentiveness was a mask. But concealing what? A bottle of wine and feet up on the sofa later might enable him to find out.

Wise was telling a joke. His voice was a throaty grumble rising intermittently above the general hubbub.

'So she's eighty-five years old, you know, the little wispy beard, more mascara than Julian Clary, and she's there at the front desk – this was when I was a sergeant, like.'

'Before the blitz, then?'

'One more smart remark like that, Jonesey, and I'll arrest you.'

'Well, you're the boss t'do it, boss.'

'Right, that's it: no more beer for you, my lad, you obviously can't handle it. Anyway, where was I? Oh yeah: there I was, green as you like, on the desk and there's this old biddy, right, eighty-five if she's a day, telling me she's been raped.'

Was it Fitz's imagination? Did Penhaligon's attention wander just a second from Skelton to Wise?

'So I goes, "That's terrible, love, when did it happen, like?" and *she* says –'

At that moment Beck arrived with a tray of drinks. He put them down on the table and promptly sneezed over them, precipitating another round of cleaning jokes. Scowling, Beck sat down in time to catch the end of Wise's tall tale.

'So anyway, I says to her, I says, "That's terrible, love, when did it happen, like?" and she says, "*Sixty-five years ago!*"' Wise waited for the sniggers to subside and continued, ' "Well it's a bit late to charge him now, innit?" I says, and she says, "Oh I don't want to bring charges, I've just come in to talk about it!" '

Fitz gazed at Penhaligon. She was giggling despite herself. He shook his head. His voice was low but it carried none the less. 'The most important part of rape counselling is "talking about it". Keep it in, bottle it up and it just comes out later, as massive personality disorders, insecurity, inability to interact with society.' He had their attention now. Good. Let his words cool that alcoholic fervour a bit. 'I knew one woman who tried to commit suicide by setting light to herself. She was trying to burn him out, she said, because even three years after the fact, he was still inside her.'

The chatter died away. Fitz found a host of stares settling on him. Prominent among them was Jimmy Beck's.

Beck sucked on his rollup and pushed Fitz's whisky chaser across to him. 'What I want to know is how come come he gets twice as many drinks as anyone else?'

Skelton flipped Fitz a wink. ' 'Cos there's twice as much of 'im, of course.'

That broke the moment.

Beck continued looking at Fitz. 'I think it indicates something.'

Fitz raised an eyebrow. 'That you're a soft sod for buying them.' He winked at Beck. *Don't mess with the master, boy.* He raised his glass to Scunthorpe and the rest joined in.

All except Beck. 'No. It indicates you think you're something special.'

Wise cut in with, 'Oh behave yourself, Jimmy, will you?'

Beck ignored him. 'It indicates –'

And there he was interrupted as Harriman finally ventured a comment. 'Bottomley.' He said, his cheeks flushed with alcohol.

'Do what?' That was Wise, rising to the bait, deflecting attention from Beck.

'Virginia Bottomley. Something about that name. Makes you want to put her over your knee and give her a good seeing to, know what I mean? A good spanking.' He led the general laughter with a high-pitched guffaw.

Chandra reached over and grabbed his chin, wobbled it about. 'If you were much younger I'd chuck you over my knee, laddie boy. And then we'd see what was what.'

That got even more laughter. The conversation degenerated back into the mess of anecdotes and wisecracks.

Beck said over his shoulder to Harriman, 'You're a twisted bloody pervert.'

Wise roared, 'He'll make a bloody good copper then!'

There was more laughter. Beck didn't join in. His eyes hadn't left Fitz.

And Penhaligon. She wasn't laughing either. Fitz ignored Beck, glanced at her. 'My round, I think.'

He returned a few minutes later with a tray of drinks. As he sat the barman brought another tray over. On it were five pints of Guinness.

Fitz pushed the tray towards Beck. 'To feed your inferiority complex.'

Beck stared at him. Fitz could feel the amazement, the anger, lapped it up eagerly. 'It's obvious to a brain-dead poodle you're more important than me. I'm *acknowledging* that you're more important than me . . .'

Beck shook his head. 'Oh piss off, why don't you?'

'With that amount of alcohol in you I rather think you'll be the one doing the pissing.'

Penhaligon grinned at that. Glanced at Fitz, mouthed the words *wicked bastard* silently. Fitz blew her a kiss. Her smile widened.

Beck clocked the exchange. 'You know I've never understood it,' he said suddenly, loudly.

'What's that, Jimmy, how to wipe your arse?'

'He doesn't need to, he's been swimming in the world's largest bidet.'

Beck ignored the wisecracks. 'I've never understood why they let it happen. Why women let themselves be raped.'

Jones sucked in a breath. 'Dangerous ground, there, mate,' he said.

Beck turned to Penhaligon, whose smile had vanished. 'You're a woman. Why do women let themselves get raped?'

Her lips narrowed. 'They don't *let* themselves.'

'Bollocks.' Beck sucked on his rollup.

'It's violence, or the threat of violence.'

'Bollocks. You can't thread a moving needle.'

Penhaligon practically jumped out of her seat. Fitz thought for one moment she might actually take a poke at Beck. 'What?' The anger in her voice was tempered only by a hint of amazement.

Beck eyed her thoughtfully, and Fitz watched him in turn. Was this the result he wanted? To anger her and get at him, at Fitz? 'You can't thread a moving needle. They let themselves get raped. And shall I tell you why?'

'Oh please do.' Her voice dripped contempt.

Beck was immune to it. 'Because, subconsciously, they want it.'

'You're talking through your arse!'

All around the table heads were nodding agreement with Penhaligon. Beck was immune to everything, arrowing in for the moment, claiming it for his own.

'Do you fantasise about rape?'

Penhaligon sat back in her chair. Fitz cast her a supportive look, but she was staring at Beck and missed it. Fitz said, 'If she does it's never *violent* rape.'

Beck twisted in his seat, 'What other kind is there?' He looked back at Penhaligon. The moment had passed now but Beck wouldn't let it go.'*Do you fantasise about rape?*'

Right. Enough.

Fitz said warningly, 'You're playing on my pitch. You haven't got the faintest idea. Women's –'

'I couldn't give a shit. Do you –'

'– fantasies –'

'– about –'

'– aren't violent!'

'– rape? *Do you?*'

And despite everything, Beck had nailed the moment.

Penhaligon looked him squarely in the eyes. 'Sometimes, yes, I do,' she said.

And left the table.

Fitz rose too, but Wise blocked his path. 'I'm her boss,' he said, aiming his next comment at Beck. 'Had a whiff of the barman's apron, have we, Jimmy?'

Beck scowled. 'I just wanted her to answer the question.'

Wise shook his head, followed Penhaligon across the room to the pinball machine.

Fitz sat, reluctantly, frustrated. He stared at Beck.

Beck stared back. 'Something to say, Fitz?'

'I've got a cancellation on Monday. Shall I book you in?'

2.30p.m.–2.35p.m.

Penhaligon nailed the flippers again, sent the ball spinning back into the heart of the machine. Again. Again.

Beside her, a sound. Wise. Jesus. Couldn't they leave her alone for a minute. It was bad enough having Fitz screwing with her head.

'Jane.'

'Sir?'

'All right?'

'Not really.' She turned to stare at him and let the steel ball gurgle down the *lose* slot. 'Do you think he should be on the case?'

'Jimmy Beck?'

'Don't you think we could find someone a bit more sensitive? Attila the Hun, someone like that?'

Wise sighed. 'You'd go before Jimmy Beck, love.'

Oh great.

'Thank you, sir.'

For your vote of confidence.

Wise studied her for a moment. She felt his eyes on her as she pulled the handle to launch another ball around the pinball track, felt him study her as hard as she studied the trajectory of the ball.

Flip.

Flip. Flip.

Numbers turning, spinning like her mind, whirling through a chaos of thoughts and emotions.

Flip. Flip.

'Go back and have a drink with the lads.'

Lose.

'I'm not in the mood, sir.' Was that her voice? So flat, emotionless. So at odds with what she felt inside. How dare Jimmy Beck do that to her!

'*They're* your mates. Not the feminists, not the hairy-arsed lesbians, those lads there.'

'One of those "lads" is a woman, sir.'

'You know what I mean. Now go and have a drink with them.'

Arrogant bastard.

'If you say so, sir.'

'I do, yeah. And while you're at it, cool off. I don't want you in charge of a rape reconstruction with an attitude like this.'

Jesus.

She flipped the last ball, let it gurgle down the *lose* slot, turned . . . and found herself face to face with Skelton, radio in hand.

'It's Molloy, sir,' he said. 'He's in hospital.'

Jesus.

2.45p.m.–3.15p.m.

Sometimes Helen Robins wondered what it would be like if she were dead. She didn't have actual thoughts of suicide, not actual thoughts, that was stupid. But still, the idea remained, wormed its way gradually into her consciousness, surfacing infrequently during the day and night. Oddly, most of these moments came during the most mundane times. During breakfast, a bowl of Bran Flakes in one hand, glass of orange juice in the other. At work, while making up a prescription for a customer in the chemist where she worked.

Anything up to three months ago the idea of her own mortality, her own *worth*, would have flashed into her head and been instantly dismissed, no more unhealthy than anyone's casual thoughts of death. She would have put it out of her head, even laughed at herself for fretting about the inevitable.

Not now.

Three months ago Helen Robins had been attacked and raped and it had changed her whole life.

Since the rape, Helen had struggled hard to understand what had happened to her. Along with her occasional morbid moments, the question 'Why me?' rattled in her head so often she thought at one point she might actually have been driven insane by the assault.

Once she even caught herself saying it to a customer at work in response to an enquiry about underarm deodorants.

Then common sense reasserted itself. A week after the rape, Helen had told her partner Kelly what had happened. Kelly had been incredibly supportive. Helen had been bottling the feelings up inside her for a week, just a week, but by the time she let them out the strength of her reaction had been frightening. Probably as much so to Kelly as it had been to herself.

Helen had told Kelly over breakfast on Saturday the week following the rape. She hadn't planned to, the words just seemed to spill out. Kelly had listened. Listened but not judged. As well as that she had not made any attempt to hold or touch Helen. She had been sensitive enough to realise any physical comfort she offered might only confuse and frighten Helen even more.

Her advice to seek aid from the rape crisis centre seemed to Helen to be sound. She had rung the number provided by directory enquiries, had got an answerphone message telling her the line was only open three evenings a week plus two hours during the day on Wednesday and Friday afternoons. There was an option to record her telephone number and name for a counsellor to ring her back. She'd thought about it for a moment, as the tape had whirred in silence on the other end of the line and Kelly had looked on sympathetically from the other side of the room. She stuttered a few words, managed to say her first name. But talking to a

113

machine about her experience proved impossible and she'd put the phone down.

Kelly's reaction had been sympathy tinged with annoyance. 'Suppose we'd better try not to get raped on a weekend then, by the looks of it.'

Helen had broken down at that point, had scrunched herself up on the couch and begun to cry. When she had finally cried herself to sleep an hour later Kelly hadn't moved; she was still there that evening, the only difference was she'd covered Helen with a quilt.

The following week was a confusion of nightmares and flashbacks to the rape. She kept seeing snatches of Centenary Park, where the rape had happened, the fountain there and the pool into which he'd pushed her afterwards. She smelled the leather of the hood he'd made her wear, heard his voice insinuating itself into her, worming its way deeper and deeper into her head, penetrating her again and no less painfully. She remembered lurching from the pool, drenched, ashamed, shocked; remembered tumbling into a taxi, almost petrified with fear; remembered the driver's jokes about swimming fully dressed, remembered getting home and throwing up, stripping and shoving her clothes in the washing machine and getting in the bath and scrubbing herself over and over again, until the bath water was streaked with blood and shampoo and her head was streaked with guilt and shame, and it all blurred together into a sickening mass and she threw up again and then she heard the front door slam and Kelly's cheerful voice and then, somehow, she managed to get herself under control.

A week passed in this way and then they had talked again. This time the conversation had been started by Kelly. She was still sympathetic, but Helen could feel the irritation beneath that. Kelly had never been one to hide her feelings. She hadn't been the one who'd had problems about coming out. She hadn't been the one who'd been married to a man for three years; a lovely man, true, but one with whom she found sex painful and unsatisfying. Kelly had no problems expressing her feelings. She was sensitive, true, but

114

sometimes she was so impatient. Now it seemed she was finding it difficult to understand how a heterosexual rape was interfering with their own relationship.

Helen didn't have an answer.

The conversation had escalated into an argument and Helen had eventually gone to bed, slamming the door and crying herself to sleep.

She'd gone to the police at lunchtime the next day, determined to exorcise this demon that was ruining her life. Ruining hers and Kelly's life together. It was the beginning of a nightmare which took her back to the edge and very nearly tipped her over.

Could she describe what had happened?

Could she describe her assailant?

Would she be present at a line-up?

Would she press charges against her assailant?

Was she prepared to testify against him in court?

Was she pregnant?

Had she been examined by a doctor?

Had she been assessed for clinical trauma?

Had she been rated on an impact of event scale?

Had she taken a rape aftermath symptom test?

Was she prepared to undergo the above?

Oh the police were sensitive enough, and they didn't make any crass jokes. But despite all their procedures, tests and assessments they simply didn't *understand*. And that, when she thought about it, was really Kelly's problem too. To understand rape you had to go through it. Anything else was just make-believe and good intentions. And at the end of two weeks she'd had enough of those to drive someone with the patience of a saint into an early grave.

Her relationship with Kelly, and that with her workmates, was beginning to suffer.

And still that question was fizzing around her head, shooting questioning sparks through her everyday life.

Why?

Why me?

What did I do to deserve this?

115

In growing desperation, she began to read books about rape. She read accounts of depression, self-blame, guilt, shame, embarrassment, loss of trust in people and family, interpersonal sensitivity, concern about others' reactions, confusion, shock, difficulty concentrating, difficulty making decisions, disorientation, fear, anger, anxiety, nervous activity, crying, tension and self-abuse.

She got very scared.

She changed the locks on the flat.

She fitted a comprehensive burglar alarm.

Another two weeks passed.

The crisis came to a head when Kelly threatened to move out. Helen had been sleeping in the spare room for three nights by then. It hurt Helen to think Kelly would give up on her after such a short space of time. Then she realised it had been six weeks since the rape. Six weeks during which, with the exception of a single abortive attempt, she and Kelly hadn't made love, hadn't cuddled, hadn't gone out to the pictures, or for a meal, hadn't chatted, played cards, watched telly together with a bottle of wine; hadn't, if she was brutally honest about it, *been* together at all.

Worse, they hadn't talked about their feelings.

The next morning after Kelly had left for work Helen gathered together all the books she had bought and threw them away. She took the day off work. That evening by the time Kelly had come home Helen had made dinner, bought some wine, rented a video. Fresh flowers were in a vase on the table.

Kelly took one look at the dining room, dropped her bag, took Helen in her arms. 'Oh Christ,' she whispered. 'I'm so sorry. I've been such a bitch.'

'It's not your fault,' said Helen. 'It's not your fault. It's *his*.'

They had taken the wine to bed.

The fact that the dinner had burned and set off the smoke alarm in the middle of their lovemaking only served to make them giggle.

From that moment on things slowly began to get better.

116

Two weeks later, when Helen had been contacted by DS Jane Penhaligon from Anson Road police station about taking part in a rape reconstruction, she felt confident enough to say yes without overlong consideration. They'd settled on today as the day. Almost as soon as she saw Penhaligon out Helen felt better. At last she was doing something constructive. Kelly wouldn't like it, probably, but that was tough.

The good feeling had persisted for the next few days. But now the time had come, she was beginning to feel the ragged edge of nervousness grate against her again. She fought the fear down as she called a taxi.

It was stupid to be scared.

Wasn't it?

'Be someone with you in a couple of minutes, love.'

'Thanks.'

When the cab turned up Helen grabbed her bag and ran downstairs. DS Penhaligon had asked her to wear the clothes she had been wearing that day, or as near as she could manage. It was colder now so she wore trousers instead of a skirt, but the jacket and bag were the same; the picture she presented, that of reasonably attractive but otherwise unremarkable business sector worker was essentially the same as it had been that day.

She hadn't looked at these clothes since the attack, had been frightened to do so; oddly the fact that she was dressed almost identically to the day of her assault provoked no nervousness at all.

She climbed into the cab, caught sight of herself in the driver's mirror. She looked pretty sorted. Maybe it was going to be OK after all.

Then the driver spoke.

'Where to, love?'

Oh Christ, oh Jesus, the voice, the voice it was the same it was the same as his!

'Uh . . .'

She felt his eyes on her. Concern? Something more?

'You all right, love?'

117

'Yeah. Anson Road police station.'

'Sure.'

The cab pulled smoothly away.

Helen struggled to get her breathing under control. It wouldn't do to turn up in a state of nervous hysteria.

But the voice, Helen, his voice. It was the same.

Helen peered into the driver's mirror, caught a glimpse of velvet brown eyes staring back at her, thick eyebrows, black skin.

The driver spoke again, chatty, no pressure. 'What are you going there for?'

Tell him. He'll keep chatting otherwise.

'A reconstruction.'

'What of?'

Tell him.

'I'd sooner not talk about it.'

The driver shrugged. 'Right.' Another little glance in the mirror. 'I'm Floyd.'

'Helen.' The introduction came automatically. Social programming. *Jesus.*

'Are you OK, Helen?'

Oh my dear Lord it is him it is!

'Can you say that again, please?'

The driver obliged. 'Are you OK, Helen?' He half-turned in his seat. '*Are* you OK?'

Tell him. It's good therapy. Like alcoholics anonymous. Hi, I'm Helen, I'm a lesbian and a rape victim. See, it can happen to us too isn't that funny? Tell him. He'll shut up if you do and then you won't have to worry about his voice any more. Not his voice, just the reconstruction.

'I was raped. I'm going to a reconstruction. I . . . I've been having a few problems with people's . . . with men's voices.'

The driver – Floyd – nodded ingenuously. 'I understand. I'm sorry. There are some mad bastards about. But, if you'll forgive me for saying so, Helen, if the only problem you're having is with men's voices, you must be recovering all right.'

What the hell do you know?

118

'If you don't mind, I'd sooner not talk about it, thanks.'
'No problem. We'll be there in a minute anyway.'
'Thanks.'

3.15p.m.–4.30p.m.

Penhaligon met her at Anson Road, introduced her to the others. Beck, Skelton, Harriman, a couple of uniformed WPCs. Penhaligon drove Helen, Skelton and Harriman to Centenary Park. Beck and the others followed in a police car.

At the park Penhaligon held Helen's door for her as she got out. 'Now it's all clear, you know what to do? Just retrace your steps from the Newbury Road entrance past the monument and the fountain towards the other exit and the bus stops, yeah?'

Helen nodded. There was a peculiar sick feeling in her stomach. No. Not peculiar. She knew what it was, knew what caused it. Knew who had caused it.

'All right. I'll be close behind you. DC Skelton and the others will be asking people in the park if they were here, or if they saw or remember anything.'

'I understand.'

My head understands. But Jesus, I feel sick!

Penhaligon noticed her expression and smiled reassuringly. 'There's no need to be frightened. You're quite safe. No-one's going to hurt you.'

That's what I thought last time.

'Yeah.'

Kelly. I want you here. I wish I hadn't asked you not to come.

'You ready then?'

Oh shit I'm scared.

'Yeah.'

'All right, then, off you go. I'll be behind you.'

And Helen began to walk. She walked along the road, past the old-fashioned wrought iron railings which had somehow escaped from the great drive for metal in the war, past the stone pillars, through the high gates. She walked into the park, feet clattering on the path, and a grey drizzle began to fall, a foretaste of winter dulling the sky, and leaves whirled about her ankles and –

– she always cut through to get to the bus stops on the high street. It was a dreary afternoon, but Helen felt great. Half day. Early closing. Excellent. Kelly had finished moving her stuff into the flat the day before. That meant they were due a bottle of wine and a vid to celebrate. Maybe a Chinese. Or maybe they'd go out. Catch a movie. Check out the new Mexican restaurant on Zetland Road. Whatever. It didn't matter. They'd be together; in this age of casual relationships and failed marriages that was what was important. Being together with the right person.

Helen smiled to herself, tipping her face up to the lead-coloured sky. Even the light drizzle felt great. There'd be a rainbow around somewhere. Maybe a pot of gold. Helen laughed at the thought. Kelly was her pot of gold. She could almost hear her voice: Oh crap, Helen. You've been listening to your mum again. *Well, what if she had. It had taken her long enough to come to terms with Helen's failed marriage, even longer to acknowledge that her daughter was gay. Now everything was square between them. It was like starting a new life. And she was only thirty-two.* Helen Robins. Here's to the first day of the rest of your life.

Helen looked around the park. Way off in the distance, past the monument and the fountain, someone was pushing a bicycle with a flat tyre. Rather you than me mate. *Apart from that the park was empty. Helen walked on, collar raised against the light drizzle, past the monument, past the fountain (the pond had a single, lonely-looking duck in it) to the place where the trees encroached on the path for a hundred yards or so creating a dim, cavernous overhang before retreating into an open space bordered by the fence and then the high street and the bus stops.*

She stared up at the sky as she walked under the trees. As a kid she'd spent hours wandering around Oxleas Woods with her mates from school. They would be playing forty-

forty or something in the bushes and she would invariably be 'it'. She didn't care. When they were hiding it was quiet, maybe there'd be a dog barking somewhere, or some kid crying, out with his parents. But mainly it would be quiet. Like now. And she liked the

world spun around her and she bit her lip as her head hit the ground, felt gravel grind into her cheek. There was a weight on her back, no – there was someone *on her back there was someone holding her down, pressing her face against the path, grinding her cheek against it, and there was a voice telling her that* she'd be OK, she'd be OK if she didn't struggle, that she'd enjoy it if she didn't struggle.

She gasped, felt herself jerked upright, had no time to call out before a hood was drawn over her head and the world was blotted out. And she cried out in panic, her voice muffled by the hood, and another blow sent her reeling, and the hands were all over her, they were ripping at her clothes, at her body, they were hitting her and Oh God he was going to do that to her he was going to rape her right here in the park only a hundred yards from the high street and the buses and if she could only scream, just scream to let someone know she was here and she was being raped just scream and scream and –

smashed her fists against the man in front of her, the man in the black hood and anorak, the man the man in the hood, the rapist who was going to do that to her was going to do that to her all over again and then there were arms around her and she turned and Penhaligon was there, arms round her, holding her, soothing her with nonsense, just soothing sounds, and Helen buried her head in the detective's shoulder and sobbed hysterically.

'Make it stop, please make it go away *please make it go away!*'

4.30p.m.–4.45p.m.

It took Helen a few minutes to calm down enough so that Penhaligon felt confident in passing her to a WPC.

'Look after her for a minute, will you?' To Helen she said, 'I'll just be a minute, then I'll take you home.'

Helen managed a tearful nod. 'I'll be OK.'

Damned if I won't.

Penhaligon nodded. Turned to where, behind her, the man in the anorak and hood was pulling off the hood to reveal the rumpled features of DS Beck. His face was a picture. Utter amazement at her reaction. Then Helen looked harder, saw even though he was talking to Penhaligon he was looking at her, at Helen. Looking at her with something almost like interest. No – more than that. Fascination.

Obsession.

Helen shivered.

When Penhaligon came back and asked if she wanted to go home now, Helen nodded. 'Please.'

Just get me out of here. Why did I do this? Oh God, Kelly, I wish you were here.

But even as Helen followed Penhaligon to her car, she felt something wither up inside her, wither up and die and be blown away like dead leaves on a wind of change. And although outside she was weeping, sobbing, unable to stop, inside her tears were no longer tears of humiliation and fear but overwhelming joy, because she knew the thing that had gone from inside her, the thing she herself had faced and driven away, was her guilt.

4.45p.m.–5.30p.m.

Beck brought Carter in. You didn't need to be a Morse or a Taggart to see that he'd done it, too. Done for Molloy. Three broken ribs, lacerations to the face, a split cheek, a broken nose, a punctured lung, concussion, severe trauma. That was OK. For Beck's money Molloy deserved it all and more. The man had killed once in his life; the odds were he'd raped as well. The man was a twisted pervert. No. He wasn't even that, a man. Wasn't even human.

Beck stared Carter straight in the eye as he held the door of the police car open for him. 'If it was down to me I'd give

122

you a medal.' He shrugged. 'As it is . . .' And Carter had come, just like that, leaving Catherine staring helplessly from the front door, pain, fear, incomprehension in her eyes lighting her face with a ghostly pallor.

Beck had brought Carter in, left him in a cell while he had taken part in the rape reconstruction. Now Carter was in interview room one, sitting opposite Fitz. Bloody Fitz. Beck had once told David it was getting so his shift couldn't shit without Fitz. Now he was round the station so often it wouldn't surprise him if he found the psychologist in bed with Wise instead of Penhaligon.

Beck felt like giggling at that, but stopped himself with a thought. Less than an hour before a woman had run screaming from him in the middle of Centenary Park and right at this moment Jimmy Beck was unable to decide precisely how he felt about that.

The reconstruction had shaken him up considerably. Old memories he'd thought well hidden were now bubbling just under the surface. Feelings chased themselves through his head; fear, surprise, pleasure, guilt, more fear. Jesus. Time for a holiday, Jimmy. Make it through this case, through the christening, then off to Spain for a fortnight. Somewhere warm, where the cold memories couldn't find you, find you and drive you one more step nearer the edge.

Beck made a tremendous effort, cleared his head of all distractions, watched Fitz instead. He had a job to do; he'd be buggered if he'd let the past come between him and the job.

Fitz sat opposite Carter, studied him minutely. Beck watched every movement, every gesture, clocked everything. Fitz would get a confession out of Carter. It was as clear as a pint of watered-down beer.

But it wasn't to be quite as simple as that.

Carter decided not to play.

'I'm here about Molloy, right?' The cab driver's voice was firm.

Beck shook his head and sucked his rollup. There. There was your admission of guilt right there. Nobody had even mentioned Molloy yet.

'How is he?'

Beck sniffed, took out his rollup. 'Intensive care. He's lying there like a cabbage.'

Fitz sighed. What was he thinking? He stared straight at Carter and said, 'Can't be that bad if he's doing impressions.' Beck watched him study Carter. The man made no response. Was he scared? Did he know what was going to happen to him here?

'Bad taste?'

Carter looked away. 'I'd say so.'

Fitz nodded.'But he's only a pervert.'

'Yes.'

'So . . . he doesn't really matter. He's beaten up, left for dead, but it doesn't really matter.'

Carter appeared to consider the point, shook his head slowly. 'It doesn't.'

'So why not confess, hm? If it doesn't really matter, why not confess?'

'Because I didn't do it.'

Fitz sighed. 'Sometimes I think I'm cursed.'

Carter stared at Fitz. Beck stared too.

'I have the curse. The curse of understanding.'

Carter sighed, looked back at the table. Tapped his knuckles there impatiently.

'I understand, you know. Why you did it.'

Carter said nothing.

The door opened. Penhaligon came in. She took in the scene in a glance, her gaze raking across Beck, Carter, then back to Fitz. She stood by the wall, close to Beck. What was she playing at? Regs only required one observer. What was she doing here?

Fitz placed his glasses on his nose, studied Carter over the frames.

'For a woman to be good she must be dead, or as close to it as possible.'

Carter let out a startled bark of a laugh. 'Jesus.'

Fitz continued smoothly, 'Catatonia is a good woman's best quality. Sleeping Beauty slept for a hundred years. The kiss of the heroic prince woke her. He fell in love with her while she was asleep. Or was it *because* she was asleep?'

Fitz sniffed, adjusted his glasses. Beside Beck Penhaligon remained motionless against the wall. Her gaze was locked on Fitz. What the hell was she thinking? She was sleeping with him and he was coming out with this crap.

Fitz said, 'Sleeping Beauty. Cinderella. Snow White. Rapunzel. All classic feminine icons. All characterised by passivity, beauty, innocence . . . and here's the killer, John: *victimisation*.'

Was that a shiver that ran through Carter's body there?

'They are all archetypal good women – victims by definition. They never think, act, initiate, confront, resist, challenge.' Fitz took his glasses off, rubbed the bridge of his nose, smiled tiredly. 'Sometimes they're forced to do housework.'

'You're sick.'

'It makes the understanding easier.'

'My wife will be worried about me. In case you'd forgotten, she's been raped.'

Fitz put his glasses back on. 'I know you did it, hurt Molloy. I know why you did it. You asked yourself, "What would other men do?" Answer – they'd kill the bastard. There's something in here, in your heart, that says don't, it's barbaric, but you need to prove something. Not to yourself or to Catherine, to other men. And it's nothing to do with justice or revenge. Property. She's your property and your property's been damaged. Damaged goods must be paid for. So off you trot to collect, don't bother to wait for a conviction, just grab the first little pervert you can lay your hands on and every punch, every kick, every time you smash his head against the steel floor of the lift, you're proving that *I am a man*. I've been raped, my wife has been raped, but *I am still a man*.

Penhaligon shuffled uneasily beside Beck. My God, what did she get out of this? Was she enjoying it? Beck shook his head. Did Fitz realise he was opening the woman up just as much as Carter? Was he doing it deliberately? Jesus.

And Carter was unfolding, crumpling inwards. Fitz's words had reached him, wormed into him, broken him open from the inside, and now it was all spilling out. 'I'd sooner be the victim than the husband of the victim.' His voice was soft, a dry rattle like a punished schoolboy. 'Her role's mapped out. Her friends come round, offer condolences, say how sorry they are, listen to her talk, listen to her cry. I can't listen to her cry. I can't cry. Someone has to be strong don't they? Someone has to make decisions, take control of the situation. Don't they?'

Carter was leaning forward now, the pain in his voice giving it a ragged edge. 'And what about me? No-one says a blind thing to me. I'm not the one who's been hurt. Am I?' And Carter was out of his chair, kicking it backwards, towering over Fitz as he sat perfectly still. '*I have been hurt!*'

Then Fitz got up, slowly, righted Carter's chair, sat him down again. Beck felt himself tense. Carter was ready to blow. Any second. It was going to happen.

But it didn't. Maybe any blow in him had gone off already. Maybe Fitz knew that, was exploiting the knowledge.

Fitz said, 'I know.' His voice was loaded with tenderness.

But Carter was off in his own world, looking inwards, not out. 'What's my role? What do I do? Do I take her in my arms, make love to her, show her that nothing's changed? No. I can't. Because it's not making love any more. It's doing what he did. What that man did. Do I avoid it? No. Because that's treating her like some kind of leper, that's admitting he's won. That pervert's won.'

Fitz narrowed his eyes. ' "Won?" '

'Yes.'

'It's a strange choice of word.'

'You think so?'

'Then you don't understand anything.'

Fitz put the nails in the coffin and began to hammer them home. As he spoke he looked around. Beck, Penhaligon. He spoke to the walls, the ceiling, anywhere but Carter. He *knew*. And Carter was just starting to get it.

'The person you love gets raped. What does that do to you, John? I'd say it makes you guilty. You should've been there to protect her. You weren't. You feel guilty.'

Carter watched the nails go in, one by one, numb, his responses almost programmed. 'Yes.'

'Something else to feel guilty about. This idea that your property's been tampered with. A man's come along and laid hands on something that's yours, that's exclusively yours. It's selfish, not very politically correct, but it's true. And it's there, the idea's there and it's just one more thing to feel guilty about. Yes?'

'Yes.'

'That's all OK. It's all wholesome, natural. But something less wholesome now. You *blame* her.'

And that was it. Carter folded like a deck of cards in a high wind. Fitz could have stopped any time he liked, could have put the confession in front of Carter; the man would have signed an admission of witchcraft.

Fitz just kept on hammering in the nails.

'She should've been more careful. She's a manager. She's in a position of responsibility, for God's sake. So why wasn't she more responsible? Wait a minute – did she *want* it? She didn't scream, John. Why not? Because she wanted it? And this is the killer, John – what did he say to her? *I promise you'll enjoy it*.

Beck shuffled uncomfortably, felt himself flush. What? What was going on here? Fitz had his dig at Beck a year ago. What the fuck was going on here?

But Fitz wasn't looking at Beck, he was looking at Penhaligon. Beck followed the psychologist's gaze, suppressed his own feelings. Maybe the result here was going to be a little more interesting than he'd thought.

Fitz went on, 'Did she? I mean, we're talking rape here, John. We're talking about a man who just *does* it. All those times when we haven't been up to it, John. She was willing, she helped, and we still weren't up to it, so how do we match this man who comes along with his stick of Blackpool Rock and *just does it*? How do we match that, John, hm?'

And Carter was out of his chair again, swinging around to face Penhaligon, his face twisting out of control, guilt and fury and pain and anguish and love and confusion all churning it into a nightmare battlefield.

And still Fitz kept on.

'That's why you beat up Molloy, isn't it, John?' Bang. Another nail. Bang bang. 'I understand it. A judge will understand it. A jury will understand it. That's why you did it, isn't it John?'

And Carter was down, suddenly sitting on the floor, hands clenching impotently, body racked with sobs.

'Yes, oh yes, oh God yes, the bastard, the bastard he did it to her and I did it back to him and I'm glad I did it, I'd do it again, oh God, oh Jesus, oh God . . . yes. I did it, yes . . .'

5.30p.m.–6.00p.m.

Beck took Carter back to his cell after the confession. As the steel door slammed shut between them, Beck stared through the observation hatch. Carter. Despite everything Beck almost felt sorry for the man. He understood as well. Understood the rage of emotion boiling in Carter's head. But the driver had broken the law. He had to be punished.

Still . . .

'You OK, Jimmy?' George Sanders, the duty sergeant, had a pleasant voice that rang in the steel-shuttered corridor.

Beck blinked. 'Yeah, sure. Cheers George.'

'No problem, Jimmy.'

Beck walked back to the duty room slowly, his mind whirling with thoughts. Thoughts from long ago and thoughts generated as late in his life as that same afternoon.

In the duty room Wise was waiting. 'Jimmy. My office.' Beck scowled. Jesus. Wise was in one.

Once behind the door Beck steeled himself for the explosion.

Wise's first punch hit hard. ' "If it was down to me I'd give you a medal." Did you say that?'

128

Beck sucked on his rollup. 'No, boss.'

'Carter said you did.'

'I didn't say anything of the kind.'

Wise scowled. 'The man's a criminal. He took the law into his own hands. He put a fellow human being in hospital.'

That was enough for Beck. 'A pervert, sir. Not a fellow human being. And no jury's ever going to convict Carter for doing that. Even now he's coughed no jury'll ever convict. Molloy was a pervert.'

Wise's lips thinned, Beck could see his whole body tense with anger. '*A fellow human being*. Molloy is innocent until proven guilty.'

Beck shrugged. 'The Criminal Justice Bill.'

'What?'

'Guilty until proven innocent.'

'What!'

'The rules have changed, sir.'

'Christ, Jimmy. You keep your bloody opinions to yourself. If I thought I had a bloody fascist on the team –'

'I'm not a fascist.'

'You keep your opinions to yourself. You've already upset a fellow officer so from now on keep your mouth shut. Clear?'

Beck felt the emotions inside bubbling upwards again, defying control. 'Who? Who said that about me? I'm entitled to know.'

'In this job you're entitled to know what I want you to know.'

'Someone's complained about me.'

'Yeah.'

'Penhaligon.'

'No.'

And there it was: the truth, glaring at him from the dark spaces behind Wise's steel-rimmed spectacles.

'I'm sorry, sir, I don't believe you.'

'Tough.'

And Beck finally couldn't take any more. 'David – DCI

Bilborough wouldn't have put up with behaviour like that, sir. A copper going behind her mate's back.'

Wise stood. 'I'm not Bilborough, Jimmy.'

'No, sir.'

You are most definitely not.

'Don't push it, Jimmy.'

But Beck was running out of control now. 'DCI Bilborough encouraged us to speak our minds. It's not me that's the fascist around here.'

Now it was Wise's turn to snap. 'DCI Bilborough's dead. He's fucking dead, Jimmy. What he may or may not have done is irrelevant. I'm in charge now. Bilborough is dead. And you know what rumour control would have to say about that, don't you?'

Beck froze. *They'd say I did it. Oh I may not have pushed the knife into him, may not have watched him begging for help, watched him start to die, but they'll say I did it none the less.*

'No, sir.' Beck allowed an icy anger to enter his voice. 'You tell me. What would they say?'

And Wise stopped then, stopped because somewhere inside Beck could see he knew he'd gone too far. 'Do one, will you, Jimmy?'

'What?'

'You heard me. I said piss off home! I'll see you tomorrow.'

Beck stared at Wise, amazement bubbling up with all the other emotions. 'Are you telling me to go home?'

'Jimmy.'

'Sixteen years I've been a copper. Sixteen years, no-one's ever told me to go home before.'

'I'm telling you now. So piss off, Jimmy. Just do one, will you?'

'Fuck *me!*'

'Don't think I'm not capable of it, Jimmy. Just go.'

Beck slammed the door loud enough to rattle the glass. The sound didn't scratch the surface of the noise in his head.

Jane Penhaligon lay in bed beside Fitz and stared at the ceiling. Way up in the corner was a tiny little spiderweb. Every so often it glimmered as the light shining through the window from the residential street on which Fitz lived reflected from the strands as tiny little gleams of yellow light.

Penhaligon felt the rumpled sheets beneath her, the cold air drifting over the window still bringing with it the distant sounds of traffic. She tried to empty her mind, let the day flow out, leave her a bit of peace and quiet in there, a respite from the emotional tumult.

'They lay traps, you know.' Fitz's voice startled her.

'I thought you were asleep.'

'How could I sleep with you in the room?'

'Hm.'

Penhaligon turned over to stare at Fitz. He was looking at the spiderweb in the corner of the ceiling.

'Some kinds of spiders. They lay traps. Build tunnels concealed by little doors. Trapdoors. They wait for something to happen along, some innocent grub, a beetle, then . . . bang! The door opens, the spider jumps out and it's beetle toasties for dinner again tonight, dear, and don't forget to check the sell-by date.'

Penhaligon giggled.

Fitz allowed his face to crumple into that appealing smile. 'You know what I'll say? When they ask me what my secret is, how I can get it on with a sex bomb like you? You know what I'll tell 'em?'

'It's the smalltalk?'

'Know her. Understand her. Be one with her.'

'Oh yeah? And what about the mystique?' Penhaligon drew part of the bed sheet across her face, like a veil, to illustrate her point.

'Load of old hogwash. Women like to know. They like to trust, and be trusted.'

Penhaligon shrugged. 'So?'

131

'Ah, but why, Panhandle? Shall I tell you? It's because the relationship can be more dangerous that way. More . . . experimental. More thrilling.'

'Oh yeah?' Penhaligon got on top of Fitz, grabbed hold of his hands, pushed them back towards the headboard.

'Like a bit of control do you, Fitz? The woman on top?'

Fitz held Penhaligon's gaze. 'Not what I meant, Panhandle. And you know it.'

'Too superficial for you?'

Fitz chewed his lower lip. He held her gaze for a moment longer, then, 'I wouldn't have had to ask you if you fantasise about rape.'

Penhaligon felt herself tense.

'Not like Beck.' Fitz sniffed. Penhaligon opened her mouth to retort, but he spoke again, cutting her off. 'I'll tell you about control. Jimmy Beck needs to control. He needs to control others because he finds it hard to control himself.'

Fascinated despite herself, Penhaligon asked, 'Why?'

Fitz shook his head. 'Don't know. I'd love to get him on the couch. Open him up a bit.'

'Pervert.' Penhaligon laughed. There was more tension in the laughter than she would have liked. Why did talking about Beck make her tense?

'That's what he'd say.'

'Did you see his face while you were interviewing Carter?'

'White as a sheet, I'll bet.'

'What do you think of him, Fitz, as a copper, I mean? Do you think he's any good?'

Fitz blew out his cheeks. 'He's a fifteen-year man, right? In the force for life? It's a family to him. You have to do right by your family. Is he married?'

'You know, I've never thought about it. No. I don't think so. No kids either.'

'Now, I ask myself, is that natural for a man in his middle forties?'

'Pot calling the kettle black, Fitz?'

'I said married, not divorced. He's a bit like Molloy in that respect.'

Penhaligon had had enough of talking about Jimmy Beck. 'How did you know Carter attacked Molloy?'

'You know me.'

' "I just have the knack. I can meet someone and within a few minutes I know more about them than they do themselves." '

'It's a fair cop, guv.'

'Shut up, Fitz, I'm not your guv.'

'Wise said that to me today.'

'Seriously – how did you know?'

'Seriously?'

'Yeah, seriously.'

'I didn't. There was a fair possibility it was true. Circumstantial evidence supported the theory. He'd been told about Molloy. He'd been wound up and then refused an outlet for his anger. He seemed like the sort of bloke who might commit violence if provoked enough.'

'Yeah – but how did you *know?*'

'Well, you watched me. You know how I work. I asked questions, weighed the answers, studied his body language . . .' Fitz trailed off, let his gaze roam over the ceiling, the spiderweb, before settling back onto her face. 'No. That's bullshit. That's what a ten-a-penny psychologist would do. I knew he did it because I know what it's like to want to do it.'

'Judith?'

Fitz nodded. 'When we first split up she slept with her therapist. I wanted to smash his face in. Came close too.'

'Close enough to scare him?'

'Close enough to scare myself.' Fitz sighed. 'What we are capable of, as individuals, as a species . . . it scares me. That's my monster in the closet. *I'm* my monster in the closet. I know. I know what Carter felt because I felt it myself. I know what he did because I came this close to doing it myself. I wasn't telling him about himself. I was telling him about me.'

Penhaligon was silent.

'Well. You asked. Now you know. I'm a violent man. Deep down inside I'm a violent man. Inside me there's a not very PC animal screaming and clawing to get out. Violent, selfish, possessive. I keep that animal part of me caged away, because I know what it's capable of. I want to possess. I want to possess violently. And the only thing between *it* and . . . well, you, say, is my control.'

Penhaligon fought for words; again Fitz spoke first. 'How do you feel about that, Panhandle? You're in bed with a savage, does it scare you? It would scare me. Come on. What are you thinking? "Jesus, how come I always end up with the nutters, the overweight, self-loathing, misogynistic, middle-aged, inadequate slobs of this world. Either that or the shop dummy with no personality of his own that isn't programmed by society?" '

Penhaligon felt herself frown. 'If you mean Peter, you're just as much affected by social programming as he is.'

'Ah, but I have the knowledge that I am a product of society. I can step outside the machine, rewrite the programme.'

Penhaligon felt anger build inside her.

Fitz glanced narrowly at her. ' "How come he always does this to me? Always winds me up like this? We were getting on so well, sex was magnificent, and now this? This anger? Where does it come from? How does he put it inside me?" I'll tell you, shall I? I don't. You do. You like it like that. There's a touch of the masochist in you Panhandle, just like there's a touch of the sadist in me. It's in everyone. Just a hint, a shadowy glimpse somewhere deep down in our subconscious, just the merest sniff of a hint – but enough to utterly terrify us. It's true isn't it? Go on: confess, I dare you. I did it. Now it's your turn. Or don't you believe in equality?'

Penhaligon felt herself go rigid with amazement. She hardly knew herself whether the anger blooming inside her was due to his assumptions about her or because he had nailed the truth and she was simply too frightened to admit it.

She struggled for words. 'Fitz, I've said it before: you're an emotional rapist.'

His smile was infuriating. 'And?'

And suddenly she knew. The truth came hammering on the doors of her mind, smashed them down, opened her up to herself in a moment of almost savagely pure honesty.

'And . . . damn you, Fitz, *I like it.*'

I can't believe I just said that.

He leaned upwards then, kissed her. It was a nice kiss. Sweet, clean. A hint of the wine they'd had with dinner. She bit his tongue.

Sex was magnificent.

11.30p.m.–12.30a.m.

Penhaligon showered alone afterwards. Fitz smiled at that, pushed a little, but Penhaligon was adamant. There was something rather nice about being in a bathroom alone. It gave you time to think. To savour that warm feeling of *afterwards.* To check out what bathroom products he used.

Fitz was a Body Shop man. That or Mark was. Penhaligon looked around and wondered what had belonged to Judith in here. Then she laughed. Judith was gone. Fitz's marriage was over bar the legal details. That was true. Or she wouldn't be with him. Would she?

Penhaligon smiled wryly. Ooh, that little voice in her head. That voice that said *wake up girl, see how he's using you, how you're using each other. Love doesn't come into it; it's all mind games.*

Jesus.

Penhaligon shivered, turned the shower up full and stuck her face under the water.

After her shower, Penhaligon squeezed most of the moisture from her hair, wrapped herself up in a bathrobe from the airing cupboard, padded along the landing towards the bedroom.

There were voices coming from the room. Fitz. Fitz and Mark.

Angry voices.

135

Her first instinct was to just barge in. Then she stopped. This wasn't her house, her family. She couldn't make any demands of Fitz; for one thing she was enough of a realist to know she couldn't change him. For another . . . well . . . she hadn't quite worked out how she felt about Fitz's family yet. Because there was always the question that if they did make it together where would Mark live? And that was complicated. Penhaligon wasn't entirely sure she liked Mark.

He was talking now, his voice muffled through the bedroom door. Hating herself for doing it, Penhaligon leaned closer to listen.

'She's in the shower.'

'Her name's Jane. Not "She". That's a book by H. Rider Haggard.'

An angry sigh from Mark. 'You want me to tell Mum about her?'

'No.' Astonishment from Fitz. The thought had never crossed his mind. Well that was good news. Kind of.

'You're doing it all to make Mum jealous, aren't you? Well, she can't be jealous if she doesn't know.'

There was a silence from the bedroom. Penhaligon imagined Fitz chewing over his son's words. Weighing them up for pros and cons. Weighing *her* up.

'I'm not doing it to make your mum jealous.'

'Then why?' The plaintive note of incomprehension in Mark's voice provoked an odd sympathy in her. 'Do you want Mum back?' Poor bloody kid. Whatever Fitz said to him was only going to screw him up even more.

'Most of the time, yeah.'

Jesus.

'I do as well. But if she comes back and finds Boadicea here, she'll be off again won't she?'

A long silence.

Finally, 'You're a joke, Dad.'

And the door was open, suddenly, before she could move he was there, angry, upset, confused.

'Look,' she began.

He scowled. 'That's my mum's,' he pointed to the

136

bathrobe she was wearing, skirted around her, went into his own room and slammed the door.

Penhaligon turned to Fitz. She shook her head. 'He's going to grow up just like you, you know.'

'God forbid.'

'You don't believe in God. Lapsed Catholic, remember.'

Fitz uttered a short, humourless laugh. 'So I am.'

Penhaligon sighed. 'I think I'd better go.'

'Yeah.'

'Come back to mine?'

Fitz shook his head. 'I can't. Not with Mark . . . well, you know.'

She nodded. 'Yeah.'

Fitz pinched the bridge of his nose. He looked at her. Seemed to fight some inner battle. 'Do you love me?'

She laughed, more a surprised cough than a laugh.

'I don't know. Maybe. Probably. I don't know.'

He nodded. 'Yeah.'

She felt like crying. Wondered how he'd respond.

'I'll see you tomorrow.'

'Yeah.'

12.30a.m.–2.00a.m.

In the Volvo Penhaligon sighed. It was freezing cold and her hair was still damp. It'd go frizzy. She hated it when her hair went frizzy.

She shoved the car into gear, pulled away. Refused to allow herself to look back in case Fitz was watching. If he was and she saw him, she'd be back like a shot – she was honest enough to admit that. As it was she didn't look back. Somehow not knowing if he was watching her was easier than having to admit he might not be.

As she drove Penhaligon felt herself begin to cry. She shoved her foot down on the accelerator. Slammed the Volvo round a few corners, ran a few red lights, face blank, cheeks sticky with tears.

Do you fantasise about rape?

137

I wouldn't have needed to ask if you fantasised about rape.

Please make it stop, just make it go away.

Something made her think of Helen Robins, the expression on her face after the reconstruction as she'd clung to Penhaligon like the proverbial drowning man and begged her to take away the pain, to take away the memories. Yet now she thought about it there was something in Helen's expression, something she may not have been aware of herself, even. As if . . . as if something inside had been liberated. As if she'd faced her fears and . . . somehow . . . found a way of dealing with them.

Penhaligon knew it wasn't as easy as that for some people. For most people in fact. Since her promotion to DS Penhaligon had personally counselled fourteen victims of rape ranging from a ten-year-old schoolgirl to a fifty-eight-year-old married mother of four whose oldest son had been two years older than Penhaligon herself. What she brought away from these experiences were the fear, the self-loathing, the depression, the guilt. She knew what Wise would say, what Bilborough had always told her: don't take it home with you. Leave it at the office. Oh God. Bilborough. She hadn't seen Catriona or the baby since the funeral. The christening would be coming up soon. She had an invitation for that at home. Jimmy Beck would probably be there. He and Bilborough were like *that*.

Had been like *that*.

How was Jimmy Beck dealing with Bilborough's death?

Penhaligon pulled the Volvo alongside the kerb and parked.

She got out. She wasn't home. She looked around. A sign on the flats read Belle Vale.

Helen Robins's home.

Penhaligon laughed. Her subconscious had brought her here. Like in that film with Robbie the Robot. Monsters from the Id.

Oh, Jane, girl, the voice in her head told her. *You are one screwed-up bitch tonight.*

She shook her head. Made to get back into the car. Stopped. Her breath steamed in front of her, bonsai cumulonimbus. Then she turned and surveyed the flats. The buildings formed three sides of a square. Between them was a small stretch of grass planted with trees. One end was fenced off. A kiddies' playground. A slide. A roundabout. A rocking horse. A climbing frame. Some swings.

She went and sat on a swing. Looked up at the wide rectangle of sky framed by the flats, tried to let her mind go blank, tried to let the odd, dull sadness she felt drain away.

As she did this she swung her legs and the swing began to move.

Backwards. Forwards.

Overhead, the stars. Inside, the dull, emotional ache.

Her breath. Clouds of moisture.

Let it out. Let it all drain out.

Cold air on her face as she leaned into the swing, wrapped her hands around the cold metal chains.

Backwards. Forwards. Higher. Faster.

Distant sound of traffic. A car parking. A door slamming. A dog barking. Then silence again.

Fitz. Mark. Judith. Helen. Catherine. Bilborough. Giggsy. Peter.

Fitz.

Footsteps.

She turned, forgetting for a moment where she was, and the swing seat twisted under her. She felt the chains bite into her hands, felt herself slipping. A moment of dizziness, weightlessness, then a jolting pain in her knees as she hit the ground.

'Jesus Christ!'

Then the swing seat came back and hit her on the shoulder, a biting pain that knocked her over.

Oh great. Just fucking great. Mud all over my clothes now. I'll have to wash them before tomorrow. Probably cut my knees too, Christ they hurt. I wonder if –

And then the footsteps, fast, pattering towards her across the grass. A hand on her shoulder, another over her mouth.

What the fuck?

She tried to yell out, felt someone push her down onto the ground, all the way, face in the mud beneath the swing.

She struggled.

Pain exploded along her jaw as

he punched me, the bastard punched me

the pressure around her neck eased momentarily before tightening again. And this time there was a gleam of light; a stinging sensation against her

knife that fucker's holding a knife to my

throat, stabbing through the mass of pain pumping through her face, the sound of blood hammering in her ears.

Fuck. Jesus. Fuck.

She struggled hard to remember her training, went limp, felt his grip ease, gave one mighty heave, managed to turn a little before his grip tightened again.

And she saw the mask he wore. A black pit in the shadow of the stars above, side-lit by sodium yellow from the street.

Saw the mask and knew what he was going to do to her.

PART TWO

Impact

FIVE

2.00a.m.–2.30a.m.

Something made her think of her father. Of how he'd been with her as a child. Always disapproving. Always angry. Always irritable. She remembered how she would smile at him, try to win his approval. He was Daddy. She loved him. But he couldn't see it. Had to
push
hurt her
inside her
always on at her, always wanting
pushing
her to be like her brothers, like Charlie, Rich and Dave, to
be quiet, keep still, remember your training, wait your opportunity and
assert herself, to be strong, and then when she was, when she'd got the kind of job he'd pushed her for years into getting, it was
hurting her oh God it was
still not enough for him, not enough to stop him wanting her to be like her brothers, like him, to just do what he wanted and be
quiet
what he wanted and
still and
he'd never
go away oh please make him like me make him
understood her never once supported her never
stop oh please stop it Daddy it hurts please stop it please

143

please stop it please it hurts and hurts and

she was yanked to her feet, turned, arms whirling, head spinning. The world spun too, the swing, the flats, the yellow streetlights, the stars, the umber clouds, the darkened windows behind which people slept or cuddled or watched satellite telly or made midnight snacks or pissed or snored or

screamed

talked in their sleep or

raped

made love or

raped she was being raped she was

turned, pushed back onto the ground, head down, legs open –

'Disease. I've got a disease. I've got AIDS. You'll catch it. You'll –'

– hands in the mud, a crushing tightness around her waist, the palm of a leather glove sealing her mouth and then pain, so much pain, and with it the humiliation, the sheer terror of penetration.

She went limp in desperation, felt herself hoisted back onto her knees.

A sickly odour filled her nose. Him. His aftershave. His leather gloves. Tobacco. His hot sweat in the cold night.

He lifted her again, positioned her, still kneeling, facing him.

She looked up; past his naked hips to the mask, the body a black silhouette amongst the clouds, the mask a black extension of his pale body, looked up at him . . . and

I love you Daddy please stop please

felt her cheeks twitch and

stop hurting me now and

her lips part and

love me back. Please.

she smiled.

Please

She smiled and

please stop hurting me

144

he reached down to her and took hold of her and filled her up. Her body. Her head. Filled her with terror and with himself.

Again.

And again.

And again.

PART THREE

Rage

SIX

2.30a.m.–3.00a.m.

She lay in the mud. The swing seat creaked back and forth above her head, chains clinking softly in the night. She coughed. Spat him out of her mouth. Felt her tights and skirt drag in the mud as she drew her knees up to her chest. She coughed again. Hugged herself. It hurt. Oh dear God it hurt, *she* hurt. Her eyes were tightly closed, the muscles of her lids and cheeks aching. She opened her eyes. He was standing over her. Pulling up his trousers. Standing over her. *Enjoying* standing over her. She closed her eyes again. Waited for the whisper of air preceding another punch, a kick, the sting of the knife. Waited. Waited.

The chains stopped clinking. A whisper of damp air across her mud-soaked hair. Distantly, a dog barked.

Apart from that, nothing.

It seemed to take her ages to screw up enough courage to open her eyes. When she did he was gone.

3.00a.m.–3.15a.m.

Now. Do it now. Run. Run now.

No, can't. Hurts to move.

Must. Must *move*.

Can't run.

Crawl then. Crawl. No. Stand. Stand and walk. Walk to the car. Get in. Get in and drive. Drive away, drive now. Drive *now*.

149

She drove fast. Foot on the accelerator. Pedal to the metal. Radio on. Late-night classics on 94.6. ZZ Top. 'Sharp Dressed Man'. She drove fast, to outstrip the memories, leave them behind in the rain and the mud.

No chance.

She flicked at the clutch, shifted up a gear. The speedo needle shot upwards as

he stood over her and adjusted his clothes. Enjoyed *standing over her as*

she steered the car out of Belle Vale Estate and onto the nearby spine road, shifted from second directly into fourth, tromped on the accelerator. The Volvo jerked beneath her, jerked and thrashed, every crack and soft spot in the tarmac jolting her from arse to brain. Jolting her as he had jolted her. In the night. Under the swing. Where the kids played.

And the hissing of the rain against the windscreen was his breath. The creak of the steering wheel was the squeak of his mask against her neck. The metallic ticking of the wipers was the clinking of chains as the swing seat rocked back and forth in the darkness; slowly winding down into silence, a silence filled with pain and humiliation and terror.

She drove onto the ring road, nailed seventy and kept on going. She looked at the dashboard clock. 3.30a.m. Two and a half hours to sunrise. Outside the car the night was dark, streaked with rain. Umber clouds stretched across the sky. The yellow lights from the town centre reflecting off the clouds made it seem like the city itself was on fire. She felt as if she were on fire herself; it was inside her head, spontaneous combustion.

She leaned across the passenger seat and wound down the nearside window. Air blasted through the car, sucking the breath from her lips. She straightened up in time to avoid piling the car through the central division and onto the lane for oncoming traffic.

She felt like grinning, couldn't. It was as if she'd forgotten how the muscles in her face could move to change its shape. As if her face had become like *his*. Like a mask.

The night blasting in at her, with the rain, brought her closer to the edge. Maybe it was time to step off.

She stopped the wipers.

Instantly the windscreen became an opaque sheet of marbled glass shot through with streaks of reflected light from the headlights. Even this reflected light was too bright. It reminded her of the fire in her head.

She switched off the headlights.

The night closed in around her, cool, soothing, a thief to steal her pain. She remembered how to smile then; caught a brief glimpse of her reflection in the driving mirror, thought it looked less like a smile than the rictus grin on the face of some week-old corpse. She was captivated by the sight of herself; the bald peeling of the lips away from the teeth, the rage of emotion furrowing the seamed skin around her mouth and eyes. A mask of mud and runny mascara, blood-black in the yellow street lights. A ghoul out of some horror flick, Argento's *Suspira*, Carpenter's *Prince of Darkness*. A thing, a special effect, something created, not a real person at all; not a woman, a creation. *His* creation.

When the air horn of a long-haul truck blasted into the Volvo she turned. A huge square shape cruised alongside her. Lights in the cab. A pennant ripped by the wind and rain.

A figure leaned across the inside of the truck's cab. The figure gestured, the open mouth working furiously. Though the words never made it past the cab's passenger door, the driver's meaning was abundantly clear.

She gave a faint smile and looked beyond her reflection into the blank windscreen; except it wasn't blank, was it? Oh no. It was simply a screen for the pictures in her mind, a mirror to the flames in her head.

The truck dropped back. Way back. Sensible fellow. She wondered how far she could drive without lights or wipers. Then the engine coughed and died; when she looked at the petrol gauge it read *empty*. That was one problem solved, then.

151

She pulled the car over to the hard shoulder. Waited for the truck to pass. Found the jerrycan that she kept in the boot. Emptied it into the tank. Got back in. Shut the door. Wound up the windows. Turned on the headlights.

Realised there was skin under the nails of her right hand.

Skin and hair.

His skin, his hair.

On the back seat of the Volvo was a burgundy plastic bag with the words *Waterstones Booksellers* printed on it in gold ink. The bag was exactly the right size for two paperbacks. It fit her hand like a glove. She sealed the bag at her wrist with her hairband.

She started the engine, drove home.

She drove *fast*.

4.00a.m.–4.30a.m.

At the flat she parked the Volvo diagonally across two spaces, left the vehicle without locking it, headed across the car park. At the stairs she hesitated. There were shadows there. Shadows beneath the lintel over the staircase. Broken glass lay on the ground. The shards glinted minutely, reflecting the first streaks of dawn clawing upwards across the nearby canal, creeping through the wired glass of the communal door.

Glass. A broken bulb. Shadows.

What if *he* was there?

What if he was waiting for her?

She chewed her lip. Sniffed. Blew out her cheeks. Her face ached where he'd punched her.

Glass crunched as she put one foot on the stair. The sound was shockingly loud in the silence, startling her. She jumped. Then shook her head, began to climb.

She hesitated again at the first turn in the staircase. The shadows were deeper here. No tell-tale light to throw a shadow, something to warn her of someone lurking just out of sight around a turn of the staircase.

'Oh fuck this.' Inside her head her voice was a defiant

yell; in reality the words were so quiet there weren't even any echoes from the brick walls that penned her in.

And then, as if the whisper of her own voice was the crack of a starting pistol, she ran.

She ran up the stairs, his breath rattling in her ears, along the landing, key in the lock, push, turn, wrench the key loose, open the door, through the door, slam the door, slide the deadbolt, the chain rattling

like a swing seat and

her breath rasping in her throat

like the rustle of his clothes of his trousers going down and

her heart

pushing

hammering inside her ribs until she thought she might cry out with the pain, but something else inside made her hold it in, made her hold the pain in, channel it, use it, force it to work for her. Squash it into a pulsing knot somewhere deep inside her and keep it there until she could

oh but what if you can't, what if you can't

deal with it.

'I can deal with it. I can deal with it. I can. I can deal with it.'

Her legs trembling, she took a step into the hallway. She turned on the light. She turned on all the lights. Only when she'd toured the whole flat, legs trembling like they used to when she was learning the drums, the muscles screaming protest at the abuse, when she'd checked every room for nerve-racking shadows and lurking figures, drawn every curtain tightly shut against the night, only then did she open the door to the kitchen, turn on the light, reach for the kettle.

Then she remembered the Waterstone's bag tied around her hand.

Her hand wavered in mid air, extended towards the kettle as if her arm had a will of its own, a whole different game plan from the rest of her body. She looked at the hand, clenched her fist, made the plastic rustle and crinkle, lifted the hand up and down. Still part of her then. Still part of her body, still her own hand. She told her arm to lower itself to her side. The arm obeyed.

She suddenly laughed, a tiny runnel of nervous energy fizzing out into the kitchen. 'I'm talking to my arm.' Another laugh, louder this time, bordering on hysteria. 'It's taken me half an hour to walk the hundred yards from my car to my flat and now I'm *talking* to my *arm*.'

Hey Jane, girl, the screechy voice inside her head whined. *What if you can't deal with it, with his thing that's happened to you? What if you* aren't *dealing with it? 'Cos, you know, if you aren't then talking to your arm would be a good sign of this, wouldn't it?*

She sat at the kitchen table, laid the arm on the varnished pine. Her jacket sleeve was torn, streaked with mud, as was the arm beneath. She became aware that her arm wasn't the only part of her to be covered in filth.

'Bath,' she breathed the word softly, a mantra against the night, a spell to ward off the memories. 'I need a bath. I need a bath. Oh God. I need a bath.'

But she fell asleep instead, right there on the kitchen table, head cradled on her arms, on the plastic Waterstones bag wrapped around her right hand; fell asleep and didn't wake for several hours, not even when she twitched with some agonising memory, toppling the plastic milk bottle full of flowers which Fitz had given her that morning onto the floor with a wet *blop!* and sending a mass of icy water lapping around the smeared and torn tights still clinging to her aching feet.

10.00a.m.–10.30a.m.

She awoke suddenly, blinked, let the kitchen come gradually into focus around her. A thin blade of
    a knife he's got a knife to my throat he's got
sunlight pierced the kitchen blinds, laid a laser-thin track across the table, the chunky glass salt cellar, the Waterstones bag covering her right hand. The beam was a pale stripe

under the kitchen neons, a ghost of light glimmering on spilled water and a few floating cuticles of greenery.

Somewhere nearby something was whining. No, shrilling, no – *ringing*. Her alarm clock. She groped her way through the fully lighted flat to her bedroom. The clock was on the floor beside the bed.

10.05 a.m.

The alarm had been ringing for three hours.

She nudged the button, switched it off. Rubbed her ears in the silence.

Bath.

She walked to the bathroom. The plastic bag around her right hand rustled as she reached for the doorknob. Her hand was itching. The inside of the bag was covered with moisture. Condensation. And mud. Her hand was cold and wet, a slippery reminder of her ordeal. The sensation was irritating. She wondered how long it would be before her skin softened, wrinkled with moisture. Wondered how long it would be before the cold, wet, itching sensation drove her completely mad.

She turned on the taps. Water gurgled into the bath. After a moment she put the plug in. The water level began to rise.

A thought struck her. Clock. Had the alarm clock been ringing? What time was it?

She walked into the living room, eyed the clock over the mantelpiece.

10.10 a.m.

Of course. She'd just switched off the alarm in the bedroom. How could she have forgotten?

God she was hungry.

She was late for work too.

She hovered indecisively in the front room for a few minutes, not thinking, just looking at things. The photo of her dad on the telly. The stereo. Her collection of film soundtracks. The drum kit. The sofa. The low glass-topped lounge table. The fruit bowl. The beige and russet fluffy carpet.

155

She sniggered. Fitz had walked dogshit into that carpet once. She'd made him clean it up. That had been last year. Halfway between their first meeting and their first time in bed.

Fitz.

She picked up the phone. Dialled. No answer. Put the handset down. Dialled again. No answer. Put the handset down. Dialled a different number.

A gravelly voice, made tinny by distance, said, 'Wise.'

Jesus. Help me. He hurt me. He hurt me. I'm confused. I've been assaulted. Tell me what to do. Tell me what to do because I think I'm going mad.

She licked her lips. Said nothing.

'DCI Wise speaking.' Faint irritation. 'Who is this please?'

Still she said nothing. Inside her head the screechy voice was whining again. *You tell him all about it. Tell your sympathetic boss. Anyone who can understand the feminists and the hairy-arsed lesbians is sure to empathise with a member of his staff who's been raped.*

The irritation in Wise's voice notched upwards. 'I'm putting the phone down. If this is you, Jones, you're sacked.'

'Sir.' Was that her voice? That pathetic excuse for a whine, her voice?

'Jane?'

'Yes.'

'Jane Penhaligon? Is that you?'

'Yes.'

'Are you all right?'

'Not really, sir, no.'

'You're calling in sick?'

'Not really, sir, no.'

An irritable sigh. 'Then why are you calling? And why aren't you here?'

'I . . . I'm sorry . . . I . . .'

She sighed, put the handset down, cutting off her own apology. Acknowledged even as she remembered the running bath that the voice in her head was probably right. The chances of Wise understanding her ordeal were so small you'd need a microscope to find them.

She checked the bath, turned off the taps, wandered into the kitchen, switched the kettle on, switched it off again, wandered back into the lounge, poured herself three fifths of whisky and took it into the bathroom. Tested the water. Too hot.

She undressed in the kitchen, bundled her clothes into a bin liner. Took the battery-driven radio/cassette player from the shelf beside the spice rack, hugged the cold plastic to her chest as she went back into the bathroom.

The water was still too hot. She ran some cold and got in. The radio clunked into the handbasin. Local radio plunking out some old tat from the previous decade. Godley and Creme, *Under Your Thumb*.

Victim music, said the voice in her head. *Jane, girl, they're playing our song.*

'Bollocks to that,' she said aloud, astonished by the strength in her voice. She reached out of the bath with her left hand, switched channels on the set until she got some halfway decent music.

Then she sat back in the bath, as if not quite sure what to do next. Logic told her she shouldn't be there. If Wise knew where she was after what she'd been through he'd light a rocket under her that would put her right up there in orbit with Columbia and Atlantis.

S.O.P. How many rape victims had she counselled? What had she said to them? And what had they said back?

I'm guilty. It's my fault. What did I do to provoke him? What could I have done to stop him? Why did I let him? My boyfriend doesn't understand me. My husband hates me. My friends can't deal with it. My family won't talk to me. My relationship is breaking up.

Oh yes, she knew the form. Had read all the textbooks, attended the crime lectures, the psychological profiles. Knew all the responses.

Intellectually.

Only now did she realise the world of difference that

existed between the theory and the fact. Only now, sitting in the bath with one hand wrapped in Waterstones' own brand of plastic bag, her mind and body tortured with vivid bruises and even more real memories, did she wonder if she'd ever really listened to any of those women, if she'd ever heard a single word any of them had ever said.

Holding her bagged hand clear of the water, she grabbed a tube of Body Shop birch and seaweed bath gel and began to wash her left knee.

A moment later she began to shake. It was as if her mind had suddenly started working again when she hadn't even been aware of it shutting down. Suddenly the pain was real. The humiliation was real. The terror was *real*.

Her face scrunched up. She blinked, her eyes full of soapy steam. But the moisture on her cheeks was simple condensation. Tears refused to come. Yet.

10.30a.m.–11.00a.m.

The bleep of an hourly time signal from the radio made Penhaligon realise that she had been brushing her teeth for twenty minutes. She put down the brush aware that her gums were bleeding, and that she had a viscous flood of
him, of his
pink foam cascading from her mouth.

She spat and rinsed.

The bath water was a muddy grey by now so she pulled the plug and watched it gurgle away. She sat in the empty bath for a while. The bag around her right hand was completely opaque now, beaded inside and out with moisture. Her hand felt sweaty and cold. She ran her finger around the soggy hairband, felt a little life return to her hand as the circulation stepped up a little. By now the bath water had drained away. She put the plug back in, ran more hot water.

She lay back, tried a few meditation exercises she'd caught on some Saturday morning breakfast TV show to slow the thumping of her heart in her head. After a few minutes of this she became aware that something had changed. The music had stopped. They were into a chat show of some kind. A chat show with a familiar voice. A male voice. Fitz.

She lay back as the slow gurgle of water into the bath made an ambient backdrop for his words.

'Show me a man,' said Fitz's voice, made tinny by the radio. 'And I'll show you a potential killer, a potential rapist. God knows I'm one myself, I was telling my girlfriend just last night. I don't do anything about it, of course.'

She felt herself relax even more. That was odd; Fitz was holding forth on his favourite subject. Himself. The words ought to drive her over the edge. Only now, perhaps because of their intimacy the previous night, she felt nothing more than a mild amusement poking through a general pall of indifference.

'But that's because I'm frightened of other men, frightened of being caught. I'm educated, I'm the product of thousands of years of so-called civilisation. And yes. I'm frightened.'

She sighed, stretched out with her toes to turn off the taps, caught her breath when the movement caused the dull ache present all through her body to sharpen in spurts through her stomach and thighs.

On the radio, Fitz blathered away, his words oddly soothing, elevator music for a brutalised mind. 'He wears a mask. That's not unusual of course. Lots of rapists wear a mask. But he tries to form a relationship with his victim. That is unusual. A masked rapist wouldn't normally do that. The mask gets in the way. It's frightening, intimidating. That suggests to me that there's something about this man's face, something he doesn't want the world to see, something he's ashamed of . . .'

Penhaligon closed her eyes. Saw the swing, a kid's pendulum in the light from the street. Chain clinking beneath the stars. Saw the mask. Heard the breathing. Felt herself turned. Positioned. Felt herself smile. Felt the shame come welling up again. Why hadn't she fought him? Kicked him?

Screamed? Punched, head-butted him in the balls, for God's sake? OK, he had a knife, could have stabbed her. But that would have been nothing compared to this sudden agony of guilt; the humiliation ran deeper than any physical pain.

Why hadn't she defended herself?

Suddenly the voice coming from the radio was her father's. She sat up, hugging herself as his voice bounced off the Japanese crane print bathroom tiles, burrowed into her head.

'... something like a deformity, a scar, something he needs to hide because it's always led to his rejection in the past, his sexual rejection.'

She began to shiver. Hugged herself even tighter. Another voice came on now. A listener, speaking to Fitz on the phone. A woman. 'My name is Marcia Reid. And when are you going to understand? When are men going to understand that rape is not sexual? That rape is about power and violence and humiliation?'

And Fitz, sounding just like Penhaligon's father, responded in predictable manner: 'I'm sorry, but that's white liberal bullshit. Rape is a *sexual* act. Throughout history men have killed other men and raped their women. Why? Because these men were particularly evil? No. Because these men wanted to people God's green Earth with little clones of themselves. They wanted to destroy other men's genes so that their own could prosper and multiply – the law of the jungle. The most natural urge in the world.'

'Jesus Christ, that's the most utter bullshit!' With no memory of the intervening moment, Penhaligon found herself out of the bath, standing shivering on the carpet. Fitz's voice was his own again, not her father's, his own and she knew what he was doing: winding them up, the listeners, out there in radio land. And the voice in her head did a number then. *Jesus Christ, Fitz, what's the matter, one on one not enough for you now? Got to take your peculiar brand of psychological torture farther afield? A captive audience? How many on the Fitzometer today then? A thousand? Ten thousand? More? And who are they? Who listens to the*

160

*radio this time of day? Mothers. Housewives. Jesus. No
wonder rape myths are slow to lay down and die!*

And as she headed for the kitchen and a towel, she knew
that wasn't even the end of it. Even through her fury she
knew it was worse even than that. She knew Fitz didn't
believe a single word he'd said. He'd done the show for the
money. And if the controversy boosted the ratings a little,
well, who was to know? Just the housewives and mothers.
Just the potential victims who might be listening in.

And the potential rapists.

She knuckled her eyes. Tried to cry. Couldn't.

Damn you, Fitz.

11.00a.m.–11.30a.m.

She shuffled to the kitchen, filled the kettle and boiled it.
Swallowed two mugs of double-strength Red Mountain and
a bowl of cornflakes. As her hunger faded she realised she'd
made a mistake. The cereal and coffee mixed with the three
fifths of whisky she'd already drunk in a way that made her
run for the bathroom.

She made it in time to avoid throwing up in the kitchen or
the hall, but only just. The worst part of all was hearing the
sound of Fitz's voice, still blathering out of the radio, a
fatalistic accompaniment to her own private misery.

By now he'd been joined by a new voice. A Jamaican voice.
A man. 'This information you got about the rapist, Doctor Fitzgerald. You got it from the victims, that's right, yeah?'

'Yeah.'

'So, do you realise what you're saying, Doctor Fitzgerald,
yeah?'

'You tell me.'

'If you hadn't spoken to the victims, you wouldn't know
about the mask, and you wouldn't know he's scarred or
deformed. That's right, yeah?'

'Yeah.'

'So if I was this rapist, you'd advise me to kill my victims
in future, yeah?'

A pause. Then, 'I'm sorry. I don't understand the question.'

'Should the rapist kill his victims in the future? Forget morality, OK? Forget that. If he lets them live there's more chance of being caught. So, should he kill his victims in future? Is that what you're advising?'

'I –'

And it had gone too far; a new voice cut in. The talkshow's host, sounding just a shade rattled. 'I'm afraid I'm going to have to stop you there, to introduce our next caller: Jane from Eccles.'

Another new voice, this one that of a young woman. 'No, it's not Jane from Eccles. It's Jane Eccles actually. From Salford. And I was wondering –'

Penhaligon lifted her head from the toilet, flushed, sniffed, shivered, slapped the *off* control on the radio cassette.

In the silence that followed the impatient ringing of her front-door intercom was insistently loud. Toothbrush in hand she went in search of her bathrobe.

11.30a.m.–12.30p.m.

At the front door she hesitated, bundled into a bathrobe two sizes too big for her and clutching her toothbrush in her left hand, as sharp memories rose to cut through her numbness. She poked the intercom switch with the handle of the toothbrush.

'Who's there?'

'Wise. Can I come in?'

A moment's thought. What would she be letting herself in for if she let her boss in now? She knew what the screechy voice in her head would say, had already said. Her lips thinned determinedly. When she spoke her voice didn't sound real, more like that of someone learning English; short, no complex construction. As if simplicity was the key to communication. Except in her case it was becoming clear that simplicity was the key to merely getting the words out in the first place.

'Yes. Come in. I'll buzz the door.'

When she finally opened the door to Wise, a couple of minutes later, it was obvious he'd made an effort with his appearance. He was still straightening his tie when she peeped through the tiny lens set into the door, prior to opening it.

He came in looking around. A copper's instinct to give any new place the once over. Well. She knew all about that. Never off duty. Eventually his gaze completed the grand tour of the hallway and settled on her face, slipped a moment to take in the dressing gown and the toothbrush, her bagged right hand, then returned to her face.

'I don't do this for all my staff, you know,' he said gruffly. There might have been a grin on his face, but if there was his beard hid it.

She shrugged. 'I can just see you going to Jimmy Beck's house every time he phones in with a hangover.'

Wise did grin then. 'Not so ill you haven't lost your sense of humour then.'

'I told you on the phone. I'm not ill.'

She watched his grin fade at the harshness of her voice.

'Yeah,' he said. 'You did, that.' A sigh. 'That was a bloody peculiar phone call, Jane. I was worried.'

'It's OK. There's nothing to worry about now. That's what I keep telling myself anyway.'

Wise sighed. 'You're making about as much sense as a punch-drunk retard. Now. You going to invite me in or will I need to get a warrant to get past the hall?'

She shrugged. 'Shut the door will you?' She led the way into the living room without waiting to see if Wise was following or not.

In the living room she idly scraped her toothbrush around one of the Zildjians on the kit. It made a metallic ringing noise.

She turned to find Wise looking at her. The brusque directness of his gaze, something she normally found vaguely irritating, now seemed almost comforting in its familiarity.

'So what's it all about then, Jane?' Wise asked without

hesitation. And she could see in his face the list of possibilities he expected her to draw an answer from. Illness. Death in the family. Pregnancy. Time of the month. All that predictable bullshit. And his fatherly interest was just as predictable, and ultimately just as annoying.

'I've been raped.'

She looked down at the kit, idly tapped the ride cymbal with her fingernail, looked up again, held his gaze for what seemed like a damned long time. If she was honest, Wise was looking a little like a punch-drunk retard himself right about now. She could see the thoughts chasing themselves across his face, could read him like a book. *What do I do about this? How do I deal with it? What do I say? Do I laugh it off? Sympathy disguised as humour? How will she respond to that?*

She said nothing, let him get on with it. After a moment he said, predictably, 'I need a drink.'

That's right: when in doubt, think of yourself.

She nodded, poured him a whisky.

She went to the bathroom, swapped her toothbrush for a hand towel and began to dry her hair. When she re-entered the living room Wise hadn't moved, except to swallow the whisky.

'It was the man we're looking for. Knife. A mask. The same kind of mask.'

Wise sat down on the sofa. 'What are you going to do?'

'I don't know.' She gestured with her bagged hand. 'I've got evidence under my nails.'

Wise was looking at her again, and that direct gaze was resuming its former annoying status. 'You've had a bath?'

No you bloody fool I've come straight from the midnight swimming gala for assault victims.

'Yes.' She waited for the explosion.

'I know you protected your hand but ...' irritation, disbelief.

Oh good. We're on familiar ground now. Familiar, even comfortable ground. Anything to avoid talking about it.

'I can't believe you had a *bath*, Jane.'

164

She ran her hand through her hair. Sighed. Felt like screaming at him, not words, just an incoherent animal scream of pain and fear, just to get through to him, just to make him understand. Just to make him *understand*. 'I had to have a bath. I'm sorry. I know there's no logic to it but I had to have a bath.'

Wise nodded.

Probably thinks he understands.

'I'm sorry.'

She nodded, went back to drying her hair.

'What were you wearing?'

Oh for God's sake, guv, I put it through the washing machine. You can take it to forensic in the clean laundry basket!

'Clothes, you know. It's all in a bin liner in the kitchen.'

Wise swallowed nervously. 'Stains?'

She nodded.

'He's never left anything before. It could be useful.'

She grinned. 'Stroke of luck, eh, sir?'

Wise sighed. 'That's not what I mean, Jane, and you know it.'

'Isn't it?' *Go on, strike out at him. He's a bloody man isn't he? He deserves it.* 'We wanted him to rape again. *I* wanted him to rape again, but to slip up, to leave us something. Well. Now we've got exactly what we wanted.' She bit her lip, avoided Wise's gaze. He would see through her, she knew that. If she looked at him he would see right through her anger to the fear beneath.

He did it anyway. 'It's no good to us unless you report it.'

She laughed, more of a snort really, a nervous little nothing-sound that was becoming frightening in its familiarity.

'Will you report it?' Wise was digging now. Back on safe ground. Police territory. Procedure. And better yet, dealing with another copper. *She knows the ropes. I won't have to beat around the bush with her. She'll respect me for that. And I won't have to worry about how badly I'm dealing with it.*

'I've counselled fourteen victims. So . . . I've got to report it, haven't I? Otherwise I've given fourteen women a heap of bullshit. And I don't think I could live with that.'

Wise nodded and she saw that he understood that much at least. He said, 'You know what we've got to do now, don't you?'

She nodded. *The rape suite. Forensics rummaging through her clothes, her body. The swabs. Oh God. How many times had she seen it before? Yet never from the victim's point of view. Oh yes. She knew what was to come.*

Wise saw from her expression that she knew as well. 'Jimmy's outside in my car. Get dressed. I'll get your gear from the kitchen.'

'No. I'll get it.'

She was adamant about that at least.

12.30p.m.–12.45p.m.

In the car park Beck wound down the driver's window of the pool car and looked at her from the driver's seat. His eyes were shadowed by the roof of the car. Was that sympathy in his gaze? Understanding? Was somebody like Jimmy Beck capable of either feeling? Any empathy at all? His head moved minutely as he took her in, crumpled face and clothes, bagged hand, the lot. He said nothing. She sighed, grateful for small mercies; there was far worse to come, that was a truth there was no denying. For now she had enough to worry about.

She licked her lips, glanced at Wise, then back to Beck. 'Belle Vale,' she said, surprised at how normal her voice sounded. 'It happened at Belle Vale. In . . . in the kids' playground. By the swing.'

Wise inclined his head in her direction, not a nod, a gesture of respect. For what it was worth. Then he, too, turned to Beck. 'Sort it, Jimmy. Get forensics over there. Nease and Copely. The works.'

Beck cast his gaze sideways to Wise. Then back to Penhaligon. Hooded eyes. A pall of smoke from his habitual rollup dappled the darkness within the car.

Wise continued, 'We'll take your motor, Jane, all right? I'll drive.'

She nodded.

'All right then. Jimmy, off you go.'

Beck nodded. She felt his gaze rake over her one last time, then he wound up the window and the car pulled away.

She led Wise to the Volvo. 'We'll have to stop at a garage. I haven't any petrol.'

Wise opened the driver's door. 'Leave it unlocked like this where I live and you'd be lucky to have the car.'

1.00p.m.–2.30p.m.

She looked around the Family and Child Protection Unit. Nothing had changed, yet it all looked so different. The walls were the same unobtrusive white-with-a-hint-of-apricot, the furniture as inviting and comfortable as she remembered it from her last visit here, with Catherine Carter. But something was different. What was it? The analytical part of her, the copper, took over for a moment, displaced the woman, the *victim*.

And then the truth dawned, smacked home, a
fist smashing into her face, a
revelation as terrifying as it was obvious.

The fact was, nothing here had changed except her. *She* was what was different. She had changed. Had *been* changed. It was her. The surroundings only mirrored the change that had been wreaked in *her*.

She sniffed. Felt her eyes sting. Nothing more though. No tears. Not yet. She was beginning to wonder if they would ever come. If she would ever again be capable of feeling the depth of emotion necessary to cry.

Wise remained in the waiting room. She allowed herself to be led away by a friendly-looking policewoman.

She followed the WPC to the examination room. The WPC took the plastic bin liner containing her torn, stained clothing, placed it on a nearby table. The WPC then asked her if she felt able to take off her clothes. She hesitated.

167

The WPC smiled. *It's OK. I know you're scared. I understand your fear.*

And Penhaligon suddenly found she wanted to believe that imaginary dialogue. Wanted to believe it very much. She took a deep breath, stepped behind the screen provided and undressed. A few moments later, wrapped in a hospital gown, she stepped out from behind the screen.

The WPC had been joined by a female doctor, grey-haired, apparently in her mid-forties. 'I'm Doctor Cantrell. DS Penhaligon, yes?'

Penhaligon nodded.

Cantrell looked at Penhaligon's bagged right hand. 'I think we'll start there. I bet it's itching like mad.' Cantrell indicated Penhaligon should sit on the examination table. 'How long have you had that on there, anyway?'

'Ten, eleven hours.'

Cantrell nodded, glanced at the WPC. 'We'll get started here. If you could make sure DS Penhaligon's clothes are labelled correctly and passed to forensics.'

The WPC nodded, glanced at Penhaligon as she lifted the bin liner containing her clothes. Something about the nurse's movement triggered a momentary fit of anxiety in Penhaligon. 'I want them back. Today.'

Cantrell frowned. 'That's impossible. As a police officer you should know that.'

Penhaligon's lips thinned. 'I'm not having a bunch of coppers going through my knickers. I want them back today or I walk out right now.'

A standoff. Then the WPC nodded. Real understanding there. Hands-on sympathy. Not like Cantrell. 'I'll see what I can do.'

By now Cantrell had unshipped a pair of scissors and snipped through her hairband at her wrist.

That was fifty pence from the Body Shop, some part of her cried. *I'll want a bloody refund.*

Cantrell eased the bag off her hand and the sudden rush of air across her skin made her wince.

'That hurt?'

168

'No. Itches like buggery though.'

'Understandable.' Cantrell deposited the dripping bag in a gleaming specimen dish. 'At least you had the sense to ease the pressure regularly. Tie it too tightly and your hand would've fallen off by now.'

Penhaligon sighed. The pale, wet, wrinkled skin of her hand looked like some kind of insect emerging glistening from its cocoon. She wanted to pull it and stretch it and wave it about just to feel the air moving over it, wanted to rub warmth and life back into it, strip away the mud and muck like a sticky little-girl scab, plunge it into a basin of hot soapy water and scrub for about a week.

Instead she managed to keep her hand quite still as Cantrell put down the scissors, guided Penhaligon's hand until it rested over a steel dish, then selected a flat-bladed scraping tool from a nearby instrument tray and began to probe beneath her fingernails.

She began with the little finger and worked inwards to the thumb. Each sample was removed with a fresh scraper, each sample of mud and skin was sealed into its own plastic tube. Each was labelled. Her name. The date. The samples were taken away by the WPC. To join her clothes, presumably.

Cantrell took a swab from each finger, the back and the palm of her hand. The movement of the cotton balls across the skin made her arm jerk. It was only with a considerable effort she managed not to scratch right there and then.

Cantrell noticed the aborted movement, asked her if she wanted to wash.

'I'd kill for a bar of Imperial Leather.'

Cantrell smiled. 'Under the circumstances alcohol and antiseptic solution is the best I can offer, I'm afraid.'

'Sure.'

Hand washed, Penhaligon was told to get back onto the examination table.

'I want you to lie down. I know you've had a bath but I'm going to take swabs anyway. Now. I know this may be distressing, so take your time. I'll be as gentle as I can. If you want to stop, or feel uncomfortable for any reason, just say so.' She smiled a little. 'Believe it or not, you're in charge of this bit. OK?'

Penhaligon nodded agreement.

'All right then, DS Penhaligon. If you could lie back, please, and place your feet in these stirrups.'

Penhaligon felt her stomach muscles stiffen as she lay back on the table. At Cantrell's touch she bit her lip hard enough to draw blood. Said nothing.

The swabs were taken, an eternity of cold plastic and itchy cotton balls rubbing against her sore skin. The samples were bottled and labelled.

'Can I get up now?'

'I'd like to check you out for internal injuries. Have you had any muscular pain? Were you hit anywhere else apart from the face? Are all these bruises attributable to the assault?'

Yes.

Yes.

Yes.

'OK, that's fine, thank you. You can put your legs down now. I'm going to open your gown. I need to check the stomach area.'

Yeah, sure, fine, just bloody well get on with it will you, and quit giving me a running commentary, I feel like I'm at the races.

She felt hands running over her skin

turning her, positioning her

palpating her stomach, gently probing for subcutaneous damage. The cold touch of

his gloves

a stethoscope on her bare midriff made her gasp. She tensed and that sent waves of dull pain flooding through her stomach and legs. Cantrell's hands moved over her swiftly and impersonally, themselves every bit as delicate and sensitive as the instruments she used.

'Is there any pain there? Yes? And there? Good. Thank you, DS Penhaligon. You can close the gown now.'

A moment, then a metallic clink, a tiny rubber *blop* and

the patter of falling liquid.

'I'm going to give you an injection. It's just for –'

'I know.'

The sting of the needle. Followed by the sting of more words.

'If I could just ask when was your last –'

'Two weeks ago.'

'Do you use any –'

'I'm on the pill. I don't use perfume. I have cornflakes and coffee for breakfast and my bloody shoe size is six and a half!' She sighed. 'Shit. I'm sorry.'

But you're not sorry at all, are you? And with every reason, too. Who is this bloody woman who's prodding and poking at you? Has she undergone what you have? Has she been assaulted? Been hurt like you have? Been raped? What right has she to –

'Um. Can I have something? Germolene or something? I bit my lip.'

SEVEN

11.45a.m.–1.00p.m.

Fitz left the radio station with another fistful of tenners and a mental buzz on like he hadn't had for weeks. The buzz was composed of equal measures of excitement and frustration. The caller. The Jamaican lad. What a mind. *Forget about morality.* That's what he'd said. *Forget about morality. Should the rapist kill his victims in future?*

And on prime-time radio. Live. Jesus.

It was the kind of caller he had wet dreams about. It was almost enough to give him a hard-on. He imagined all those armchair or kitchen-dweller listeners sitting up ramrod straight, newspapers flopping to the floor, or jerking to attention beside the ironing or the washing up as if zapped by a solid 240 volts. Fitz knew what Wise would have said if he'd told the DCI he was going to talk about the case on air, knew what he was sure to say when he found out. But screw that. The buzz was worth a bollocking. It was worth a bollocking ten times over.

Jesus.

He stopped at Valubuys on the way home, bought two new bottles of Bell's, his mind revolving at breakneck speed around the call. The cashier had to remind him to pick up his change.

His next stop was Eddy's, the high-street bookie, where he chucked a wad on Chaos Theory in the first run at Newmarket.

Chaos Theory came in at five to one. The buzz coursed through his veins, rattled his body, zapped his head. He bet

172

again. Won again. Slapped two hundred and fifty quid down on an accumulator. The first two horses crossed the line in fine form; the chemical dance in his head made him reel. That giddy feeling, better than drink, better than sex, better than any damn thing at all, made him forget everything. The caller. The rapes. Judith. Panhandle. Everything. The high strengthened as the horses took to their boxes for the last race of the day. Purified, a blast of flame scouring the inside of his head free of all thought, leaving just feeling, just need, just gratification. There was no way he could lose. No way on earth.

The last horse fell at the second fence, tumbled its rider onto the ground and Fitz back to reality. He stumbled out of the bookie's, the welter of emotion fading, the buzz greying out into a dusty numbness.

He opened the first bottle of Bell's on the bus, gulped the equivalent of three fingers before he reached home.

The first thing that hit Fitz when he opened the front door was the smell of Mark's socks. He shook his head, closed the door, stashed the Bell's in the kitchen, followed the sound of a buzzsaw rhythm guitar to the lounge.

Mark was stretched out on the couch, feet propped up in front of the telly, rollup in one hand, ashtray perched precariously on his stomach. Fitz thought he could detect a familiar odour – something beyond the bouquet of tobacco smoke and old socks. Something that brought back memories from his own youth. Was that a little weed in the rollup? A little Black? Fitz shook his head. And what was he supposed to do about it if it was? Judith would know. Judith always knew how to deal with Mark. But then she didn't think of it as *dealing with* her son. Whatever, she was gone now. Gone, and he had passed the boundary layer, the divide between the extinction of his marriage and the rise of a new relationship. Fitz shook his head. That line of thought became too disturbing, too near the truth, for comfort. So Edward Fitzgerald, doctor of psychology and sometime detective, opted for a little emotional displacement instead: Mark was here. He was spliffed out of his head. Fine. He'd be angry then. Anything was better than lonely.

The lounge was a mess. Well, that was no surprise. He looked around, drank it in, let it fuel his anger. The remnants of a kebab slopped over a plate; an empty can of Coke next to it. Knife, fork, ketchup and butter were spread across the coffee table in wild disarray. Tossed casually on the carpet next to Fitz's stereo was a stack of record sleeves and records. Playing was State of Grace, 'Love, Pain and Passion'. The lyrics clashed annoyingly with the soundtrack playing on the telly. Mark's left trainer snuggled against the foot of the curtains bordering the French windows. The other was nowhere to be seen. Fitz wondered idly if it had got bored with the company – or the music – and left of its own accord.

Mark looked up lazily as Fitz entered, clocked his look of disapproval. 'Like father like son, eh, Dad?' he mumbled with a vacant smile.

Fitz felt his scowl deepen. 'I'll get a mouth-organ, we'll do a duet.'

'What?'

Fitz sighed. He nodded at the rollup in Mark's hand. 'That stuff scrambling your brains again is it? Your feet *hum.*'

'Oh. Right.' Mark thought about it. 'That's funny, Dad.'

'Not from where I'm standing it isn't, believe me.' Fitz felt anger rise inside him. Mark had been provoking this reaction in him for more than a year now. Fitz picked the record sleeve up, placed it beside the remnants of Mark's meal. Stood between Mark and the telly. Mark blinked but said nothing. More laid out than laid back, Fitz thought. 'Fleming beat you to penicillin.' He nodded pointedly at the dead kebab. 'Though you're a very convincing second.'

Now that his view was blocked, Mark closed his eyes. Other than that he made no response. Faced with his son's apparent indifference, Fitz felt his anger build, a feeling he didn't struggle too hard to control. 'How long have you been up?'

'Dunno. Hour and a half. Couple of hours, maybe.'

'Couple of hours? Why haven't you tidied up?'

'I'll get round to it.'

'You got round to going out for a kebab, didn't you?' Fitz stared at his son in disgust. 'You could be a member of the lost generation, Mark. The Crisis of Western Capitalism's deprived you of work, ambition, motivation, self-esteem.'

Mark kept his eyes shut. The music cranked up a notch louder. Now it sounded like an aeroplane taking off.

Fitz looked at his son, saw himself butting his head against the brick wall of youth, of indifference, continued anyway. What else was there to do? 'That could be the case, yes, but personally I just think you're a bone-idle little git!'

Mark opened one eye lazily. 'Lost on the horses again, did we?'

Fitz reached boiling point. He was on the verge of replying when the front doorbell rang.

Somehow he managed to control himself before he got to the door. When he opened it he saw a short, rather pretty black woman dressed in jeans and an overcoat.

'Doctor Edward Fitzgerald?' Her voice was vaguely familiar.

'Yes.'

'Jane Eccles.' She essayed a tentative smile. 'We spoke on the radio this afternoon. I . . . I have to . . . Look, do you mind if I come in?'

1.00p.m.–2.00p.m.

Fitz nodded, studied the woman whose call the producer had used to interrupt his conversation with the Jamaican, the lad who'd wanted to know if the rapist of whom Fitz had spoken should kill his victims in future.

'Of course. I wasn't expecting you. Come in.' Fitz opened the door right up and invited the woman in.

'Sorry to just dump myself on your doorstep like this, but . . . Well. What you said on the radio rang a few bells, and you were in the phone book and, well . . . I wanted to come and talk to you about it.'

Fitz nodded as he closed the door, led the way to the

175

lounge, stopped when he remembered Mark's feet and the aeroplane music and the penicillin competition. 'My son,' he said by way of explaining his sudden halt. 'Going through his James Dean phase.' He gestured to Jane to follow him to the kitchen. 'Drink?'

Jane glanced at the bottle of Bell's. 'It's a little early in the day for me.'

Fitz shrugged. 'Tea? Coffee?'

'Tea would be nice.'

Ten minutes later they were both seated at the kitchen table. Fitz was on his second glass of Bell's and Jane was sipping nervously at her tea.

Fitz studied her, decided on the direct approach. Thump the wall hard, see if it falls. 'When we spoke this morning on the phone you said you'd been raped.'

Jane sipped her tea, shuffled uncomfortably on the straight-backed kitchen chair.

'I understand. On the phone it's impersonal. No face to the voice. You stay anonymous. One to one it's different. No chance of anonymity now. He knows me. Knows my name, what I look like. And now that I've seen him, how can I be sure he can help?'

Jane took another sip of tea. Fitz watched her glance around the kitchen rather than reply. Eventually her gaze fastened on some of Katie's pictures which were still Blu-tacked to the wall above the fridge. Great colourful clots of crayon over watercolours. Expressionistic.

'Your son's?'

'My daughter.' Eleven going on twenty, Katie was everything that Mark wasn't. Creative. Imaginative. Cute. 'I can't bring myself to take them down.' *Because all the time they're there, something of the family still remains.*

Jane's expression told him she'd heard the silent addition to his spoken words. She put down her tea cup. 'He wore a mask. Used a knife to threaten me. Just the way you described it on the radio.'

Fitz nodded, absorbing her words, cataloguing them, filing them for later consideration. 'Anything else?'

176

And suddenly her expression was hard, her voice sharp. 'You think I'm lying?'

Fitz made no response. Aggression. What was that hiding?

'You think I'm lying. Some kind of crank. You want me to come up with something I didn't hear over the radio. Something that fits in with what you already know.'

Fitz shrugged. 'Yeah.'

She seemed to relax then, now that the truth was out. The truth as she perceived it. Fitz knew what he was doing. Let people hear what they wanted. That was the way to get a result. Except in this case what Jane wanted to hear also happened to be the truth.

'He asked me my name. I said Bernadette. God knows where I got that from but I said Bernadette. He wanted to know who was the first person I screwed. What it was like. He never stopped talking. And he sang to me. He sang *When You're in Love with a Beautiful Woman.*'

As Fitz watched Jane lifted the tea cup to her lips, hesitated, then let it clunk back onto the table again. He sipped from his own glass. How far would she go?

'All the time he talked and sang, he combed my hair. Then he dragged me into a stream and washed me.' She lifted her eyes to Fitz, held his gaze with a strength that was almost frightening. 'That fit?'

'Yes.' Fitz nodded. 'When was this?'

'Two years ago this December. December the seventeenth.'

'You didn't report it?' A standard question. He knew the answer already. Though the figure was growing, still, only a tiny percentage of all rapes were ever reported to the police.

'No.' Jane momentarily glanced back at Katie's pictures. 'Say it.'

'Say what?'

And the litany came, just as expected. 'If I'd reported it he might have been caught. I'd have spared those other women all that pain.'

'That's not what I was thinking.'

Jane nodded and smiled, the quick, glassy smile of the

disbeliever. 'For two years I haven't read a paper. I don't read the paper, I don't find out he's done it again. In exactly the same way, I don't feel all this guilt. Then you come on the radio and you . . .' She licked her lips, fell silent.

Fitz didn't need words to fill in the gaps.

You come on the radio and you open me up, spill out all my secrets. I had it under control, the past. I had it beat, and then you came along with your supercilious attitude and punchy rhetoric and laid me open like a bloody surgeon. You're as guilty of rape as he is and you didn't even have to be anywhere near me to do it!

Fitz blinked. Jane was talking again.

'They'd have done nothing anyway. That's what I keep telling myself. I'm black. He's black. I report a rape and the coppers think I'm a prostitute who didn't get paid.'

Fitz put down his glass. 'You have *absolutely nothing* to feel guilty about.'

'Don't I?'

'No.' Fitz hesitated. Something was troubling him. Hovering just out of reach. Something . . . Then he had it. ' "He's black." ' A silent widening of her eyes. 'You said he was black?'

'Yes.'

Fitz frowned. 'But you also said he wore a mask.'

Again that glassy, humourless smile. 'So how could I tell he was black, right?' She bit her lip. 'I could tell from the way he spoke.'

Fitz frowned. Connections were being drawn here. A voice. The way he *spoke*. A *voice*.

'A Jamaican accent?'

'What makes you say that?'

He shook his head. 'Nothing. Just an idea.'

But she was sharp. She'd got it already. 'You think it was that bloke on the radio, don't you? The bloke on before me. Christ.'

A moment's silence, broken by abrasive music from the lounge, as Mark cranked the volume up again.

Fitz smiled disarmingly.

Jane said, 'You think what I'm saying is rubbish?'

'Not for a trained voice analyst, no.' *But I doubt you're that.* Fitz saw the expression on her face and knew without question she'd divined his unvoiced thought. And he knew that whether she was telling the truth or not, it was the only answer he would get from her.

2.00p.m.–2.30p.m.

As Fitz expected, Jane Eccles refused his suggestion that she repeat their conversation to the police. But a little pushing resulted in her making a provisional appointment for a half-hour counselling session the following week.

His mind buzzing once again, Fitz called a cab to take him to Anson Road. He had blagged a copy of the radio broadcast from the station engineer once the producer had left, meaning to listen to it at his leisure; now that tape was burning a hole in his pocket. He wanted to get a voice expert to go over it, analyse the Jamaican caller's voice, determine whether there was any information to be gleaned. Any information he could use to pole-axe Wise's inevitable tantrum about his taking the case onto the radio in the first place.

Mark sloped out of the living room then, record in hand, grabbed his coat, headed for the front door.

'What about the tidying up?'

'I gotta take this record back to Dave by six.'

'There's four hours between now and six!' Fitz yelled at his son's retreating back, adding silently, *though by the look of you it'll take you that long to find the garden gate.*

Mark vanished without further comment.

When the cab turned up, Fitz remembered he'd blown the radio money on the accumulator at Eddy's. There followed an argument with the cab driver about whether he should pay a cancellation fee, which the cab driver ended by pulling away in the middle of one of Fitz's juicier digs. Denied both a ride and the last word, Fitz dug into his pocket to see if he had enough change for a day rider bus ticket. He did. Just.

Fitz walked to the high street and got on a bus. It wasn't until he got off that he realised his mind had been going places without him again. He was at the end of the street where Penhaligon lived.

He cruised along the street, stumped up to the communal door of her flats, pushed the intercom button for her flat. There was no reply. He pushed again. Still no reply. Oh well. It was just a thought, she was probably at work anyway. There'd be time enough to apologise for last night later. He'd see her at the station.

He turned to leave, then, on a sudden impulse, walked around the flats to the garages at the back. Beyond the garages was a plot of communal ground. In the middle of the ground, in direct contravention of the *No Bonfires* notice posted on the nearest wall, Jane Penhaligon was throwing clothes one by one into a dustbin full of burning newspaper.

Fitz scratched his head. Odd. He walked slowly towards Penhaligon, hung back for a moment to watch her. She was burning her clothes. Burning her *clothes*? And her body language was all wrong. Something was up.

A pair of tights vanished into the dustbin and bright orange flames flickered briefly over the rim, sending a fresh pall of greasy smoke drifting towards a nearby row of washing lines.

Penhaligon watched the flames. As she watched she rested her weight on first one foot, then the other. That was really strange. She looked almost nervous. Penhaligon was the only person Fitz had ever met who had the capability to stand absolutely still if the need arose. Now she was fidgeting like a schoolgirl caught smoking in the playground loos.

A skirt vanished into the fire. A jumper. Now something else struck Fitz as strange. The clothes Penhaligon was burning were those she'd been wearing the night before.

Shaking his head, Fitz ambled closer. 'You gonna burn that bra?' he called by way of greeting.

Penhaligon didn't move. Just turned her head slightly, held Fitz's gaze for about a second, then looked back into the dustbin as the bra vanished into the flames.

Fitz decided a little push was in order. ' 'Cos, if you are, it's a bit sixties, wouldn't you say?'

Penhaligon said nothing. The bra was the last item to be burned. Now she just stood, still rocking slightly from side to side, staring into the flames. She wrapped her arms around herself, as if to protect herself from a cold wind. The gesture was odd considering how close to the fire she was.

Fitz frowned. Something was wrong. OK. A little humour then. 'Personally I'm in favour of women's movements. I hate it when they just lie there.'

She turned then, and when Fitz saw her livid expression he knew he'd overstepped the mark. She made as if to walk past him, back towards the flats.

He reached out to take her arm. 'Hang on, what's up?'

She wrenched her arm away, glared at him. *'Get off me, Fitz!'*

And she walked off without a backward glance.

The door to the flats was shut by the time he'd collected his wits enough to follow. He leaned on the doorbell for ten minutes but there was no response.

2.30p.m.–3.30p.m.

Head spinning, Fitz ambled back down the road to the high street and got on a bus heading for town.

When he arrived at Anson Road the duty room was unusually quiet. Even Jones had his head buried in some report. And though Fitz was no sluggard when it came to picking up on moods, the reason for this collective depression managed to elude him in a way he found utterly compelling. When you got right down to it the old saying was true: there was indeed nowt as strange as folk.

Put a whole bunch of individuals in a room together, hit them with a few common factors and watch the Gestalt presence emerge, each individual taking his or her position in the new social machine. Well, if this room full of people was a social machine, it had slipped a few cogs today, and no mistake. As he looked around the duty room, past Jones, Chandra, Jennings, Skelton, Beck, Harriman, to the glass divide between the room and Wise's office, Fitz found it all too easy to imagine the clashing of gears in a machine on the verge of running right off the rails.

In this confused depression Kevin Riley seemed almost as out of place as Fitz felt himself. A thin, bony individual, Riley was the voice analyst who liaised, on request, between Manchester University and the local police. Fitz found it a source of continual amusement that Riley had been gifted with over-large ears that stuck out comically from the side of his head. Well. Pipe-cleaner man or no, Riley had a reputation for producing solid vocal analyses that invariably panned out.

It took him only one listen-through to Fitz's tape to reach a conclusion.

'The Jamaican accent's false. This is a local man. Young. Um . . . probably working-class. I could go further if you like. I'd need the tape though. And it would take a day or so.'

Fitz shook his head. Riley had already given him the information he needed. 'Why Jamaican?'

Riley shrugged. 'Search me.'

Fitz chewed his lip. 'He wants us to think he's black?'

Riley nodded. 'Seems like a good bet to me.'

'Is he black?'

Riley pursed his lips and scratched one over-large ear thoughtfully. 'I'm gonna need more time on that one.'

'But you wouldn't rule it out.'

'Mmm . . . no.'

It was good enough for Fitz. He rewound the tape and hit play. *'If he lets them live there's more chance of being caught. So should he kill his victims in future?'*

Wise shook his head, blew out an impatient breath. 'It's a hoax.' He looked directly at Fitz and his expression spoke louder than any words. *You're an idiot. Taking the case on the bloody radio. Now you're following up another wild guess and we're picking up the tab.*

Fitz sighed, peered around the duty room. 'Anyone got a

fag?' He took one from Bobby Skelton, lit up, blew a cloud of smoke and returned his attention to Wise. The DCI still hadn't got it. It was time to lay it out for them. 'People phone radio stations for fifteen minutes of fame. They want their family and friends to hear them.' And here it was, the truth, so simple it was like a law of nature. 'But this man disguises his voice.'

Skelton was first to get it. 'You think it's him.'

Fitz nodded. 'I think the voice on this tape belongs to the man we're looking for.'

Skelton frowned, his dark skin creasing around his eyes as he thought it through. 'That would make sense. And it explains the mask. A white rapist would assume nothing would throw us further from the scent than hiding his face and putting on a black voice.'

Fitz frowned. 'Who said anything about him being white? He's black. I've got evidence. Another victim.'

Wise was shaking his head. 'A black guy putting on a black voice? No Fitz, you're wrong. The man we're looking for is white.'

Fitz felt the mood in the duty room lurch out of control. He looked at Wise, met his gaze across a sea of watching faces. 'Who says he's white?'

'Well Penhaligon does for a start, and she should know.'

And suddenly it made sense; the whole duty room had been telling him, in everything but words, telegraphing the blow like a punch-drunk boxer.

'He raped her last night.'

And then, as Fitz was reeling from that blow, the door to the duty room opened and Penhaligon herself walked in.

3.30p.m.–4.30p.m.

The duty room fell silent as the door swung shut behind her. A silence broken only by the quiet whirr of the tape deck and the recording of his voice.

'Should the rapist kill his victims in the future? Forget morality, OK? Forget that.'

There was a click as Riley switched off the deck. The silence was complete. Penhaligon made no response, either to the taped voice or to any of her colleagues. Ignoring them all equally she moved to her desk and sat down.

Fitz watched her move. The body language told him everything he needed to know; like the mood in the duty room itself, her behaviour was obvious when you had the right information. Back at the office. Back on the horse. Except for her getting back on the horse was likely to be more difficult than she could possibly imagine.

Penhaligon pulled out a report sheet, grabbed a pen and began to write. As she did so the phone rang on her desk. She picked it up and spoke. 'Duty room. DS Penhaligon speaking.'

As if this was a sign the room seemed to breathe again. Fitz didn't need to imagine the collective sigh, the release of tension. Yet it wasn't quite gone. There was still an edge beneath the surface, something abrasive and nervy.

Harriman was first to succumb to it. As Riley began to pack away his tape deck, the detective sauntered across to Penhaligon's desk. When he reached her he hesitated, hovering as she finished her conversation and put down the phone. Fitz watched this all without comment. He knew what was going on here. Harriman felt guilty. Guilty by implication, because he was a man and a man had raped his colleague. He was guilty and wanted absolution, but didn't know how to articulate the need. Instead he expressed concern, sympathy. Dumb kid. He didn't even know he was doing it.

'Jane. I'm . . .' He licked his lips. 'We'll get the bastard.'

Penhaligon looked up briefly from her report, flashed that same glassy non-smile Fitz had seen most recently on the face of Jane Eccles. It was as effective a snub as he'd ever seen. Harriman sloped away to his desk.

Riley said goodbye to Fitz and Wise saw him to the door. When the DCI returned he collected Penhaligon from her desk. 'My office, Jane. Right now, OK?'

She didn't reply. But she put down her pen. The

superficial normality of the duty room was filtering away again, new tension replacing the comfortable answering of phones, typing of reports.

Wise passed Fitz and went into his office. As Penhaligon drew level with Fitz, he said, 'You should have told me.'

She spared him a look then. A look that said everything and nothing, a mute expression of emotion, a confusion of shock, fear, outrage; a challenge, and Fitz wanted to reach out to her, hold her, comfort her, make it right for her.

Impossible, he knew that. No-one could make it right. For some people healing never took place.

The moment passed and she walked by. She didn't look, but merely held open the door to Wise's office. It was enough. He went in. Peripherally he was aware of others following him. Beck, Harriman, Skelton. The rest stayed outside, unwilling to intrude, perhaps unable to deal with the situation any other way.

Inside the office, Wise offered Penhaligon his chair. She refused. He sat behind the desk.

'Coffee?'

'No thank you, sir.'

And they waited. Fitz, Wise, Beck, Harriman, Skelton. The only difference was that he, Fitz, was the only one that knew what was coming.

Harriman perched on the edge of Wise's desk. Beck leaned against the filing cabinet. Skelton stood, ramrod straight before the door.

Fitz thought it was interesting that no-one but Wise had the nerve to sit.

Then she began to speak.

'It happened in the early hours of this morning. At Belle Vale. I was . . .' she gave a little laugh. 'You'll think this is stupid. I was out for a drive . . .' a quick glance at Fitz. 'Thinking things over. I found myself there. Went to the kids' playground. Sat on the swing. Must have been thinking about the reconstruction, I suppose.' She noticed the blank expression on Beck's face. 'Helen Robins lives there. Anyway. I was thinking. I pushed the swing but, you know,

185

it was too small, and there was a light drizzle. My feet slipped in the mud. I fell. That's when he attacked.'

There was a seat this side of Wise's desk. Now Penhaligon sat in it, perched right on the edge, tense, afraid of reliving the memories, but sure in her own mind it was the only way to begin dealing with them. Fitz saw all this in a moment, was proud of her, knew he could never tell her that for fear of sounding condescending.

She went on, 'He punched me. On the cheek. Then he held a knife to my throat. Then he . . . he must've . . . uh, pushed me down again, or turned me round . . . uh . . . I can't really remember.'

'Why didn't you scream?' Harriman. Idiot.

She ignored him. 'I . . . tried to speak but my mouth . . . I had mud in my mouth. I remember the taste . . . uh, I told him I had a disease. I had AIDS. That he'd catch it . . .' She hesitated.

Harriman stepped into the breach, blissfully ignorant. 'There were people living there. Why didn't you scream?'

And she looked at him then, and Fitz saw her helpless fear mirrored in her eyes. '*Because I was frightened, you stupid –*' She broke off, tried to gather herself together. 'I was frightened, all right? He had a knife and I was frightened!'

Harriman reeled from her words. He licked his lips. Glanced at Wise. The DCI gave an impatient shake of his head. Harriman knew what that meant. He got up to leave. Skelton stood aside to let him go.

When the door closed Penhaligon remained silent. When it became obvious she wasn't going to add anything more Fitz said, 'Can I ask you something?' He kept his voice carefully neutral. No sympathy. No special concern. It was enough.

She nodded.

'You said he was white.'

Again a nod. But she wouldn't look at him, stared instead at her hands clasped in her lap, the ashtray on Wise's desk, the calendar on the wall, anywhere but Fitz.

'You saw enough of him to know?'

Now she looked at him. Began to push back. 'Yeah.'

'What did he say?'

Penhaligon pursed her lips. 'Nothing.'

Fitz frowned. 'Nothing at all?'

'No.'

And then he had it, the nagging thought crawling around in his subconscious had finally poked itself up far enough to be caught. To Wise he said, 'It's not the same man. The guy we're after is black.'

Wise sighed. It was obvious he wanted to stamp on Fitz, control the situation for Penhaligon's benefit. He spoke fast. 'No. You said he was black. You were wrong.'

Fitz said, equally firmly, 'He's black.' To Penhaligon he said, 'Did he use water?' He could see by Wise's expression that he already knew the answer, but Fitz pushed again anyway. 'Did he make you wash?'

Penhaligon shook her head. Fitz could see how his conflict with Wise was affecting her. But this had to come out now. Or it would be buried forever in the healing process. 'He didn't talk. He didn't use water. Different MO. Different man.'

Wise cut through Fitz's words. 'Jane. Have you got your car?'

'No.'

'Jimmy. Take Jane home, OK? Now.'

Penhaligon frowned. 'I don't want to go home.' Her voice was firm. About this she was sure, at least. That old devil displacement again. At work she wouldn't be able to dwell on the event. Fitz couldn't let that happen. It was time to puncture the wound, suck the poison out. 'Panhandle. A significantly high proportion of all rapes are perpetrated by someone the victim knows. You know this man. He has a very distinctive voice. That's why he didn't speak.'

'Thats's a load of bollocks.' Beck, sucking on his rollup, blowing smoke. Fitz spared him a quick glance. He was dealing with the situation about as well as Harriman.

Beck began to go on, but Wise cut in. 'That's enough

Jimmy. Take Jane home as I asked you.' To Penhaligon he added. 'You're going home. That's an order. Put your feet up. I'll be in touch.'

And she looked at Fitz then, her gaze unfathomable, and suddenly it was a three-ring circus, Fitz versus Wise and she was caught in the middle, shell-shocked and vulnerable.

'It's a different rapist. Two men. You have to acknowledge that.'

'Sure. One black, one white. And they share the same mask.'

'Ooh, sarcasm. That's helpful.'

'Go home, Jane. Go home now.'

And Fitz had had enough. He took a step towards the middle of the room, towards Wise, ensconced behind his desk. 'Language is a tool. You rape a woman, you use every tool at your disposal. A rapist *talks*. Sometimes it's to charm the victim, flatter the victim; other times it's too terrify the victim into submission. But he always talks. He always talks. But not this guy. This guy stayed silent. Not even a moan of pleasure, of release. There's got to be a reason for that.' And he stared at Penhaligon, willed her to understand him, to believe him, willed Wise to believe him too. 'The reason is *she would have recognised his voice.*'

And the moment broke as Penhaligon rose, her face blotchy but free of tears, rose and strode to the door, left the office without speaking at all.

Beck stubbed out his rollup, left the room with a glance that seemed to say, *Nice one Fitz.*

He was left alone with Wise. Fitz began to speak, closed his mouth as he finally acknowledged the futility of it. But he wasn't going to let this drop, couldn't let it drop. Not while Panhandle was at the middle of it. No way.

He opened the door and walked out of the office.

4.30p.m.–5.00p.m.

Harriman was entering the lift as Fitz approached. There was no-one else in sight. On a sudden impulse Fitz ran into the lift after the detective, pushed him roughly against the back wall of the elevator, pressed his face against the steel wall so he couldn't turn or look back, held his Parker ballpoint against the struggling detective's exposed throat.

In a bad Liverpool accent, Fitz said harshly, 'Don't struggle. Don't fucking struggle! I've got a knife against your throat so don't struggle, all right?'

Harriman became instantly still, a tiny moan of fear escaping from his lips, his breath steaming against the elevator wall. Fitz reached out and pressed the button for the ground floor. The doors closed.

He dug the pen a little harder into Harriman's neck.

'Wallet.'

'What?'

'Your wallet, give me your fucking wallet.'

'Sure, OK, don't hurt me.' Harriman got out his wallet, bent his arm backwards so Fitz could take it from him.

'Good boy. Now give me your wristwatch.'

'I don't believe this, we're in a police station!'

'*Shut the fuck up and give me your wristwatch!*'

Harriman complied.

'Trousers round your ankles.'

'What?'

'Do as you're fucking told!'

Fitz jabbed with the pen, felt a perverse sense of satisfaction when Harriman, without another word, undid his belt and let his trousers slide down to his ankles. He was making tiny little sobbing noises now. Fitz grinned. Inside the flame was billowing out, the frustration, the anger, it was all bubbling up, pouring out, an exorcism.

He took the pen from Harriman's neck. Turned the man round. Showed him the pen. Showed him his face.

'Fitz, you fucking –'

Fitz put the pen away, lifted one finger to his lips and tut-tutted. ' "Why didn't you scream?" '

Harriman recognised his own words as Fitz made him eat them whole. He said nothing. What could he say? And then the lift slid to a halt and the doors opened onto a group of women police officers. They looked at Fitz. Looked at Harriman. Looked at his trousers.

Fitz walked out of the lift. As he passed the women, he turned. 'All I said was, "Going down?" '

His words were aimed at the women but he never took his eyes off Harriman's face. Had he got it? Was there an inkling of realisation there?

Fitz sighed, suddenly tired. He turned, walked away, leaving the women to stare at Harriman as the detective hurriedly pulled up his trousers, face burning with shame. Shame and, yes, a tiny glimpse of the truth.

Fitz left Anson Road police station feeling cold, unsatisfied; his anger unpurged. Because the truth was he identified totally with Harriman. And he knew that all his anger, all his frustration, confusion, everything, was all rooted to his guilt. His guilt at being *a man*. At being a man like the *man* who had raped his woman. And despite twenty years of professional experience which assured him that he *wasn't* guilty, that he *wasn't* the same as this man, about that feeling there was simply nothing he could do.

Nothing except go to her, be with her, try to offer support, and hope – no, pray – that she was able to accept it, that she was able to accept him, as her friend, her lover, after what had been done to her.

EIGHT

9.30a.m.–10.30a.m.

First thing that morning Floyd Malcolm had paid a second visit to his local benefit office. Stuffed into his wallet was his birth certificate. His face was burning with embarrassment and anger. Anger that he had been made to produce such documentation, anger that he was being discriminated against simply because of the colour of his skin. He was no different from the other half a million unemployed in Manchester. He was skint, blagging a job because the government wasn't able to help. Whose fault was that? Bloody whites that's who. They were in charge. Look at the mess they were making. Somewhere in the back of his head a voice was saying, *You wound that clerk up; you put on a false accent and you wound him up. Maybe he wouldn't have been so pedantic if you'd simply answered his questions, ticked the boxes. You know the deal – abide by it and you'll get by.* He ignored the voice the way he ignored his mother, the way he ignored everything in his life that he hated, with an ease developed through years of pent-up anger.

Twenty minutes after his arrival at the building, he was sitting across a desk from a familiar face. Andrew Wiley. The claimant adviser who had spoken to him on his previous visit. Andrew Wiley. Middle-class. Middle-aged. White. A clerk's clerk. A fusser. A red tape-er. A by the book, tick in the box man. Floyd stared at Wiley across the desk, the neat rows of stationery, once more aware that he, Floyd, was at a disadvantage. Aware that he had to come cap in hand to ask this middle-class white man for help that should have been his by virtue of his birth.

Wiley performed the usual tricks, asking Floyd for his national insurance number, name, address, if his circumstances had changed. He was a trained seal bouncing balls on his nose, juggling with elements of Floyd's life. That annoyed Floyd. The anger grew, and with it the knowledge that Wiley's quietly antagonistic behaviour stemmed from his fear of Floyd. His fear of Floyd's skin; the colour of his skin. The colour that, for Wiley at least, was a sure indication of the way Floyd operated, his intentions towards other men like Wiley, other white, middle-class men. And their women. Oh yes. Mustn't forget their women. Their women and what he, Floyd, might do to them if the white, middle-class men like Wiley didn't keep him firmly in his place.

The men in power, they could do this by preventing Floyd from working in well-paid jobs, by denying him promotion if he should ever land such a job. Wiley, though, he was different. He was little more than an office boy himself, at the beck and call of those who bought and sold the system. His only way of keeping Floyd in his place was by observing the letter of the law and placing pitfall after clerical pitfall in the way of Floyd's claim, while at the same time maintaining a façade of bland helpfulness.

Floyd could see through the façade. To him Wiley was as transparent as the windscreen of his cab. He saw fear in the clerk's eyes as he handed him his birth certificate, crumpled from its ride in his wallet, watched it bloom on his face as Floyd spoke, in that fake Jamaican accent he knew was his only way to score against the clerk.

'Passports cost money. And you won't give me any money without a passport. But passports cost money. This is my birth certificate. Got it off me mum. It says Manchester. *England.*' And Floyd grinned, because the look on Wiley's face told Floyd he had produced the necessary documentation for his claim to proceed.

Wiley nodded as he smoothed out the crumpled birth

certificate. Floyd saw the faint irritation overlaying the fear on his face and grinned. The grin faded as Wiley looked back at him. Faded because the irritation on Wiley's face had faded, and with it, the fear.

Wiley said, 'I'll need to check if this is valid. If you could wait in room two, please.' He indicated a door leading off the main benefit office.

Floyd frowned. 'Why you want me to wait in trap two, man?'

'I'd like to talk to you in private, Mister Malcolm.' Wiley stood, still holding the birth certificate. 'Room two, please. It's just through there, on the left.'

Floyd rose slowly. His immediate reaction was to run, to grab his birth certificate and get the hell out, pick up a few more fares, get some money in his pocket. But something held him. Something seemed to be driving him towards a confrontation. And if he was honest with himself he wanted that confrontation. He wanted it. Him versus Wiley. Him versus the state, the world. He wanted the conflict. Wanted to swing fists, pound faces. Wanted to bruise. To draw blood. He *wanted* it.

And he could see from the change in Wiley's expression that it was what Wiley wanted too.

Once again the common sense in Floyd screamed at him to get out while the going was good. Floyd had never been one for common sense. He ignored the voice inside him like he had ignored the voices that had taunted him as a child. The voices belonging to other kids, kids who had grown into men like the one standing before him. Like Wiley. Middle-aged. Middle-class. White. Racist. Bastards.

And Floyd went for it.

He walked into room two.

Wiley followed him in a few minutes later. The change in the clerk made Floyd blink. His body language was different. He leaned forward as he walked, aggressive, dominant. But there was something beyond this, something more: the bland look he had worn until now had been replaced by a kind of self-righteous fervour. The face of a man in the right, who knew he had the power to do something about it.

And Floyd realised he'd been hooked then. Baited and hooked and reeled in, a prize catch for Wiley's superiors. A head for the wall, a trophy for the men who walked the halls of power.

And he knew what Wiley was going to say. A split second before the words came, he knew. There was only one thing which could have engendered such a change in the bookish clerk. And Floyd knew what it was.

'Mister Malcolm. I'm giving you the chance to withdraw your claim. I'd advise you to take it.'

'Why?'

'Because, Mister Malcolm, you drive a minicab?'

The words came without any inflection, any emotional colouring, but still Floyd sensed the emotion behind them. The triumph. He felt his head spin. 'Who told you that? Was it Carter? I'll kill him. Who told you that? *Who told you that?*'

Now Wiley was calm again. He was in control and knew it. The knowledge angered Floyd even more. But it also frightened him a bit too. 'It was a police officer, Mister Malcolm. So you see, the source was reliable. And my offer to withdraw your claim still stands.'

'A police officer? He's a liar! Who was it?'

'I strongly advise you to withdraw your claim, Mister Malcolm.'

And Floyd passed the point of no return.

He stared at Wiley, let the clerk's supercilious smile fuel even further rage. 'I know where you live,' he said quietly.

Wiley's smile dropped. 'What was that, Mister Malcolm?'

Floyd found himself smiling now. 'If I was a cab driver, right, I'd know where you live, wouldn't I? I'd know where everyone lived.' He leaned closer to Wiley, who took half a step backwards, a bright star of fear gleaming for a second in his eyes. 'I know where you live.'

'Is that a threat, Mister Malcolm? Mister Malcolm, are you threatening me?'

But Floyd was outta there, moving fast, his body struggling to catch up with his raging mind, the flood of anger carrying him through the main office and out into the wet streets of central Manchester, where he stood, lost, alone in the crowd of mid-morning shoppers, every one of whom walked around him as if his anger was a visible aura that they had to avoid.

11.00a.m.–11.30a.m.

So he made the call to the radio station. The call to the psychologist. And he said, '*Forget morality, OK? Forget that. If he lets them live then there's more chance of being caught. So, should he kill his victims in future? Is that what you're advising?*'

And Fitz answered.

In the second before Floyd's call was cut off, Fitz answered, his silence a reply only Floyd could hear.

And then, from the phone box where he'd placed the call, Floyd caught sight of Andrew Wiley emerging from the benefit office. Emerging with a woman. A woman he took to lunch. A woman he kissed goodbye half an hour later, a white, middle-class woman. A woman he called *darling*.

And as he placed the now impatiently buzzing receiver back on its cradle, Floyd found he had decided what he was going to do next.

11.30a.m.–12.30p.m.

Debra Wiley felt her marriage was a good one. Oh, there were the occasional moments of boredom, of stress, but generally speaking she was happy. Sometimes she wondered if Andrew was as happy as she was. Well, he deserved to be. He got the pick of the bunch when he married her. Then again, there was no-one to blame for that but herself. Well, maybe her mother. Debra grinned when she remembered her mother's advice. *Never marry an attractive man. Or if you do, make sure all your friends are less attractive than you are.* Well, that part at least had been easy. Even now, approaching the big four-oh, Debra found she had no complaints about her face or figure. She certainly knew that Andrew didn't. The funny thing was that although her mother's advice had worked for her and Andrew, she would never dream of giving that same advice to her own daughter. At fourteen and a half, Connie Wiley was apt to give her mother, or anyone else for that matter, a lecture on feminism that would leave their brains steaming like a burnt joint. Connie with her Doc Marten boots and her fashionably striped leggings, her blonde dreads and plaited beads, was the complete opposite of everything her grandmother had ever believed in. And more often than not Debra felt herself caught in the middle of this conflict of generations. Whoever said having kids was easy was full of the proverbial. Oh yes. It was her mother who'd said that. Hum.

Debra grinned as she finished the shopping. Life was good. And if her daughter or her friends ever mentioned subtly that a woman's place was no longer necessarily in the kitchen, that there were careers waiting for her out in the big wide world beyond taking care of her home or family, Debra was not discontented. Her mother's advice had worked for her. She was happy. And she was happy that Mum had gone to her grave knowing that she, Debra, was happy.

Now Debra made a second-to-last stop at the local model shop. The coming weekend was Andrew's birthday and she planned a special surprise for him. Tamiya had just released a one-thirtieth-scale 1948 Bentley kit for matchstick modellers. The completed model would be twenty-six inches long and would, according to the instructions on the box, be composed of nine hundred and eighty-six match-sized sticks of wood (plus fifty spare). Something in her heart skipped a beat when she imagined his expression when he unwrapped the present on Saturday afternoon.

Saturday night was to be a special present too. Connie was staying over at a friend's for the weekend; Debra had booked a table for two at the same expensive French restaurant where he had proposed to her, fifteen years before.

Debra made her final stop at Ann Summers along the high street. She hesitated outside the shop for a moment, then walked in. What would her mother think now, Debra wondered, if she knew what she planned for Andrew's birthday surprise?

12.30p.m.–1.00p.m.

Floyd watched from his cab as the blonde woman who he was sure by now was Andrew Wiley's wife left Ann Summers with a bag full of interesting packages and started up the high street towards the bus stops.

Floyd had waited for over an hour. He had watched the woman and thought hard about what he was going to do to her, although in reality he was already absolutely sure what was going to happen between them. Andrew Wiley himself had narrowed all his choices to one more than an hour ago, in the unemployment building.

His eyes peeled for strolling coppers, Floyd checked the false back of the glove compartment, made sure the toilet bag containing the knife, the comb and the mask and gloves were still in place. Then, flouting traffic regulations, he did a U-turn across the high street and pulled up alongside the bus stop just as Debra Wiley took her place at the end of the bus queue.

She looked at the cab and he could see her mind working. It was convenient, a ride home after a morning's shopping. All right, it would cost a couple of quid, but she could afford that. The amount of shopping she had just bought Floyd thought she could probably afford to buy his bloody cab.

She caught his eye through the windscreen. On the roof the *for hire* light was flashing. She made up her mind. Picked up her bags. Took the step towards the cab.

Her hand was on the passenger door handle, had turned it and begun to open the door, when all hell seemed to break loose in front of his cab.

197

The commotion seemed to centre on the driver of a hackney cab which had pulled across the high street to block his way forward. The driver was a smallish man, somewhere in his late middle age. White. Naturally. And he was screaming abuse.

Floyd became aware he was the target of the abuse.

'Fucking minicab drivers! You don't pick up on the street, right? I've got your number, pal, and I'm fucking reporting you. I'm gonna see you get done, right? Fucking minicab drivers. You think I don't have to eat? I don't have to put food on the table? Jesus!'

Floyd glanced at the woman. She had taken a step away from the cab, gave him a friendly shrug and a grin. *Sorry. Not my argument. Maybe I'll stick with the bus.*

Shit.

Someone wrenched open the driver's door of his cab. He turned, face to face with the furious hackney cab driver. 'You don't pick up on the street, right? Coming over here and stealing our jobs. I'm gonna see you get done, you greedy black bastard.'

Floyd blinked. 'What did you say? What did you call me?'

Something in the hackney driver's face changed then, perhaps aware that he'd gone too far. Floyd didn't see it, saw nothing but the anger. The rage. 'What the fuck did you just say to me? Did you just call me a black bastard? Did you? Did you call me that?' He made as if to get out of the cab, and that was when the police car screeched to a halt in front of the hackney.

Shit and double shit.

Floyd pulled his door shut, reversed a few yards, slammed the cab into first and shot away from the kerb, leaving the spluttering hackney driver to confront the police alone, to the amusement of the watching pedestrians.

By the time Floyd had circled the town centre and come back to the bus stops, the hackney and the police car were both gone.

So was the blonde woman. Floyd saw her getting onto a

number thirty-nine bus heading out of town.

He smiled, slipped the cab into gear, pulled away from the high street after the bus.

1.00p.m.–1.30p.m.

When Debra Wiley got home the first thing she did was dump the shopping on the kitchen table and fill the coffee percolator with fresh beans and switch it on. Then she packed away the shopping. Meat into the freezer, veg into the cupboard. Andrew's present she'd take upstairs in a minute. Along with the packages from Ann Summers.

She grabbed the last items from the bag – a couple of tins of Whiskas Premium Meaty Chunks.

'Thomas! Gizmo! Dinnertime.'

Thomas and Gizmo failed to appear.

Debra shrugged. 'Your loss, guys.' She looked around the kitchen and spied the open window above the sink. She opened the back door, left a couple of bowls of Whiskas on the floor by the dishwasher. They'd be back soon eough when they caught a whiff of that.

Grabbing the parcels left on the table, Debra headed upstairs. She dumped the parcels onto her bed, made a quick detour to the bathroom to run a slow bath, returned to the bedroom. As the back door creaked gently downstairs, she imagined the pad-pad of paws across the kitchen and the busy champing of cat jaws that would follow soon after. 'Don't forget your napkins, boys,' she called through the open bedroom door.

Then she took the 1948 Bentley model from its bag and shook it. The sound of nine hundred and eighty-six matches (plus fifty spare) rattling inside made her smile.

The smile widened when she looked back at the parcels left on the bed.

She opened one of the parcels, held up the contents, giggled. She went to the full-length mirror on her wardrobe and held the garment up in front of her. Her giggles deepened into a laugh. Cute.

She wound her hair into a sophisticated bun, posed again in front of the mirror.

Happy birthday Andrew.

Then something moved at the edge of her vision, a darting movement that crossed the mirror while she was concentrating on herself.

'Tom? Giz?' She began to turn. 'You greedy buggers, have you eaten all that food already?'

Someone grabbed her around the throat, spun her fully around. She had a moment to register the sight in front of her. A tall figure. A man. Mask. Gloves. A knife.

Dropping the clothing she held, Debra lashed out with one fist. The movement was instinctive, and caught the man by surprise. She let out a cry; not fear, pain as her knuckles split on the cheek of the mask. Her cry was matched by one from the man.

'Get the fuck out of my fucking –'

She never completed the shout.

The masked figure grabbed her, swung a fist into her face. Pain exploded through her cheek and jaw. The room spun around her; for a moment she saw stars. Another blow landed, this time on the point of her jaw. Her teeth clacked together on her tongue and she screeched. Her mouth filled with blood. Another blow came and she fell across the bed, landed on the 1948 Bentley model. The box split. Her last sight, as she tried desperately to turn and crawl away across the bed, was of nine hundred and eight-six matches (and fifty spare) spilling across the covers and onto the floor.

1.30p.m.–2.00p.m.

It was no good. It was no fucking good. It was no good. It was *no fucking good!*

He couldn't hurt Andrew Wiley if his wife was unconscious. She had to know. *He* had to know. It was no good. No fucking good at all.

He lifted the woman's unconscious body from the bed, rocked her in his arms, slapped her face a couple of times to

200

try to bring her around. Nothing. Her mouth filled with blood and she dribbled pink saliva onto his sleeve. He shuddered and dropped the woman onto the bed, wiped at his sleeve until the offending stain was gone. On the bed the woman snored. Fucking *snored*. As if she were bored. Bored with him. Oh this was no good, this was no fucking good at all, no way.

Floyd turned her over. Undressed her. Tried to get it on. It should be better like this. Should be. She couldn't see him. Couldn't hate him, couldn't laugh at him.

Then again she couldn't respond either.

He tried again to take her. She flopped. More blood dribbled onto the bed covers. The matches crunched beneath her buttocks.

Oh fuck. This was crap. This was bollocks. What was going on here? This wasn't working out. This wasn't working out *big time*.

He paced the room.

Sucked her breasts.

Masturbated.

Nothing.

Fucking nothing.

And then he realised. In a moment of blinding clarity it hit him. And he understood, for perhaps the first time, understood that it wasn't the sex that turned him on: it was the fear.

The fear his women felt for him.

He bit his lip. Thought for a moment. Hunted through a nearby chest of drawers, found a pile of monogrammed handkerchiefs. Grabbing the top one, he wadded it up and forced it into her mouth. Now there'd be no blood to worry about. She gasped a little as he gagged her, but other than that showed no signs of coming round.

He stood upright. Checked his watch. Wank. This was a pile of wank. He shook his head. Fuck. Fuck. Fuck.

Then he heard the sound of running water. A bath. He picked the woman up, carried her into the bathroom, laid her on the beige carpet, let her head rest on the foot of the toilet pan.

He splashed water from the bath onto her face while she awoke, gasping and spluttering, eyes wide with fear, choking from the cloth wadded into her mouth.

She began to struggle, tried to spit out the handkerchief.

He showed her the knife.

She froze.

This time when he tried to get it on there were no problems. No problems at all.

And afterwards he told her what he was going to do to her.

2.00p.m.–2.30p.m.

Having him inside her was awful, but his voice, that was worse. He droned on and on. And he sang. Badly. In time with his thrashing body, but flat. 'When You're in Love with a Beautiful Woman'.

Christ he was sick. Sick to do this to her. Sick to hurt her, to infect her with himself like this. Sick. She turned then, crawled to the toilet, emptied her lunch into it. And as she was being sick he held her, stroked her back, muttered soothing words to her. All the while she felt the cold edge of the knife at her side, the rasp of leather at her neck as the mask moved on his face.

'There,' he said sympathetically. 'It's nearly over.'

She spluttered, grabbed for the tissue he passed her, wiped blood and vomit from her lips. 'Oh Jesus. Fucking go will you. Just go.'

'I can't do that, Debra.'

She groaned as he turned her, propped her against the side of the bath as he flushed the toilet. Steam swirled around them, thirty minutes of slow-running hot water. Downstairs the coffee percolator was bubbling merrily.

'Don't tell me that, you've had what you wanted you fucking pervert, now will you *just get the fuck out of my house!*'

His voice was still gentle when he said, 'I said, I can't do that, Debra.'

And he pulled the mask from his face.

She winced, but it was for nothing. He was quite attractive actually. A lean, young man, stubble, brown eyes. Intelligence.

She'd have no trouble recognising him again.

That's when she realised.

'Oh. Oh God. Oh please. Please. No. You've had what you wanted. Please go. Oh please just go.'

But he was shaking his head. 'I don't normally show my face. But, you know what? I was chatting today, to this guy I know. He's a psychologist, by the way, so he should know about these things. He said I was scarred. That I was ugly. Well that was a bad guess wasn't it? Anyway. I was chatting to him, and I asked him, postulated, you know, that this rapist should kill his victims in future. Because it was safer for him, for the rapist that way, because that way his victims couldn't tell anyone about him. Do you know what my friend the psychologist said?'

Debra shook her head dumbly. She blinked, felt tears pour down her bruised cheeks. 'Please,' she mumbled thickly. 'Please.'

'You're not interested, I can tell.' The man shrugged. 'It doesn't matter anyway.'

'Please let me go. I've got a kid. A daughter. She's only fourteen. Please. Please let me go. I won't tell anyone, I promise. I promise. Please.'

He took a deep breath, as if of bracing mountain air. The air in the bathroom was loaded with steam, smelt of sweat and blood. An animal smell, like a run-over cat.

'It's not down to you, Debra.'

'It's my husband's birthday on Saturday.'

'Oh really? That who the model car was for?' The man nodded. 'Andrew'll like that.'

'You know him?' Stupefied. Disbelieving.

He grinned. Nice, even, white teeth. *Never marry an attractive man.*

'Oh yes. I know him. The way he treats people down the social. Black people. Me in particular . . .' A big sigh.

Casual. Conversational. 'I have to hurt him, Debra. I'm sorry but there's only one way I know of doing that.' He shrugged. 'Think of yourself as an early birthday present.'

Debra felt her eyes bulge. Something hot and wet cascaded down her legs. *Pissed myself I pissed myself I'm going to die he's going to kill me, kill me with that knife, going to kill me with that –*

She moved. Unable to believe there was any strength left in her she lashed out again. And once again caught him unawares. His head cracked against the side of the bath, leaving a sticky mess of blood and hair. He didn't scream. He grunted. Like an animal. Like when he'd been inside her. Like when he'd raped her.

She struggled to her feet.

He reached out and grabbed her ankle. She slipped on the wet carpet, slipped in her own piss, fell against the bath. Something cracked along her right side. Pain shot through her chest. She was moving again, but not quick enough. Not nearly quick enough. She felt his hands around her throat. He was angry. Furious. The knife was nowhere in sight. He'd dropped it. She tried to scream. Found she was unable to breathe. Felt herself bent double over the bath, found herself face down in the water. It was hot. She felt his grip slacken as she convulsed. She screamed; a flood of water sucked into her throat stifled the noise.

Things started to go grey then.

Water. Inside her. In her lungs. That was silly. She couldn't breathe water. Only air. She had to breathe air if she wanted to live. And she did want to live. Oh yes. Because Connie would be home from school in a bit. And it was Andrew's birthday. And there were the cats to feed. And his present to wrap. The 1948 Bentley. Or was it '49? And the stuff from Ann Summers. He'd find it, then the surprise would be spoilt. She had to do these things. She had to live to do these things. She had to breathe to live. But there was no air in her lungs. Just water. Grey water. Hot. Grey.

2.30p.m.–3.00p.m.

He washed her, of course. Working on automatic. Tipped her into the bath and washed her. Her skin was like wet cardboard. Flushed with the heat, loaded with moisture. The steam kept her hot, you could almost believe she was still alive. But Floyd knew better. He'd heard the surprised groan, seen the last outrush of breath from her bloodied mouth and nostrils, watched the breath form bubbles in the skin of soap floating on the now still bath water, watched the bubbles burst one by one, the last bit of her, giving itself up to the wet air.

Steam ran through his hair, washed sweat into his eyes. That stung. The pain was good, enabled him to focus.

The *slosh* of water.

The *pad-slop* of his feet on the carpet.

The smell of hot piss in the wet air.

Something scrabbled at the door.

Floyd yelped, jumped. He turned. A fluffy black and white cat was peering round the door, investigating the interesting smells and noises coming from the bathroom.

'Christ, cat!' Floyd kicked the door shut in the cat's face, finished washing Debra, retrieved his knife, his mask, the gloves, the comb, stuffed them back in the toilet bag.

He was practically crying as he came down the stairs. At the bottom another cat prowled, this one a sleek black tom. He almost tripped over it. Laughed when he realised they would have found him there, impaled on his own knife, the cat's revenge, a touch of the Edgar Allen Poes.

Oozing laughter that was almost indistinguisable from hysterical tears, Floyd ran through the house towards the back door.

The black cat followed him for a few paces, then was distracted by the still half-full bowls of food by the dishwasher.

3.00p.m.–3.30p.m.

Floyd's cab was parked halfway along the next street. He jumped in, dumped the toilet bag with the mask, gloves, comb and knife onto the front passenger seat, started the engine.

The back passenger door opened and a man got in.

Floyd turned wildly around. 'What? What do you want man? What do you want?'

The man, neat, tallish, business suit, stared at him in some surprise. 'You are a cab, right?'

Floyd nodded, sweating, his eyes bulging. 'Sure. Yeah man. I'm a cab. Right.' He struggled to get himself under control.

The man nodded. 'Manchester Victoria then, please. I've got a train to catch.'

Floyd nodded, dazed. He began to pull away, stalled, gave the man in the back a queasy grin, started the engine again. As an afterthought he reached across and stuffed the toilet bag into the glove compartment.

He pulled away.

After that everything seemed to happen very quickly. A burgundy Volvo came out of nowhere, pulled in front of him with a screech of tyres, coming to a halt diagonally across the residential street and blocking it. At the same time a blue Ford Escort slid sideways across the road behind him. The two events were timed so perfectly there was little more than a second for Floyd to think between them. But a second was enough to inspire panic. These cars were unmarked police cars. They'd sussed him. Somehow they'd sussed him. Now they were going to get him, bang to rights.

No way.

In the second the thoughts went through his head, Floyd slammed the cab into reverse, accelerated backwards the ten feet that separated his car from the blue Escort, slammed the brakes on just in time to avoid collision with the Escort's bonnet.

The glove compartment popped open.

He shoved the cab into first, tried to get round the burgundy Volvo. The driver of the Volvo reversed to block Floyd's course. Floyd drove up onto the pavement, scraping the cab against a garden wall, and back onto the road on the other side of the Volvo. Floyd stamped on the accelerator. Sent the cab shooting forward.

Into a dead end.

Into the wall at the end of the road.

The car slammed to a halt, the engine stalled as the bonnet popped open, both Floyd and his passenger were rocked hard in their seats.

The toilet bag popped out of the glove compartment, bounced from the passenger seat and dropped into the footwell amid a pile of loose items.

Dazed, Floyd reached for the bag, planning to make a run for it, and that was when the man in the rear passenger seat casually leaned forward and showed Floyd his ID.

'Floyd Malcolm?'

And they had him. Bang to rights. Floyd looked at the man in the rear seat, saw in his expression a bored hostility that told Floyd he was going down for a long stretch.

Then his fingers, groping for the toilet bag containing his rape kit, found instead a cab driver's licence. Wilson's licence. He smiled.

'Ah, no man, shared cab. Floyd does use this cab, but my name's Wilson. Wilson Parry.'

'Mister Parry, Edward Brent, Detective Sergeant, South-fields police station. This cab has been seen on three occasions picking up fares from the public highway. That contravenes the Local Government Miscellaneous Provisions Act of 1976.'

And Floyd was laughing, tears streaming down his face, the toilet bag forgotten as he parked the cab and locked it, as instructed, opened the doors, left the vehicle and handed over the keys, submitted to a breath test. 'I suppose you'd like me to accompany you to the station?' he giggled as they waited for the little green light to change colour.

It didn't, of course.

'No, Mister Parry. That won't be necessary.' Brent glared at Floyd. 'Since this is a first offence, and since your breath test proved negative, I am prepared to let you off with a fine. And of course, you will have to produce your documents at a police station of your choice, within seven days.' Floyd laughed even harder then, till his sides ached and his eyes ran with tears.

3.30p.m.–5.30p.m.

Of course he had to tell them about it at dinner. The tow home by the garage truck was enough to trigger any number of questions.

They took it just as badly as he expected.

'Two police cars, five coppers.' Bev, airing her view as normal. 'Why? Because the hackney drivers are paying coppers to do their dirty work for them.'

'Bev, you're a hypocrite.' Marvin, playing devil's advocate, as usual.

'Marvin, your sister is nothing of the sort.' Mum, mediating as usual and, as usual, succeeding only in winding everyone up.

'Mum!'

'Mum's right, Marvin! You tell me what Floyd did wrong.'

'I'm not talking about Floyd, I'm talking about you. You're always on about coppers, but when our house gets done over, like last year, remember? And who phoned them right away? You, that's who. You're a bloody hypocrite.'

'That's different. Doing over houses is serious. All he's done is pick up on the street. It's not exactly rape, is it? It's not exactly murder – picking up off the street.'

'It's breaking the law, Bev. The coppers are just doing their job.'

'That's crap, Marvin, that's not the point and you know it. There's people getting raped out there, that's the point. People getting raped and murdered and what are the coppers doing? Arresting cab drivers for picking up on the street! And another thing –'

But Floyd could take no more. He rose, headed for the door, blew out into the street, silent, but inside his head he was screaming, screaming and there was no-one to hear him, no-one but the gathering night.

208

NINE

By the time Fitz reached Penhaligon's flat the confusion and anger provoked by Harriman's reaction to her rape had faded, to be replaced with a sort of giggly humour. The thought of Harriman himself standing in the lift, trousers round his ankles, big splotch of blue ink on his neck from the pen, watched in total bemusement by the women waiting for the lift, did much to lift Fitz's spirits. With his finger on the intercom button, Fitz felt nothing but confidence. Oh, maybe a little guilt, but intellectually he could file that under *inappropriate* and worry about it later. He was just what Penhaligon needed. Together they'd get through this.

The faint sound of clashing cymbals seemed only to confirm his opinion.

He leaned on the intercom button long enough for the buzzer to filter through the sound of the drum kit, then waited as she came to the door.

The intercom crackled, disguising any emotion that might have been apparent in her voice., 'I want to be alone.'

Fitz grinned. This was expected. 'Mae West,' he responded obtusely. He'd get her with that one. She always fell for the obscure references.

Again the intercom crackled. 'Before my time.'

Fitz's smile widened to a grin. ' "Every man I meet wants to protect me. I can never figure out what from." Mae West said that. Want to guess which movie?'

'Can't remember.'

'I'll give you a clue: it wasn't *Star Wars*.'

'Oh for God's sake, Fitz. Come in if you must.'

The lock buzzed. The door clicked open.

Inside her flat she stood apart from him, wouldn't come close. Led the way back into the living room without waiting for him to follow. He closed the front door. Followed her into the living room.

The lights in the room were dimmed, the curtains open. Well that was a good sign. At least she wasn't hiding.

He kept his face carefully neutral. He didn't want to come across as sympathetic or unsympathetic. Just supportive. They stood apart, she behind the drum kit, he by the window, and stared at each other for a few moments, without speaking.

Eventually she said, 'I want my dad.' And she laughed. Fitz knew how she'd got on with her family, and she knew he knew.

'Your dad's dead. Huntington's. You can't have him.'

Her voice hardened. 'But I can have you?'

'If you want me, yes.'

'Big of you, Fitz.'

A little grin, just a crinkle of the cheeks. 'That's me. A big man.'

She didn't respond, except to bash the snare a bit. 'My dad bought me this snare drum when I was seventeen. It was a bribe. I think he wanted us to be closer. I was furious. I stuffed it in the loft. Forgot about it for years. Then when he died . . .'

A pause.

'You want to talk about it?'

And there was a look in her eyes. A hardness he'd never seen before. Perhaps he'd never looked for it. 'I blame you.' Her words cut him deeply. But he understood.

'It's someone you know. He's seen you with me. Overweight. Skint. Drunk. Middle-aged. "If she can go with him, she's anybody's." '

A silence, except for the irritable tapping on the snare. Then she said, 'Yes.'

Another silence.

210

And Fitz knew what it was like to have the truth of the matter and be cut by it again, hurt more deeply than he could bear. And the confidence went, the guilt came rushing back, and despite every good intention he pushed back. 'It's that old devil displacement again. You're angry with the man who raped you. He's not around. You vent your anger on the first available male. The one you care most about –'

And the look in her face became even harder, icily polite. 'I'd like you to leave, please.'

'Clench your fists.'

'What?'

'Clench your fists.'

'Get out!'

'Trust me.'

'Jesus, Fitz!'

'All your pain, your anger, your guilt, your humiliation, all in those fists. Concentrate on the fists. Look at them! That's better. Clench them tighter. Tighter. Tighter. Tighter. Good.' He looked at her. 'Now hit me.'

And she did, leaning across the kit and landing a classic right hook against his cheek.

He staggered back, collapsed on the couch. 'I didn't mean that hard.'

She was still looking at her fists. Slowly she unclenched them. She looked at Fitz. Shook her head. 'Edward Fitzgerald you are a complete asshole.'

'Broke the ice though, didn't it?' He grinned, felt his lip begin to bleed. 'Talking of ice, I don't suppose you've got any?'

6.30p.m.–6.45p.m.

Penhaligon took some ice from the fridge, poured it into a plastic bag, wrapped that up in a tea-towel. She fetched the improvised ice-pack back into the living room, gave it to him without speaking.

He held the pack to his cheek and told her what he wanted to do.

At his words her stomach lurched as if she were in an express lift. 'You want to hypnotise me?'

'Yeah.'

'You've done this before, right?'

'Yeah. I am a psychologist.'

'An asshole.'

'Psychologist.'

She thought about it again. 'And it's safe?'

'Sometimes.'

'Thanks for reassuring me, Fitz.'

'You want reassurance, or the truth?'

'You know what I want.'

'To catch this man. To send him to the dock. Put him away. Well, my hypnotising you might enable us to do that.'

'When?'

'How about right now?'

'Jesus!' *And what if I can't handle it? What if I can't handle the memories? What will you do then, Fitz?* She took a deep breath. 'And before you feel you have to convince me, yes. Let's do it. Let's do it now.'

7.00p.m.–7.30p.m.

Fitz used the Extended North Carolina Scale to get Penhaligon to assess her own level of trance state. 'How deep are you now, Jane?'

'Twenty-three.'

'Good. We'll hold there for now.'

'OK.' Her voice was almost perfectly normal, just the smallest trace of hesitation between question and answer. The hesitation might increase if he took her any deeper, but for now he had no intention of doing that. The further she went from zero state, or normal waking consciousness, the less the truth factored into the proceedings. From level forty plus a delusional state existed where reality and fantasy were interchangeable. Fitz had no intention of taking Penhaligon anywhere near thirty, let alone forty. Forty plus were

212

the deeps. The abyss. The place Nietzsche talked about. It was no place to go alone. For now twenty-three was a quite comfortable level. At this level he could suggest she feel no pain if it became necessary, and she would obey.

All right then.

'It's last night. We're in bed.'

She smiled. 'Spider. On the ceiling.'

'That's right. Then we talked. Now you're in the shower.'

The smile became dreamy.

'Now you're listening to my conversation with Mark.'

The smile faded, replaced with confusion, then anger. Fitz took a breath. This was going to be as bad for him as for her.

'Now you've left the house. You're in the car, driving home.'

'Not home.' The anger was clear in her voice. 'I'm not driving home.'

'Where then?'

'Belle Vale.'

Interesting. 'You're aware of this?'

'No. It's subconscious.'

'Describe how you feel.'

'I'm concerned, frightened, angry.'

'Confused.'

'Yes. Confused.'

'And you drive to Belle Vale.'

'Yes. It's raining. A light drizzle. The stars are poking through the clouds like little Christmas lights. Like bright little Christmas lights. There's a playground. I sit on the swing. I sit and listen to the wind. It's peaceful. I hear a dog barking. I sit and think.'

'What about?'

'You. Helen Robins. Being raped. Sex. Judith. You.'

'What else?'

'Work. The reconstruction. Beck scared her. Scared Helen. I took her home.'

'To Belle Vale.'

'Yes.'

'And now you're at Belle Vale. Sitting on the swing.'

'Yes.'

'What happens then?'

'I slip. Oh. I'll get my clothes dirty. That's a bloody nuisance. I'll have to – what? Get off me! Stop that! What? What are you doing? Get off me! Stop! Jesus! Jesus!'

And Fitz spoke quickly, as much to calm the fear in himself as the fear in her. 'Jane. You won't feel any pain. You're perfectly safe. You'll remember everything I ask as if you were watching it. On telly. Do you understand?'

'Yes.' Calm, no inflection.

'What happens then?'

'He hits her. Knocks her down. Rips off her clothes. There's . . .um . . . it's difficult to see, he's got a knife. A mask. He's wearing gloves. He's got one across her mouth, she can smell it. New leather. New gloves.'

'What else?'

'He hits her. He turns her, tears off her clothes, tears her tights, pulls down her skirt. Penetrates her. She's not ready. She doesn't want to. It hurts. She moans, tries to scream. The glove over her mouth stops her screaming.

Jesus. Oh Jesus, Oh Christ. 'What else?'

'He moves. Inside her. It hurts her. It hurts her. She struggles. He presses the knife to her throat. She stops moving. Stops moaning. He moves again. Again. She can smell him. Smell his breath. He's been drinking. Whisky. He lifts her. Turns her. She's facing him. On her knees. The knife. The mask. He's inside her again. Pushing. Pushing. Pushing. Pushing.'

Fitz shivered as her voice droned on, calm and inflectionless as ever, yet provoking a rage of emotion in him. 'What else?'

'The mask. Leather gloves. Whisky.'

'What else?'

'Cigarettes. He smokes cigarettes. She can smell them.'

'What else?'

'Another smell.'

'What is it?'

214

'Aftershave.'

And that was it. He had it. The clue that would put this bastard in the dock. Very slowly and carefully he said. 'The aftershave. You'll remember it. The smell. You'll remember it. Until we find him. And we'll find him. I promise.'

'I'll remember the smell. The aftershave. I'll remember until we find him.'

'Good.' Fitz gathered himself together. 'Now I'm going to bring you back up to the zero state now. You remember the zero state? That's where you're fully awake.'

A moment later her eyes blinked and she gasped. He reached for her but she was up, running past him and into the bathroom, reaching for the toothbrush, hawking into the sink over and over again, until she was sick into the basin. And Fitz could do nothing but stand behind her and stare at her back and her reflection in the mirror, the tears running down her cheeks. Tears that were matched by his own as she turned to stare at him accusingly.

'You bastard. You made me remember. *You made me remember!*'

'Jane, listen to me. We've found out so much. He's got new gloves. Bought them specially. This was his first time. And he smokes. Drinks whisky. He's not short of money. He's got a decent job. We're gonna catch this man. The aftershave. We're –'

'Shut up, Fitz!' Her shout was wild, an animal's howl.

He began to speak again but she cut him off, backed away from his outstretched arms.

'Shut up and get out of my house before I . . . just get out!'

7.30p.m.–8.00p.m.

After Fitz left Penhaligon sat on the couch, head in hands. Why had he done it. Why did he make her remember? And in such vivid detail? Oh God. She remembered everything. The cold, the drizzle, the clinking chain on the swing, the

215

rattle of window blinds a hundred yards away, the dog barking. Remembered the pain, the terror, the humiliation. Remembered the taste of him, the smell.

The smell.

The aftershave.

She checked her watch. 7.30. Right.

She drove to the high street, parked illegally on the double yellow lines outside Boots, emerged from the shop twenty minutes later with a shopping bag crammed with bottles and boxes. A month from now Barclaycard were going to scream at her but for now she couldn't care less. There was something, a smell, burning a hole in her memory; a chemical dance in her brain and the music made her jitter and bop. She had him, the man who had raped her; somewhere in the bag of boxes and bottles she *had him*.

She had Fitz to thank for that. He'd hurt her, yes, maybe beyond healing, but he'd also given her a second chance. A chance to nail the bastard who'd raped her.

She wasn't going to let him get away a second time.

8.00p.m.–8.30p.m.

Fitz caught up with Beck and Harriman in the Robin Hood. He knew they'd be there. He didn't want to talk to them. Not about Penhaligon. They wouldn't understand. He had no evidence. Nothing they would consider evidence, anyway. Their evidence was still in forensics. Beck would get that in the morning. For now Fitz just needed to allow the thoughts and feelings to percolate into the lower levels of his brain, let them mull for a while. To do that he needed alcohol. The problem was he had no money.

Harriman was buying a round. Fitz stood next to him at the bar, until the young detective noticed him, then pretended startlement.

'Sorry. Never recognised you with your clothes on.'

Harriman sighed. He reached into his pocket for some money.

Fitz pulled out his wallet, started to open it. 'Let me. My way of apologising.'

Harriman stared at Fitz. 'No, Fitz, that's OK,' he said at length. 'I was probably asking for it. Let me buy you one, eh?'

Fitz closed his empty wallet, grinning inwardly at how easily Harriman had fallen for his simple blag. 'Thanks. Scotch and dry. Double.'

Harriman nodded. Ordered Fitz's drink and his own, a rum and Coke.

Fitz nodded at the drinks. 'Had you figured for a whisky man.'

Harriman snapped his fingers. 'Right. Forgot.' He turned to the barmaid and ordered a whisky. 'For Jimmy.'

Fitz nodded.

Interesting.

8.30p.m.–9.00p.m.

Penhaligon lined the bottles up next to one another along the coffee table. She looked at them. Aftershave. All different. One of them was his. Fitz had let her remember. He had hurt her to let her remember. Hurt her badly. She mustn't allow that pain to go to waste.

She unscrewed the top of the first bottle. A few drops onto a tissue, under the nose, quickly before she had a chance to change her mind. A heartbeat, then *inhale*.

Is it him? No. Cap the bottle, dump it back in the bag. Try the next. And the next. And the next. Nothing.

A half hour passed. Still nothing. She had a break. Had a cup of coffee. Tried to relax. Impossible. He was here somewhere. His scent. His aftershave. *Him*. He was in this room, she knew it. She knew it.

Five minutes. She started again. A new bottle. Pop the cap, a few drops on a clean tissue. A deep breath. *What if it's him this time? How will I deal with it? What will I do then?*

She'd started with thirty-four different brands. There were now only five left. Five contestants in this game on

217

which she'd pinned her very sanity. Five finalists.

She picked up the first bottle.

Nothing.

The second.

Nothing.

The third, the fourth.

Nothing, nothing.

She stared at the last bottle.

What if I'm wrong? What if this isn't him? Oh God no. Not that. Please. Not after such pain. I'll go mad, I know I will.

She stared at the last bottle.

How can I not smell the aroma from this bottle? If I do and it's not him, I'll go mad. If it is I'll go mad. If I don't do it I'll wonder if it would have been him until I go mad.

She stared at the last bottle.

Either way I'm fucked. And it's down to you, Fitz.

She picked up the bottle.

9.00p.m.–9.30p.m.

When Fitz got home from the pub the message light on the answerphone was blinking. Fitz poured himself a drink, brought the glass back into the hall, pressed the button that played the tape.

He sipped his drink as the tape rewound. The burning whisky turned to ice in his throat when he recognised the voice on the tape, the fake Jamaican accent.

'*Doctor Fitzgerald, right? From the radio. I took your advice, man. Go to nineteen Stevenage Drive. You'll see what I mean. You'll see a woman in the bath. She's dead.*'

Fitz put down his drink.

The tape went on, '*You gave me advice man. You gave me advice. She's dead and it's down to you 'cos I took your advice.*'

'Christ. Oh Christ.'

The front door banged open and Mark breezed in. 'Any calls?'

218

'Shut up!'

The tape continued playing, now to an audience of two. *'It's life for rape. And life for murder. So what's the difference? And a smart arse like you, I've seen what a smart arse like you can do when you talk to these women. These profiles. So they're dying. They're dying and it's down to you.'*

'Christ. Oh Jesus. Oh Christ.'

The tape clicked as the message ended.

Mark was staring at him. 'It's a hoax, right?'

Numb with horror, Fitz ignored his son, reached for the phone, dialled.

'Get me DCI Wise. No, I don't care if he's gone for a shit in Shanghai! Just get him!'

9.30p.m.–10.00p.m.

Penhaligon held the bottle for all of ten seconds before making a break for the bathroom, leaving the bottle to fall, capless, to drench the carpet with the smell of *him*. A smell it would take her hours to remove.

She made it to the bathroom just in time, knelt beside the toilet and tried to retch, though by now there was nothing to come up. Nothing, that was, except another dose of memories. The flats. The playground. The swing. The dog barking. Memories of him. Of what he had done to her. Memories. All encapsulated in the smell from that one bottle. She didn't know the name, didn't need it. The smell would be etched on her mind for ever now.

She knelt beside the toilet and dry-heaved time after time, until her stomach was racked with cramps as bad as the previous night, pain that ran twice as deep because, despite the regression, the renewed fear and humiliation, despite all that, finding out which aftershave was his was almost entirely futile.

This particular brand must be used by a thousand men throughout Manchester.

She had the information she wanted, but neither she nor, she suspected, Fitz would have any idea what to do with it.

219

TEN

10.00p.m.–10.15p.m.

Afterwards it seemed incredible to Andrew Wiley that he spent so much time doing the ordinary things: feeding the cats, cleaning the coffee percolator, which someone (probably Connie) had allowed to boil dry hours before. And just wandering around the house, relishing the quiet now that Connie herself was sleeping over at her best friend Sarah's. Then again, Andrew was a neat man. He fussed a little, he knew that, but it was all for the best. He always said that, and Debra always agreed.

Now she would never agree with him again. Or disagree. Never argue, never make up, never cuddle, never make love, eat a meal, watch a video, go to the theatre, never do anything again. Ever.

Now, collapsed in the bathroom cradling his dead wife in his arms Andrew Wiley knew why the coffee percolator had boiled dry. Also why the back door was open a crack. And why none of the house lights had been on when he'd arrived home.

He stared around the bathroom, breathed in the smell of old piss as if that would bring her back. It wouldn't. Nothing would bring her back. He rocked her and kissed her. She was wet, her skin was slippery and her hair smelled of bubble bath. But she was cold. So cold. He kissed her again. Felt something inside his head rip loose and sail away on a mad midnight wind when her lips remained still and cold.

He knelt and cradled Debra in his arms and cried, and kissed her, and yelled at her because she'd left the bathroom

220

in such a mess, such an awful mess, it would take him ages, hours to clean it up and how could she be so selfish as to leave the bathroom in such a mess?

Debra didn't reply.

Water from her body drenched his suit.

The back door clattered lightly.

Somewhere a cat made an inquisitive, hungry, not-really-that-bothered-about-anything sort of noise.

She was cold. Wet. Bruised. There were cuts in her neck. Blood diluted by old steam on her shoulders and legs.

Andrew took her to the bedroom, swept the mess (who had left all these matchsticks here anyway, didn't anyone have any consideration at all?) onto the floor, laid her on the bed.

Halfway to the phone he began to wheeze. He made a grab for his briefcase, pulled the inhaler from it, sucked hard, once, twice, felt his heart pound as the Ventolin took effect.

By the time he had the asthma attack under control, the front door was opening all by itself and a bear of a man was pushing through the gap.

The man produced a police ID. 'DCI Wise, Anson Road police. You're Andrew Wiley?'

Andrew gasped. It was a bad attack. Eventually he forced out words. 'Up. Up. Stairs. My wife. Debra. She's –'

Dead! Oh God she's dead she's dead my wife is dead, Debra's dead oh dear God oh God what will I do? What will I tell Connie? What will I do now?

10.15p.m.–11.00p.m.

Fitz made sure the kitchen was empty of all police officers. Wiley could give a statement later. For now it was important that Fitz keep him steady. Because Andrew Wiley looked like a man who might just jump the rails big time somewhen very soon.

And Fitz knew exactly how he was feeling.

The clerk was sitting quite still. A black and white

fluffball of a cat wound itself deliberately around his ankles; he ignored the cat. He ignored the sounds from upstairs, the thumps, the sound of draining water, the dull voices from the police officers, the pathologist, forensics. Scene-of-crime men. Andrew Wiley was not a scene-of-crime man. He was just the victim's husband. He sat in the kitchen chair, at the kitchen table, ignoring the cat wrapping itself around his ankles, and said nothing. Instead he stared at a potato knife lying on the chopping board on the table between them.

Fitz saw the look. Knew what was going through Andrew Wiley's head.

'Impotence. Rage. Fear. Loss. Emptiness.'

No reaction.

'You're looking into the abyss and it's looking back with her eyes.'

No reaction.

'The rest of your life is that abyss. Empty without her.'

'Uh.' Not a word. A sound, half strangled, more like a choked-off sob.

'You can't run from it. It'll follow you wherever you go. It'll be with you wherever you go. And then it'll claim you too. And you'll be in it. You'll be dead.'

'Dead . . .'

'You have kids?'

'Connie. Sleeping over at Sarah's.' Andrew Wiley suddenly shivered. Fitz jumped, thinking for a second he was going to make a grab for the knife, but it was just a reaction to the cold.

'Connie always made such a mess. Such a mess. Debra worked night and day to keep the house nice. For visitors. For our friends, and Connie's.' Now tears did come, great racking sobs that shook the clerk's slight frame. 'I'm scared. Oh God I'm scared. I'm scared.'

And Fitz was right there with him. 'It's OK to feel scared. But you're not going to die. Debra's dead, but you're alive. Alive. You have to stay alive. For Connie.'

'Alive?'

The tremulous question told Fitz all he needed to know. He reached the knife a bare second before Wiley, snatched it away, put it back into the knife holder on the draining board while the clerk's fingers were still curling around thin air where the knife had been.

'Fitz.' He turned to see Wise standing in the doorway. 'Word in your ear, mate.'

Skelton came into the room, sat with Wiley while Fitz followed Wise into the hallway.

'What the hell do you think you're doing, Fitz? The man's wife has been murdered and you sit him at a table with a bleeding bread knife.'

'I had to find out if he was the type to develop suicidal tendencies.'

'Bollocks. This is the scene of one death. You want to make it two!'

'Frequently in cases like these, the urge to suicide remains buried. Sometimes for years. Ten years down the line he could have killed himself. Or others. I need to know if he's likely to do that now.'

'Jesus.'

'And it was a potato knife. I'm not entirely stupid.'

'Fitz. I reckon you must like playing God.'

'Yeah.' Fitz sighed. 'Got a fag?'

Wise shook his head. 'Trying to give up.' He glanced up the stairs to where the sound of a body bag being zipped up could faintly be heard. 'Bruising to the rear of the skull. Severe bruising around the throat, consistent with strangulation. Internal and external bruising to the vagina. A hell of a lot of water in her lungs. She's been raped, half strangled and drowned.'

Christ.

And Wise was staring at him now, staring at him as if he was some kind of organism, a germ caught underneath a powerful microscope. 'Did you have to go blabbing on the radio? "Look, everybody, look how clever I am, what a right bloody smartarse I am?" ' He took a breath. 'We're dealing with human beings, for God's sake. They've been hurt. One of them's been killed. But that's nothing to you. It's some kind of intellectual bloody game to you, just a chance to show off on the radio.'

Fitz sighed. 'Finished?'

'You are.'

And Wise turned to walk back upstairs, leaving Fitz alone. He wandered back into the kitchen. Andrew Wiley looked up from the kitchen chair. 'When will they finish upstairs?'

Fitz shrugged.

Skelton said, sympathetically, 'Probably not till tomorrow.'

'I'll need to use the bathroom.'

'Could you use next door's?'

'I suppose so. Will I have to sleep down here?'

'Is there nowhere else you could spend the night? Family? Friends?'

'I'll have to get Connie.'

'We can send a car if you give us the address.'

Fitz's mind greyed out then, the words washing over him and numbing him. He saw Andrew Wiley's expression and knew that Andrew wasn't asking where he could sleep, or go to the toilet. His voice rang as clearly in Fitz's head as the loudest church bell, and it said, *Why kill her? He didn't kill the others, so why kill her? Why kill my Debra?*

And to that Fitz had only one answer.

11.00p.m.–11.15p.m.

Fitz met Wise again on the way out, as the DCI was overseeing the movement of the zipped-up body of Debra Wiley into the mortuary van. He caught the DCI's gaze and held it, determined to get in a return salvo before the night was done. 'The man that did this. He's a young black male. He's got his own transport. He's physically and emotionally scarred. Left school at sixteen with no qualifications but he's bright. Very bright.'

And Wise rounded on him then, possibly the first time that Fitz had ever seen the DCI display real anger, anger directed at him. 'For Christ's sake, Fitz! A young, working-class black guy? That's the best you can come up with? It's a fucking myth, Fitz! A myth they exploded years ago! We're in the nineties now, not the middle ages. Open your eyes.'

Fitz spluttered.

'And besides. Penhaligon's seen the man and he's *white*.'

'All right, maybe she did see a man but –'

Wise let him get no further. 'I dunno, Fitz. A black guy, then two guys, one black, one white, what is this, some kind of multiple choice? Go home and get some sleep. You obviously need it.'

Fitz heard the contempt in his voice and finally it was all too much. Wise. Wiley. Penhaligon. *Him*. Too much.

He was on the point of walking out, away from the accusing stares and the guilt, right on the edge of surrender, when the rules of the game changed again.

Andrew Wiley's voice held him back. 'Doctor Fitzgerald. Wait. I've remembered something.'

11.15p.m.–11.30p.m.

Fitz turned, caught sight of Wise out of the corner of his eye. The DCI was turning as well, both of them moths to the clerk's flame.

'A man threatened me today. At work. I didn't take it seriously, of course, because things like that happen all the time in one form or another. You know. Unhappy people on the dole, looking for a way to vent their helplessness, their frustration and fear.'

'What was his name?' Fitz saw the moment, the truth, reached in to grab it with both hands.

He was rewarded as Wiley said, 'Malcolm. His name was Floyd Malcolm.'

And Fitz practically grabbed Wise around the waist and danced him around the lawn. 'Young. Black. Poor. Drives a cab.' He stared at Wise. 'And best of all: he's got previous. We've had him in already.'

Wise bit his lip, called Harriman out of the house as

Skelton took Andrew Wiley inside to take a full statement from him. Harriman ran, breathless from the house. He practically stood to attention before Wise. Fitz looked at him and mugged, his best *Thunderbirds* Parker: '*Hew rang, b'lidy?*'

Harriman looked at Fitz as if he were mad, switched his gaze to Wise. 'Boss?'

'Take statements from occupants in all the houses in this street and, oh I dunno, a couple either side. See if anyone saw a cab here today. See if we can get a match to the cab Floyd Malcolm drives.'

'Right, boss.' Taking a couple of uniformed constables, Harriman vanished into the night.

Fitz turned to Wise. The look on the DCI's face told Fitz he didn't need to say anything.

When Harriman returned half an hour later with a positive ID on the cab, Fitz was still grinning from ear to ear. Wise was right. He was playing a game. A game in which he'd just nailed himself some serious penalty time.

11.30p.m.–Midnight

Floyd got the call at fifteen minutes to twelve.

'Floyd. It's Helene. The police have picked up Wilson. Something about the cab. He told me to ring you. Are you OK, Floyd? What have the two of you got into now?'

But he was already muttering into the phone. Some nonsense. He slammed the receiver down, ran to his room, dressed hurriedly. As he left the room again, he heard sounds outside the door. His mother.

'Floyd. What's going on?'

Floyd ignored her, panic making his heart bang loudly in his ears, ran for the front door, yanked it open, blew out into the night.

His mother followed him as far as the porch, her voice rattling on, irritating. He ignored her. Made for the cab. Grabbed the toilet bag from the glove compartment.

The sound of cars at the end of the street made him look

226

up; the cab wasn't going anywhere – it was all he had been able to do to get it towed back here. He got out of the car, jumped the fence into the next door's garden, scooted down the alley between the houses, jumped the fence at the back, raced across a hundred yards of waste ground and scaled the fence that was supposed to prevent access to the railway lines.

He scrambled down the embankment, his mother's voice ringing protests and denials in his ears, lights coming on in houses all down the street. He ran alongside the tracks, ran north, as far as he could into the night, until the lights and sirens and the sound of his mother's voice faded into the wind and the hiss of grass against the tracks and his own laboured breathing.

Midnight–1.30a.m.

They took Wilson Parry back to Anson Road, placed him in a cell. As a prize he was a poor second. No-one was prejudging anything, but Jimmy Beck thought Parry was going to wash out. A big fat zero. He was Floyd's best mate, wasn't he? He was going to say nothing with a capital 'N'.

After typing up his preliminary notes, Beck clocked out and went home, where he made a meal, picked at it in front of the telly, watching with the sound turned down until the day's programming finished and the screen flooded with static.

He made a rollup. Lit up. Blew smoke at the screen.

Static fizzed out into the room, tiny points of light like frost glinting across the furniture, walls, stereo, mantelpiece. The static made a soft hiss, insidious, almost soothing. Jimmy Beck let the sound filter slowly into his mind, let it fill him up until there was no room left for memories. No room left for fear and guilt, no room for hatred.

Just the static.

Then he got up from the couch and he went to the Welsh dresser and opened the bottom drawer. Inside the drawer was his dad's gun. He got it out. Also in the drawer was a box of bullets. He loaded the gun. He went back to the sofa. The telly was still fizzing. He lit another rollup. He held the gun up in front of his face, between his eyes and the telly, let the metal and wood become a flat silhouette, focused past the gun, onto the screen. He blew smoke. Onto the gun, past it, to the telly.

After a while his arm began to ache. The gun was heavy. He turned it over, switched it to his other hand, held it again until his arm ached. This was no good. The gun was heavy. Too heavy. Too heavy to bear, certainly too heavy to carry. But what could he do with it? He couldn't put it down. What would happen then? It would be anyone's guess. Except he knew. He knew what would happen if he put the

guilt

gun down. Oh yes. He knew all right. Could see the faces, the accusation, the condemnation, the pity, the rage.

He changed hands again. Held the gun upright. Brought it a little closer to his face. Now he could smell the gun oil. His dad had kept this gun immaculately. It had saved his father's life once.

His arm was beginning to ache again. He blinked. The smoke and the fizzing static from the telly were making him tired. The meal he had cooked sat on his stomach like a greasy slick of oil on a puddle of rainwater. It shifted whenever he moved, rolled around inside him, slopped and slurped like something out of that old Steve McQueen film, what was it called? *The Blob*.

He picked up the phone. Weighed it in his left hand. Phone in the left. Gun in the right. Balanced. He looked from one to the other. Smoke from his rollup drifted up from the ashtray. He looked from the phone to the gun, back to the phone. He put the gun down. Dialled a number.

Picked the gun up.

Balanced again. All forces held in balance. Gun, phone. Phone, gun. Guilt, phone, gun.

The ringing tone.

My boss died a while ago. I don't really fit in without him. We were looking for a skinhead. I found one. But this man told me he had cancer.

The gun. The phone. A balance.

And because I felt sorry for him, I believed him. And he killed my boss. He killed my friend.

A balance. David was balanced. Across the kerb, back arched, stomach open to let the rain in, steaming in the drizzle.

Compassion, you see. I showed compassion. There's no place for it in my world. There's no place for me *in my world.*

The gun.

The phone.

A balance.

Then a click. 'Hello. This is the Samaritans. Please do not hang up. In a moment you will be given a phone number where you can contact the emergency –'

He slammed the phone down. A crash as loud as a gun shot.

And there was just the gun.

The balance was gone.

He looked at the gun. He smelt the gun. This gun had saved his father's life. His arm was aching. But he couldn't put it down. Couldn't put the

fear

gun down. Because he knew what would happen then.

He brought the gun closer. Closer. Turned it. Stared at the barrel, saw the gleam of oil, backlit by the telly, the tiny corkscrewing of the rifling inside the barrel, vanishing into the –

– darkness of his bedroom, where his father had taken him, had sat him on his knee, cuddled him, told him he was special, that he was Daddy's special boy, that he should be good and do what Daddy said, because Daddy was right, and Jimmy was Daddy's special boy and if Jimmy was good he'd get to go to the football on Saturday and Jimmy wanted that, because he'd never been before, because it was grown-up to go to the football, so if Jimmy did what Daddy wanted and –

– put the barrel of the gun against his head.

He put his finger on the trigger.

The phone rang.

He blinked, dropped the gun, heart banging in his chest. Fully expected it to go off, blow a smoking hole in the sofa, maybe shatter the telly, maybe even hit him, open an artery in his leg, leaving him bleeding to death.

Nothing. Just the phone.

The gun fell, landed on his dinner plate, splashed gravy across his trouser leg, lay there facing away from him, just a lump of metal and wood. Inert. A slice of carrot balanced across the trigger guard.

He looked at the phone. Picked it up. 'Hello?'

A voice, young, a bit embarrassed. 'Hey. Sorry, man. Wrong number, I guess.' A click and the line went dead.

Jimmy Beck sat quite still for a long time, his gaze switching from the phone to the gun and back again. The balance. Something was shifting the balance. Something was tilting.

He got up, walked to the mantelpiece. Took a match from the crib board there, the board which had belonged to David's murderer.

He lit the match. Let it burn a little. Blew it out. Placed it back into the board.

He didn't know if the match was for David, for Floyd, for her.

Or for himself.

He cleaned the gun. Unloaded it. Put it and the bullets away. Hit redial on the phone. There was a number he'd be needing. An emergency number. He thought he'd be needing it quite soon.

1.30a.m.–2.30a.m.

Twenty-four hours. It was such a short time, really, when you got right down to it. Twenty-four hours. A day. One three hundred and sixty-fifth part of a year. One twenty-six thousandth part of the average human life. A day. Such a short thing, really.

Jane Penhaligon sat on her sofa, staring at the telly and channel-hopping through the satellite stations, sat there and thought how funny it was that so much could be crammed into such a small thing. So much hurt. So much fear. So much humiliation.

She channel-hopped.

A sitcom. Sport. An old black-and-white movie. A chat show. A video show. More sport. A cartoon. The news. And adverts. Hundreds of adverts, electronic pulses that were blasted into her mind. That held her immobile and *penetrated* her.

She held the TV remote in one hand, a bottle of aftershave in the other. Aftershave, TV remote. TV remote, aftershave. A balance.

A balance she was going to change. Somehow.

She switched off the telly.

ELEVEN

8.00a.m.–9.00a.m.

They left Wilson in the trough until the next morning, then brought him to interview room one. Harriman was there. His first interview. Wise had let him go all the way since it had been his work that had confirmed the presence yesterday of Floyd's cab in the area of Andrew and Debra Wiley's home. Now Wise sat with Beck, a little to one side, and watched as Harriman switched on the tape deck and cautioned Wilson.

The interview began.

'Your name is Parry? Wilson Parry?' Not a hint of over-eagerness. That was good.

'Yeah.' Sullen. But cute. It was obvious from the outset this could go either way.

'You work for Trantor's Cabs?'

'Your point being?'

Harriman took the push with surprisingly little effort. With no inflection at all he said, 'There was a minicab seen. Yesterday. 2.45p.m. On Stevenage Drive. The description and registration number match that of the cab you share with Floyd Malcolm.'

'And?'

'Were you driving the cab, Mister Parry?'

'What, you mean yesterday? At 2.45p.m.?'

'Yes.' Patient. Good boy. 'That's exactly what I mean. Were you driving the cab yesterday, at 2.45p.m., when it was seen on Stevenage Drive?'

Wilson nodded ingenuously. 'Oh yeah.'

Harriman referred to his notebook. 'You went up and down?'

232

Wilson shrugged. 'Yeah.'

Harriman compared the answer to the facts recorded last night in his notebook, nodded thoughtfully. 'Why?'

Wilson smiled. 'Why do you go up and down any road in a cab? I was looking for number 202. Couldn't find it. Called in. I'd got it wrong. It was Stevenage *Road*.'

'I see.' Once again Harriman referred to his notebook. 'And what would you say if I were to tell you that I checked with the controller on duty at Trantor's Cabs and discovered that there were no recorded pickups for either Stevenage Drive or Road, or even Avenue last night. No pickups at all. Furthermore, there *was* a record, logged at 3.45 p.m. yesterday at Southfields police station, that you were, in fact, arrested and cautioned for picking up on the street – only one street away from Stevenage Drive. What would you say to that, Mister Parry?'

And Wise had to admit that Harriman had him there. Ice cold. Maybe the kid would work out after all. He exchanged glances with Beck. The older detective's expression was clear. *I suppose the promotion board must have seen* something *in him*. Wise grinned.

Wilson Parry said nothing.

Harriman referred to his notes and added, casually. 'We're investigating three rapes and a murder. A murder that took place on Stevenage Drive at 2.45 yesterday afternoon.'

Parry's face cracked then, first surprise, then alarm, as Harriman went on, 'So, Mister Parry. Three rapes and a murder and the evidence from your own mouth puts you in the right area at the right time for the worst of the lot.'

Wilson licked his lips. Glanced towards Wise and Beck. No help there.

Harriman waited in silence for Wilson Parry's response. It was a long time coming, but it was worth the wait.

'OK. I lied, all right? I lied. I didn't know it was anything to do with murder or rape. So I lied.'

'Why?'

'Because Floyd is my mate.'

'Brothers in arms?'

'And what is that supposed to mean?'

Harriman shook his head with a little supercilious grin. 'Nothing. Just, you know . . . cab drivers all together.'

Wise and Beck exchanged tiny grins at the implied slur.

Wilson Parry ignored it. 'I'm innocent.'

'Yet by your own admission you were driving the cab seen in the area at the time of a rape and murder.'

'I told you, I lied. I didn't rape anyone! I'll take any test you like! I didn't murder anyone either. I didn't murder her!'

Harriman smiled. 'Who said it was a woman that was murdered?'

'Well . . . I . . . You said there was a rape. You implied –'

Harriman was shaking his head. 'Men get raped too, Mister Parry. It's a fact.'

Wilson was getting more flustered by the minute. Wise said nothing. If Harriman got any better at this they'd be able to bootleg the tape.

'All right. Whatever. It was a man that was raped and murdered. I don't care. I didn't do it!'

Harriman's smile broadened into a grin. 'You haven't booked any holidays for the coming year have you?'

'No.' Puzzled. Confused. Oh Harriman was very good today.

'Good. Because you told me you were driving the cab, and that cab was seen outside a house where a woman was raped and murdered by a young black man.'

'Jesus.' Wilson licked his lips. Wise saw it all on his face. The fear. The anger. The helplessness. 'What'll I do?'

'About twenty-five years.' Now the grin was gone from Harriman's face. He was dead serious. Wilson knew it.

'I mean now. What do you want me to do now.'

'Tell us who was driving the cab.'

'It was Floyd. You bastards. It was Floyd.' And then it hit him. 'You knew that already didn't you? You never suspected me for a minute, did you? You just used me to confirm your own suspicions!'

'Thanks for your help, Mister Parry. It's appreciated.'

Harriman terminated the interview and switched off the

234

tape. When Wilson had been taken back to his cell, Wise and Beck exchanged grins.

Wise said. 'You been taking lessons while we weren't looking?'

All three laughed.

Harriman asked, 'What next?'

'Go and see how Fitz and Penhaligon are getting on with Floyd's mother, I suppose.'

Beck said, 'I'm going to Forensic. We're due the results of Penhaligon's tests about now. And this afternoon I'm due at the christening.'

Wise nodded. 'Bilborough's kid.'

'Ryan. Yeah.'

Harriman said, 'No, I mean what are we going to do about Wilson?'

Wise considered. 'Ah, let him stew. He'd only warn Floyd if we let him go.'

'Yeah, you know what it's like,' Beck sucked on his rollup. ' "All cab drivers together!" ' And he left the room, smoky laughter ringing in the hallway.

Harriman grabbed the tapes from the recorder and followed. As he followed Wise caught his eye and noticed that the lad seemed to be thinking the same thought: there was an edgy tone to Beck's laughter. A tone that seemed to cry out for attention. Ah well. That was Jimmy Beck for you; probably missed his shot of Irish this morning. It wouldn't kill him.

9.00a.m.–10.00a.m.

An hour with Sue Malcolm had shown Fitz he was going to have to use an unusually large array of weapons to get through her defences. Floyd's mother was a thoroughly determined woman, stubborn, pedantic, utterly convinced her son was as innocent of evil intention as the day he was born. She was wrong of course. Fitz was convinced of that, although he had no hard facts yet. But he would get them. The first thing to do was have Penhaligon soften her up a little.

Penhaligon had reported for work first thing this morning.

Wise had let her stay. In truth Fitz had taken one look at her face and thought to himself that Wise couldn't have kept her away with a bulldozer. As to how he himself felt about that, about her being here, well, he didn't really want to have to decide about that yet. But she was here. And he had an idea she was going to be useful right now.

'Tell us about your father,' Fitz said quietly.

Penhaligon knew what he wanted, he could see it in the sharp look she gave him. The look that said, *Don't be guilty of using me, Fitz, or you'll regret it.* Fitz clocked that look, ignored it. There was no time for niceties now. They were up against it. Time was the enemy now. And it was on Floyd's side.

Penhaligon took a breath, began to speak. 'Well. There was this time. I was about five, six. I'd been naughty. Cheeky. He smacked me round the back of my legs. My father had never hit me before.'

Oh no, Fitz thought. *Physical abuse was never his style was it? Not physical?*

'So I grinned. He was so angry you see, and I wanted the dad I knew, not this angry man, and that's why I grinned. But that just made him madder and he smacked me again. I cried then, which is what I should have done in the first place. Because he stopped then.'

For a couple of days, anyway. Fitz scowled. He could see the toll this was taking of her, knew he had to press on anyway. Because while the memory was eating into Penhaligon it was also having an effect on Sue Malcolm.

He nodded to Penhaligon to go on.

'Why am I telling you this? Because when that man was hurting me. Raping me. When that man was raping me, I grinned. I did it to make him like me, so he wouldn't hurt me as much. But he just hurt me even more. And it made me think of my dad. And the time he smacked my legs.'

Her story finished, Penhaligon fell silent. She wouldn't look at Fitz. Looked only at Sue Malcolm. And now their expressions were drawing closer, closer, twins joined by an umbilicus of painful memories.

Fitz let the silence that filled the room when Penhaligon

236

had finished speaking stretch out.

Eventually Sue Malcolm said, 'You want me to respond to that?'

Fitz lit up a high tar, blew smoke. 'If you want to.'

The response was anger. 'My son didn't rape you!'

Penhaligon's response was weariness. 'I know. The man who raped me was white.'

More anger from Sue Malcolm. 'Then why tell me the story?'

Fitz knew. And he knew she knew. But he told her anyway. 'Because your son has raped other women. He's put other women through that sort of trauma.'

'He hasn't!'

'You're sure?'

'Yes.'

'Positive?'

'Yes. Stop playing games with me.'

'Then tell us where he is.'

A sullen look. The anger subsiding beneath the surface, bubbling away under there, ready to smash through the surface at any moment.

'Mrs Malcolm, I could bring in a dozen rape victims. They'd all have stories like that to tell. The women that can't deal with it, that turn to drugs to escape, that inflict self-abuse to gain attention. The women that can deal with it who then have to deal with the secondary victimisations. The guilt from their friends and family. The blame laid at their door. And for what? Wearing the kind of clothes they wanted? For being the kind of person they wanted? These women – and men sometimes – are victimised for being themselves, and then victimised again afterwards by their loved ones who can't deal with the traumas themselves.'

Sue Malcolm bit her lip.

'Tell us where Floyd is. Please.'

Nothing.

'Please.'

'My son is innocent.' Stubborn, blind, the last hope.

Fitz pushed back. 'Stick your head in the sand, Mrs

Malcolm. Stick your head in the sand and hope the problem goes away. Well. It'll never go away. Not for me. Not for you. Not for Sergeant Penhaligon here. Not for all Floyd's victims.' A moment. 'All his future victims.'

'My son is innocent.'

'So what have you got to fear?'

'He's innocent. But he's mixed race. So being innocent isn't going to help.'

Fitz sighed. An old story. But true. True until now. 'Times are changing, Mrs Malcolm. It might have been like that once. It isn't now.' But in his heart Fitz knew that would only be true when the whole police force had been rebuilt from the ground up. There were still too many old-school coppers, the Jimmy Becks, those stuck in the rut of fighting fire with fire. And there would always be those who abused the power they had, the responsibility. Oh yes. Changes were coming, but far too slowly. Too slowly for Sue Malcolm to see, anyway.

He said, 'If Floyd's innocent, I'll prove it. I promise. If he's guilty we've got to catch him. Before he rapes again.' *Before he kills again.* 'You're not just helping us, Mrs Malcolm. You're helping Floyd. Because he's got to live with himself when all this is over.'

'Live with himself.' Her voice was hoarse with emotion, abrasive, practically a bark. 'You talk about him living with himself. Why would Floyd need to rape? He's got a lovely girlfriend. They've been going steady for months. Why would he need to rape?'

Fitz thought about that one for a moment. Actually it was a very good point. 'She's black?'

'Yes.' Anger.

'You're sure. Not white?'

'Yes. I'm sure.' Confusion now, overlaying the anger. She couldn't see where he was going. Well, that was OK, Fitz wasn't entirely sure he knew where he was going himself. Yet. But he would. Very soon. He could feel something stirring here, some tension in the air. Tension from her, fizzing out into the air like electricity before a storm.

It was going to be a big storm.

He sucked hard on his high tar, stubbed the butt out in the ashtray. 'You think you're protecting Floyd?'

A sharp look. If she was protecting him, she knew he didn't want or need her protection.

He went on, free-associating now, lightning speed, letting the words come to him unbidden, using them, making them work for him, letting his subconscious take over the show. 'Because I don't. I think you're protecting yourself.'

Another sharp look. A narrowing of the eyes. Tension in the set of the body. All right. Let's home in on this fear a little. 'It can't be very nice to know that this . . . this *monster* came out of your womb.'

Sue Malcolm bit her lip hard enough to draw blood.

'I'm sorry. Did that hurt you?'

'You're not sorry.' Cold, her voice dripping with contempt. But laced with fear. Because Fitz had nailed the truth, and she knew it.

'Suppose I said that monsters aren't born, Mrs Malcolm. They're made. Would that hurt you even more?'

'You know it would, you smug bastard.'

The words were carefully if tearfully articulated, but Fitz heard something else. *You know it would you smug white bastard.* He filed the knowledge for later use, pursued his original line of thought instead. 'Because who makes a child into a monster? The person with most influence over him. And who is that person? His mother.'

'Yes.' How much hurt was there in that one simple word? Fitz couldn't even begin to guess.

'It's bullshit. Every killer, every rapist in the world, Mrs Malcolm, they all blame their mothers. And they're all talking bullshit. Floyd's father was Jamaican?'

'Yes.'

'He left you when Floyd was very young?'

'Yes.'

'You raised Floyd on your own?'

'Yes.'

'You did the best job you know how. The best a mother

239

could. Took any work to pay the bills, to keep food on the table, to ensure he had a good education.'

'Yes. Yes, yes!'

'Then it's not your fault, is it?'

'No.'

'I don't blame you. Society doesn't blame you. *You've done nothing wrong.*'

'No.'

'And yet every time you're with him you see it in his eyes. The accusation. "I blame you. I blame *you*, Mum." '

'Yes.'

'So you blame yourself.'

'Yes.'

'Even though you know you've done nothing wrong.'

'Yes!'

Fitz let the moment freewheel away into silence, lit up another high tar. Across the room Penhaligon was tense, her body rigid, her lips compressed to a thin line. Was he hurting her with his words as much as he was hurting Sue Malcolm? It didn't matter, nothing mattered except the truth. The truth was here, it was here in this room, and he was going to have it.

'Where's the scar?'

'What?'

'I think the man we're looking for is scarred. Hence the mask. If Floyd's not scarred, he's not the man we're after. That's good news isn't it?'

'*For crying out loud, don't play games with me!*'

Fitz said nothing. Inwardly he was jumping up and down and waving a winner's cup over his head.

After a moment Sue Malcolm asked for a cigarette. Fitz handed her one, lit it for her. Another little connection there. She was crumbling and fast. Maybe he wouldn't need the tapes after all.

'I haven't smoked in three years,'

Fitz nodded sympathetically. 'Don't inhale, then.'

And she stubbed the cigarette out. 'I can't.' Fitz had a bad moment then, reached into his pocket for the tapes, but she was only referring to the cigarette.

'How did it happen?'

'He got in a bath when he was eleven.'

'Scalded?'

'Scalded I could live with.' She took a breath. 'Have you got kids?'

'Boy and a girl.'

'Both still at home?'

'Yes.'

'Your son wants to be like you?'

'Right now he just wants to kill me. But there was a time when he wanted to be like me, yes.'

'Floyd wanted to be like me.' She looked at Penhaligon, who returned her gaze neutrally. 'So he sat in a bath of bleach when he was eleven years old.'

Christ. Jackpot.

'Your child has an accident. That's bad enough. The guilt. The pain. But your son locks himself in the bathroom, sits in bleach, deliberately sits in bleach, and you see what he's done to himself, and he's screaming and you're screaming and he looks at you and then later, as the anaesthetic's beginning to work, as they're taking him away to theatre, he looks at you and says, "I just wanted to be like you, Mum. Just like you." '

And suddenly she was crying, the release of tension in the room overpowering, a storm, one Fitz had controlled, directed. And the lightning struck dead centre, exactly where he wanted. 'Floyd's got a friend. Gerry. Gambier Road. If he's anywhere, that's where he'll be.'

'Thank you.' Fitz was sincere. He shot a glance at Penhaligon. She'd approve. They were one step nearer catching the rapist now. Penhaligon wouldn't look at him. And of all the emotions churning across her face the most obvious was anger. He knew who that anger was directed against.

He walked over to her, tried to speak. *I'm doing it all for you. Oh, we need to catch this guy, but I'm doing it for you.*

Somehow the words wouldn't come. She waited a moment, then took Sue Malcolm from the interview room. Fitz moved after her, but was waylaid by Harriman. 'Fitz.

241

Phone. I think it's your wife,' he added in an overloud conspiratorial whisper.

Fitz glanced at him, forced a grin. 'Thanks.' *A whole bunch.* He tried to catch Penhaligon's eye, but she was gone.

10.00a.m.–10.30a.m.

Floyd was in the shower. Singing. He didn't know why he was singing. Maybe because it was out now, all the stuff inside, spilled out into the light of day, and he was happy about that. But he was sick too, it made him feel sick. Because when you got right down to it, there wasn't a whole lot to really like about himself, was there? A boy should love his mother. Love her, respect her, care for her, as she had cared for him.

Should never hate her.

Well that was OK for normal people.

Floyd looked at his reflection in the steamy glass of the shower. Looked at the scars. The scars his mother had caused. Caused by being white. And the song he was singing changed timbre, became deeper, slower.

'When You're in Love with a Beautiful Woman'.

Mother.

Scars.

Fear.

Pain.

Humiliation.

Mother.

The door to the shower opened quietly. No fuss, no bother. Floyd turned, startled. A bear of a man faced him. A man he recognised even before he held out a police ID.

And he stopped singing. Watched Wise's face change from smugness to horror at the sight of Floyd's legs. A moment then back to the smug grin. The annoying grin. The grin that said, *Got you mate, bang to rights.*

And Wise said, 'Do you do requests?'

TWELVE

10.30a.m.–11.00a.m.

While Wise supervised the search for Floyd, Fitz blagged a ride home in one of the pool cars. By the time he reached home the fact of the call, the fact that *she'd* called, was echoing inside his mind like a shout in a cavern, multiplying, reflecting, sending millions of little clones of itself bouncing around his head. She'd called. Judith had called. She was at home. She had something to tell him. Would he come now?

He had half a mind to laugh, a Vincent Price laugh, *you've made your bed, my dear*, a mad cackle before throwing down the phone and cutting her off.

While you're at it, he thought, why don't you book a one-way ticket to Australia? Both were equally likely.

He didn't laugh. He didn't throw the phone down. He listened. And then he came home.

Mark met him at the door. His son wore a somewhat dazed look. But he was grinning. In Fitz's book the two didn't sit easily together. 'Been on the spliffy again have we, son?'

Mark's grin just widened. 'Mum's in the front room. You're gonna need a drink.'

And he did. A bloody large one.

Judith was five months pregnant.

'I'll spare you the arithmetic,' she said by way of greeting. 'It's yours.'

243

Jimmy Beck stubbed out his rollup and walked into Saint Luke's. The turnout for Ryan's christening was . . . he looked around. It was disturbing.

The church was full of people. People who were friends and family to David and Catriona. Each one brought back the memory. David jack-knifed across the kerb. Stomach open. Steaming in the drizzle.

Catriona was by the font, with the priest. He was splashing baby Ryan's face with holy water. As if that would save him from a fascist's size elevens, a knife wielded with intent to kill.

Beck shivered. The ceremony was over quickly, for which he was thankful.

It ended on a light note from the priest. Taking a lighted candle from a nearby stand he handed it to Beck. Beck looked at it, totally bemused.

'It's a symbol, Jimmy. You're to make sure Ryan sees the light.'

The light dying in his eyes, in David's eyes, jack-knifed across the kerb, stomach open and blood everywhere –

'Supports City, not United.'

Beck managed a noncommittal reply. A gentle wave of
blood
laughter rippled around him
like drizzle pouring into his stomach and
Jimmy Beck clutched the candle, wrenched himself back to the present with an effort. The ripple of laughter faded. Both Catriona and the priest were looking hard at him.

The priest smiled. 'I think our Jimmy's a bit overcome with the moment.' That provoked another gentle round of laughter. 'Traditionally the emotional scene is supposed to be the woman's job.'

'What?' The word snapped out before Beck could stop himself. Then, 'Ah, sorry. Don't go to church much. I'm a bit nervous.'

'Aren't we all in the sight of the Lord?'

And, thankfully, to that the priest seemed to require no answer.

The priest took the candle back from Jimmy ('Before you set fire to the nave') and finished the service. 'Ryan, go in peace and the Lord go with you.'

A round of Amens.

After the service Beck stood with Catriona while the friends and family made the ritual congratulations. He was silent for a long time.

Catriona said, eventually, 'He looks like David, doesn't he?'

Beck forced a smile. *Not quite, Catriona, no. It's the intestines. They're still in the right place.* 'He's the image of him. Does it help?'

'Yes.' A moment of silence. A tear, poised on her cheek. 'Oh yes, Jimmy, it helps. It really does. I don't know what I'd do without him.'

Beck could understand that. He took a breath. There was something he had to say. He had to say it now, while the impulse was there. Before he buried it again, squashed it back inside, controlled it. The truth wanted out, wanted out now.

'There's something I've got to tell you.'

Catriona looked up then, but it was too late. Control had re-established. The truth was gone. The guilt was back. 'I miss him.' Self-consciously Beck wiped moisture from his cheeks. 'I miss him so much.'

And Catriona was there, sympathy, strength, understanding. 'I miss him too, Jimmy. And . . . I dream about him. That helps too.'

And Beck gathered himself then, felt himself stiffening away from her sympathy. Because the truth was back again, bubbling up from inside, carried on a tide of guilt, and the truth was that he, too, dreamed about David Bilborough, friend and boss.

But his dreams were nightmares . . .

Twenty years of marriage. Eighteen years as a practising psychologist. Neither of these things prepared Fitz for the state he now found himself in: fatherhood. Third time around. No. This was going to take some getting used to.

A flood of emotion raced through him. He could have quantified each one; something inside stopped him, something told him now wasn't the time. That same voice said, *Now's the time for holding, for loving, for welcoming back into the fold, for forgiving.*

'I need a drink.'

'You just had one.'

'I need another one. I need lots.'

Judith smiled. Just a hint of the old Judith, the woman he'd fallen in love with all those years ago, the woman he now found himself confronting on an emotional level he never thought to reach again.

'Allow me.'

He took the drink she offered, felt the warmth of her fingers touch his, and that broke the moment, shattered it into a million glittering fragments, each a reflection of her face. Judith when they'd first met, bright with the fervour of women's rights, Judith when they'd married, still bright, a little puzzled, as if to say, *Was that really me that just said, 'I do'?* Judith when Mark was born, exhausted, terrified, agonised, but oh, the wonder there. The pain and the wonder. And Katie. The same. And now it was going to happen again. The pain and the wonder were back. She was back. Oh God. She was back she was back she was –

'Judith.' The drink went onto the dresser, forgotten in the moment. Moments. 'I've missed you so much.'

'Me too.'

And then he was holding her, her body pushing against him, familiar yet strange, something extra in there. A boy or a girl. His child. Their child.

'Fitz. Sit down before you fall down. And finish your drink. You look like you need it.'

The next hour or so passed in a blissful daze. Mark had the sense to stay out of the way. Katie was in her room, rearranging a cupboard full of furry gorillas and pinning up the *Twin Peaks* and Nirvana posters. Fitz talked rubbish. He blathered. He grinned. He glowed. He had no idea how to deal with the situation and for once didn't care.

The first thing he remembered with any clarity was Judith asking him if he was pleased.

He nodded, unable for the moment to remember a suitably over-the-top film quote.

She nodded. 'Pleased about the baby? Or pleased that I've come back.'

'Both.'

She looked at him, and something of her rosiness faded, to be replaced with concern. 'You think we're too old. I'm too old.'

'I don't.'

Judith thought this through. He could see the gears working inside her head. She wasn't as fazed as he was about the pregnancy. Then again she'd had five months – well, four months – longer than him to get used to the idea. It suddenly occurred to him that she'd waited to tell him until the chance of a safe abortion was long past. He wondered if that was deliberate, calculated, or if she really had been uncertain about his reaction for so long?

'No,' he said again, more firmly. 'Turtles can do it, so can we.'

Judith smiled, another little hint, just a shade of the old Judith there. 'I love it when you lie. You think your best quality's your honesty. It isn't. I love it when you're kind enough to lie.'

And Fitz couldn't help thinking how many people would disagree with her on that. One in particular.

'I'll get my bags from the car.'

'Let Mark do it.'

'He's out, Fitz. Family isn't his scene, remember?'

'Then I'll do it. You're pregnant.'

'Fitz. I've got the equivalent of a seven-pound penalty in

247

here.' She patted her bulging midriff lightly. 'I'm still at the bottom of the handicap compared to you.'

Fitz grinned. 'Where did you learn that language?'

'Wouldn't you like to know.'

Fitz shook his head. 'I dunno. My wife walks back into my life. Tells me she's pregnant. Tells me it's mine.' He shook his head. 'I need a fag.'

Judith's smile faded. 'No smoking Fitz. Not until the baby comes. Promise me?'

Fitz shrugged. Put the high tar back in the packet without lighting it. 'I treated a guy who'd packed it in. He found it easy – except after sex with the wife. A massive craving then. I told him: "Smoke. Three a year won't hurt." '

Laughing, they went to get Judith's cases from the car.

1.00p.m.–1.30p.m.

They were still laughing five minutes later when Penhaligon's car pulled across the drive. Judith saw Penhaligon as she got out of the car. Fitz looked quickly from his wife to the detective, registered the looks on their faces, began to get an idea of the depths of the hole he'd dug for himself. A hole he knew he was going to find it all but impossible to climb out of.

Judith smiled, 'Jane, isn't it?'

Penhaligon nodded. Looked at Judith. Looked at Fitz.

Oh Jane, don't do this to me, not now, not that look. What have I done? I can't help it if she's come home now! I thought we were done, I thought it was over. I'm just as confused as you are!

'Would you like a drink?'

Penhaligon shook her head. 'We've got Floyd. I'll wait in the car.' She shot a quick, somewhat insincere grin at Judith as she turned. 'Congratulations.'

Judith nodded. Grabbed a suitcase, headed back into the house. Helplessly Fitz followed.

He followed her through the hall and into the lounge, where she dumped the suitcase. 'Mark can take it up later.'

Fitz hesitated. 'Um. Do you mind? I have to go back to the station.'

And Judith hit him with the look then, the old look that had become so familiar in the months and weeks before their break-up. The look that said, *Don't mess with me Fitz, I deserve better than that.*

And she did, of course, that was the killer.

Judith said, 'You're screwing her.' No question. Simple fact.

There was no question of his lying. 'I was.'

Until the day before yesterday. Now she's been raped and you've come back and you're pregnant with my child and suddenly I don't know what to think or do any more!

'Mark knows?'

'Yes.'

'So it's been here. In our bed. The bed we made our baby in.'

And that was enough for Fitz. All his confusion and fear, all his humiliation, his pain all came out then, came out as anger, and he pushed back. 'Our house? You were selling our bloody house, Judith!'

'She's young.'

'Yes.'

'Beautiful.'

'Yes.' Fitz sighed. ' "Is her father alive?" No. "Am I a father substitute?" Probably. You get a four-eyed wanky therapist, I get a sex bomb, is that fair? No. "Will it last?" No. "Am I flattered?" Yes, yes, yes.' He smiled coldly. 'Have I missed one?'

He had of course, and Judith knew it. 'Do you love her?'

And to that, Fitz had no answer he could give.

1.30p.m.–2.00p.m.

Rain dappled the windscreen of Penhaligon's car as she pulled away from the kerb, grew quickly to a torrent as she accelerated sharply away.

'In training for NASA, are we?' Keep it light. There may

still be a way through.

No response.

'The shuttle pilots only have to go seven miles a second. You've got them all beat.'

He looked at her. Willed her to respond. A smile, a look, anything. But there was nothing. No sign. No give.

He sighed. 'I'm sorry. I'm sorry you found out that way. But it was as much of a surprise to me as you.'

She didn't answer, merely cranked the speed up a notch.

'Please. Let me explain.'

She switched the radio on. Loud, drowning out the rain blatting against the windscreen. She changed gear. The speedo crept higher.

'Can you slow down a bit? I'm allergic to crashes. I come out in lumps.'

A touch of her foot and the car leapt forward, accelerating again.

'Panhandle, please. I don't *know* what to do!'

And then she did look at him.

'For God's sake look where you're going!'

She glanced back then, for a moment, as if to make sure the road was where she'd last seen it, then switched off the windscreen wipers. The road vanished behind a wall of water. She smiled. She was playing with him.

'I've seen this one before. You're angry. You're taking out your anger on me. You want to scare me. You want some control back. I understand that. But you can't control anything from a hospital bed and that's where we'll both end up if you don't *switch the bloody wipers on and watch where you're going!*'

And, still smiling, she switched the wipers on.

The road ahead was clear.

Fitz breathed a sigh of relief.

The rest of the drive to Anson Road was completed in silence.

Penhaligon parked the car, turned to Fitz. 'What are you going to do?'

'About Judith?'

'Yes.'

'I said. I don't know.'

'That means you'll do nothing.' The contempt in her voice was every bit as damning as the look in Judith's face had been.

And Fitz was well and truly stuck on that one. Because she was right. He knew it, and saw that she did too.

'Now will you get out so I can lock up, please?'

THIRTEEN

2.00p.m.–4.00p.m.

Floyd was brought into the interview room by PC Skelton. Fitz studied them for a moment, both young, both black, so similar, yet so far apart. A balance. To Fitz that balance, that *neatness* was almost beautiful.

Penhaligon brought Floyd forward and sat him down. Fitz took out a high tar, offered one to Floyd. Nothing. He lit up.

'My name's Fitz.' He offered his hand. Floyd took it. Cool one. Going to take a lot of digging to loosen this guy up.

Floyd's hand was warm, dry. Not a hint of nervousness. He smiled. 'I've heard you on the radio.'

'I know.' A little dig. Just to establish the ground rules. 'You phoned me.'

Floyd shook his head. 'Not me.'

Fitz shrugged. 'I suppose they introduced you to DS Penhaligon.'

Floyd looked at her, extended his hand. She wouldn't take it, shot Fitz a look that said, *Stop playing games.*

Fitz ignored the look. 'And this is PC Skelton.'

Floyd glanced dismissively at the black constable. Skelton remained totally impassive, the complete professional. Fitz respected that self-control, wondered how hard it was for Skelton to resist rising to that sort of bait.

'Sit down.' Another ground rule. 'I'm in charge here.'

Floyd gave a little half smile. 'Sure, man.' He sat. Another little glance at Penhaligon as he did so.

Fitz clocked the glance. *Interesting. Maybe even useful.* Looking at Floyd he said, 'I don't think you two are going to hit it off.'

252

Neither Floyd nor Penhaligon responded to that one. Ah well. Time enough to probe old wounds later. For now it was time to rub salt in a more recent one.

He looked at Floyd. Held his gaze. 'I've met your mother.'

Nothing. No response at all. 'Yeah?'

'She's white.'

That got a reaction. Feigned surprise. 'Yeah, tell me about it.'

Fitz stayed silent, sucked on his high tar, blew smoke.

Floyd frowned. 'She's white. So what?'

Interesting. I wonder how far we can take this. Fitz stayed quiet. Tapped ash from his high tar into the ashtray.

'So what?'

OK, the record was wearing a little thin now. Time for another push. 'I was wrong about you, Floyd. I said you'd be scarred. You wear a mask so the mask has to be better than the face God gave you. But I'm wrong. You've quite a nice face.'

Floyd smiled. No cracks in the dam yet. 'Thank you.'

'But it's black.'

That got a reaction. A narrowing of the eyes. Fear? Anger? Hatred? Oh yes. All of those. Fitz could feel the heat, saw it churning in there, behind those bland eyes. Felt it, wanted it. Needed it.

A moment, then the flash of heat was gone. Controlled. Fitz wondered for how long.

Floyd said, 'You've noticed.'

'Is that why you wear a mask, Floyd? To hide your black face?'

And Floyd smiled then. 'Look. What is all this about a mask? I don't wear one. I don't need one. OK?'

As God is my witness, I swear he could be innocent. 'I wasn't far wrong though, was I Floyd? You are scarred.'

'Am I?'

'You sat in a bath of bleach as a child.'

Again a flash of heat. Fitz saw it, linked it in Floyd's head to the word *mother*.

Floyd said, 'It's a birthmark.'

Fitz laughed out loud. 'A career on stage is indicated. I didn't realise you were a comedian, Floyd.'

But Floyd wasn't laughing, wasn't even smiling, and Fitz saw the heat building, felt it fizzing out into the room, began to circle it, looking for an opening, a weak spot, a way through to the truth.

'Were there fat boys at school?'

'What?'

'The school you went to. Were there any fat boys?' A look. A push. Careful blandness in Floyd's eyes, but underneath it, was that bewilderment? A touch of confusion? 'Fat boys, Floyd? Layers of white flesh? Why didn't they pick on them, the bullies, the hard boys? They were fat, they could diet, they could do something about it. Not you. Not you Floyd. You were black. Nothing you could do about the colour of your skin.'

Floyd swallowed hard. Fitz was reaching him. Time for another push. Draw a connection. 'You felt that. I know you felt that. Because I was that fat boy. I heard black boys say it: "Pick on someone else; pick on the fat boy." I know what it's like. I know where that kind of pressure leads. It leads to fear, and hatred, and guilt, Floyd. And it leads to people like you sitting in baths of bleach.'

Floyd blinked. Fitz's words were blows. He could dodge one, maybe two, but eventually they would tell. Already he seemed unsteady, as if he might tumble from his chair. His gaze roamed restlessly around the room, avoiding Penhaligon, latching aggressively onto Skelton for a long moment, raking past the clock, the tape deck and back, inevitably, to Fitz.

Fitz waited until he had Floyd's attention then pushed again, harder this time. 'What kind of society is it that drives a young boy into a bath of bleach? What kind of sick, twisted society is it? Eh, Floyd? What kind of society is it?'

And Fitz got his answer.

'White.' Floyd was trembling as he pronounced the word. 'Sick, twisted, *white* society.' And the heat was blooming

254

inside him now, seeking an outlet, fizzing out into the room like static before a storm, and having no other outlet, Floyd stood and he stared. He stared at Skelton, and all of his rage was in that stare, all his fear, his anger.

Skelton took it, soaked it up, said nothing. Said nothing even when Floyd pressed the point, nodding in turn to Fitz and Penhaligon and saying bitterly, 'He's Tarzan, she's Jane. What's that make you?'

Skelton said nothing, merely stared at Floyd, unflinchingly, until he sat down again.

And Fitz felt it was time for another dig, a proper push, the first proper push of the day. 'How does it feel, stalking a victim?'

'How would I know?'

How indeed. Aloud, Fitz said, 'We'll talk about *him.* He's out there right now, stalking a victim. How does he feel?' Fitz snapped the last words out, a command to which Floyd responded.

'I haven't got a clue.'

Fitz smiled, lit up another high tar. 'We're talking hypothetically, Floyd. What are you frightened of?'

'Nothing.' Arrogance. Aggression. But underneath . . . underneath . . . Fitz could feel the fear, fuelling that heat in Floyd, that heat still looking for an outlet.

'So he's out there, stalking a victim. How does he feel?'

Floyd shrugged, feigned indifference. 'Bit of a commando maybe.'

Fitz pounced on the analogy. 'Bit of a commando. Battle of wits, maybe?'

'Yeah.'

'He sees her, watching him. He thinks she's leading him on, teasing him. She wants it really. And she's gonna get it, the cheeky bitch, stringing him along like that? Yes?' Again the last word snapped out, a command, demanding a response from Floyd.

'Possibly.'

Fitz sighed. 'Why does he do it?'

'He's black?'

'Yes!' *At last.*

But Floyd was up again, up again and moving this time. Circling the room to confront Skelton directly. 'Why does he do it?'

Skelton remained perfectly still.

Penhaligon glanced at Fitz. *Should this be happening?*

Fitz shook his head, a tiny movement. *Let it run.*

Floyd pressed the point to Skelton. 'You think he's letting the side down. This rapist is letting the side down. He's black and you think he's letting the side down.'

That was enough for Skelton. 'Sit down.'

But Floyd hadn't finished yet. 'All that sucking up to your white friends. It's all wasted because a big black man's come along and raped their women.'

'Sit *down.*'

And Floyd did sit. Stared directly at Fitz and said, 'What do you dread most? You and every other white man? Your nice white wife getting raped by a big black man.' Floyd leaned back in his chair, emulating Fitz for a moment. 'It's a racist myth. I know it. PC Plod over there knows it. But it's there, isn't it? In your head. And in your heart too. And maybe that's why he does it.'

'So he rapes white women as revenge against white men for inventing the myth of the black rapist?' Fitz blew out his cheeks. 'Sociologically speaking, that's a big mouthful to bite off before lunch.'

'Too big for you, eh, mister white psychologist? Too big because you'd have to reinvent yourself, devise new myths, new things to be scared of.'

Fitz sucked on his high tar, tapped ash into the ashtray. 'Why be scared of anything?'

Floyd couldn't answer that except with mute anger, the heat building steadily now.

'So.' Fitz took out his glasses, placed them on his nose, peered over them at Floyd. 'He rapes white women as some kind of revenge against white men?'

'Possibly.'

Fitz shrugged. 'Well it's that or he's queer. Something to

prove. You know the form.'

'No!' Floyd's answer was too fast, too sharp. Fitz saw that and went on, 'I've got a patient, you see, Floyd. He can only make love to other men's wives. Single, unattached women, can't do it. Can't get it up. Married? And it's wham bam thank you ma'am.'

Fitz sighed. Affecting tiredness, as if the words were the punchline to an old, old joke, he said, 'Likes to do it in the other guy's house, on the other guy's carpet. Wash himself down in the other guy's shower. He's screwing the other guy.' Fitz found his gaze held. Let it happen. Let the words come.

'I'm not gay.'

'Who's talking about you?' Fitz sucked on his high tar. 'We were speaking hypothetically as far as I remember.'

Floyd frowned. 'Is my lawyer here yet?'

But Fitz was away on a new angle. ' "He rapes white women as a revenge against white men." There's a problem with that, though, isn't there? He's raped a black woman too.'

'No he hasn't.'

Again, too sharp with the answer. Fitz had Floyd on the run now, coming down the last stretch. 'Two years ago. Bernadette. He dragged her into a stream afterwards. Why should he do that? I reckon he was just practising, perfecting his technique.'

'Possibly.'

'You know what that tells me, Floyd? This is a man who despises the colour of his own skin.'

A reaction from Floyd. A spark of heat in the eyes. It was coming now, Fitz could feel it, his words fanning the anger into rage, wanted the explosion.

'He thinks a black woman's nothing. Just something to practise on. A white woman. That's the ultimate prize.'

'No. That's what you think. That's what the police think. He raped black women because the police don't bother if the victim's black. You're looking for a man who's proud of his colour.'

257

Fitz closed his eyes for a moment, opened them, fixed Floyd with a tired stare. 'Two things, Floyd. Firstly, your information regarding the police is way out of date. That's not you speaking. It's someone else.'

'Yeah, right.' Contempt. Anger and contempt. And . . . perhaps just a hint of . . . what? Resignation? Had he scored a point there? 'And secondly?'

'And secondly . . . you said "Women".'

'What?'

'You said "black women". So Bernadette wasn't the only one. Was she?'

Floyd folded his arms and looked away, said nothing.

'And you said we're looking for a man who's proud of his colour?'

'Yeah!'

'Like you?'

'Yeah!' A moment then, a moment when Floyd saw the trap, but it was too late; he'd started to fall and he knew it. 'Not me. Someone like me.'

And Fitz knew he was close. So close he could feel the heat spilling out from Floyd in sick waves, flowing across the desk making little ripples in the smoke from his cigarette. He glanced at Penhaligon, held her gaze for a heartbeat. *I'm doing it for you. All for you.*

'And you've always been proud to be black?'

'What do you want me to say? Yeah. Course I have!'

'Even when you sat in a bath of bleach?' And Fitz grinned then, grinned inwardly because Floyd's reaction was the first wedge in the door, the first chink in the armour, and he could see the truth in there, squirming, desperate to escape, but he'd have it, he'd have it yet. 'OK, you've rationalised it. It was racism. White society put you in that bath, but at the time, Floyd, at the time you despised the colour of your own skin.' The truth. A moment to let it sink in. 'You were not to blame. They made you feel like that. I understand that. But you can't forget it, can you? Because it's left those scars. A permanent reminder. And who sees those scars, Floyd? *Every woman you ever sleep with.*'

Floyd reeled from the words. Fitz saw the effect his verbal blows were having and decided it was time to change the angle of attack. 'How did we find you, hm? At Gerry's. How did we find you?'

'I don't know.'

'Your mother told us where you'd be.'

Floyd licked his lips. 'Yeah?'

'Why do you think she did that, Floyd? For your sake? No. You won't accept that. I know what you're thinking. I know what's going on in here.' And Fitz reached across the table and tapped Floyd on the temple.

Floyd flinched away from Fitz's outstretched hand. 'She told you 'cos she's white. That's what I'm thinking. That's what's going on in here. This guy's raping white women. Women like her. So she turns me in. When it comes down to it, it's her colour. Even before her own son, it's her colour. White.'

And Fitz slid forward in his seat, let his voice notch upwards a little, building the tension, fuelling the fire in Floyd's head. 'And now it all fits in, doesn't it, Floyd? You come home from school, the taunts ringing in your ears; the bath of bleach is ready, but there's your mother, this white woman, pretending to love you, but how can she love you, Floyd, when even you despise yourself? She's a lying bitch, Floyd. A lying bitch –'

'– is right! A lying bitch is right.' And there was a moment then, a moment of utter helplessness, utter hopelessness, when Fitz thought he might have pushed Floyd too far. But no. Like a good fighter he was up for the last round, the final round. ' "Wait till your father gets home." She's white. She can twist my father round her little finger. He gets home. She starts acting. Performing. She's giving it everything she's got because she wants him to hit me. And he hits me. But it's not enough. She carries on. Makes what I've done ten times as bad. All that energy and it's just to get my father to hit me again and again. And he does. He hits me again. It's why he left us. He couldn't stand the manipulation. The pain. The humiliation.'

'I understand your anger.'

'*You understand nothing!*' Floyd spat out the words contemptuously. 'You're white.'

'I'm not talking to a black man, Floyd. I'm talking to a killer. And I understand killers. I understand the anger that drives a man to kill.'

And Floyd had it, darted in with the punch line. 'Because you can kill.'

Fitz nodded.

'But you can never be black.'

Fitz thought fast. There must be no hesitation now. He was so close. 'OK. I can never understand a black killer.' Quickly, before he recovers: 'A black killer like you, Floyd.'

Floyd said nothing.

Fitz said, 'We haven't told them, Floyd. The husbands. We haven't told them we've picked up a black man. We know what that'll do to them. Victims of their own mythology. The pain they'll feel. The fear. But that's the point, isn't it? You want them to know. So you have to confess. Then we can tell them. Then they can know the fear and pain. The same fear and pain they inflicted on you. Confess and your revenge will be complete.'

And Floyd was falling, crumbling inwards, arms on the table, all arrogance, all brashness gone, just pain and fear and terrible loneliness left to outline a face running with tears.

And Fitz pushed again. 'Tell me you did it, Floyd. Because it's important for those white men to know it was you, it was Floyd Malcolm, a black man, who raped their women. To know that the myth we've fostered for years, white men like me, has suddenly come true *where it was never true before.*'

And that did it. Floyd looked at him then and Fitz saw that look on his face, that look of inner peace overlaying the anger, the look that said, *You're right. I did it. I confess.*

He began to speak.

The door opened and Wise came in. 'Your lawyer's here.'

And Floyd was up and heading for the door, a triumphant grin etched over his tears, and the moment was gone, shattered, the trap was sprung but the prey gone and Fitz practically yelled aloud with frustration, because that heat for which he had dug so carefully, so diligently, for which he had exposed so many raw nerves of his own, and others, had got away. The truth had got away, the pain, the fear, the rage, got away and buried itself back inside this man, this killer, where it was now able to wait a chance to emerge again. Rape again. Kill again.

Fitz didn't know where or when, but sensed it would be soon.

Very soon.

4.00p.m.–4.30p.m.

They followed Floyd and Barbara Charles to the custody desk, where she oversaw the return of Floyd's personal possessions. His anger was a living thing, fizzing out into the room, filling it, spilling over, nowhere else to go but out, out, somewhere, anywhere, just *out*.

Floyd picked up his tobacco, cigarette papers and lighter. He stared at Fitz. 'All those innocent people banged up. No bloody wonder. It's down to you. To arrogant white bastards like you.'

Skelton handed him a fistful of change. Floyd counted it. Still looking at Fitz. 'You don't give a shit about the truth. You just want to show off in front of everyone. In front of *her*.' A nod towards Penhaligon.

Skelton handed Floyd his wallet.

'You're white, I'm black. You're clever, I'm thick. You're nothing but a racist. An arrogant bloody racist.'

Floyd looked away then, to check his wallet at Barbara Charles's urging. He signed for his things.

The outer door opened and Sue Malcolm entered. 'Floyd? I've got a cab.'

Floyd gave her a look of such contempt and hatred that she gasped and lurched backwards away from him, and that just fuelled the anger. 'You can keep your cab, you scheming white bitch!'

And Floyd walked out of the police station.

Sue Malcolm spared Fitz a single agonised glance and followed her son.

There was a moment of silence. Barbara Charles turned to follow her client. As she did she glanced at Penhaligon. 'Something on your mind?'

Penhaligon said nothing. And Barbara Charles said nothing either. But Fitz knew what she was thinking, the words that would articulate her own anger, words that she could never speak: *I'm black first, a woman second, OK?*

And to Fitz that was the most terrible, the most tragic thing of all.

4.30p.m.–4.35p.m.

Fitz stumped into Wise's office.

'I was this close. *This* close!'

'So was I, Fitz. To a bloody lawsuit. We had no ID. No forensic. Wilson Parry admitted to driving the car . . . You don't mess around with a lawyer like Barbara Charles. She talked to the Chief Super, for God's sake!'

But Fitz wasn't listening. And he knew that Wise was thinking exactly the same way. 'All that anger, that rage. It'll have to come out somewhere.'

And when it does, it's down to me.

FOURTEEN

4.35p.m.–5.00p.m.

Penhaligon stopped Fitz with a look as he came out of Wise's office. She wasn't sure why she did it; the duty room was brimful with officers, every one of whom would be able to hear any exchange. She did it anyway, stopped him, wanted the confrontation, needed it.

Fitz saw that she did, too, she could see the understanding on his face, just one more layer on a mask of confused emotion. She faced him as he closed the door to Wise's office, tried to guide her to one side, away from the centre of the room. She refused to be guided.

He sighed. 'What can I say?'

She thought, *It's perfect. I don't know what I want you to say, you don't know what you want to say. We're a perfect match.*

'I didn't know she was pregnant. It was as big a shock to me as to you.'

Penhaligon smiled, a chilling expression. She felt him back away from it, in his head, if not in person. 'Old story, Fitz. Seem to have heard it before somewhere.'

She could see Fitz knew she was pushing, but couldn't seem to fathom why. She wasn't so sure she knew herself.

He said, 'I've slept with her once in the last six months. Made two dirty phone calls mind you, but I don't count those.'

Christ, Fitz, do you think you're funny? Do you think I'm funny? That what's happened to me is funny?

'It doesn't matter.'

And Fitz took that as a sign to continue. 'You're right

263

when you say I'll do nothing. But I'll do nothing because I don't *know* what to do.'

Of course you don't. You never think beyond the next game, the next cheap thrill.

'I never meant –'

'– to hurt me? To hurt Judith?' And then she had it, clear as daylight. The simple fact was that he was paying more attention to the case than he was to her. More attention to anything, to anyone than to her. Because he couldn't deal with it. 'It doesn't matter, Fitz. Nothing matters now. Nothing compares to the fact. The fact that I've been raped.'

And she saw the truth emerging from the gestalt of emotion running riot across his face. Saw it for just a moment before leaving him in the duty room amidst a crowd of carefully neutral faces.

5.00p.m.–5.30p.m.

Coffee. I need coffee.

The canteen was on the ground floor. She took the lift. The lift stopped on the second floor and the doors opened to reveal Jimmy Beck. They faced each other for a moment, then he turned away. Something about his face provoked a reaction in Penhaligon. Oh God. Today was the christening. She'd forgotten. She'd missed it. Something else to feel guilty about.

A moment before the doors slid shut, Penhaligon ran out of the lift. She caught up with Beck on the stairwell.

'Jimmy?'

He ignored her, kept moving up the stairwell. Late afternoon sun shone through dusty glass panels, illuminating everything in a flat grey light. Grainy. Like a television picture.

'Jimmy, wait. It was the christening. Right?'

He turned then, looked at her with something akin to hatred. 'It's Bilborough. Catriona says she dreams about him. I felt like saying, "I have nightmares, love. And in every one of them he's blaming me. He's bleeding to death and he's blaming me." '

Beck licked his lips. The look on his face changed, swept through a whole range of emotions, fear, guilt, pain, back to anger, back to *rage*.

He spoke the words she still remembered clearly from the afternoon on which David Bilborough died. ' "I want you to get this bastard, Jimmy. For me and Catriona. Get this bastard." '

And Beck was down then, collapsed onto the bare concrete stairs, his face crumpling and his eyes filling with tears, down and sobbing, the rage coming off him in a wash, fizzing out into the stairwell, flooding her, pushing her away.

She resisted it, came closer, put her arm out to him.

'Jimmy . . .'

'Everyone knows. They blame me. I know they do.'

And then she had it. Clear as the daylight filtering in through the dusty windows.

'I didn't tell anyone.' The words came quietly, but inside she felt her own anger rising. Beck had fucked up. He'd fucked up big time – and she'd covered for him. That made her guilty by association. But it was useless anyway. There had been upwards of a dozen people in the incident room when she'd called the hospital to check the ID of Beck's suspect, found out that he'd been given a false name. By then of course, it was too late. Bilborough was already dying in the gutter of a lonely surburban street, miles from Anson Road, miles from any possibility of help.

'Oh Jimmy . . .' Penhaligon felt her heart go out to Beck. Stubborn prick though he was, his heart was in the right place. He'd shown compassion and made a mistake. A mistake she thought he'd be repaying for a long time to come.

She reached out to him, drew him closer, a moment of compassion. A moment of shared guilt.

And then she smelt it. The aftershave. *His* aftershave –
– was Beck's aftershave.

And in one moment reality corkscrewed away from her, left her teetering on the brink of madness, swaying on the concrete stairwell.

Beck reached out to her, his offer of help hopelessly late as his voice dopplered downwards into the bass register.

She blinked. A moment in reality but an eternity in her head *where she was on her hands and knees in the mud with her skirt and tights around her ankles and* him *inside her, pushing, pushing, and she was smiling,* smiling *up at him so that he wouldn't hurt her any more, but he was pushing, just pushing against her, inside her, again and again, hurting her,* raping *her* –

And then the blink was over. Her eyes were open. Reality snapped back into sharp focus. And he was there in front of her. On his knees. On the stairs. Right there in front of her. And in her mind there was not the slightest doubt that Jimmy Beck was the man who had raped her.

A moment.

Grey light through dusty glass.

Motes of dust swirling in the light, tiny particles of dirt and skin and *the smell of his aftershave*.

A moment to consider the hopelessness of the past, the futility of the future.

A moment of surprise. Shock. Incomprehension. Disbelief.

Then the moment ended and it all turned to rage.

'How could you do it? How could you fucking do it, Jimmy? You bastard. You bastard. How could you do it?' And she was screaming at him now, hurling the words at him as if they were jagged pieces of broken glass, to hurt, to maim and kill, to do to him what he'd done to her, and her words became an incoherent scream of anger, pain, humiliation, and she ran at him, charged up the steps, brought her fist across his cheek in a savage blow that had him reeling. 'Bastard! You bastard you *bastard!*'

Another moment, one moment filled by his voice, too calm, no surprise, loaded with resignation. He'd expected this. He wanted this. 'We'll have the boss in. If you're accusing me of rape, we'll have the boss in. Then I'll take any test you want. DNA, anything. But we'll have this out in front of the boss. Right?'

The rage was bubbling out of her now, fizzing out into the

stairwell, so thick she couldn't see straight or think straight. With a tremendous effort she controlled the rage. Squashed it down inside her. Turned to go, to leave him there, unable to look at him, not for fear of what he might do to her but of what she might do to him.

5.30p.m.–6.00p.m.

Wise was bollocking Harriman and Skelton when she entered his office without knocking.

'The wrong man? I told you to follow Floyd and you, you walking pair of bloody brain donors, you tell me you spent quarter of a bloody hour following the wrong bloody man?'

'They swapped clothes, sir. In the house. They must have done.'

'Gormless pillocks. Check his cab. No, forget that. It was damaged. Check all stolen vehicles. He won't rape without transport. And send officers to the addresses of all his rape victims. The mood Floyd's in he's not gonna waste time stalking a victim. And talk to his mate. Find out what Floyd's wearing now. Check this guy's ashtrays, check his bloody electric meter, do him for something, teach him a lesson. Christ! Just get back out there and find him, OK? Just get out of my sight the pair of you.'

Wise looked at Penhaligon as Harriman and Skelton left the office. 'Yes, Jane. What is it?' He interrupted himself to shout after Harriman, 'And get someone round to his mother's!' He turned back to Penhaligon, gave a token apology. 'Sorry, Jane.' He thought for a moment. 'Look, sit down will you?'

'Sir, there's something I have to –'

Wise shook his head impatiently. 'Sit down. I've got something to tell you.'

She sat.

'I've got the lab report. From your examination.'

'And?'

'The slides are blank. Every one of them.'

The bastard.

'I don't believe it.'

Wise sighed. 'There's two explanations. One there's been a mistake. Two, no rape took place.'

She looked at him then, saw her own rage mirrored in his eyes.

'All right. You were raped. In that case there's been a mistake.'

A sick feeling was growing inside. 'Who sent the swabs off? Who collected them?'

Wise scanned the evidence label. 'The last signature on here belongs to –'

'Jimmy Beck.' Her voice was cold, full of anger. Even Wise noticed it.

He looked up. 'Beck's an experienced man. He wouldn't make a mistake like this with evidence.'

'He made a mistake like it with a suspect, though, didn't he, sir? A mistake that resulted in DCI Bilborough's death!'

Wise really studied her now. 'You think Beck raped you?' It was clear from his voice that he in no way considered the thought far-fetched.

Penhaligon frowned, surprised at Wise's perceptivity. 'Yes, sir. I do. He smokes, drinks whisky, uses the right kind of aftershave. And he handled the swabs.'

Wise considered. 'That's not evidence.'

'He saw me get into your car with my hand in a plastic bag. He said nothing! He drove straight to Belle Vale.'

'He'd been there before, to collect Helen Robins. You went together.'

'Yes, but sir, he could have destroyed the evidence at the site.'

Wise stood. This was serious. Penhaligon could tell he didn't like what he was about to say. 'That's not evidence. You get me evidence and I'll do him –'

Yes!

'– if you fancy life as a traffic warden.'

The words hit her like a punch. 'I beg your pardon, sir?'

Now Wise turned, as full of anger as she was, anger at himself, at the system. 'Do I have to spell it out?'

'Yes, sir. I've been raped. Yes, you have to bloody well spell it out.'

'Jimmy Beck's been on the force for years. OK, he's a little old, OK, he's a little hard, OK he can be a bit of a prick. But as a general rule he gets results. The high-ups like results. So they like Jimmy Beck. You follow me?'

Oh yes. 'I'll be the one who sent him down.'

'Yeah.'

'I can live with that.'

'Maybe so. Your mates can't. If they're on their own with you, you might start screaming rape again. It's a load of bollocks, yeah, but that's what they're gonna think. Take it from me, love, and I've been on the job longer than Santa Claus.'

She tried to speak then, but nothing would come. After a minute, she managed to choke out a few words. 'What am I supposed to do then?'

'You want my honest opinion?'

'Yeah.'

'Jane. You're a bloody good copper. You're better than Beck, you're better than nine tenths of the people I've worked with. You're special. You're going to have a special career, assholes notwithstanding. You don't want to jeopardise that career. So my advice to you is *do nothing.* Put it behind you. Put it down to experience. Write it off. Whatever you need to do to get past it. Whatever it takes. Just let it go.'

And that was the last straw. She stood abruptly, turned to leave. The room wobbled around her, a heat haze, a mirage. Rage. All she knew was rage. The bastards. The utter, arrogant male bastard pricks. How could they do this to her? To her?

She turned at the doorway, spoke in a controlled, icy voice. 'You want evidence? I'll get it. I'm going to see him done. If you won't help me, I'll do it on my own.'

She had heard the truth in Wise's words, but chosen to ignore it. The truth was no longer a factor in the equation that was Jane Penhaligon, Detective Sergeant in the

Manchester CID and victim of premeditated rape.

No truth. Only anger.

Only rage.

6.00p.m.–6.30p.m.

Fitz got Wise to authorise his use of a pool car and had himself driven to the Malcolms' address. Now he stood with WPC Lewis and waited for his impatient knocking to be answered.

The front door opened. Sue Malcolm peered at him over the security chain. Her face was streaked with tears she hadn't bothered to wipe away. 'What do you want?' Her voice was bitter, abrasive, edged with a mixture of fear and guilt.

'Can we come in?' An ingenuous smile. Keep it light. Just a little push, no more, not yet.

Sue Malcolm shook her head. 'No you bloody well can't. Don't you think you've caused enough harm already?'

Stay patient. 'Mrs Malcolm, we need your help.'

'I've helped you all I can and my son *despises* me for it. You had me convinced, do you know that? You even had *me* convinced he was guilty. Well he's not. You've asked him all your questions. You've played all your games. And you've still had to let him go. So *why don't you just leave us alone?*'

She should have slammed the door then, ended the conversation with the final word. She didn't; she held Fitz's gaze a heartbeat longer than necessary. For Fitz that was enough. Already he was turning her words over in his mind, flensing them away to reveal the meat, the subtext, the truth. And then he had it, and it was time for the push. 'You don't believe a word of that. Floyd doesn't despise you because you helped me to accuse him, falsely or otherwise. He despises you because you're white.'

'*And whose fault is that!*' It wasn't a question, simply an articulation of her fear and pain, her humiliation, her guilt.

Fitz smiled inwardly. He had pushed; she was toppling. 'Mrs Malcolm, I think you're in danger.'

270

'From who?' Too fast. The question came too fast. She already knew the answer.

'I think Floyd wants to hurt you.'

'He's my *son*.' Again that almost strangled outrush of emotion.

And Fitz had her. 'That's why he wants to hurt you.'

And she did close the door then, a final slam that rattled the frame, left Fitz and WPC Lewis exchanging tired smiles.

Fitz waited. A few minutes passed. The door opened.

'Did he tell you that?'

The moment. 'He didn't need to.'

She let them in then. Unhooked the chain, closed the door behind them, ushered them into the sitting room in a daze of social programming. 'Tea? Coffee?'

'Do you have anything stronger?'

She shook her head.

Lewis accepted a cup of tea. Fitz abstained.

Ten minutes later she was settled in the front room; as settled as anyone can be who is beginning to believe their son may be a rapist and killer.

Fitz watched her indirectly as she sipped at a cup of tea. 'Tell me about Floyd.'

'He's my middle kid. Bev's older, Marvin's younger. They're fine. They were all fine. Even when Den left us. Until Floyd was fourteen. Oh, there was the usual stuff. Taunts at school, that sort of stuff. Bullying. Even when he was little, eight, nine. Some of the kids wouldn't play with Floyd, wouldn't do activities with him. I think one time they were supposed to all hold hands. Tell each other about themselves.'

Fitz nodded. 'A group exercise. Tied strengthening.'

'Whatever. A couple of the other kids wouldn't hold Floyd's hand.'

'The white ones?'

Sue Malcolm uttered a short humourless laugh. 'That's a bit naïve. Floyd was mixed race. I was white, his dad was black. Floyd was both. Everyone hated him. And do you know why?'

'Because their parents hated you?'

She nodded.

'Hated you for daring to break the rules. Their rules. For daring to love.'

She nodded again, lost in memories. 'It all changed of course, when Floyd was eleven. He stopped telling people his mother was white when he started secondary school. He kept me secret, put me in a closet. Then he was only bullied by white kids.' Another sip of tea. 'As he grew older he got militant. Put on this Jamaican accent. Black was great; white was suspect. But I wouldn't call him black. I wouldn't call any of my kids black. They're mixed race. I call them black and I deny my part in making them, my white part. That was OK for the others, Bev and Marvin. Not Floyd.'

Fitz nodded. 'And the scars?'

'That happened in first year secondary. Floyd was the youngest in his class. He was only eleven. Only eleven!' She rubbed her face; Fitz could sense she was holding back more tears. He waited. Eventually she continued, 'He discovers black pride. That was Gerry, that was. And Wilson. They both got him into it.'

And Fitz was ahead of her, the mental gears churning forward implacably, 'Discovers black pride, embraces it, all the fervour of the religious convert. But he's got those scars. Once upon a time those white boys made him despise himself. And those scars mean he can never forget it. Never heal.' He tapped the side of his head. 'Never heal up here.'

'Yes.'

'So it's the other part of himself he despises now. The white part. Your part.'

'Yes.' And now Fitz could sense something more than guilt in Sue Malcolm's voice. Anger. Bubbling under the surface. Waiting to spill out, pushing him back.

'Did you talk about it?'

'I tried. I couldn't. He wouldn't.' She hesitated, the anger bubbled a little closer to the surface.

Fitz let it come. 'Mrs Malcolm. We need your help. Can you think of anyone Floyd had a grudge against? White

272

men? Teachers? People he was at school with? People at work? People in authority?'

And she was looking at him now, and he saw her anger for what it was, rooted in fear and directed at himself. Rage at himself. Because he was white. And then she said the words. And he knew.

'He hated a lot of people, Doctor Fitzgerald. White authority figures. People like you, Doctor Fitzgerald. People like you.'

He knew then. Began to shake.

You're in the book.

Floyd knew his phone number. That meant Floyd knew his address. What was it Floyd had said to Andrew Wiley on the day he'd murdered his wife?

I know where you live.

He'd said that and then *he'd raped and murdered Andrew Wiley's wife.*

Sue Malcolm was saying, 'I was everything to Floyd. Everything that a mother could be. But I wasn't black.' And her voice was altering now, stretching to let the anger out, the rage, but Fitz had gone beyond the moment, was racing ahead, racing to escape a blinding rage of his own.

I know where you live.

Without asking, he picked up the phone, dialled his home number. He was shaking, ignoring the curious looks from Sue Malcolm and WPC Lewis.

She's fine. Judith's fine. The baby's fine.

Fitz let the phone ring for two minutes but there was no reply.

He put the phone down, turned to Lewis, his words tumbling out in a confused torrent. 'Floyd. Judith. My house. Floyd's at my house. *For God's sake use your bloody radio!'*

And he was heading for the door at a run, that fat-boy waddle he'd had no call to use since the age of twelve; running, awash with guilt and fear of his own, emotions that changed as he ran, as he thought of what he might find at home, through anger to a deep, searing rage.

FIFTEEN

If anyone had asked her afterwards Jane Penhaligon would have had to say that it was anger that made her do it. No. Not anger, it was more than that. It was rage, like an unquenchable thirst that drove her on.

To smash the window beside the door. To reach in, spring the lock. To come into his rooms, his flat. To penetrate him.

The flat was unremarkable. A typical bachelor pad. Maybe a little neater than some she'd seen. One curiosity was the crib board on the mantelpiece. The matches. Six burnt now. Six dead. She knew instantly where the board came from, wondered who the extra matches represented in his mind, wondered if one of them was supposed to be her.

She touched the board, no fear of leaving prints; she wore gloves. New leather gloves. She lifted the board, examined it closely. Put it back on the mantel. Moved around the rest of the flat, examined things.

Beck had still been at the station when she'd left. Confused. Frightened. And Fitz. He'd been there too. A sympathetic look. She'd clocked that look, seen how quickly he'd hidden it; stay neutral, she'll respect you then. Well she wasn't going to wear it. She had her own problems to worry about now. No time any more for Fitz, for the mind games he played. Oh no. Now it was about her. Her and Jimmy Beck. It was about revenge. It was about regaining control.

But most of all it was about rage.

She went through the rest of the flat like a professional. Drawers open, contents out on the floor. Under the bed, in the bed. Kitchen cupboards, old cardboard boxes, wardrobes, all yielded to her anger.

She found what she was looking for in less than ten minutes.

Nestled in the bottom drawer of the bedside table; a pair of black leather gloves. One still had a price label curled up inside it.

The bathroom cabinet yielded a half-empty bottle of aftershave. The right aftershave. *His* aftershave.

The kitchen had a rack full of knives. Any one could have been the weapon he used to terrify her into submission.

No hood though. Perhaps he'd got rid of it.

She emptied the kitchen bin onto the floor.

Nothing.

She went back into the living room. Something about that old Welsh dresser beckoned her. It was dark wood, chipped slightly, a family relic. She tried to remember if Jimmy had any family. She knew he wasn't married; that had failed years ago. But what about parents, brothers, sisters? She didn't know. She opened the drawers one by one, pulled out the contents. Cutlery. Napkins. Place mats. One drawer full of pens and pencils, another with a leather box containing two medals. One for long service in the Manchester Met, one a decoration for conspicuous valour. The box was covered in dust; hadn't been opened in years.

She found the gun in the bottom drawer.

It was old. From the war. A service revolver. She wondered if it had ever saved anyone's life. She held the gun up. It was heavy. She pointed it at the mirror hanging over the mantelpiece. Aimed at her own reflection. Held it there until her arm began to ache.

The door to the flat opened. She turned then, saw a body silhouetted in the doorway. A silhouette she recognised. A man. Him.

She pointed the gun at the figure in the doorway.

6.45p.m.–7.00p.m.

Jimmy Beck left his smashed car beside the battered VW Microbus in the high street. Walked away from the irate

275

drivers, the screaming passengers. What did they know? Who gave a fuck anyway? It wasn't important any more.

He walked slowly, weaving. He walked in the road. Other drivers avoided him with angry shouts and blasts on horns. He ignored them all. They sped around him, yelling abuse, only to be forced to stop a hundred yards further up the road, where it was blocked by the jammed-together mass of his car and the Microbus.

He walked, blood running from his cheek where he'd cut it on the steering wheel. As he walked he replayed the conversation of the night before. The conversation he'd been thinking of when he'd put the car into neutral and let it simply roll from the side road into the rush-hour traffic streaming along the high street.

'My boss died a while ago. I don't fit in without him.'

'You were fond of him?'

'What's that mean? Was I fond of him? Of course I was fond of him. He was my boss. He was my mate. It was my fault he died. I showed a bit of compassion, you see. And there's no room for compassion in my job. My job's full of women. Full of rape counsellors. Full of Victim Support counsellors. And I want to shout at the lot of 'em. Tell 'em to forget it. To get back to the old ways. Because compassion only gets you killed.'

There had been a silence then. A thoughtful pause. Then the voice had asked, *'Is there anything else you want to tell me?'*

'What do you mean? Anything else I want to tell you? Like what?'

'Sometimes it's hard to talk. Sometimes a recent trauma can trigger memories of an older experience. If that happens the memory can be as distressing as the original event.'

'What are you saying? What are you trying to get me to say?'

'Nothing.' Quickly. *'I just thought –'*

'Aye, well that's what I did. And look where it got me.'

And he'd put down the phone.

The words echoed in his head as he walked.

He walked home. He opened the door and entered the flat. A cup of tea. Better yet a whisky. A whisky and then bed. A long sleep. Maybe a week off sick. Get his head together. Get his life together.

Then he saw the intruder. The woman. It was *her*. Penhaligon. She had the gun. His dad's gun. She pointed it at him.

7.00p.m.–7.15p.m.

She pointed the gun at him. It was heavy. It hurt her arm, and she didn't like that. But she couldn't put it down. Not while she had control. But she could put it down if she pulled the trigger. Then she would be able to put the gun down and still retain control. Just pull the trigger. That was all. Aim it at him and pull the trigger. The trigger.

But she couldn't.

The rage told her to, screamed at her to, begged her to. But she was stronger than the rage.

For the time being.

'Come in, Jimmy.'

He came.

'Shut the door.'

Mesmerised by the gun, Beck did as he was told.

'Get down. On the floor. On your back.'

He did it.

She looked at him. The gun was even heavier. Her arm aching even more. 'It's heavy, you see. So heavy. This gun. This burden. This burden you've put on me, Jimmy. If you're on the floor I don't have to hold the gun up so high. My arm doesn't hurt so much. I'm not quite so inclined to pull the trigger.'

He made a noise. Not words, an inarticulate moan. A mixture of fear, anger, other emotions she couldn't identify, didn't care about.

She lowered her arm. Pointed the gun at him. The moan stopped.

'You let me hold you. On the stairs, at the station. You let me comfort you, feel sympathy for you. All the time you

277

knew. You'd done that to me and you knew.' She began to shake. 'You're dead, Jimmy.'

Another moan. A reflexive jerking away from her, from the gun.

'You're dead inside.' She saw his fear, felt it fizzing out into the room. 'Sorry. Did I scare you? Never mind. This'll make you feel better.'

She knelt astride his hips, lowered herself onto him. He writhed, the fear blossoming into terror. She rode him like that, rode his fear, controlled it, pushed it, pushed him.

She put the gun against his lips. 'Open up, there's a good boy.'

He couldn't. He was too scared. She prised his mouth open with the gun barrel. Pushed it inside. Felt it click against his teeth. His eyes were rolling back, jittering around in their sockets. Terror made them do that. He was off the edge. Off the edge and falling.

'Suck it.'

He mumbled pathetically, began to choke. Then he began to shake. Then to spasm. The gun rocked in his mouth. She felt her finger bounce on and off the trigger. That quiet *tick-tick* of the pad of her finger hitting the metal trigger should have terrified him into submission, but he was beyond it, gone away somewhere inside.

A memory? A memory of penetration, of raping her?

The rage surged in her, as Beck surged beneath her. She felt his fear through the bones of her legs, felt it jitter into her own nervous system, juice up her brain. And she was frying too, like a junkie in terminal OD, like an experimental animal, skull open and bucking against the electrodes, frying, fizzing, screeching like some kind of animal, joined together at some fundamental level with Jimmy Beck as beneath her, the detective –

7.15p.m.–7.25p.m.

– pulled down his trousers and lay down like Daddy said on the bed and let Daddy push just there, just a little bit and then a little bit more, and then a *little bit more* then he'd get to go to the football because he was Daddy's special boy and Daddy loved him and if he just let Daddy push him and push him and push and push and –

7.25p.m.–7.30p.m.

– pushing against her, heaving, thrashing against her, hard enough to bruise, and as he jerked and thrashed he mumbled words past the barrel of the gun clacking against his teeth.

'Dad. No. Football. No. Please. Dad. No.'

Wrong words. Wrong word. *Dad*. It triggered her own anger.

Father. Rape. Father. Smile. Rape. Smile. Father. Rage.

And then it was over, like *that*, and he was still, and the words came clearly past the gun barrel, clearly because she didn't just hear them, she felt them, she *lived* them.

'You and me. We're the same. Jane. We're the same. *I've been raped too.*'

But they were too late, those words. Too late by a second and a lifetime. Because the rage was already loose in her. And it was the controlling force now.

In a moment of savage clarity she realised she didn't know if the gun was loaded or not.

She decided it was probably time to find out.

She pulled the trigger.

279

SIXTEEN

6.30p.m.–6.45p.m.

If anyone had asked Floyd afterwards why he killed her, he would have had to say it was down to the anger. The rage. Rage at his mother, his white mother. White society. Rage at Fitz. White, middle-class, alcoholic, gambler and headfuck supreme. Oh yes. Rage at Doctor Edward Fitzgerald of 14 Locksley Road, Southfields, Manchester. And by implication, of course, rage at Fitz's wife, Judith.

He torched the stolen car at the end of the street. Set light to his cigarette packet and stuffed it under the petrol cap. On an afterthought he stuffed his cigarettes in there too. He wouldn't be needing them any more. And then he was off. The explosion blew windows out a hundred yards away, set light to a nearby hibiscus.

It didn't even scratch the roaring in his head.

He ran round the back and into Fitz's house through the open back door while Judith was peering over the front garden hedge, gawping with the rest of the neighbours.

He recce'd the house. A bit of a commando. The thrill of the chase. The house was empty. The stereo was on in the lounge. Radio Four. He shook his head. That was no good. Switched it to Black FM. Jittered to the beat until he heard the front door swing open, then closed, heard her come into the lounge.

He turned. She was there. He showed her the knife. He took her as she turned to run, pressed the knife to her neck, breathed in her scent, whispered to her as she struggled in his arms.

'Be still or dead, man. Your choice.'

Her brain screamed gibberish. The trees. The trees were on fire. The Slatterlys' hibiscus was burning. Had she left the fridge open? Was that the phone ringing? Who switched channels on the radio?

She felt herself jerk as he reached out with one foot and kicked the door shut. Felt herself fill with rage. 'Get out of my house.'

'You raise your voice and you're dead.'

'Take your hands off me and get out of my house right now.' Stay calm. Let the anger come out in the voice. He'll hear that. Hear it and go. He'll go if you tell him to.

He didn't go. He laughed. Then he began to sing. 'When You're in Love with a Beautiful Woman.'

She began to shake. That was no good. He'd feel that. Feel her trembling. Know she was scared. That would give him what he wanted. Power. Power over her.

She felt the knife press harder against her throat. The cold sting was more irritating than painful, a wound she couldn't get at, a scab she wanted to scratch off.

'Get out of my house!'

He stopped singing then. 'Rich middle-class white bitch. Used to getting her own way. And here's some uppity nigger. Well, she'll soon put him in his place. That's the way you think, yeah?'

Idiot! I help people like you. I work at the Salford Project, for Christ's sake!

'I'm pregnant.' Was that her voice? That terrified whine? Her voice?

'Is it Fitz's?'

'Yes.'

He knows him, this bastard knows Fitz, knows my husband.

Floyd smiled then. 'Normally I rape my victims. I don't do that now. Fitz told me there was no future in it. You want to know what I do now? To my victims?'

And to that question the pressure of the knife against her

throat was answer enough. She felt it jerk reflexively against her skin as the sound of a car skidding to a halt outside preceded the crunch of footsteps on the driveway and the opening of the front door.

7.00p.m.–7.15p.m.

He knew where they were without looking. Judith never listened to anything other than Radio Four. The urban rap jittering out of the lounge now held more than simple lyrics, drove before it the sound of desperately quiet speech, the stink of sweat, the smell of *him*.

Indicating to Sue Malcolm that she should stay back, he pushed open the door to the lounge. Wise and Harriman hurried away silently.

Judith was on her knees beside the wide French windows. Crouched behind her was Floyd Malcolm. He had one hand round Judith's belly, the other was holding a knife to her throat. Her face was blotchy with unshed tears; her neck was blotchy with smeared blood.

Fitz went a little mad then, inside, imagined himself striding across the room, wrenching the knife from Floyd, imagined smashing his head against the wall until the plaster cracked with Floyd's skull. He imagined this, did nothing. He couldn't afford to let the rage take over. Not now. Now he had to play for time.

Judith was looking at him. Her throat worked against the knife blade but she said nothing. Floyd said nothing too.

Fitz took a breath. 'It's the end of the line, Floyd. Forgive the cliché, won't you?'

Floyd was blinking rapidly. His pupils were distended; the space between the lids filled with endless darkness.

'What do you want, Floyd?'

'Can't you tell, man?'

'A helicopter on the roof, five million in unmarked notes, a pass for the border guards?'

'Fitz!' That strangled cry came from Judith. He ignored it. Floyd was his target. He was the one marked for the push.

And he was susceptible, Fitz already knew that. It was just a question of selecting the right weapons. The right words.

'A black revolution? Power to the people? Gunpowder under the Houses of Parliament?'

And Floyd was crumbling. 'I'll kill her, man, I swear I will. You know I'll do it!'

'So kill her.' *What have I done?* No sign of Wise and Harriman. No uniforms.

Silence then.

And a look from Judith. A mixture of desperation and anger. Anger at him. Rage, in fact. Seemed to be a lot of it going around lately.

The silence maintained, stretched out wire thin, wrapped around the moment and strangled it. What damage was he doing to Judith with this war of nerves? He had no way of knowing. All he knew was that it wasn't a game any more. And that was the truth. No game this, no rules. It was all calculated guesses. A life bet on an accumulator where the horses were rigged and the price for failure was a lifetime in hell.

Time to shake up the odds.

'I've been married twenty-odd years, Floyd, and I'm sick of it. Kill her.' There. Keep it simple. Unarguable. See how he deals with that.

Floyd said nothing. Judith was moaning now. Wriggling in his grip.

'I've wished her dead loads of times, Floyd. Never had the guts to do it myself, of course. An accident maybe. A little car crash. I've dreamed of it, Floyd. Of course I could always tell her it was over but that takes emotional courage and as you've no doubt observed I've none of that. So do it. Go ahead, Floyd! Do it!'

The knife trembled.

A single bright red bead of blood, trickling down her neck.

A desperate moan, could have come from either of them.

'*Kill her.* It's what you do best, isn't it? It's all you do! Not like your mother. Not like her, Floyd.'

Another moment of silence.

Then, 'What about my mother, man? She's just another white bitch like this one here!' And Floyd shook Judith so that tiny droplets of blood flew from her throat, pattered across her blouse, the carpet.

'You think your mother hates you. Because you're black. "When it comes down to it, it's women like her. Even before her own son, it's her colour. White." That's what you said. You hate her because she's white. The corollary is she hates you. She has to hate you. Because if she doesn't hate you, then it all falls apart, right?' A push. 'Right, Floyd?' The words snapped out, lashed out, claimed a response.

'Right! Yeah, right. She hates me. It's fucking obvious. She's white and she hates me!'

'But if she doesn't, Floyd. If she doesn't, then it all falls apart and you're staring into the abyss and the abyss is you. It's you, Floyd. And you've no reason to rape. No reason to kill. No excuses and no-one to blame. Just nothing. Unless she hates you.'

The knife trembling.

His arm, trembling.

Judith, trembling, bleeding. *Where was Wise. Where was Harriman?*

'She's here isn't she? My mother's here. You've brought her here!'

'Because she doesn't hate you. She doesn't hate you, Floyd.'

'She does, she hates me, she hates me because I'm black!'

And that was it, the moment presented itself and Fitz took it. '*If that's the case why did she marry your father?*'

Another moment. A faint movement from the garden: Harriman seeing if he could take Floyd through the windows. All too late. Too late now, because his arm was moving, the knife was moving, and Fitz knew he'd pushed too hard, that he'd lost Floyd, lost Judith forever and she was screaming, his wife was screaming, and that brought the knife tighter against her throat and into her skin and she was

284

bleeding, dear God she was *bleeding* and Floyd was jerking helplessly in the throes of some memory, some memory of –

7.15p.m.–7.25p.m.

– pain. A lifetime of pain jammed into a moment that stretched out forever, beyond the schoolyard, beyond the kids and their taunts, beyond the natural arrogance of kids whose belief in their own parents' ideals was so much stronger than his. Beyond all that, past the bricks thrown in the alleyway, past the gibbon screams and scratching of armpits, all the way home, to his own home, to his room and his mother, his mother who was so different from him, different from him but the same as them, as their parents. Past all that to the locked door, the plastic bottles, the air heavy with fumes, the bath, the bleach. Beyond even that to the pain, the surprise and the pain of the bleach, of being black, of not being white, the pain of knowing he could never change, never change his skin, his black skin, never change himself no matter how much it hurt, and it hurt, oh God, Mummy, it hurt, it hurt so much and all he wanted was to be like her, like Mummy and he –

7.25p.m.–7.30p.m.

– jerked behind Judith, his arm bruisingly tight around her swollen waist now, frighteningly tight, and the knife was –

– still. And he was still. Quite still. Staring.

Next to Fitz the lounge door had opened. Sue Malcolm had come in. She was crying. Tears streaming from her eyes. She was staring at Floyd. Staring with a profound horror Fitz knew she would take with her to her grave.

And she said, 'I married your father because I loved him. Black and white, they didn't matter then, not to us. To other people yes, but not to us. We dared to love in the face of the hatred of others. Your father and me. Black and white, together. And you. You're of both of us. You hate black or

285

white and you hate yourself. Don't hate yourself, Floyd, and don't destroy others because of it.' She took a step into the room and said the three words that changed everything. 'Dare to love.'

And the moment shattered then, everything flying in different directions, as the French windows burst open and Harriman threw himself at Floyd, changed direction when he saw he'd let Judith go, knocked her aside as Floyd stumbled forward to meet his mother in the middle of the room and both sank to their knees, sobbing wildly as they embraced, and the room was full of police officers and suddenly the phone was ringing and the sound brought Fitz to his senses with a terrible shock.

'Where's the knife?'

And then Sue Malcolm sank to the floor and he saw where the knife was, knew from its angle and depth of penetration that there was no hope for her, heard the words she whispered with her last breath.

'Dare to love.'

Then she was gone, and Judith was in his arms and Harriman was sitting on Floyd's chest while Wise cuffed him and the room was full of uniformed officers and radio jammed on Black FM and the bloody telephone was ringing and ringing and ringing.

7.30p.m.–7.35p.m.

And when he eventually picked up the phone it was Penhaligon. And Judith stared at him, eyes wide above a bandaged throat, somehow able to read the fact that it was her on his face as if she could hear the words she spoke into his ear.

'Fitz? It's Jane Penhaligon. We have to talk. Now.'

And that was all.

Except, of course, that it wasn't all, not by a million miles. Something in her voice pulled at him the way Judith's expression pulled at him. And he was caught in the middle, stretched beyond any reasonable expectations, and he looked from the phone, to Judith, to the smashed French windows, the corpse of Sue Malcolm cooling on his carpet, to Floyd being taken away like some chained slave, all choices gone, and what he felt was tiredness.

That and an overwhelming rage.

ACKNOWLEDGEMENTS

The Recovery Phase

In many ways the picture of a police force unsympathetic towards victims of rape is out of date. I am especially grateful to Detective Sergeant Jill Williams, who allowed me access to Locklease Family and Child Protection Unit, and took the time to explain just how the attitude of the police towards victims of rape and child abuse has changed over the last ten years, and indeed is changing all the time.

Hot from the presses is the acknowledgement that victims of rape are not necessarily women. Men can be raped too. As yet the reported incidence of male rape is much lower than that of women. This is changing.

Thanks are due to the following people: Jill Williams, Paul Hinder, Michelle Drayton, Mum and Dad, Jo and Steve, Jop and Andrea, Peter and the merry crue at the grinding industrial wheels of Virgin Publishing (today the typo, tomorrow the werld).

A special mention to Theresa, Tim, Andrew, the boys and girls of mammal, Lynne and Lizzie (PMT and Chocolate – a killer combo).

Thomas and Gizmo appear by special permission.

The resemblance of any characters, places or tank engines to anyone, where, or thing you may know is entirely coincidental.

Be cool to each other, dudes: outtahere –

Jimbo

The Cracker Writers

Jimmy McGovern

Jimmy McGovern's scriptwriting career began in the early 1980s with plays for Liverpool's Everyman and Playhouse theatres. His Merseyside association continued with scripts for over eighty episodes of Channel 4's soap opera *Brookside* between 1983 and 1989. During the 1990s he has written for over a dozen films and television series, including *El CID*, *Backbeat* and, of course, *Cracker*.

Jim Mortimore

Jim Mortimore was born in London in 1962. At various times he has enjoyed employment as a rubbish shoveller, library assistant, social services clerk, printer, commercial musician, and graphic designer. His interests include: origami, cycling, reading, writing, painting, music, and video/computer art/animation.

Jim lives in Bristol, and has reluctantly agreed to the removal of all jokes from this biog.

The Cracker Stories

Based on the original scripts, Virgin's Cracker novels add depth and detail to the televised stories and provide a permanent record of Fitz's involvement with the police and of his relationships with his wife Judith and with Detective Sergeant Jane Penhaligon.

Series One

The first three Cracker stories, first broadcast on British television in 1993, were all written by Jimmy McGovern.

The Mad Woman In The Attic
Adapted by Jim Mortimore

Dr Edward Fitzgerald, who insists that everyone call him Fitz, is a psychologist with an apparently conventional life. He teaches and practises psychology; he has an attractive wife, two children, and a big house in a pleasant suburb of Manchester. But he's also addicted to gambling, booze, cigarettes, and pushing his considerable bulk into any situation he finds intriguing. His wife Judith has had enough. She leaves him. Fitz's life is beginning to fall apart.

When one of his students is murdered, Fitz can't resist becoming involved. The police have a suspect; they are sure he's the serial killer, but he's claiming complete amnesia. The police reluctantly hire Fitz to get a confession.

As Fitz investigates, he finds that the police theory

doesn't fit the facts. He discovers, in solving murder cases, a new focus for his life. And he meets Detective Sergeant Jane Penhaligon.

To Say I Love You
Adapted by Molly Brown

People do strange things for love.

Tina's parents had nothing but loving intentions when they turned her into a talking guide dog for her blind sister. Sean, full of bitterness and fury, is prepared to kill for the love of Tina. And Fitz, psychologist and occasional catcher of murderers, would do anything to win back the love of his wife Judith – if only he didn't find himself working so closely with DS Jane Penhaligon.

In this, the second Cracker thriller, Fitz can find a murderer, prevent a catastrophe, and still find time to flirt with a pretty policewoman. But he also knows only too well the motivations that drive Judith into another man's bed and that push him to the edge of self-destruction.

Compared to the complications of Fitz's own life, tracking down a team of cop-killers is simple.

One Day A Lemming Will Fly
Adapted by Liz Holliday

Everything's going to be all right. Judith is back home, Penhaligon's falling in love, and Fitz has a new problem to solve from the police.

It's an open and shut case. A schoolboy – a young, effeminate, scholarly and often bullied schoolboy – is found murdered. His English teacher – male, single, lives alone – tries to commit suicide. It's obvious: the teacher killed his pupil. The police think so. The boy's parents think so. Everyone in the family's neighbourhood thinks so. And Fitz thinks so. It's just a matter of obtaining a confession.

But the truth is as elusive as trust and honesty, and the case goes badly wrong.

In this, the third Cracker story, Fitz reaches the crisis in his personal drama. He has to choose between Judith and Jane. And that's the least of his problems.

Series Two

Cracker's second series was first broadcast in 1994. Two of the three stories were written by Jimmy McGovern.

To Be A Somebody
Adapted by Gareth Roberts

Having argued with DCI Bilborough and abandoned Jane at the airport, Fitz isn't welcome at Anson Road nick any more. He's back on the booze, his gambling is riskier than ever, and Judith's had as much as she can take. Fitz is at a new low.

When an Asian grocer is stabbed by a skinhead, the police assume a racist motive. Fitz knows better, and as usual he's right. But he can't convince Bilborough to let him help until the murderer has struck again.

Albie and his dad, Liverpool supporters, were at the Hillsborough disaster. Five years later, Albie's dad has died. And Albie wants revenge. He'll kill anyone who makes assumptions about white, working-class scousers. But he particularly wants to kill coppers.

The Big Crunch
Adapted by Liz Holliday

Kenneth Trant is a headmaster and the leader of an evangelical Christian group. He's above suspicion. When one of his pupils and church members – a teenaged girl – is found dying, her body covered with arcane symbols, suspicion falls on the disturbed young man who works for Trant's brother. It's an open and shut case.

Fitz doesn't think so, of course, but at first there's not much he can do. Anyway, he's distracted: Judith has moved out, the house is up for sale – and Jane Penhaligon is still very interesting. And interested.

Men Should Weep
Adapted by Jim Mortimore

This story brings the second series to a shattering conclusion. The Anson Road detectives tear each other apart, and Fitz's life dissolves into chaos, as a serial rapist terrorises Manchester. This is the hardest-hitting Cracker story yet.